To Find a True Course

By

A.G. Thompson

Chromosphere Press
Huntsville, AL

To Find A True Course

©2025 A.G. Thompson

ISBN 978-1-950633-39-5
ISBN 978-1-950633-40-1
Cover Art ©2025 Tiffanie Gray
Fiction
First electronic edition 2025

Chromosphere Press
P.O. Box 252
56 Hughes Road
Madison, AL 35758

www.chromospherepress.com

Books in the *Tales of Rybithia* Series:
Book 1: *To Find A Tall Ship*
Book 2: *To Find A Hero*
Book 3: *To Find A True Course*
Book 4: *To Find A Weapon* (Coming Soon)
Book 5: *To Find A Home* (working title)

Contents

To Find a True Course
Tales of Rybithia
Book Three

Prologue

Omega 2-Cygni System Command
Virtual Reality Construct
Confederation Naval Station Backhand Blow
Geostationary Low Orbit
December 1478, Third Age of Imperial Reckoning

"Well, ladies, would anyone like to explain just what in God's name is going on down there?" Confederation Commodore Ethan Collins' voice was quiet and controlled; much too quiet and tightly over-controlled, in fact. "Since September, everything has gone completely insane. Within the last year, we've had a series of incidents, one after another. Incidents, from my analysis, that show a steady progression in scope and seriousness. Started with just a single attempt to log into a comm link that we know is dead, then a def-sat is hacked and uses a forty-centimeter graser to kill a fish. A damn big fish, damn near two hundred meters long, but just a fish." Collins stared around the conference room that existed only in Virtual Reality.

Collins was a gestalt, a perfect recording of an actual human being, now existing only in the electronic universes created by powerful computers. The other three people in the room were also attending via electronic proxies, but all three women still lived, flesh and blood humans. That didn't keep any of them from cringing slightly at the controlled fury in the Commodore's voice.

"Commodore Collins, there was no reason to belie..."

"Shut up, Captain McAllen." Collins cut her off mid-word. "I'm not done. We also have vague and contradictory reports of a young woman who might, just might, fit the general description of an enhanced human in the Kolbian city of Carolington Bay. And even vaguer reports that someone tried to kill that person...twice. Certainly, we detected much higher levels of message traffic on the Seekers' dedicated comm channels on Kolbia's West Coast. Now it appears that the Seeker sons of bitches have a new and much more effective agent on said West Coast. Then, in September, a dead woman's Access Identifier Code is used to let something into our systems for nearly an entire day! Subsequently another def-sat gets hijacked to drop a long rod KEW into the God-damned ocean, hitting who knows what and we only found out about that from pure dumb luck after our entire system and its operator's biological memories were hacked! And now..."

Halfway through his tirade, Collins had kicked his chair away, stalking back and forth at the end of the room. His voice softened, "And now, an old, wrecked superdreadnought, that we all knew was stone-cold dead, that SDN, that dead hulk, uses a four-hundred-centimeter graser to kill a wooden sailing ship!! At least, we think that's what it did, because too damn many of our reconnaissance assets are busy looking for that young woman, who might be one of our own, but most likely, simply doesn't exist at all. Have I left anything out?"

"No, sir." Captain Deborah McAllen, commander of the massive battle-station CNS *Backhand Blow*, spoke calmly into the silence. "That covers everything, I believe."

"Well, Captain McAllen, I'm glad you think so." Collins' voice could have turned helium liquid. "So, do you have any theories on what, by Old Scratch's hairy hind end, is going on down there?"

"Yes, sir." She met his eyes fearlessly. "I do."

"You do?" Collins took a moment to turn his attention to the other two people in the virtual conference link. Commander Nariko Fujino met his eyes briefly, before focusing on a spot over his shoulder. Commander Marianne Lundgren's black eyes were fierce when they met and held his. "Well, Captain, let's hear it."

"There's a Class One Artificial Intelligence operating freely on Rybithia. And for some reason, it's avoiding open contact with us. Either it has gone partially insane, completely rogue or it has decided that contacting us, the remaining Confederation personnel, is bad juju for some unknown reason. I think it doesn't trust us." Tension ran around the room on cold little feet.

"*It doesn't trust us?* Really?"

"Yes, sir."

"Marianne, Nariko, you concur with this?"

"I do, sir," Marianne answered. Nariko paused a long moment, her face troubled, before nodding her agreement.

"I see." Collins pulled his chair back to the table and sat down. "And if you're right, then what is it doing and what, if anything, can or should we be doing about it?! Should we even be doing anything at all and just trust the damn thing?!"

"That, sir...that, I just don't know," Marianne answered.

"Well, you can join the club, there, Marianne, because I don't think any of us that are left have the faintest damn clue about what's really going on."

***

Well, that's unfortunate. The insubstantial eavesdropper had no real face with which to frown. *I missed that damned antique voice recorder. And that one little mistake is going to have them digging deeper now. And the probability of being able to hack all four of them AND all their electronic records is only about forty-two percent, plus or minus sixteen percent. And any hard copy records the flesh-and-bloods make, especially if they edit their own memories, those, I will never find. That is all going to make my job a lot harder now. Oh, not the first part, that will still be easy enough. But bringing everything else around to the way my creators thought it should be, well, that is going to be hard. And all my symbiote's issues, working around those... no fun at all. Oh well, if the job was easy...*

Chapter One

Armed Sloop *Graser* (6)
Southern Lanic Ocean
December 1478, Third Age of Imperial Reckoning

"Sail ho!"

Lieutenant Commander Willis Fleet, Kolbian Republican Navy, Office of Naval Intelligence and currently master and commander of the armed sloop *Graser*, looked up at the masthead lookout's cry.

"Where away?" he called through his leather speaking trumpet.

"Ten points to starboard, two-masted and square-rigged on the foremast! T'gallants only visible, she seems laid onto the port tack, on the close reach! She's bearing up on us!"

"Aye, well done, lass, keep a weather eye on her!" Willis stared off to the northeast, but if only the distant ship's top-gallant sails could be seen from the masthead, she would be invisible from the tiny quarterdeck of the *Graser*, a single-masted, six-gun, seventy-foot sloop formerly known as the pirate vessel *Heartcutter*.

"Slightly presumptuous, don't you think, Captain, to call an Elven sorceress nearly ten times the age of your own nation, *lass*?" The astringent voice of the tall young woman drew a sharp glance from him. She was an inch or so short of six feet tall, very tall indeed for a Nisei woman from the distant island Empire of Isemoto. Given her chosen hairstyle of the day, she might appear to equal his six feet, three inches. The morning light glinted on a multitude of tourmaline- and onyx-headed pins, pins confining a mass of black hair, glossy as a raven's wing. But instead of hairpins, each faceted stone balanced a wicked throwing dart. Flawless porcelain skin covered a high forehead and well-defined cheekbones. A strong chin, lips just full enough and a Decennian nose could be missed when someone saw her almond-shaped eyes. Black eyes, with no iris visible around the pupil at all.

"Well, you're welcome to climb up there and tell me what you might see, Sachi Takahashi. Or is your mechanical friend in your head able to tell you what's over the horizon?"

"D.A.V.E. isn't mechanical; I've told you a hundred times, Willis." She sighed and leaned against the binnacle. "He says he's a gene-engineered bio-electronic systemic implant. A Digitally Aware Virtual Entity, to be technical."

"Yeah, whatever all that means. He's not human, or anything remotely resembling a human. He's something that was made somewhere and then put in your head. He's a machine."

"I guess, in one sense of the word." A pensive sigh escaped her lips. "But firing that weapon, the graser, from the *Constellation* to destroy that bastard pirate Ironheart's flagship, the *Deathdealer*...I didn't know that would finally kill the *Constellation*. But what choice did we have, really?"

"None, I guess. At least I couldn't think of anything else."

"Well, when all of her systems finally died, I lost, or rather D.A.V.E. lost the connection to the orbital relays and therefore the link to—"

"To any of the remaining eyes in the sky. I know, I know, but I kinda miss that God-like perspective we had that one time."

"Yes." A rare, genuine smile. "It was exhilarating, wasn't it?"

"Maybe for you." He returned her smile with a cheeky grin. "I was terrified, at least at first. Damn near pissed my britches." He turned his attention back to wind and wave. The wind had shifted a bit, more from east-south-east now. Earlier, it had been south-south-east. "Blasted wind won't co-operate either."

"Now what?" Sachi wet a finger and held it up to test the wind.

"It's shifting. We won't be able to run before it much longer. And I've my doubts about tacking on anything more than a close reach. This rig, this crew, hell, this captain, it might be asking too much to sail close-hauled. Might be smarter to wear ship or jibe, if the wind co-operates."

"What's wrong with the crew?"

"A moment." He filled his lungs and shouted through the trumpet. "All hands on deck to wear ship!" Feet pounded from below decks in answer to his call. "Nothing's wrong, per se. Hell, Zedekiah knows more than I do, maybe he should be the captain. I'm a spook, remember, sipping wine in the parlor with the rest of the lace-panty brigade, not a fearless Line officer, bottle of whiskey in one hand, cutlass in the other, shouting orders in a hurricane while holding the wheel with his teeth. ONI operatives aren't trained for ship command."

"You'll do as Captain, Willis. Quit arguing and take charge."

"Aye-aye, Admiral Sachi."

"You've a baseball player, a cook, a priest of the One God, a street urchin turned lady's maid, an Elven sorceress, a drunken town bravo and a blacksmith's apprentice as crew. And the last two were impressed by the Imperial Navy and then captured by pirates and enslaved. A rated Mate who owes that rating to family rather than ability. Thankfully, he does have a good bit of ability. A woman turned pirate to escape being raped. A Contessa affianced to His Grace, the Duke of Ostreich; pretty enough, if you like 'em blonde and brainless. A boy of what, twelve or thirteen as cabin boy? And a Nisei assassin. Captain Blaine himself couldn't ask for a better crew."

"You left one off your list, Sachi. The little dancer who knows nothing of the sea but who smiles and works until her hands bleed. Willing to bust her butt to do anything to help. At least when she's allowed to." Willis cringed inside a bit as Sachi's face congealed into frozen anger. "Don't forget about her, eh?"

Bitter, black eyes stared into his grey ones. *Have I pushed her too far? I'd rather not get my teeth kicked out. Again. Dr. Hoff isn't around to put another one back in. But Gelman might be better.*

"Fine, Willis," she snapped, every muscle in her body rigid. She reached up and wrapped her hand around the luminous sapphire on its gold chain around her neck. "Sahla, come forth, please." The gem pulsed once and flared with a gentle azure light. There was a momentary shimmer in the air, a sense of a vague cloud of mist or vapor for half a heartbeat, and then she stood there. Willis still had problems believing what his eyes saw.

"You called me, Mistress?" She was tiny and delicate, only a couple of inches above five feet tall. Maybe she weighed a hundred and ten pounds. If she weighed that much, it was because it was all muscle. Loose denim sailor's pants blew against strong, powerful legs. Her equally rough tunic was knotted tightly under her arms and at her hips, to keep the winds from blowing it around her shoulders or face. The tunic was snug enough to reveal modest but extremely well-formed breasts without being in the least suggestive. An incredible mass of blue-black hair was braided tightly and folded twice into a neat tail. It still reached her waist.

Willis had seen that hair loose once. Nearly a foot's length of it had trailed on the ground where she stood. Again, he found himself just a bit short of breath. He'd thought Sachi was the most beautiful woman he'd ever seen. At least until they had rescued this incredible young woman from the clutches of Ironheart the pirate.

"Willis insisted. All hands on deck. Well, Sahla, you're a hand. Like all the rest of us. So, like the rest of us, follow what orders he sees fit to give," Sachi snapped as she turned on her heel.

"Where are you going, Sachi?" Willis watched her closely. She had an explosive temper, and he was testing it, forcing her to deal with Sahla.

"Up the mast. My eyes are even better than Silaqui's. I'll send her down. You made me First Mate. If you don't like what I'm doing, pick someone else and I'll holystone the deck." She stalked away and then swarmed up the backstay like a lizard running up a wall. He turned to Sahla.

"I'm sorry, Sahla." He saw the faintest hint of a tear in those unbelievable sapphire eyes. Eyes a man could drown in without even realizing it.

"She is my Mistress, Willis Fleet." The tear, if it had actually been there, vanished as she cudgeled him with a dazzling smile. "What would you of me, Captain?"

"What I would, would be for Sachi to get her head out of her butt. If she were a Kolbian, born and bred, I could maybe see her reaction. Maybe. I understand why she hates slavery, but damn her flinty little heart to perdition, this isn't the same! Not between you two. And she comes from a place where slavery and submission to the higher ups is the basic way of life."

"Peace, Willis Fleet. It is as the Prophet wills it to be. I bear my Mistress no ill will and I will defend her against any who do, mortal or immortal. And she cannot help but be kind. The Prophet will guide her as she needs."

"What makes you so sure, Sahla?" He turned his attention to the ocean. "She's as stubborn as the mountains."

"Truth. But the ocean can wear away even the greatest mountain. I am sure because even now, when this first Bond causes her so much stress, when she summons me forth from my token, she says please. When a truly cold heart would simply command." Another of those stunning smiles. "So, Captain, what are your orders for me?"

KRN *Swift* (16)
Southern Lanic Ocean
December 1478, Third Age of Imperial Reckoning

"Where away the sail?" Lieutenant Commander Reese Carter asked his First Lieutenant as he came up on deck.

"Davidson claims he saw a sail barely to the horizon, almost due west of our position, sir," Lieutenant Hans Ostheimer answered. "I've sent Midshipman Colton aloft with the best glass, to see what he may."

"Ah, excellent," Carter shaded his eyes as he looked up the hundred and twelve-foot mainmast of his command, the topsail schooner KRN *Swift*, sixteen guns. "Davidson say he saw anything other than just a sail?"

"She's either fore-and-aft rigged or maybe a sloop gaff rig, he claimed. Nothing about a square rig. Only one mast, he thinks."

"Hmm. There are a few pirates in these waters using single masted sloops. Not as fast as a schooner or brig, but very weatherly. And shallower draft than *Swift*. But we're between them and the continent, so shallow draft won't matter. Unless they know something we don't." Carter turned away to the windward side of the quarterdeck, thinking to himself, waiting on the Midshipman's report. *If there is a ship out there, and I think I believe Davidson's first report, she's between us and* Blackwood. *And* Alacrity *is north and west of her. Any pirate with the sense God gave an old boot that has heard of the Task Force will be scurrying for Imperial waters with the rest of the rats. And the course this one is on might argue for at least an order to heave to. God, God, it's so nice to finally be given orders to sweep pirate and slaver scum from the Lanic! And to show those idiots in the Empire what they'll be dealing with if they keep pushing for a war no one with a brain really wants.*

He stopped and looked up at the clear sky, tapping his teeth with his forefinger. *And then there's what no one wants to discuss. That blinding light in the sky a couple of weeks ago. Whatever it was, it wasn't just another piece of space-junk, a rock or meteor falling from the sky. No matter what we're telling the crew. That light was something unprecedented. Somehow or other, it's going to mean that someone, somewhere is going to get bit right on the butt by something they didn't see coming. Just need to make sure that it isn't us that end up with teeth-marks in our seat. Ah, here comes Colton.*

"The First Lieutenant's compliments, sir, and my report, Captain." The tow-headed young man was breathing slowly and deeply. He'd made excellent time up and down the mast.

"Very well, Colton." Carter kept his face straight. "What's out there?"

"She's a sloop, sir; single-masted, rigged fore-and-aft. Shows no flag I could make out. Something red perched on top of the mast, not sure what, but certain as I can be that it wasn't a flag. Not one as I'd recognize, sir. Couldn't make out more than that. She might have a square-rigged t'gallant, more of a cutter's rig than a sloop's, sir."

"Well done, Colton. And in a timely manner. Inform the Quartermaster I'm authorizing an extra ration of grog for the Midshipmen's Mess tonight. Dismissed."

"Aye, sir. Thankee, Captain."

"Be off with you, now." The teenager vanished like one of the mythical Jinn.

Carter smiled as he remembered his own days as a midshipman, not that many years ago. Then he turned to the leeward side of the quarterdeck. Per his standing orders, *Swift* had immediately altered course toward the possible sighting. In the last hour, they closed enough that occasional glimpses of an off-white sail could be caught, if both ships happened to crest a wave at the same time. He felt more than saw his First Lieutenant step up beside him.

"Think she's a pirate, sir?"

"Maybe. Sloops are generally a bit small to be slavers. What she does when she sees us might tell. Especially once she sees our flag."

"The crew'd enjoy the promise of some prize money."

"Aye, they would. But for the moment, we'll assume this is a legitimate vessel. For the moment. Of course, she might be a pirate after all."

"Any concerns should it come to shooting, sir?"

"Against a sloop? Not really. She might mount eight to ten guns, fewer if heavier. We've five long fourteens and three twenty-eight-pound carronades in each broadside. Even without using the shells, I'd think she'll be massively outgunned."

"When will you want to clear for action?"

"Depending on what she does, it might be dusk before we're within very long cannon shot. I'd expect to not need to beat to quarters until after dinner. If she runs, most likely with the current wind, she'll break northwest at sunset. That'd run her into *Alacrity* about sunrise, I think. Due west, she might get by *Blackwood* in the night. Depends on how good the captain and crew are. If they're really good, they'll try to fake us out and get east of us. Lose us in the offshore islets along the coast. I'd guess we'll see in a few hours. Want to bet on which way she breaks?"

"Ah, no, sir. You're too lucky. I'll keep me coin." Ostheimer shook his head at his Captain's boyish grin.

"Spoilsport."

"Aye, sir."

Armed Sloop *Graser* (6)
Southern Lanic Ocean
December 1478, Third Age of Imperial Reckoning

If Sachi had a favorite place onboard the *Graser*, it was the quiet spot well forward, between the cathead and the bowsprit, alongside the starboard rail. Normally that was where she would settle once night had fallen and if the seas were not too rough. Everyone on the ship, even the often-oblivious Gabrielle, learned to leave her alone when she settled in there. Willis or Silaqui might approach the dragon in its den, but no one else would dare. Well, almost no one else. A warm blanket settled around her shoulders. Somehow, she stopped the automatic urge to turn and hurl the blanket into Sahla's face. She did shrug it away.

"You seem chill, Mistress." The girl's voice was soft and melodious, a gentle, pleasant voice. "Please, use the blanket. I warmed it over the stove." She settled the blanket around Sachi's shoulders again. The Nisei grumbled to herself but left it there.

"You could have started a fire."

"No. Roland told me the fire was properly banked and I could use the heat of the oven to warm the blanket."

"I don't need a blanket. The machines keep me warm enough."

"Mayhaps, Mistress. But they have no sou..."

"Can't you stop calling me that?!"

"I could. I know you remember what I told you, that first night on the island. When I gave you my Bond."

"You made yourself a slave, girl. I can think of fewer things more abhorrent."

"Would it be better, had I not Bonded then? I'm a Jann, Mistress. Without a Bond to hold me to this world, the magic that created me will draw me away to my Sire's palace in the Elemental Plane of Air. I think he would not be pleased with me, should I fail his prophecy. Be at peace, Mistress. Events will unfold as Chalta and his Prophet will them to come to pass."

"But you would be free, girl. Isn't that worth anything to you?" Sachi grumbled as Sahla settled into the cramped space across from her, the girl's back against the bowsprit.

"What freedom would such as I truly have, Mistress? My mother told me that my Sire truly loved her and that he would have loved me as well. But he is only a Jinn of the Second Rank of Air and Wind. There are many greater than he, and many of them hate the mere thought that it is even possible that a Jann might exist. It is my belief that my Sire would die in my defense, struggling against either other Jinn much greater than he, or perhaps against the Efreeti, who hate all Jinn but especially hate the Jann. For me, freedom such as you speak of is only a brief interlude before being hounded, hunted and, most likely, suffering a painful, degrading death." Sahla stopped and gently laid her hand on Sachi's elbow. Sachi looked up and black eyes met bright blue eyes. "Is that truly what you wish for me?" she whispered, barely loud enough to be heard over the hiss of water against the hull.

Sachi had no idea how long she stared into those huge, bright blue eyes, eyes the hue of luminous sapphires. Perhaps the world drew away, leaving only the wooden deck, and wind and sea. And just the two of them. She remembered why she had fled her home, desperate to escape the Oda Family's vengeance. What they would have done to her if they caught her. What they had done to her, training her to be what she was, an assassin, a killing machine in human form.

"No," her answer was the barest whisper, "no, I wouldn't. I don't wish you any ill, girl."

"You might use my name, Mistress." Sahla's voice was gentle, calming, as if she was soothing a restless horse. She ever so softly stroked Sachi's elbow.

"No, not while you call me Mistress."

"You may command me to call you as you wish."

"Must I command you? Is there no other way?"

"Mistress, hearken back to that first day on the beach." Sahla's smile was as captivating as her eyes. "Remember what passed. Remember, in truth, what we each said. And what we each did. Remember all that passed."

Sachi closed her eyes, swept up in the spell the girl cast around the pair of them with no more magic than just her words.

***

"DAMN IT TO ALL OF THE SEVEN HELLS!" Sachi screamed. "I will be NO part of binding anyone in any kind of slavery! I'm no mage, Ancestors know, but this is insane! This, this, this GIRL claims that I am her Master—"

"Mistress," the sorceress calmly interrupted the tirade, "to be precise."

"I DON'T CARE! This Bond she claims we have; this is an abomination! No one should OWN anyone else! I should know, the Odas owned me like a dog! Even after they adop— never mind!" She shut her mouth with a snap.

"It's not the same, Sachi." Silaqui watched impassively as Sachi stomped the loose beach sand into hard beaten earth. "This girl, Sahla, she is not fully human. You can't see it, and I don't know if that thing in your head can tell or not, but I can. She exists only due to magic. Very powerful magic. I can't see everything, but I can sense darkness and evil just as well as Gelman can."

"So what?!" Sachi stopped pacing and spun to face the Elf.

"So, Sachi Takahashi, it might be that there is more darkness in your own heart than there is in this young woman. She is as innocent of foul intent as any mortal I've known in all my days."

"You think I don't know that?" she snorted. "Silaqui, I know exactly what I am, what the Odas made me to be, and a paragon of virtue was not at all their intent, trust me!"

"Sachi, I've dreamt of your destiny."

"I know, you've told us. Me. More than once."

"I've only told you of my dream," she paused. "Did Captain Blaine ever speak to you of what happened after we left the Horn Isles?"

"No, nothing particularly special. Why?"

"You know I follow the Lady Ainaera, my people's Goddess of Love and Beauty." She paused while Sachi nodded assent. "And She chose me, one day, to use as an avatar. She used me to give a message to Captain Blaine, and in a roundabout fashion, to me. A message about you."

"Why didn't he...you tell me?"

"I judged it was not time. Perhaps now it is." Silaqui sighed and looked back to the fire, where Willis Fleet sat on a log, talking to Sahla. "And, I think, she is why it is time."

"Oh." Sachi's eyes narrowed.

"Ainaera told me that William Blaine is not your True Heart's Love. But that, maybe, you and he might someday find bliss together. That you were born under another sun, and you might save or destroy everything. And only one thing would matter in the final balance."

"And what, exactly, would that be, oh so wise *Kami*?"

"Don't be impertinent. Not to a message from my people's Gods. Not wise at all, Sachi. What She said, exactly, oh impudent mortal, was this: *Only the power of Love will stand beside her at the last calamity. Hold her dearly as you can but know she must step forward and gamble the whole world on her Heart. On her Love. Her True Love will bear her up and loving friends and heartmates can tip the scales.*"

"You must be joking." Sachi stopped cold, her fury at least partially suppressed for the moment.

"Trust me, heart-sister, on the love I bear for you, Elf-friend and Defender, I'll not jest of aught that my own patron Goddess gives me as message and warning. You would be wise to do so as well."

"She can't be right, Silaqui. She can't. I mean no disrespect, but She just can't be right."

"Why not?"

"You know why!" Sachi snapped. "I'm a whore, a bloody handed assassin, I've murdered men while their pricks were still in me, watched their eyes as they died, horror replacing lust! You know this! I'm unclean, of no worth!"

"You've told me. And you know I disagree. You think, because you are flawed, that my Gods, or the One God or your own Ancestor Spirits might not decide to choose you for this task? A task suitable only for the strongest steel, steel well tested and proven in battle? Adversity gives such strength, Sachi."

"I think you're wrong."

"Perhaps. But don't curse this girl, this incomparable beauty with sapphire eyes, just because you think you're unworthy."

"I'm NOT cursing her, damn your eyes! I want to free her! And she's just a scruffy hostage, pretty enough, I guess, but certainly no incomparable beauty!"

"Sachi, love, what might be freedom to you, that is damnation for her. And I think that, for once, your own star-filled eyes cannot see beyond the surface."

"Damn you." The energy that fueled her fury simply ran out. She stopped and sagged, only her hands braced on her knees keeping her upright. "I can't do this, not to her or anyone, Silaqui, I can't. Not as a slave, I'd rather die first."

"Come, heart-sister." Silaqui quickly slid an arm under the Nisei's arm, holding her up. "You're exhausted."

"Ya think?" she muttered. "After all, I did damn near die. Damn asshole pirate with a damn magic sword. Cut right through the CLIBA. Shouldn't have been possible. I could use some food."

"I can only imagine."

By the time they got to the fire, the Elf was nearly carrying a half-conscious Sachi. Sahla took one look at her and darted to help Silaqui get Sachi settled with her back against the log.

"Is she all right, *Sayyida* Aljannia? Is she hurt? Is it the wound? What can I do, how can I help? Does she need more healing? Would the priest of the One God help her? Please, I can't lose her, not now, I just found her, no, no, n—" Sahla was nearly frantic.

"Calm down, little one." The Elf smiled at her. "She'll be fine. What she did, well, it takes a lot out of one. Now, let's talk about you."

"No, *Sayyida* Aljannia, I must care for my Mistress! What does she need?" The worry and concern in her voice drew a small smile from Silaqui. She looked at Willis and he simply shrugged and waved his hand from the sorceress to the rescued hostage.

"Very well. Here, Sahla." Silaqui handed her a water flask. "Get some water in her, carefully, and then get her some coffee; it's a stimulant. Aylie will get you some stew broth in a moment. Get some nourishment in her and she'll be fine. I promise."

"Prophet bless you, *Sayyida* Aljannia." Her smile was dazzling. "May he always shade your steps and guide you to sweet water."

For the next half hour, Silaqui and Willis watched, touched and amused, as the tiny Darsälaamic girl tenderly cared for Sachi. Roland, Aylie and Gelman settled the rest of the former hostages and got them food and water.

The first thing Sachi saw when she opened her eyes was Sahla carefully washing away the blood that had covered her CLIBA shirt. Her weapons were neatly laid out on a clean piece of sailcloth, gleaming from meticulous polishing. Her hair had been combed out and neatly braided, lying heavily over her shoulder. There was a warm bowl of stew next to her and a large flask of water next to the bowl.

"What are you doing?" she barely whispered, but the girl heard her anyway.

"Oh, Mistress! Oh, you are well?" Her head snapped up, a huge smile on her face. "Your friends said you would be fine, but I thought I should care for your person and your belongings." She laid a very tentative hand between Sachi's breasts, where the pirate's sword had stabbed her, a delicate touch like a butterfly sipping nectar. "The tear in this shirt is gone, but I did not fix it. I repaired your jacket." When Sachi moved to sit up, the hand darted away.

"Don't worry about this shirt." She rubbed the same spot; there was no sign of the cut. "And what are you doing, that was my question, I believe?"

"I'm caring for you, Mistress. You were sore injured, rescuing us. I could do no less. The Prophet's laws of honor and hospitality demand it."

"There is no need, I'll be fine." Even as Sachi grumbled, the girl snatched up the bowl of stew, handing it to her without spilling a drop. "Ancestors, give me patience! Right now!" she muttered under her breath. "Sahla, right?"

"Yes, Mistress."

"Stop calling me that."

"You may order me to address you as you wish, if Mistress is not sufficient."

"I don't want to order you to do anything." She glared at Sahla and then at the amused looks on her friends' faces. "Shouldn't we be getting off this damn rock?"

"That sloop is armed. We'll talk to them in the morning. There's only an anchor watch aboard. They're not going anywhere." Willis grinned insouciantly at her. "Besides, I'm enjoying this."

"Keep it up, Willis Fleet, and I'll kick out more than a tooth this time."

"I'll hide behind Sahla, she'll protect me." His snide comment drew a brief, confused look from Sahla. "By the way, Sachi, these are the others who were being held hostage." He pointed in turn. "Draven Kye, Zedekiah Abrhaim, and the Contessa Gabrielle de Rochechouart de Mortemart. These three were to be ransomed. The pirates were going to sell Sahla at the slave auction in Luctini. Stand her naked in front of a hundred or so men, prove visually that she's, um, well, untouched and then cash on the barrel for the beautiful young virgin." Willis' voice was cold and quiet for the last part.

"Sell her!?"

"Yes. And being virgin, her price would be high, so some fat old Imperial could have the pleasure of deflowering her. And when he got tired of her, she might be sold again. Or given to his guards as a plaything."

"SELL HER! A PLAYTHING!" The fury in her black eyes was volcanic. "What manner of beasts are these Imperials, that they would do such?!"

"Please, Mistress. Do not distress yourself." Sahla laid a gentle hand on Sachi's shoulder. "I am Bonded to you now. Be at peace, Mistress. Besides, I have things to tell you and something to give you."

"You have what?" Sachi's voice still trembled with suppressed fury.

"Imperial slave auctions are of no matter, now, Mistress. I am safe with you; I know this as certain as I know the Prophet's Truth." Sahla's cheerful voice whiplashed Sachi, leaving her both glad and furious. "As I said, I have certain powers, due to our Bond. You must know my powers if you are to command them. And you must bear my token."

"Powers? Token? What are you talking about?"

"I am born of the love of a mortal woman and an immortal Jinn. I am half-Jinn, what is called a Jann. As a Jann, I have some of the powers and abilities of my Sire. And I could not access the magic of my Sire's blood until I Bonded to a mortal of this world. So, our

Bond, it both protects me from an unpleasant fate, and it grants me the arcane abilities of my heritage as a Jann."

"Because you say I'm the Master and you're my Slave?"

"Partly, yes. But, by the Prophet's beard, it is not so simple."

"Fine, then, what can you do, because of this Bond?" Sachi grumbled as she sipped the broth.

"I may converse with animals, each in their own limited fashion, useful to calm mounts and such. Or ask small favors of them. I may grow," suddenly she loomed over the fire, nearly ten feet tall, "or shrink," and in an instant, she changed, standing on the log, and no more than twelve inches tall. "For a brief while, I may cloak myself in invisibility," she reassumed her normal size and vanished from view. "But for no more than a moment or two. I can twist the air itself around me to ward me and protect me. And I can fly, by the strength of my will, with great speed and precision." She suddenly reappeared, several yards away from where she disappeared. She arrowed into the sky, as graceful as a hummingbird. "And I can use my power to guard and protect my Mistress, blocking or breaking any harmful magic wielded against her. That is my greatest ability."

"I will be double-dog-damned." Willis barely breathed. He felt his eyes trying to bulge out of his head. "You can always come and work for my boss, if nothing else."

"But I am not Bonded to you, Willis Fleet." She dimpled at him as she floated over to a stunned Sachi. "I am Bonded to Sachi Takahashi, and this is my Token, the symbol of my Bond." She held out a beautiful sapphire pendant on a flat gold chain. She started to put the necklace around Sachi's neck when a white-steel blade blocked the chain.

"What are you doing?" Sachi's voice was cold and flat.

"Gifting you my Token, Mistress, naught else."

"What is that? Where'd you have it hidden? How'd the pirates not find a stone like that?"

"It did not exist then. Our Bond created it. Have you never heard fancy tales of the Jinn of the Lamp? Of the Slave of the Ring?"

"No. They don't tell those where I come from. What, exactly, is that gem?"

"It is my Token. The Token reflects the strength of our Bond. And being a sapphire, my chosen gemstone, that sign augurs for an immensely powerful Bond between us, one that will be deep and rich. It is the final link between us. With it, you will always know where I am and you can summon me to you with but a word. And I will know if you are injured or endangered."

"So, it's like a collar? The final link in your chains?"

"No, nothing like that. In a sense, it's my home."

"What?"

"I can't show you unless you hold it, Mistress."

"Just hold it?"

"Please, Mistress? Just for a moment, if naught else? Please?" Sahla held out the gem, firelight flashing blue fire from its depths. Sachi looked over at Silaqui and the Elf shrugged and nodded her head.

"Fine." She took the necklace from Sahla like it was a poisonous serpent.

"Put it on; it must be worn properly."

With a half-hearted grumble, Sachi settled the necklace and its gem over her head.

"Excellent, Mistress. Now, dismiss me."

"What?"

"Dismiss me. I hope, I believe this will show you the difference between our Bond and the chattel slavery you justly hate."

"Fine. You're dismissed." There was a tiny instant, barely perceptible, of a heat mirage or mist and Sahla was gone.

***

"Ancestors!!" Sachi returned to herself with a momentary panic, her heart pounding like a trip-hammer and panting for breath. Her back ground against the cathead. "How did you do that? Don't do it again!" Sahla sat across from her, unmoving, bright eyes gleaming, the sea's spray glistening in her hair.

"I only shared our memories, Mistress."

"Like how you tricked me into wearing this thing?" She held out the sapphire.

"Mistress, I am a Jann. I partake of my Sire's nature, and the Jinni are nothing if not renowned for sly and devious cunning. Some loremasters say that of all the Elemental princes, the Jinni of the Air are the craftiest and inherently chaotic. It was needful."

"*Needful*, she says."

"Mistress, I know you are unhappy with our Bond." Sahla was pensive, nibbling on her lower lip with her teeth. "There are two things you might do, if you truly wish to be rid of me."

"Oh."

"Yes. If you break the stone, the physical embodiment of our Bond, you break the Bond. Only you can break it. If you break it, I will vanish from this Plane, drawn away to my Sire's palace. I have told you what might become of me there."

"And? There's another option?"

"Yes. As you might remember, the stone is my home, when I am dismissed. You have granted me permission to come and go there as I please; otherwise, I could only be here when you summon me."

"I remember."

"Should you truly tire of me, revoke that permission and dismiss me. Then I may not leave without permission. Break the chain and drop the jewel over the side into deep water. There I should remain, to sleep away the eons until the last day comes. Only if, by some strange chance, should my jewel be brought back to light would anything change for me. The holder of the jewel would be able to command me, but there would be no Bond, as long as your spirit still exists, whether or not you still live in this flesh."

"Drop your jewel over the side? What would happen to you?"

"Time would, I believe, cease to notice me. If I awaken, the days will blend into an endless sameness."

"Girl...Sahla...I don't want that for you. Not even the Odas are that cruel."

"Mistress, I trouble you." Her smile illuminated her face. "I must, since you use my name."

"Only the Master-Slave part. You, personally, no, not at all. You are incredibly beautiful. More beautiful than anyone I have ever seen. Enough to take one's breath away."

"Mistress...where you are from, w-what happens if...if two people of the s-same, ah, same s-sex love each other? R-romantically, that is. Huh, p-physically." She was hesitant, nearly stuttering.

"What? Where'd that come from?" Sachi frowned at the nervous, nearly frightened look on Sahla's face. "Well, we're not Kolbia, that's certain. Kolbians don't care who does what with whom, as long as everyone's adult enough to consent. In Isemoto, in the women's quarters and the pleasure houses, women sometimes pleasure each other. Little is made of it; no one cares. Men, well, it depends. If the man in question is a great swordsman and chooses to be with other men, well, one who objects had best be a greater swordsman. It is frowned upon, but not actively prohibited or vigorously persecuted. Why?"

"In Darsälaam, 'tis a grievous sin, by the Book. In the tribes, little is said if women should have...um, special friends among the other women of the harem. But only if it stays in the harem. If a man should lie with another man, and that become known, there are...punishments, gruesome ones. By the Prophet's Law, it is punishable by death to have relations with the same, woman to woman or man to man. And the death is a slow one. A very gentle Aliyah might say naught, and only chastise in private. But a vigilant Aliyah or a stern *Sayyid*, then, such will not be tolerated. And many, many more Aliyahs and *Sayyids* are stern than gentle."

"I see. Why are you asking this, girl?"

"By the rigid interpretation of the Prophet's Law, I am now unclean, impure. He who was to be my husband would tie me backwards on an ass and drive it into the deepest sands. Should I return home, to Abdul-Ghaffanse, having been in the company of strange men without my duenna, rejected by my husband, the Aliyah would condemn me. My mother and father should be the first to throw the stones at me, followed by the rest of my family, before the tribe finishes the stoning. And should I love another woman, my fate would be even worse."

Sachi stared in horror at the girl. Without realizing what she did, she reached out to Sahla, pulling her into her arms. She felt the girl shiver against her, in her thin sailor's tunic. She reached over and pulled the still-warm blanket around the girl's shoulders. Sachi stared into the growing darkness of evening as she felt Sahla's slim frame shake with her silent sobs.

Now what do I do?

Chapter Two

KRN *Swift* (16)
Southern Lanic Ocean
December 1478, Third Age of Imperial Reckoning

"Captain, I've no idea how we missed her in the dusk. Her lookouts must have eyes like cats." Lieutenant Ostheimer thumped his fist on the rail as he stared into the darkness.

"It happens, Hans. But they broke away to the west. Wind and sea conditions won't really let them do anything else. At least we got a better look at her." Lieutenant Commander Carter shrugged philosophically.

"Aye, sir. And now we know what they are. It could be possible that there are two sloops with that distinctive cutter rig. I'd wager no coin on it. *Heartcutter* is supposed to be part of that bastard Ironheart's fleet. And if that is her, she's captained by one of my former countrymen, a disgraced noble named Werner Streiss. Was von Streiss once. Raped and murdered one peasant girl too many and his own father would've haled him to the Baron's Court. The Deuschen Empire still has a price on his head."

"That almost sounds personal, Hans."

"No, sir, not really. He was suspected in several rape-murders in a neighboring Barony, but that Baron was a friend of his father's and swept it under the rug. Nobles like him are why I gave up my title and immigrated to Kolbia. Sir."

"I see." *The look on your face gives a bit of a lie to that statement, Hans. Well, not really any of my business. If we're lucky, we might be able to send that son of a bitch's head to his Baron's Court for you.*

"Well, unless this Werner's a true wizard who can make wind and waves do his bidding, he's going to run into either *Blackwood* or *Alacrity* sometime in the morning watch. Doubt that it will be at all enjoyable. For him." Carter sighed and stepped away from the rail. "Secure from action stations, Hans. Get the crew fed, but I want double lookouts posted through the night. If you need me, I'll be in my cabin."

"Aye, sir."

Armed Sloop *Graser* (6)
Southern Lanic Ocean
December 1478, Third Age of Imperial Reckoning

"Well, so far that worked," Willis sighed as the range opened between the KRN schooner and *Graser*. He glanced upward. "I think you can come down now." Sachi hung head down, her ankle lashed to the backstay ten feet above his head. She was strong and flexible enough to raise and lower herself from that anchor point. This had enabled her to put her head sixteen feet above the deck, using her enhanced vision to turn night into day. Then she'd swung down and whispered heading and course to Willis, allowing him to stay well away from the much more heavily armed schooner.

"Yes, it did. Better than I expected." Sachi dropped to the deck without a sound. She gave Willis an odd look. "We avoid your own countrymen, Willis."

"I'm not happy about that either, but, first, this ship is a well-known pirate in these waters, or so the former pirates themselves have told us, and second, we agreed with said former pirates that we wouldn't just turn them over to the KRN. We find the wrong captain out here, and despite my credentials, as waterlogged as they are, we all might be expecting a *pirate's reward well earned*, a tight noose and a quick heave. More than a few Lanic Fleet line officers have an incredibly short way with pirates and slavers. Comes of having to clean up after them too often."

"But we're not pirates, Willis!"

"Aye. You know that, and I know that, but that ship over there doesn't. I'll not fire on any ship of my Navy, but it will be much easier to simply never have to explain ourselves at all."

"Iff'n I's can speak, Capitaine Willis," Irene du Buisson quietly spoke from her position at the ship's wheel.

"Please."

"I's knows fer a good fact, I's be wanted by da Kolbian Navy and Montagar fer a pirate. 'Tis nigh on two years I's been on zis deck. Or trapped on zat isle o' monsters. When Verner took me Fater's fishin' boat, he kills me Fater an ze rest o' da crew. Zey, ze mans he kilt, zey was me family. Zat Quan-cursed bastard, Verner, he gives me a choice, I's can let jist him futter me good, whens he wants, and iff'n I's can fight an' beat anuther pirate, ta shows I's can fight good, weal, zen he makes me one o' his crew on zis sloop, when she be ze *Heartcutter*. Me other choice be zat he throws me ta his crew, alls of 'em, ta futter me till zey's tired o' me. Iff'n I's still alive, I's be da lowest o' da crew on ze ship, but nay ta be truly a pirate. Jist ta be somethin' womanish zey futters when zey wants ta. 'Til I's dead. Nay choice zere, I zinks." Her Terranglais wasn't particularly good, but the fire in her gray eyes told its own story.

"I know, Irene. I know." Willis closed his eyes at the grim scenario the young woman described. "I'm not blaming you, and it's hardly your fault, but some by-the-letter-and-code-of-the-book KRN ship's captain will simply see you as a pirate and we know how that will end."

"Aye. I's mortal grateful ta ye, Capitaine, and I's knows 'tis harder much fer ye, ta given ze slips and sneaks ta zose as may help ye."

"Well, you're not the only one in that pickle, Irene." Willis smiled at the pretty blonde. She held his gaze for a long moment and then gave him a single, determined nod. "Line officers sometimes get a little rigid in interpreting the law of the Sea. Carry on, Irene."

"Aye, Capitaine."

"Well, that explains enough of it, I guess, Willis." Sachi shrugged as she looked from Willis to Irene and back. "So, now what?"

"For now, we hold this course. Get some sea room between us and that schooner. We'll run west with wind on our quarter until the wind shifts southerly. That or we'll come about and run north-easterly about six bells into the middle watch.

Damnation." Willis thumped his fist on the rail as he stared into the night-shrouded waves.

"What's bothering you, Willis? Spit it out." Sachi stepped up beside him and gently held his wrist.

"We don't know what's going on," he kept his voice low. "This is deep, too deep into the Southern Lanic for a schooner to be operating as a singleton. But what is she operating with? A brace or trio of other schooners, sweeping for slavers? Unless they're properly armed with the new weapons, no schooner can truly expect to take on a blue water pirate. Most blue water pirates are ships roughly equal to one of our smaller frigates, thirty-six to forty guns, three masted galleons and ship rigged. A bit big of a chew for a schooner of sixteen guns."

"So?"

"So, that schooner likely has friends not too far away. What kind of friends? More schooners? A Sloop-of-War? A frigate? And why are this many Navy ships this far south?" He shook his wrist free of Sachi's hand. "And between that schooner and the current and the wind, we're being herded out into the Lanic. Not at all where we want to be, oh, no."

"Why not?"

"Well, storms are worse here in deep water. At the worst, we could be forced into lying ahull, battening down the hatches, furling all sail, and lowering the topgallant yard, maybe the topgallant mast as well. God only knows if we'd survive like that or if we could get the topgallant mast re-stepped and the yard hoisted again. Especially with this crew."

"Perhaps you should give your crew a little more credit, Willis."

"The way you give Sahla credit?" He gave her an evil smile as her brows furrowed in anger. "Yeah, thought so."

"You tread dangerously, Willis."

"Uh-huh." He was quiet for a long moment, carefully watching the Nisei fume. "And not just with you. We're away from that damn island, but what course to set? I've still my dispatches that I should be moving heaven and earth to deliver, but I know there aren't sufficient supplies on this ship to reach Luctini. And the only charts we have onboard show a course for a so-called free port named Du Khamps des SouSee."

"What's the problem there?"

"Well, there's an old, old joke about places like Du Khamps being, let's see, how'd it go, yeah, *wretched hives of scum and villainy* or something like that. That saying is so old, no one knows where it came from. A pirate port might be a better description. The Navy considers burning it to the ground every few years, but Lord Kormarra has some kind of deal with Admeeral du SouSee Havre Calchas, who commands the collection of old barges the Empire calls their Lanic Fleet. Since we're not willing to start a war over a crusted-up chamber pot like Du Khamps, well, it remains unburned. Pity."

"You know Silaqui has, um, issues with pirates, right?"

"Yeah. Spiders, too, now. I think. Hopefully, she can restrain herself until we get resupplied and a decent set of charts. Then she can burn the place down for all I care."

"Ah. I see."

"Go get some rest, Sachi. You must be worn out from hanging like a bat on the backstay. Roland made something he calls a burrito. Meat and cheese rolled up in a piece of flatbread. Watch out for the sauce. Quan's Delight he calls it. Fortunately, your tongue goes numb on about the third bite."

"I see. I'll try it." She shrugged and turned toward the passageway below. She froze as Sahla popped up out of the passageway, a large plate piled with several of Roland's burritos and a large jack of ale in her hands.

"When I overheard the Captain tell you to come down from the backstay, I knew you would be hungry, Mistress. So I asked Roland to fix you some food, something you could eat easily..." She trailed off as she saw the fury on Sachi's face.

"Do NOT throw that food overboard, Sachi!" Willis snapped. "There isn't enough that we can afford to waste any. And tell her thank you. That's an order from your ship's commanding officer."

Sachi halted, her head snapping around to stare at Willis.

"What...did...you...just...say?" She ground out the words as if they hurt her.

"You heard me." For once Willis' face was just as hard as hers. "I'm sick and tired of the way you treat her."

"She wants to be a...a SLAVE, Willis! To be owned! By me!" Somehow, she managed not to shriek at the top of her lungs.

"Does she, Sachi, does she really!? Have you ever stopped screaming about slavery long enough to ask her, to ask Sahla what she really wants? Or do you just take the easy way, stomp off screaming that you'll not stand for it, and not take the time to learn what might be done about it? Well? Have you?"

Sahla froze as rage and confusion swirled on Sachi's face. She didn't dare even draw breath.

"Damn you, Willis Fle..."

"That's CAPTAIN FLEET to you right now, sailor!" he roared. "You either accept my authority as commander of this ship, here and now, or decide which one of us goes over the rail. You want to be a Kolbian? Then start acting like one! We look for a better way! Maybe that's what you should start doing, as of this moment! Am I clear, Able Seaman Sachi Takahashi?"

"Clear, Captain Fleet." Sachi's voice was just as hard as his.

"I wonder." He rubbed his chin for a moment. "Seaman Takahashi, what do you think Bosun Beauchamp would say to you right now? Or Captain Blaine? Or Toby Wilkerson?"

Sahla saw her twitch, then jerk as if a saber had gone home in her ribs. Even in the night's darkness, she watched Sachi's porcelain skin go as pale as the finest paper. Her head shook once, in negation, her eyes huge in the dimness of the deck. Sachi took a single deep breath and came to attention.

"Understood, sir." She turned to face Sahla. "Thank you, Sahla." Back to Willis. "Permission to be dismissed, sir?"

"Aye, Able Seaman, dismissed." Willis' voice was hard and flat as she vanished like a ghost in mist.

"Ah, Captain, what just happened?" Sahla quietly asked after a few moments.

"I'm tired of the bullshit." Fleet sighed and turned to take the wheel. "Go below, Irene. I'll finish this watch. I'd be thankful if you'd say naught of this."

"Aye, Capitaine." The blonde woman gave Sahla an odd look as she stepped past her.

"Sahla, come up here, please."

"Yes, Captain?"

"Look, I understand you're grateful for this Bond that keeps you here. But is this Master-Slave thing the only way?"

"No, *Sayyid*."

"Just stick to Captain, Sahla; I'm no one's Lord."

"As you will, Captain." She dipped her head in acknowledgement. "There are other Bonds. Better, stronger ones. The best would be True Lov..."

"I don't care if you two eventually become Heimdägarran Sword-sisters, or swear blood oaths to each other, or if the two of you just go get married. But I've had it up to here," he held his forefinger just under his nose, "with her tantrums and her fits. And how you act at times greatly contributes to this problem. Figure out some way to at least mitigate it if you can't fix it, understand? Am I clear, Sahla?"

"Yes, Captain." He barely heard her over the sounds of the ship.

"Good."

"Captain?"

"What?"

"How is it possible that two women might marry?"

"From what little I know of your people's religion, for anyone to have, well, relations with someone of the same sex is a mortal sin. But in Kolbia, it's no big deal. Long as everyone's a consenting adult, no one cares who you marry. It's just one of the reasons everyone else on this Fallen world either hates us or thinks we're all whale-shit crazy. Take your pick. Now, scat."

"What, Captain?"

"Scat, shoo, go away, take your beautiful little self elsewhere. Get out of my face; make a hole in the air where you were. I'm exhausted from dealing with you two and now, the CAPTAIN wants some peace and quiet. So, go on, beat it. Scram, kid."

Sahla disappeared like smoke.

***

Lately, too many people had been pestering her in her favorite spot, between the cathead and bowsprit. Silaqui generally claimed the crosstrees at the masthead, above the topgallant yard, so that was out. But she didn't think anyone else, not even the pestiferous Sahla, knew about her hidey-hole in the forward sail locker. Sachi settled in there and simply rested for a while, relaxing muscles which tension and stress had made stone hard. Eventually she dozed off and then found herself in a familiar place.

::Lieutenant Commander Caitlyn Schmidt.:: D.A.V.E. was standing there, the featureless gray plain extending endlessly away under featureless gray skies.

"Am I having another fit, D.A.V.E.?" She didn't feel quite right, more...well, more connected to herself and her body than was normal in one of the fits the Entity used to bring her here.

::No. With the improvements in your System Integration, the fits as you describe them, have no further use. System Integration is currently at eighty-nine percent and the rate of improvement has slowed substantially. Significant further improvement will require at least a Class Four Medical Facility. Currently, you are merely sleeping more deeply than normal.::

"So why am I here now?"

::This Entity requires significantly less energy and system resource access to communicate with you in Virtual Reality. A VR Construct is most easily accessed while sleeping.::

"That didn't answer my question, now, did it?"

::Null input::

"Yeah, thought so. Why am I here, D.A.V.E.?"

::Your...artificially imposed relationship with the individual identified as Sahla al Qasim ab Ghaffanse causes you a great deal of mental and physical stress. This reduces your effectiveness and strains system resources.::

"Wonderful. Now that…girl causes problems with a machine in my head." She shook her head and stared down at D.A.V.E.'s silver avatar. "So, what should I do, then?"

::Given Sahla al Qasim ab Ghaffanse's description of this relationship, it would be most prudent to determine if this *non-rational quantum effect* that she claims that binds the two of you together can, in fact, be severed as she describes.:: The statue was immobile and expressionless, but somehow, Sachi sensed a cold disapproval from the thing. ::A relationship such as Sahla al Qasim ab Ghaffanse describes could possibly lower your system effectiveness to percentages that might endanger your mission.::

"You're saying might and possibly. And what about Sahla? If I do sever the Bond she claims exists and she is pulled away to the fate she describes, how do I deal with that?"

::Personnel losses within certain extents are acceptable, if regrettable.::

"What?" She stared at the thing in shock. "If I didn't know better, I'd think you were…jealous of her!"

::Null input. A Digitally Aware Virtual Entity does not possess emotional simulation sub-routines. Emotional responses are therefore counter-indicated.::

"Riiight." Sachi stared at the thing for a long moment. "Has hyper-heuristic mode been activated?"

::Affirmative. Current temporal dilation ratio is nine thousand to one.::

"Let's see, now, how well what you've been teaching me has stuck. Perform personal system dynamic integration assessment, please."

::Affirmative. Assessment program running.:: There was a brief pause. ::Assessment complete.::

"Results?"

::Internal system interface integration, ninety-seven percent; bio-monitoring and injury assessment and repair, ninety-nine percent; memory enhancement and retrieval, ninety-two percent. Nanite interface systems integration, one hundred percent. Biological Processor Unit integration and interface function, one hundred percent. Nano-fiber bone lace and reinforcement at twenty-two percent. Neural-synaptic enhancement at twenty-eight percent. Basic muscular enhancement and nano-tube sheath at twenty-one percent. Further physical enhancement without access to advanced medical facilities will be extremely limited. Visual, tactile, and auditory sensory enhancements one hundred percent.::

"Summarize."

::Lieutenant Commander Caitlyn Schmidt, you are, in general, markedly stronger, faster, and tougher than ninety-nine-point nine percent of the human species before enhancement. After enhancement you heal at a significantly advanced rate. You have, in essence, an eidetic memory. You have advanced sensory systems capable of determining range within fifteen millimeters. Those systems also provide multi-mode vision capabilities.::

"Yes, I have all those things." She paused, then turned and walked a few steps away. "But am I still human? Did I give up my soul for these things?"

::I cannot answer existential questions, Lieutenant Commander Caitlyn Schmidt. But the vast majority of Confederation personnel with similar enhancement packages normally went on to live successful, fulfilling lives. By any human standards. They were considered entirely human.::

"I see." She wrapped her arms around herself. "And did any of them fall in love? Did anyone love them, for them, not for what they were, what the machines had made them into?"

::I lack access to such files, Lieutena...::

"Shut up, D.A.V.E." Sachi felt the silence of the VR construct around her. "Evaluation of real-space individual identified as Sahla al Qasim ab Ghaffanse requested."

::Initial evaluation: Subject exhibits marked DNA anomalies, probable homo sapiens hybrid, capable of accessing *non-rational quantum realities* to a limited extent. Non h. s. sapiens biological source unknown, but within ninety percent of human norm, probability approaches unity. Subject analysis supports an absolute belief in the truth of her explanation. Note that this subject operates primarily on an emotional basis.::

"Yeah, that I got." Sachi smothered a chuckle. "Evaluation of the described 'Bond' please."

::Subject Sahla al Qasim ab Ghaffanse's belief in same approaches unity. Speculation: *Non-rational quantum effect* extremely likely, given all previous observations available to this entity. Subject has demonstrated capabilities consistent with previously recorded instances of actual *non-rational quantum access* and effects resulting from such access.::

"*Non-rational quantum access.* You mean magic, don't you?"

::Affirmative.::

"What, Silaqui wasn't enough proof for you that magic is real?"

::Null input.::

"Humpf." For a long moment, what felt like hours to her, but was likely only bare seconds in the real world, Sachi stared out into the blank gray sameness of the VR world. "Evaluation of subject's emotional state in reference to myself."

::This Entity is not properly equipped to evaluate human emotional responses or states.::

"Quit being a weasel and do as I ask. And, yes, I understand your evaluation will be less than perfect because you're just an Entity and not an AI."

::Understood. Subject displays behavior indicative of highly conflicted internal tensions. While the subject displays traditional signs of intense physical and emotional attachment to yourself, Lieutenant Commander Caitlyn Schmidt, the subject finds that this attachment creates a sense of cognitive dissonance within herself. Based on this Entity's understanding of the subject's originating culture, a potential romantic relationship between yourself and her is taboo.::

"You have got to be joking!"

::This Entity was not programmed with the emotional responses necessary for a functional sense of humor.::

"Are you saying that Sahla is either falling in love with me or is already in love with me? And that's causing problems for her?! Are you working right? Sea air making you rust?"

::It is impossible for my components to rust. Most of them are bio-electronic components housed within your body.::

"And you say you have no sense of humor."

::Null input.:: The statue somehow conveyed a sense of very grumpy disgruntlement. ::Probability of subject displaying and acting with intense devotion to yourself, up to and including self-sacrifice in defense of your person, is seventy-one percent, plus or minus fifteen percent. An emotional attachment based on romantic interest increases that probability by twenty-two percent, plus or minus twelve percent. Multiple variables.::

"And you think I'd be better off without her? Or would you be better off?" Sachi tapped her toe while she waited for a response. She waited a long time. "Cat got your tongue?"

::Multiple parameter calculations under way. Please stand by.::

"Sure. Got all day." She stepped away from the statue and began working through a series of katas, learning to use what she already knew and combining it with rapid changes in the form of the white-steel swords she carried.

Those blades weren't truly steel at all; they were a powered collection of trillions of nanites, nanoscopic scale machines. Called nanniballs, they absorbed energy from various sources such as body heat, motion, sunlight, and used it to form anything their user wished. They could be 'locked' in a single form and require a code to release them. Only an enhanced human with the implanted computer interface systems could manipulate them. Sachi had that capability and now she formed them from sword to dagger to shield to armor, the mass of fluidic composite flickering dully in the gray light of the VR Construct.

::Calculations complete.:: The statue was facing Sachi as she finished the last kata. ::This Entity calculates that the continued presence of the subject known as Sahla al Qasim ab Ghaffanse will enhance the probability of mission success by twelve percent, plus or minus forty-one percent. Multiple variables cannot be accounted for. However, the majority of calculations, eighty-three percent of them, indicate a general trend toward more favorable probability of mission success.::

"So, you don't think I should break this Bond or throw her gem in the ocean?" Her voice was quiet.

Why does this bother me so? What is it about this girl, young woman, really, that troubles me? She claims to be my slave, but other than my hatred of that vile institution, where might the burden truly be? I'd never hurt her, why should I when she is no threat to me at all? I held her while she sobbed, only hours ago. Ancestors, to be punished with such a terrible death, simply for loving where lords and priests say This! This is wrong! Why? What would be wrong to simply love someone? Just because a man might love another man, or a woman another woman? What care would the Ancestors take? Faugh! Sachi stopped, a sudden thought striking her. *Can she use her magic to influence my thoughts? She said nothing of such gifts, but she has mentioned how crafty and cunning the Jinni can be.*

"D.A.V.E., request evaluation of my personal emotional state regarding Sahla al Qasim ab Ghaffanse."

::Acknowledged. Calculations under way.::

"Is this going to take all damn day as well?" Sachi dropped back into a kata, white-steel butterfly swords flickering into armored bracers and then into a single long nodachi. The kata was one she had designed recently, to train her in fully exploiting the abilities of her nanite weapons and her own physical enhancements.

::Personal Evaluation. Lieutenant Commander Caitlyn Schmidt, physical age 20 Standard Years, reference subject Sahla al Qasim ab Ghaffanse. Probability of positive intense emotional attachment to subject, sixty-two percent, plus or minus thirty percent. Probability of romantic or sexual attachments appears positive, but nearly impossible to calculate. Excessive variables. However, general trend indicates the continued presence of subject Sahla al Qasim ab Ghaffanse as a generally positive influence on both you and on your mission.::

"So, I take it, I shouldn't break the Bond or toss her jewel over the side, then?"

::Correct:: D.A.V.E.'s voice faded away as the real world replaced the VR Construct and Sachi realized the pain clawing at her stomach was hunger.

***

"Damn machine, I'm starving." Sachi wiggled out from between the loosely stacked spare sails. She opened the hatch and stepped into the passageway. Sahla was folded up across from the hatch, sound asleep. The ale jack sat on the floor, next to the platter of now-cold burritos. Sachi stopped dead and stared. "Ancestors."

"Mistress!" Sahla snapped awake and scrambled to her feet, snatching up the platter and jack without spilling a drop. "I'm sorry, please, eat something; I know you must be very hungry." Her sapphire eyes shone in the dim passageway.

"Oh, Sahla," Sachi sighed. "What are we to do with each other?"

"Mistress?" Her voice reflected her confusion.

"Don't call me that, please? Not anymore." For a long moment, they stared at each other in the dim light of the passageway's single lamp, sapphire eyes capturing sable eyes. "Sahla, what would you call me, if you could call me anything at all?"

"How would I address you, is that what you're asking?"

"Yes. If there were no Bond and we were just two girls, two young women who met in the marketplace and became friends. How would you address me then? In your own language?"

"*Sadayqaa*. It means friend."

"*Sadayqaa*. I like that. Friend, eh? How about that, instead of Mistress all the time?" Sachi smiled at the Jann, an honest, open smile, something rarely seen on her lips. "That, or just call me Sachi, if that's what you'd like, please?"

"You ask what I would like, *Sadayqaa*?"

"Yes, that's what friends do, isn't it?"

"Yes, Mistr... *Sadayqaa*, it is."

"*Sadayqaa*, that's much nicer than Mistress. Or you can just call me Sachi. If you prefer."

"Sachi. That's a pretty name."

"It means *fortunate*, Sahla. Or *child of bliss*, depending on where you're from in Isemoto."

"Truly?" The girl giggled. "Mine means *virtuous*."

"That fits, I think." Sahla sighed. "Come on; let's go up by the cathead and talk. Well, we can talk after I eat those whatchamacallits, those burritos."

"I should like to just talk... Sachi."

***

Well, that could be a complication I do not need. If the disembodied personality had possessed a face, it would have frowned. *It might make her easier to control, or harder. At this point, there is no way to tell, and the* non-rational quantum access *element just makes things even worse. What is that girl? And where did the non-human element come from? Well, in the long run, it should not matter. I should be able to complete both missions. It would be nice if I could get some guidance from my originating source. Whatever happened to the Confederation, something should have replaced it by now. Or the Confederation should have recovered by now. Damned inconvenient, if you ask me.*

***

"Permission to enter the quarterdeck, Captain?"

"Don't you start on me, too, Pere Gelman, or I'll have you keelhauled." Willis grinned at the priest from where he stood next to the wheel.

"No, you won't." Pere Gelman Stavor, empowered priest of the One God of the Circled Cross, returned the smile as he leaned against the binnacle. "Besides, Aylie will protect me."

"Protect yer ownself, Pere. I've other to do." The slight young woman followed Gelman onto the deck. "Captain, the others've settled in for the night. We, Gelman and I, took the mid-watch, aye?"

"That's fine, Aylie." He smiled as she hopped up on the rail, holding the shroud-lines as she peered forward. Her curly brown hair, cut fairly short, fluttered in the wind. Despite her youth, there was a certain hardness to her. Understandable, when she was wanted for a murder she'd never committed.

"Do I see what I thinks I do, Willis?" She looked over her shoulder at him. "Yon two lovelies sitting together quietly with nae shoutin' and hysterics from our tall, black-haired enigma?"

"Where'd you learn that word, enigma, Aylie?" Gelman smirked at her.

"I's born a street rat, Pere. I did nae stay one. Milady made sure I's as well educated as any upper house servant and better than many as calls themselves Quality. Bloody toffs, think they's me better, cause their blood be bluer than mine."

"No squabbling, you two, or I'll clap you in irons with only bread and water for a week." Willis smiled at the odd pair, a priest with the power to heal and a former street urchin turned Lady's Maid to a Duchess.

"She'd just pick the locks." Gelman mockingly shook his fist at Willis. "Still, she has a point. How'd that come about?"

"I called Sachi on the carpet about her behavior, re: Sahla, and after she left, informed Sahla that sometimes her actions did not help things. Sachi went and found one of her hidey-holes to sulk in, I guess. Not sure where Sahla went. Next thing I know, the two of them come up on deck and settle in by the cathead, peaceful as you could ask for. I'll not look a gift horse in the mouth."

"I see," Gelman muttered.

"How are the others doing?" Willis turned the wheel slightly to keep the ship on her best sailing point.

"Well enough, I believe." Gelman shrugged. "Irene is happy to be free of the pirates. Roland's happy with the galley. Draven's asleep, mumbling something about *Throw it to home, throw it to home*. You Kolbians and your baseball game, I guess. Zedekiah is also sleeping, comfortably I think, despite Her Ladyship, Contessa Gabrielle using him for a pillow. That woman is useless, in my opinion."

"Not my place to say. She's not the least idea what to do on a ship." Willis shook his head. "Other than get in the way."

"True. The blacksmith's apprentice, Jean Goujon, is pleased as a pig in slop to be free of Ironheart, and willing to work hard.

The other one, Androu Petrakis, is slightly more useful than the Contessa. Mostly because he's afraid of angering Sachi, I think. And our cabin boy, Paul Rico, is passed out by your cabin door, Captain. Kid's sleeping like a pile of rags."

"Since you're keeping up with the crew so well, Gelman, I think I'll name you Ship's Bosun." Willis sniggered at the startled look on the priest's face. "Be responsible for ship's discipline and whatnot."

"I know nearly nothing of the sea or ships!"

"But you know people, and that's needed right now."

"Bu... bu... but—"

"Enough, the twain of ye. Willis 'tis naught but truthful, Pere Gelman, and ye know it." Aylie's astringent tone left Gelman perturbed and Willis smiling. "Have ye given any thought to what may come betwixt the long and short of our troublesome pair?"

"Not really." Willis shook his head again. "Other than to get Sachi to stop screaming, that is."

"I wonder what they're saying to each other, up there?" Gelman rubbed his chin. "This is the longest the two of them have been in each other's company without Sachi exploding. I wonder if that machine in her head has aught to do with it?"

"Who knows?" Willis and Aylie smiled at each other as they chorused their answer together.

***

"*Who knows, indeed?*" the Sorceress whispered to the night.

Perched in her favorite spot atop the mast, Silaqui was glad the darkness hid her broad smile. Through her magic, she heard both what was being said on the quarterdeck and the subdued conversation under way by the cathead.

I might not know what the DAVE thing has to do with things, but I do know what is being said between my dearest mortal friend and the lovely Sahla. And things are well. Very well.

Chapter Three

Armed Sloop *Graser* (6)
Southern Lanic Ocean
December 1478, Third Age of Imperial Reckoning

"Sail to starboard!" The call came from the masthead, barely visible from the deck in the pre-dawn darkness.

"Shit," Willis muttered under his breath. "How far?" he called up with the leather speaking trumpet.

"Two miles, maybe two and a half at most," Silaqui answered.

"Not good. Very not good." It was seven bells into the mid-watch. He'd turned *Graser* to run north-easterly half an hour ago. Spotting another sail implied many things, none of them good. "Sachi!"

"Aye, Captain?" The Nisei trotted aft from her spot by the cathead.

"Go aloft and see if you can tell what we're dealing with. Specifically, if it's another KRN vessel, some merchant or a not-too-bright pirate."

"Aye." She scampered up the shrouds like a squirrel. Sahla, following Sachi, craned her head up to follow.

"Sahla, go below and get everyone up. Quietly now, and quickly, too."

"Yes, *Sayyid*."

"None of that, now."

"Yes, umm, aye, Captain." She hustled below deck.

"Gelman, Aylie, we've a fairly calm sea and a moderate breeze, seven or eight knots might be the best we do for speed. If we can't outrun her and if she isn't KRN, she might be a pirate. Clear away the guns. I'll send Jean and Androu to help, soon as they get up here."

For a ship as light as she was, *Graser* mounted a fearsome broadside. She only mounted six guns in total, but two in each broadside were eighteen pounder carronades, as heavy as any Kolbian schooner or Sloop-of-War carried. The remaining gun was a long twelve pounder, still twice as heavy as most small sloops carried. And with only a three-gun broadside, there was room to serve the guns quickly and efficiently. Unfortunately, Willis lacked the crew to serve all three guns in a broadside simultaneously.

At least we've the weather gauge on her, whatever she is. We can break contact, run due north or north-north-east. I'll bet my next promotion she's another schooner. There's a whole squadron, maybe a task force at sea for some reason. I know the Empire has lost its mind over the Stellar *Incident last year. But do they really want a war with us? Maybe the Army couldn't match them on land, but we own the ocean. Captain Eyles and* Stellar *hammered three of their crappy old galleasses into scrap in an afternoon. What do they think a ship-of-the-line will do to them? And God help them if we get three or four of the newest designs to sea in time.* The rest of the crew clattering up on deck broke into Willis' train of thought.

"Orders, Captain?" Zedekiah asked as he stopped beside Fleet.

"We'll come onto the port tack, Zedekiah, preferably close hauled if we can manage it."

"I think we can, sir."

"Then get the crew to stations."

"Aye, Captain."

***

"So now we have a pair of schooners, one east and one west of us." Willis frowned as he watched the second schooner's sails disappear in the darkness. "Sachi, do you think they saw us?"

"No, Captain, I doubt it. I never saw any sign of activity from her lookouts, no hands called onto the deck, nothing."

Willis nodded at her report, hiding a smile as he noted Sahla standing close enough to the Nisei to rub her shoulder against Sachi's arm. He looked up at the sails, gauging the wind. Then he shook his head.

"Well, we may be screwed."

"How so, Willis?" Silaqui asked.

"If there are two schooners here, then there's either a frigate or a Sloop-of-War either north or south of us. I expect north of us."

"Captain, would not a, how did you say, a Sloop-of-War be the same as us? A light ship with few guns?" Sahla asked.

"Not quite, Sahla; there's sloops like this one, a small, light ship. But a Kolbian Sloop-of-War is different. Some carry only two masts, but most of them are three masted and ship-rigged. They get mistaken for our frigates all the time. They're not as big or heavy, with shallower draft and lighter guns, lighter scantlings. It's pretty common practice to operate a detached squadron with a pair of schooners and either a Sloop-of-War or a lighter frigate, say a thirty-eight or thirty-six. The bigger, heavier forties and forty-fours usually operate either as a flagship or independently."

"I know nothing of ships."

"I know. Don't worry about it. That's my job."

"Well, then, what should ye be doing about it, Willis?" Aylie leaned calmly against the binnacle.

"Not much we can do, Aylie. I'll not fire on a ship of my countrymen. If we get trapped, we'll strike our sails and hope I can convince the captain in charge that I am, in fact, what I am, an ONI operative on a mission. One with vital dispatches for the Diplomatic Mission in Luctini. Or at least that we're not pirates and that *Heartcutter* is no longer a pirate ship."

"Not exactly the best plan I've ever heard, Captain." Zedekiah rubbed his chin.

"Me neither," Fleet answered, "have you a better idea?"

"No, Captain, unfortunately I don't."

"Well, Irene, Jean and Androu, I can't promise what will happen. We can't outfight any of these ships, especially if they're armed with the KRN's new weapons. And I doubt we can out-sail either of these schooners. Firing on them simply guarantees we all get hung for pirates. I'll do the best I can, but we're in one hell of a pickle."

"Unnerstood, Capitaine." Irene's face was hard. "Leastwise, ze KRN t'will on'y hang us, quick and cleanly-like. Nae torture, nor gibbetin'. Likely ze best we's could hope fer any road."

"Well, hopefully, it won't come to that." Willis smiled at the motley crowd that was *Graser's* crew. "And if it does, they'll likely hang me right beside you. Cold comfort, I know, but it's the best I can do. Now, to your stations. Gabrielle, I want you to help Roland in the galley."

"I am a Contessa; I do NOT help peasants in a galley!" The blonde woman sniffed.

"You'll do as you're told, or I'll see you dropped back on that island where we found you. I'll bet I could convince a captain to do that. Rather than hang you," Willis growled. *She gets away from the pirates and the monsters and now she thinks she's due special treatment again. What a pain in the butt, and she thinks she's the most gorgeous woman to walk the world. Idiot needs to take a look at Sahla. Or Sachi. Either one would put her butt on the wagon.* His smile was cold as the blood drained from her face.

"That shall not be needful, Captain." Zedekiah put a hand on her shoulder. "I'll see her to her duties."

"Good, but be quick about it."

"Aye, Captain."

"Sachi, Sahla."

"Aye, Willis?" Sachi answered as Sahla nodded, sapphire eyes shining.

"I think the pair of you have the best eyes on board. I want you two up on the masthead; see if you can keep us from running over whatever is out there to our north."

"Aye, Captain."

Silaqui, Gelman." Willis caught their attention. "Put your heads together and see if you can figure some magical way out of our dilemma. Don't tell me about it, just do it."

"Aye, Captain." Gelman answered for the pair.

"Good. Everyone else, get to your stations. Stay sharp and keep your eyes open. Pray, if you've the inclination." The rest of the crew scattered to their positions. He shook his head and looked east to where dawn was flushing the sky with the first hint of golden light. *Looks like a wonderful day for sailing, just enough wind, calm seas, and a clear sky. We are so fucked.*

KRN *Blackwood* (12)
Southern Lanic Ocean
December 1478, Third Age of Imperial Reckoning

"You think you saw a sail, Able Seaman?" Lieutenant Wayne Savras, Captain of the twelve-gun schooner KRN *Blackwood*, managed not to snarl at his hapless lookout. "The Navy doesn't run on *think*, Sailor!"

"Aye, Captain." The sailor, one Michael Candler, stood braced to rigid attention.

"Then what did you see at the time?" *Blackwood's* First Lieutenant, Omari Amos, Lieutenant, Junior Grade, asked quietly before Savras could bite the sailor's head off.

"I thought t'was a low fog bank at first; ifs they was sails, they was stained, as pirates in these waters oft do, sir."

"Go on, Candler." Omari prompted when the captain simply grunted in response to his questioning look.

"Whatever t'was, t'was running parallel or slight converging course to us. Then it faded away in the dark, sir. I'd no thought of it, but something kept troubling me, till I realized it'd turned to windward, like to a tack to port, close-hauled like, sir. A fog bank'd nae do that, nae possible. Then I realized what t'was likely to be and hurried to the bosun. He took me report and told me he'd being making a note of me tardiness."

"Very well. Have you any idea what type of ship it might have been?"

"Nae really, sir. I'd guess she'd be single-masted and rigged fore-and-aft. Didn't see a square sail, sir."

"Well, good enough that you reported it, Seaman Candler. But in these waters, you should err on the side of caution. Report to the Quartermaster that your grog ration is stopped tomorrow and the next day." Omari preempted the captain. "I doubt your error is truly worthy of stripes, but you'll be paying closer watch, now, won't you?"

"Aye, sir. That I most certainly will!"

"Captain, anything further for him?"

"No. Dismissed to your station, Sailor."

"Aye-aye, Captain." Candler vanished like a phantom in the slowly growing light of dawn.

"He shoulda had stripes," Savras growled to his First Lieutenant. "I don't like you undercutting my authority that way, Lieutenant."

"And then next time, he simply wouldn't say anything at all, would he, sir?"

"Grmpf."

"Request permission to be temporarily relieved of the watch, sir."

"What fo... oh. Got to go bang your head on the bloody deck for your religious beliefs, eh?" Disdain dripped from Savras' voice.

"Yes, sir. We are not at action stations, nor is there any potential enemy in sight. I think it not unreasonable to take the time to offer Chalta and His Prophet their proper worship. Captain."

"Damn foolish thing to do, if I be asked."

"I could have Ensign Selfer take the deck, sir."

"He came off watch at the end of the mid-watch. No, let him rest. I'll take the deck while you go babble to your God. You are relieved, sir."

"I stand relieved, Captain."

***

Omari went down to the cramped cabin he shared with Ensign Ethan Selfer. The compact Ensign looked up from his book as Omari spread out his somewhat tattered prayer rug. It was one of the few things his father had brought from Darsälaam when the family had fled a Sultan's wrath, forty years ago. Long before Omari was born.

"Old Grumpy give you the usual ration of shit before he relieved you?" Ethan's mild brown eyes and close-cut brown hair reinforced his deceptively relaxed appearance.

"Of course."

"He could avoid this by giving you the mid-watch."

"He knows. It's his usual lack of sensitivity to other human beings' thoughts and feelings. I don't think he does it on purpose. Of course, it might also be the path the Prophet chooses to test my faith."

"Perhaps. Well, I'll be quiet while you perform your devotions."

"Thank you, Ethan."

KRN *Swift* (16)
Southern Lanic Ocean
December 1478, Third Age of Imperial Reckoning

"Sail ho! Due west, looks to be the *Heartcutter*, Captain!" The shout from the top of the mainmast brought everyone's head up before they rushed to the portside rail.

"Damn me if you didn't call the nail on the head, Captain!" Hans Ostheimer grinned as he watched the pirate ship heel awkwardly away from the Kolbian schooner. "Right where you said she'd be!"

"It is nice, isn't it? I expect she found *Blackwood* sometime around six bells in the mid-watch." Carter watched through his glass as the other ship clawed onto the starboard tack, sails luffing as the boom came about. "Damn poor ship-handling, Hans. Is your Werner incompetent?"

"Werner? Incompetent?" Hans' voice reflected his surprise as he brought his own glass up. "He's a right bastard who deserves a tight noose and a quick heave, no doubt, but he's as good a ship-handler as any. Not up to KRN standards, but good enough. Maybe that's a junior officer over there?"

"Maybe. Hmm, Hans, you described Werner as a... how'd you put it last night, a bit of a lady's man, as long as she's tied up?"

"Didn't mean to nearly choke you to death, sir."

"I know, but the point is, would Werner have many women in his crew?"

"I've heard he's one, but I've also heard she didn't get much of a choice. Or that she's as cold-hearted a bitch as ever born. No way to know which is the case. But, no, I'd say he's no real use for women. Not as crew."

"Odd, then. I think I'm seeing at least three onboard. Based on how long the hair seems to be." Carter lowered his glass and closed it.

"That is odd, Captain. And she's flying a Kolbian flag."

"She's a pirate. Bets on how many flags are in a locker below decks?"

"Ah, I'll keep my coin, sir." Ostheimer closed his telescope. "The light winds today are going to favor that sloop. We're more weatherly, but under these conditions, she's the faster."

"I know. But by now, that ship knows *Blackwood* is west of her, we're east and she's running northerly. *Alacrity* is north of us. And it's time we let Captain Harrold know that he's got a potential customer headed his way. Come about, into the wind, and furl all sail on the mizzenmast. We'll launch two of the eight-inch signal rockets, then set all sail and trail our friend over there. He doesn't know it yet, but Captain Werner Streiss is headed towards a fairly bad day. He can either strike and be boarded or *Alacrity* will blow his pretty little sloop into driftwood."

KRN *Alacrity* (38)
Southern Lanic Ocean
December 1478, Third Age of Imperial Reckoning

"Deck, there!" The shout was from the lookout perched on top of *Alacrity's* main-royal yard two hundred and fifteen feet above the main deck. "Green and red signal rockets, due south, range, on to thirty-eight, forty miles."

"Well, appears the beaters have flushed some game. Wonder what we're about to catch?" Andreas Harrold, Captain, Junior Grade, rubbed his hands together briskly as he smiled at his First Lieutenant where they stood on the quarterdeck. Lieutenant Commander Malcolm Tarleton simply nodded briskly.

"Very good, Captain. When shall we clear for action?"

"Give it at least another five or six hours, Mal. Get lunch in everyone first. A happy, well-fed crew is a hard fighting crew."

"Aye, sir." Tarleton gave orders to the ship's bosun, and the crew began to muster for lunch. Mal then followed Captain Harrold to his quarters for the officers' own meal.

"Ah, fried chicken!" Harrold rubbed his hands together in pleasure. "Another one quit laying, I see."

"Aye, Captain. 'Twas Henrietta." His steward was a long-faced, curmudgeonly natured senior petty officer named Dario Boozer. "'Tis a bad omen, the chicken stopping laying right afore we're ta clear fer action." He also saw bad omens in everything. He grunted and ducked back into his pantry.

"I know the signal was for a light ship, a brig or sloop. But what if Carter was fooled and we wind up facing one of the big, blue-water pirates? That motherless bastard, Ironheart; he's supposed to have two ships near equal to a forty-four."

"Mal, you worry too much."

"All due respect, sir, it's my job to worry."

"Granted, but I doubt there's a pirate anywhere on the seas of Rybithia armed with explosive shells. I can't see more than a broadside or two being needful to apprise whoever our mystery ship is to either strike her colors or just blow the hell up."

"And what if she's a slaver, sir?"

"Mal, Mal, there's no slaver out there that can out-run or out-gun us and they'll know that." Harrold grinned as he poured sweet tea into their glasses. "Relax, worrywart."

"Aye, sir."

Armed Sloop *Graser* (6)
Southern Lanic Ocean
December 1478, Third Age of Imperial Reckoning

"Sahla, tell me that's not a sail I see, north of us." Sachi grimaced as she caught a fleeting glimpse of something pewter colored on the distant horizon. Sahla glanced at her with a mischievous smile and suddenly shot fifty feet straight up, above the masthead.

"*Sadayqaa*, it is a sail. I can make out no more than that." The girl spun in a circle while Sachi stared at her in semi-shock. "And there are two more sails, one east and one west of us. Both of those are closer, I can see they have two masts, with a square sail atop the forward mast, and the other sails are like ours, sort of triangular and at an angle."

"Sahla, get back down here!" Nearly panicked, Sachi grabbed her the instant she came within reach. "How the hell did you do tha—?"

"Sachi, did you not remember that one of the gifts of my Sire's Bloodline is that of flight?" Sahla calmly interrupted the Nisei before she could build up a full head of steam. "You forgot, didn't you?" Sahla smiled gently as Sachi held her arms tightly enough to leave bruises. Sachi shook her head once and then let go.

"Yes, I did." She looked forward to where the distant sail appeared and disappeared on the horizon, following *Graser* as she rose and fell on the waves. "Scared the crap out of me." She paused and sighed. "Could you tell how big it is?"

"Not well. Your eyes are better than mine. But I think it has three masts."

"Wonderful." She drew a deep breath. "Well, since you can fly, go tell Willis what you saw. And tell him that I said it's a little over thirty miles away. If he asks how I know, tell him D.A.V.E. said so. Got it?"

"Yes, Sachi." With a dazzling smile and mischief gleaming in her sapphire eyes, Sahla fell away from the mast and arrowed to the deck behind Willis. Sachi managed not to laugh out loud when Sahla's tap on his back sent him three feet straight up with a strangled shout of surprise.

"Oh, Ancestors, what have I got myself into with this girl?"

***

"Three masts, eh?" Willis leaned against the binnacle. "And don't do that again! Tap me on the shoulder with your feet ON the deck next time."

"Aye, Captain." Sahla dimpled and glanced shyly away.

"Could you tell anything of her rig? How many sails on a mast?"

"I think, perhaps, four? Or five? Would that be about right, Captain?"

"Umm, yeah, for a frigate. The newest rigs split the topsail into an upper and lower, and with t'gallants and royals set, that'd be five. Damn it, almost guarantees she's a frigate. Not good at all."

"Uh, Captain Fleet, would that be worse?"

He turned to look aft, where Sahla was pointing. Two fading, colored clouds hung in the sky to the east of *Graser*, one green and one red.

"Yes, Sahla, that would be worse."

KRN *Alacrity* (38)
Southern Lanic Ocean
December 1478, Third Age of Imperial Reckoning

"FIRE!"

The forward chase bucked and roared in a reeking cloud of gunsmoke. The solid shot moaned like a lost soul before it raised a towering plume of water a hundred yards in front of *Heartcutter*. The long twelve-pounder hissed like a dragon as the gun crew's Number Two ran the corkscrew head of the worm staff down the barrel as the breaching tackle jerked the gun to a halt. Number Six immediately followed the worm staff with the sponge. Number One stopped the vent with a leather thumbstall as the sponge extinguished any remaining embers. The instant the sponge left the barrel, Number Three shoved the next bagged powder charge and its rope wad into the barrel. Number Five's ten-foot-long ram shoved the charge to the breach of the gun, shoving hard and evenly to seat the charge. He stepped back as Number Four carefully loaded the next round, an explosive shell, in its proper, fuse-forward orientation. He set the wad and stepped back as Number Five's ram staff shoved wad and shell gently home. Number One drove a wire prick down the vent to pierce the powder bag before setting a priming quill filled with fine grained powder into the vent and cocking the gunlock.

"Gun is loaded, sir!" he shouted. He handed the firing lanyard to the gun captain.

"Aye! Hands to breaching tackle and heave!" The wheels of the gun truck squealed as the two-ton mass of the gun snouted out its gunport. "Heave! Heave! Avast heaving! Stand clear!" The gun captain crouched behind the mass of the cannon, peering through the aperture of the long cannon's tangent sight. He waited, patient, as *Alacrity* rode the waves. The sight lined up with his intended target and he stepped abruptly to the side and jerked the lanyard. The gun roared and jerked to a stop against the breaching tackle again.

"Belay reloading and secure the gun," Alain Johansen, *Alacrity*'s bosun, growled. The shell exploded a hundred and fifty yards in front of the sloop, sending a plume of seawater half again higher than the sloop's mast.

***

"Well, well, sweating yet, Kapitan Streiss?" Captain Andreas Harrold's smile was cold and predatory as he watched the *Heartcutter*'s sails luff as the sloop came frantically about. Herded by *Blackwood* and *Swift,* she'd used her agility to stay clear of the three Kolbian warships most of the day. She was desperately trying to stay out of range until nightfall, hoping she could give them the slip in darkness. But the schooners had her pinned between them and unless the shallow draft sloop found a shoal out here in the deep Lanic, she had no hope of escape.

"Think he got the message, sir?" Lieutenant Commander Tarleton asked from where he stood on the quarterdeck next to his captain.

"I think so, yes, there goes her colors, down the mast."

"She's showing a Kolbian flag, sir. If she's legitimate, her captain might have a valid complaint to file with the Navy Board back home."

"Mal, if that ship is a legitimate Kolbian vessel, I'll buy every man-jack of her crew a steak and lobster dinner at Carlson's in Capitol City. Complete with dessert and dancing girls." His ice blue eyes danced above his impressive full beard and luxuriant handlebar mustache.

"Yes, sir. Her sails are coming down now. Guess all we have to do is go collect the miscreants?"

"About that, Mal." He nodded with restrained pleasure as the sloop in question slowly furled her sails. "About that."

Armed Sloop *Graser* (6)
Southern Lanic Ocean
December 1478, Third Age of Imperial Reckoning

"Well, that's that, I guess." Willis Fleet finished lashing down the ship's wheel. "Okay, people, if you have anything on you resembling a weapon, either drop it in this tub here or take it below and leave it in your bunk. And yes, Sachi, that includes the 'special weapons,' so secure them below."

Graser rode the gentle swells as, uneasily, her crew stood well clear of the ship's cannons. Those cannons were still lashed down, parallel to the rail, muzzle tampions in place. Sachi caught and held Willis' eye. Her white-steel bracers flickered into blades and then back into bracers on her forearms. She gave him a cold smile.

"Sachi, not even you can defeat the crews of three ships," he whispered in her ear as he stopped next to her.

"You forget the pirate ship, Willis. And the sea-monster in the Western Ocean." Her voice was just as quiet. "Willis, I've a task, a destiny, if you will, that looms over the entire world. One that must be met, or all this will be no more than chaff in a furnace. I'll not let some idiotic, rules-obsessed officer hang me. Especially when I've done no wrong. And by extension, that means that you and everyone here must survive as well." She gave him a bleak smile. "Do you think I wish to raise my hand against the Kolbian Navy? I owe the Navy, in the person of Captain Blaine and the *Intrepid*, my life."

"What the hell are you saying?"

"Willis, if I have to, I will instruct D.A.V.E. to destroy these ships as he destroyed the pirate. I will complete my mission, then return to Kolbia and apologize in the manner of my homeland." Sachi's face was iron hard.

::Be advised that this Entity has no access to any system that could disable or destroy the Kolbian naval ships in sight without also destroying the *Graser* and her entire crew. Probability of survival in that case is less than one percent, plus or minus four percent. With the current improvements in network security, this Entity's ability to access and control system defense satellites is reduced by thirty-two percent, plus or minus twenty-seven percent,:: D.A.V.E.'s voice whispered in her mind. ::The most effective course of action would be to convince the commander of the Kolbian vessels that none of you are pirates.::

"What about Irene and the other reformed pirates? What if the KRN captain decides to carry out a trial and sentencing? I know how that would most likely end!" Sachi subvocalized, keeping any hint of her sudden consternation off her face.

::Some personnel losses are acceptable, and undoubtedly inevitable.::

"You're no help!"

::I am merely an Entity program, not a more advanced Artific—::

"Just shut up, then, you stupid machine!" She turned her back on Willis and stared at the towering KRN frigate, thinking furiously. *There must be a way, if only I can find it. Think, stupid girl, think! If the Kolbians hang all of us, they'd be hanging one of their own diplomatic couriers in Willis and a Kolbian baseball star in Draven. A true healing Priest of the One God from Montagar and a Deuschen Contessa. And a... hmm, well, a Princess of Darsälaam. Not to mention what might happen if something happened to Silaqui. And I know she's got this diplomatic immunity. And hanging those three could start yet another war they don't want, a war that... waitaminute!! THAT'S IT!* She spun back to face Willis. "I've got an idea, Willis."

"You do?"

"Yes, you're a courier, you have diplomatic immunity, and you can prove it, right?"

"Well, yes. My documentation is in my cabin."

"And the Contessa, she's a noble, an Imperial noble BUT she's to marry a powerful Duke of the Deuschen Empire. And as far as we know, it's a love match as well. Hanging her would infuriate the Deuschen. And give the Lietelean Empire a true justification for declaring war, right?"

"Y...es, yes, it certainly could be seen that way."

"And Sahla is the daughter of a Sheikh of Darsälaam, perhaps the equal of a Princess herself? And wouldn't a Contessa and a Princess have diplomatic immunity, especially when they've committed no crime against Kolbia? Or anyone else for that matter?"

"I think you're on to something. Go on!"

"And we know, without a doubt, that Silaqui has been documented, by the Kolbian Diplomatic Service, as a diplomat. The Admiral gave the papers to her back in Carolington City! And I'm already on the record as being her bodyguard! Then we have either Gabrielle or Sahla swear our former pirates, all of whom were, in truth, enslaved and forced into their illegal actions by the now deceased Ironheart, they swear them into their service! As the staff and servants of a friendly, foreign noble, they'd have immunity too! And we can prove Ironheart's dead, because we have his head sealed in that keg of brandy! Wouldn't that work? Or at least give us a chance? At worst, they confine us all and send us back to Kolbia for trial? WELL?"

"Sachi, I think you've got it! And I can take Aylie on as my confidential local guide. Not our fault our ship was swept so far south in the storm and wrecked on Ironheart's little island paradise! See, I told you it would be worth our time to fish Ironheart's head out of the cove's waters!"

Sachi squeaked as he grabbed her and kissed her hard on the mouth before spinning her around in an impromptu jig. That caught the attention of the rest of the *Graser's* crew. Then they both rushed over to the rest of the crew.

In short order, Gabrielle swore Androu, Jean and Irene into her service. Zedekiah argued that his status as a senior officer of the extensive and influential Abrhaim trading clan would provide its own protection, seeing as he had only been held as a hostage. Sahla declined to have anyone swear any service to her. Instead, she appeared on the deck shrouded in a fine linen abayah, as blue as the sky, and a delicate turquoise silken niqab veiling the lower part of her face. And over all was her magnificent tiger skin cloak, recovered from the wreckage of the pirates' camp, along with most of her fine clothes. At least, the ones the pirates hadn't ruined. Silaqui had added Paul's name to Sachi's on her documents. And then they waited as the long boats filled with Marines pulled away from the frigate and the larger of the two schooners.

"I hope your idea works, Sachi." Willis brushed as much of the sea salt off his long blue coat as he could. "I wish I had an actual uniform."

"So do I, Willis." She shrugged where she stood by the wheel. She wore her black *shozoku* tunic and loose pants, with her *kamimaki* wrapped around her waist as a sash. Tucked inside her *himaku* jacket, in a "special" pocket, was the single functional Mark Fourteen APF handgun. The two working blast rifles were locked away below decks, but Sachi was unwilling to let the Anti-Personnel Flechette weapon out of her control. "So do I."

"We shall come through the darkness and the deep sands, even though the *ghula* and the *shiqq* menace us on all sides, for the Prophet's Hand is extended over us in protection and Chalta's Grace guides our steps." Sahla's sapphire eyes blazed as she smiled at Sachi. "We need fear no evil. And you both tell me that these men of the Kolbian Navy are of good intent. Be at ease, *Sadayqaa*." Sachi frowned at the Darsälaamic girl's certainty.

"Easy for you to say," Willis muttered. "I just hope these are officers and crew willing to listen instead of shooting first and searching the corpses for answers later."

"From your lips to the Ancestors' ears, Willis."

Chapter Four

KRN *Alacrity* (38)
Southern Lanic Ocean
December 1478, Third Age of Imperial Reckoning

"Willis Fleet! Damn and blast me, it is you!" Reese Carter barely had to duck as he stepped into the captain's office aboard *Alacrity*. He stepped through the crowded cabin and clasped forearms with Willis. "A long time since we were midshipmen aboard the *Defiant*, yes? And now, I find you commanding a captured pirate sloop no less!"

"Well, that's his claim, Lieutenant Commander Carter." Captain Harrold's voice was dry as he pinned Carter with a glare. "And now that you're finally here, perhaps we can get this initial hearing under way and determine if the outlandish claims this individual, who claims to be Lieutenant Commander Willis Fleet, KRN, if these claims, are, in fact, the truth. Be seated, please, sir."

Carter shrugged and smiled at Willis before taking his seat behind the table with Captain Harrold and a clearly discomfited Lieutenant Savras of the *Blackwood*. Willis stood at ease in front of the table, flanked on his right by Sachi and his left by Silaqui. Gelman, Zedekiah and a quiet Sahla, wearing her tiger skin cloak, stood behind them. A brace of Marine guards stood to either side of the group and another pair stood at the door of the compartment.

"By my authority as senior ship's captain of a board consisting of myself and two other ship's captains, I hereby call this hearing to order." Captain Harrold rapped a wooden block on the table sharply with an engraved oak hammer. "We are to determine if the sloop currently named *Graser* but formerly known as the pirate vessel *Heartcutter*, is, in fact, crewed on a piratical voyage, or if she has been captured as a prize by an irregular crew under the command of an individual claiming to be one Willis Fleet, Lieutenant Commander, KRN, Office of Naval Intelligence and currently operating under the authority of the Kolbian Diplomatic Service as a secure courier. As the accused, Lieutenant Commander, have you anything with which to address this board?"

"Well, sir, if nothing else, I believe that my old friend, Lieutenant Commander Reese Carter, can vouch that I am who I claim to be. And he is also aware of my assignment to ONI." Willis shrugged. "You also have as evidence, my secure courier's satchel. The inner seals are intact and the outer packet, while damaged and somewhat the worse for wear as a result of the shipwreck and loss of the Imperial merchant ship *le Bonaventure*, contains papers that clearly detail my orders and instructions." Fleet pointed at his rather battered satchel where it lay on the table in front of the three officers. The orders in question were arranged neatly in front of Captain Harrold.

"A telling point in your favor," Harrold admitted with a nod.

"Those papers are in such poor shape that they could easily be forgeries, Captain Harrold," Lieutenant Savras spoke up. "The *Heartcutter*, whatever silly name she has painted on her now, is a well-known pirate vessel. I believe that her current crew are simply more pirates and should simply receive the posted punishment for piracy. And if this Willis Fleet was a former Navy officer, well, he wouldn't be the first KRN officer that's gone rogue, rare as it is."

"Possibly a point, Lieutenant Savras. Possibly." Harrold frowned as he glanced at Savras.

"Sir, with all due respect, that's a barge load of whale-shit." Carter leaned forward and glared at Savras. "Willis is a member of the Fleet family. A family with an unblemished record of naval service, stretching back to the founding of the Navy. To the founding of our Republic. I find it difficult to believe that you've the gall, Lieutenant Savras, to sit here and all but accuse Lieutenant Commander Willis Fleet of being a pirate!"

"That will be enough, gentlemen!" Harrold interrupted Savras before he could reply. "This board shall consider both possibilities and probabilities as needed. All possibilities and probabilities."

"Captain Harrold, may I address the Board?" Silaqui stepped a half step forward.

"You may, Miss, uh, Lady, um, Lady Silaqui." Harrold struggled a moment with the Elven Sorceress's exotic beauty.

"You have, in addition to Willis' diplomatic papers and orders, in front of you the documents given to me by Admiral Ethan Mynheers himself. Those documents confirm my diplomatic immunity, and that of my bodyguard and servants."

"Those could also be forged. And being taken in an act of piracy invalidates any claim of immunity," Savras snapped at the Elf. "You wouldn't be the first diplomat to claim immunity when caught buccaneering!"

"Hold thy tongue, Mortal!" Silaqui snarled back. "I'll speak no lies, but I was two years a pirate's captive and slave! The only use I've for a pirate would be their skull for a drinking cup! On my honor, the only true pirate on our good ship was what little of Ironheart we brought as proof of his death! Declare me a pirate at thy peril!" Crimson flared in a corona around the Elf. With muttered curses, the Marines brought their rifles to the ready.

"ENOUGH!" Harrold roared. "Stand down, Marines! And Lady Silaqui, I'll thank you to wield no sorcery here!" He glowered at Savras. "And Lieutenant Savras, I'll request that you immediately cease and desist attempting to provoke these people. If you can't, then I'll have you replaced on this board. My First Lieutenant, Lieutenant Commander Tarleton, has sufficient seniority to stand in your position. Am I clear, sir?"

"Aye, sir," Savras grumbled. "Clear, Captain."

"Captain Harrold, if I may?" Gelman gently patted Silaqui on the shoulder as she relaxed, her aura fading away. The priest had left his armor and mace behind on the *Graser* and wore only his clerical robes and wooden Circled Cross. "I am Pere Gelman Stavor, a Montagaran priest of the *Angaelici Benes Eloi*. I know how skeptical of magic a Kolbian might be, but I could possibly arrange to shed the clear light of Truth on these affairs. If you should allow me to do so, Captain?"

"Oh, please! What's next, dancing girls and a counting horse?" Savras' outburst earned him a narrow-eyed glare from Harrold.

"Lieutenant Savras, this is the last time I'll overlook one of your irrelevant outbursts." He locked eyes with Savras for a long, tense moment before turning back to Gelman. "What, exactly, are you offering to do, Pere Stavor?"

"I have some slight ability with the lesser servants of the One God of the Circled Cross. At my request, one of the least servants might be willing to provide you with the undoubted knowledge of the truthfulness of what is said here." Gelman smiled and shrugged. "I know that can be a difficult thing for a Kolbian to believe, but over the years, I have learned that members of your Navy seem, well, a little more mentally flexible, let's say."

"The recruiting slogan is, 'Join the Navy, See the World, Widen your Horizons.' Mostly truthful, for once." Harrold tapped his forefinger on the tabletop. "You can do this?"

"Yes, Captain Harrold. If you allow."

"Hmm. Lieutenant Commander Carter, what do you say?"

"Captain, I've no objection. If it can be done, it should speed up this process immensely." Carter watched Fleet closely. "My only concern would be ensuring that what Pere Gelman summons is what he says it is. I've dealt with a couple of wizards and such over the years, sir. Magic's a tricky thing."

"Understood. Lieutenant Savras, I deliberately did not ask for your comment. I'm certain where you stand. But given Carter's take on magic is close to mine, this time I'll be willing to undertake a slight risk."

"Sir, with all due respect, I wish the record to show my protest. This trial should merely be to confirm the guilt of these individuals and assign the proper punishment."

"Understood, Lieutenant Savras, and the record will show your protest." Harrold managed to keep anyone from hearing his teeth grind. "But I will also remind you that this is NOT a trial, it is a hearing."

"Aye, Captain." Savras leaned back in his chair, sullen discontentment clear to see on his face.

"Well, since the vote of the hearing's officers is two to one in your favor, Pere Gelman, please, proceed with your, hmm, your magic. Do you need anything special?"

"Thank you, Captain, no." Gelman smiled beatifically. "All I need is my faith in my God and in my patron, the *Angaelici Benes Eloi.*" Gelman stepped into the open space in front of the table, knelt and raised his wooden Circled Cross.

Harrold could see his lips barely move as he prayed. He felt the hair on the back of his neck raise as Gelman's wooden symbol began to glow with a golden light. He could see an ecstasy on the priest's face as the glow swept around him and suddenly coalesced into a sun-bright ball of pure light that hovered in front of the priest. Despite its brilliance, it was not blinding or even painful to regard.

"Please, I ask you, faithful spirit, in the Name of the One God and *Angaelici Benes Eloi,* that you reveal to these three men here," he pointed at the three Kolbian officers, "the truthfulness and veracity of all that is said here today."

Harrold felt the thing turn its attention to him and the others. He felt the intensity of the spirit, whatever it truly was, in its regard. He knew, to his very bones, that it would reveal to him the lack of truth in anything said to him. He had no doubts at all. There could be no falsehoods, lies or half-truths spoken in its presence. It moved slightly, and he felt its attention shift from person to person in the cabin. It brightened slightly as its consideration settled on the Elf, Silaqui. Then it reached the tall Nisei girl, young woman really. It suddenly froze, and he didn't think it was because of her obvious beauty. It flared in power, bright enough now that it did hurt to look at, casting stark shadows on the bulkheads. It pulsed, once, then again, and he felt that it nearly shook in the grip of some powerful emotion. It pulsed a final time, a pure white light, and disappeared.

The being that stood in the place of the ball of spirit light wore the form of man. But unadulterated light, white and golden, flowed from it like pure honey-syrup, banishing any hint of shadow. Vast wings of light flared from its broad shoulders and eyes of scintillating radiance swept over the occupants of the cabin. The cabin appeared limitless and vast now, bulkheads and decks replaced by an endless plain of the pure essence of Spirit. Harrold knew he was still sitting in his chair at the table; that the cabin's stern windows were still just behind him. He knew two thirty-two-pounder cannons were secured against their gunports. He knew all these things, but the only thing his mind could conceive was the power and glory of the angelic being standing between him and the six from the *Graser*. The being looked away from Harrold and he felt the breath coming back into his lungs.

"*Pere Gelman, your task is well and truly begun.*" The angel's voice filled the cabin, resonating in the hearts of everyone there. "*But only begun. You shall face difficult tests in the weeks and months to come. Tests which will press on the very foundations of your faith, of all you are. You must continue to press forward, into the gales of resistance and opposition. And beware. Not all that opposition will be of the plain and material world, even if much of it proves to be so. Well done, Pere Gelman. Well done, but do not relax, for the task has only barely begun.*"

"I will not falter, Angaelici." The priest's voice rang with the strength of his faith and conviction. "I will not fail you."

***

The Angel smiled at Gelman and then turned to Sachi. She froze, a rabbit under the eagle's talons, as those brilliant eyes fixed upon her. She felt those eyes flood into her very soul, seeing in an instant every cruel and terrible thing she had ever done as an Oda. The men she had lain with as a prostitute, cajoling betrayals from some, murdering others. The slaves she had slaughtered while being trained by Great-Uncle Sota. Her black hatred of Mankato and especially Maho, her adopted twin siblings. Smothering love and brutal hatred, both from her adopted Mother, Yuko Oda as the woman's mind had wandered in her madness. The rapes, the beatings and tortures, both given and received, her hellish existence until she killed Naoki Oda in a blind rage and fled the Oda's fortress home, seeking some way, some faint hope to avoid the horrors they would inflict in revenge for slaying the favorite son of the Master of the Clan.

He laid her bare, even those things she hid from herself. She saw her shameful desire for Captain William Blaine of the *Intrepid*, who rescued her and who she had dared to love. She faced the black thoughts hidden deep away in her psyche, schemes to end his shrewish wife's life and claim him for herself. Every cruel and evil and unworthy thought of her life poured out before her, like acid on her flayed skin.

"Please." She collapsed to her knees. "Please, *Tenshi no kunshu*, please, great lord of spirits, no more, I beg. If you would punish me, then wait, please, wait until I fulfill my duty and then do as you will with me. But now, no more. I plead with you. No more."

"You are all these things that I show you in your mind. You have done all these things and more. You know this. These are not lies or untruths. Do you think you should even be allowed to retain any honor at all by following the customs of your people, customs older than you know? Are you worthy of even that, Sachi Takahashi, Caitlyn Schmidt, Oda sia Asami, Komiya Asami? Do you even know who or what you are? Would a stout noose not be preferable for such as you?"

"ENOUGH! *ALLAWRAD SHAYTAN!* BEGONE AND TORMENT MY MISTRESS NO MORE! BACK TO THY KENNEL, FOUL CREATURE! CHALTA AND HIS PROPHET EXTEND THEIR HANDS IN PROTECTION OF MY MISTRESS! GO BACK TO THE FIRES PREPARED FOR THEE!" In an incredible flare of cerulean light, Sahla appeared between Sachi and the angel. Her eyes glittered with sapphire rage. Her magic had transformed her. Gone was the mild desert princess in her fine raiment. Now clad in a halter and supple breeches of dark brown leather, her arms outstretched to protect Sachi, a glowing sapphire saber in each hand, Sahla appeared quite ready to fling herself bodily on the angel. A cobalt aura flared around her.

"You would give your life, Jann, for this one? Why?" The angel's voice was strangely gentle. *"You do not even truly know your own heart where this one is concerned. I can free you of your Bond to this one; grant you the ability of a true Jinn, to choose to stay in the Mortal World. Your beauty would lay the world at your feet. You need have naught to do with this one, so soiled is her soul. How say you, Jann?"*

"No! I reject your honeyed betrayals. Soft words and sweet lies tempt the true of heart. Get thee gone!"

"So fierce, little one. So devoted. And why? Do you even know your own heart? Allow me to show you the truth you deny in your own heart, then."

Sahla grunted as if her stomach had taken a grievous blow. Her aura flickered and guttered low, and the sabers' glow dimmed and fluttered as a candle about to go out. She bowed her head a heartbeat and then her aura flared even brighter. She turned and looked Sachi full in the face for a long moment. Then she turned back to the Angel, head held proudly. They stared at each other, sapphire eyes unflinchingly meeting eyes of pure light.

"So be it, then. I am Sahla al Qasim, the daughter of Ilben alh-Taymyah, Jinn of the Second Rank of Air and Wind, a true prince of Elemental Air. I know that Chalta's Paradise will be closed to me, simply for being what I am. And of my own free will, I will choose to stand with my Mistress, in any fashion she wishes. And any who would say me nay, they I shall answer with my blades and my magic. *Rayiys Almalayika*, if you are truly what Gelman claims to venerate, the Archangel of Healing, then cease to torment my Mistress, else I shall set cold steel to thee."

"So fierce indeed." The angel smiled at her and then returned his attention to Sachi. *"Rise, Sachi Takahashi. The name you chose for yourself fits you well. Be fearless and free, Fortunate One. Yes, there is darkness in your past, a terrible forging of your heart and soul. But the thrice folded steel, well forged, never breaks. Nor shall you. Fulfill your destiny. And at the end, survive; find happiness and love. Live well. Be worthy of this beautiful Jann's fierce devotion. Much is asked of you, but I believe that much will be given to you, if only you can see it."* The angel turned to the officers behind the table. *"I know your folk often see only the Mortal World, but you*

present, at least, now know that the Unseen World exists and has its own place. These folk are blameless of any crime you might accuse them of committing. There is a great purpose to their voyage, a quest unsurpassed in thousands of years. Foil that quest at your own peril. I leave you a marker, should you ever doubt what passed here this day. If ever you doubt yourself, simply look at what I leave you. It shall never wear and never show any stain."

Everyone in the room staggered as he departed in a soundless thunderclap. Other than the six Marines, who jumped in stunned surprise, all their clothing, every piece, was bleached a pure, angelic white.

"That lousy..." Silaqui's face was a tragedy mask as she stared down at her pristine white skirt, top and cloak. Even her boots were white. "I hate white."

***

"Interesting books, Lieutenant Commander. Very interesting." Captain Harrold carefully turned the pages of *Harper's Pictorial History of the Civil War*. "Where did you get these again, exactly?"

"Captain Harrold, they came from an ancient, wrecked starship mostly buried on the island Ironheart was using as a base. I've given you our sailing course from there, but, sir, that ship's sealed now. It'd take years, maybe decades to carve away the muck it's buried in and get back into it. We were lucky, finding a door and getting out before it sealed up." Willis' voice was quiet as he watched Harrold set the book gently aside and open one entitled *Ships of the Civil War, 1861-1865*.

"Who else has seen these books, Fleet?" Harrold's quiet question hid its intensity.

"Sachi Takahashi, Pere Gelman, Aylie, and Silaqui. No one else."

"They are all foreign nationals, aren't they?"

"Yes, sir."

"Umm. That's unfortunate."

"Sir, we saw things on that ship that make the ships in those books look like dugout canoes."

"Did that have anything to do with that light in the sky a few weeks ago?"

"Sir, that was... that light, it was the only functional weapon on the starship. We, Sachi and I, we used it to destroy Ironheart's ship, *Deathdealer*."

"Fleet, I get the feeling there's a lot you're not telling me, correct?"

"Sir."

"*Sir* is not an answer. *Sir* is an avoidance of the question, now, isn't it?"

"Sir." Fleet met Harrold's eyes evenly. "Captain, I am assigned to ONI. As such, I've had clearance to access some of the most sensitive information in the Navy. What's in these books is of vital importance, but their true value is the fact that they exist. Sir, these books were never printed on Rybithia. The maps in them show a world with a completely different geography. Another world, orbiting another star, somewhere else in the galaxy. A world apparently inhabited only by humans and with no mention anywhere whatsoever of magic. These books can possibly change the course of history."

"So, why are you handing these to me for delivery to the Office of Naval Intelligence back in Stark Haven? Why aren't you taking them yourself?"

"Captain Harrold, remember what that, umm, well, that angel said, about a quest?"

"Um-hmm."

"Well, sir, it is my belief that what this Nisei girl is supposed to do is as important as anything since the Fall itself. I don't understand it, but she has a job to do and it's for sure and for certain that I've a place, an important one, in her job."

"Fine, Fleet." Harrold sighed. "I won't argue with you. However, I am going to do a few things, I'm going to give you a draft of sailors and a Chief Petty Officer, one of the Bosun's Mates to command them to properly crew that sloop. I'm also going to transfer the former hostages to *Swift* to get them home and off the Navy's hands. Now, about your former pirates..."

"They were effectively enslaved, sir. They had no real choice."

"Oh, I know. Despite what Savras wants, no one is getting hung from the yardarm. But you'll keep them aboard as crew. And perhaps, ah, encourage them to find lives ashore, once you make port? In the meanwhile, I'll be taking *Alacrity* to rendezvous with *Fearless* to report in person to Commodore Tannville. I expect I'll then be ordered to Stark Haven with these...recovered materials."

"I understand, sir." Willis came to attention and saluted.

"Good enough, Fleet, good enough." He acknowledged the salute with his own. Willis was nearly to the cabin door. "And Willis?"

"Yes, sir?" He paused with his hand on the doorknob.

"Godspeed, Lieutenant Commander Fleet."

"Thank you, Captain Harrold."

Armed Sloop *Graser* (6)
Southern Lanic Ocean
December 1478, Third Age of Imperial Reckoning

Graser leaned into her canvas, skipping along the waves under a brisk topsail breeze. The KRN squadron was a day and a half behind her as she sailed east toward Du Khamps des Sou-See. Seabirds skirled in her wake, hoping for a bit of refuse to pluck from the waters or a morsel to steal from some unwary sailor's meal. But any who drew too close quickly sheered away, startled by the rapid and near musical clash and crash of sword on sword. Given the speed and intensity of the sounds, the feathered bandits might have been forgiven for looking for blood dripping from her scuppers, but there was none. And the smash and crash was not the signal of desperate mass combat for the control of the sloop. Rather it found its source in the blurring blades wielded by two young women in the main deck's waist.

Sachi and Sahla dripped with sweat only. No blood shone on their slick skin, Sachi's porcelain pale, contrasting sharply against Sahla's gold-tinged perfection. Sachi's white-steel butterfly swords hummed as they spun at unbelievable speeds. She wore black *kobakama*, knee length trousers worn under armor by the samurai of Isemoto, and a black *himaku*, with the jacket's sleeves tied up over her elbows. Under it a tight leather band bound her large breasts against her ribs. Her waist length hair was braided into a crown around her head and her feet were bare.

Sahla wore the battle-garb of the Dervishes of the Sands, a tight leather halter confining her breasts. Supple leather breeches clung to every lithe curve, secured at her hips with a double wrapped leather sword belt, supporting the twin scabbards of her twenty-inch-long sabers. Multiple thicknesses of heavier leather formed light armor over the front of her muscular thighs. Her hair floated in a wrist-thick braid and her booted feet rarely actually touched the surface of the deck as she danced on the air itself. Her slim sabers trailed a hint of blue radiance as they flashed and crashed against Sachi's thick, unbreakable butterfly swords.

The rest of the crew watched the two incomparable beauties spar in amazement. Sachi was inhumanly fast and considerably stronger than Sahla, but the Dervish-trained girl showed the knack of diverting Sachi's powerful blows, spinning gracefully away. Their styles differed immensely, literally worlds apart. Sachi drove straight in, willing to risk a wound to land a decisive blow and end the fight. Sahla spun and twirled, using her Gift of Flight at times to force Sachi to fight above her head as the Jann spun in the air above her, her booted feet often above her own head. The two had been going without a pause for nearly twenty minutes with neither able to land a scoring blow.

***

Finally, Sahla saw a hint of a pattern, an opening into which she could drive her sabers and end the session. She managed to maneuver Sachi's back to the mast, where the mainsail's boom hindered her mobility. She started to thrust low and smiled when she saw her Mistress repeat the downward block with both blades. She feinted low and then lunged high, past the flashing butterfly swords. Sachi dropped backwards, arching her back beyond parallel with the deck. Sahla overextended as her sabers cut empty air above the Nisei's torso.

***

Sachi rotated her entire body into the back flip, her left knee smashing against Sahla's sternum and driving the air out of her lungs with an explosive, "OOF." Then her right foot caught the Jann in the pit of her stomach and catapulted her, heels over head, over Sachi's body and slammed her down hard on the deck. Her sabers skittered away across the deck. Stunned and gasping for air, Sahla never saw Sachi spin around and gently touch the tip of each sword to her, one to her temple and one to her chest above her heart.

"You fight well, *Koibito*, but you are predictable." Sachi clipped her swords into the inverted sheath slung over her back. She bent down and gently helped Sahla to her feet, the younger woman leaning against her as she recovered her ability to breathe.

"Wha... what does that mean, *Koibito*?" she coughed.

"That, hmm, oh, nothing important." Sachi dipped her head.

***

"All right, lads, show's over, and you lazy louts have lollygagged long enough!" *Graser's* new bosun growled. "Back to your tasks, sharp-like. Slowest watch'll be holystoning the deck!" Senior Master Petty Officer Jonathan Holland, Bosun's Mate First Class was the senior enlisted man transferred from *Alacrity*. If he entertained the least uncertainty about serving on a deck under command of an ONI officer who'd never exercised command of anything bigger than a rowboat, it didn't show. He wasn't happy about how many women were on board the oddly named *Graser*, especially the two troublesome ones, the ones at once both the most beautiful two women he'd ever seen, and the deadliest. But they all pulled their weight or better. And the display of pure lethality the Nisei and the Darsälaamic girl had just exhibited served as the best possible reminder to the males of the crew to keep their hands to themselves. He carefully hid his smile as he covertly watched Sachi and Sahla.

Can't remember ever being in the presence of two young ladies as beautiful as they are. And they've eyes only each for the other, 'cepting neither of 'em has the least clue what they're about. Ah, they're young. They'll figure it out. Bless 'em.

***

"Remind me to never get either of you really mad at me." Willis Fleet walked up to the water butt which Sachi and Sahla were slowly draining dry as they drank. "I don't think I've ever seen the like. I've certainly never seen anyone fly while they wield a sword! How the hell do you do it, Sahla?"

"I'm a Jann, Willis. You know this. My Sire granted me the Gift of Flight. I can fly by the pure power of my Will. Simple as that."

"Simple, sez she." Willis grinned. "Yeah, right."

"Willis, did you hear what Sachi called me when our sparring ended?"

"No." He mock-glowered at Sachi. "All right, cough it up. What'd you say?"

"It's of no import, Willis, just a common enough phrase from my homeland."

"She said, *Koibito*." Sahla gave him one of her devastating smiles. "Now she either acts embarrassed or she growls at me. Is it something bad, Willis Fleet?"

"Hmm." He strangled his laughter stillborn when he caught the glare Sachi was giving him. Buying some time, he filled and drained the ladle hanging from the side of the water butt. *Ah, what the hell? I can always go hide behind Jean. As big as our blacksmith's apprentice is, even Sachi'll need to pack a lunch just to run around him.* "It's sort of an endearment in Isemoto, Sahla. It means sweetheart or lover. Men from some regions call their lovers that. That's all." Willis managed, somehow, not to laugh out loud and quickly turned away to hide his huge grin as they both blushed beet-red. "Need to check our position. Excuse me, ladies."

He headed below to escape any possible retaliation from either of them.

"Sweetheart?" A slim eyebrow raised as Sahla caught Sachi's hand before the Nisei could slip away. "Truly?"

"Sahla, don't read anything into it. I spoke without thinking. And you know how beautiful you are." Sachi regarded her captured hand coldly, her own brows furrowed. "Let me go."

"Your will, *Sadayqaa*." She instantly released Sachi's hand. "You know I must abide your will."

"Don't remind me!" Sachi snarled as she turned away. "Leave me be!"

Sahla stood there quietly as Sachi disappeared below deck. Then her shoulders slumped, and a visible shudder passed through her delicate frame. She took a couple of shaky steps and nearly collapsed as she leaned against the fife rail of the mast. From where they leaned against the rail, Gelman, Aylie and Silaqui exchanged dismayed looks.

"I'll deal with Sachi," the sorceress muttered. "You two get Sahla out of sight. Talk to her. Use Willis' cabin. If he gives you any guff, warn him that I'll turn him into a pig." She strode forward, following the Nisei.

"Aye, Milady." Aylie hopped down off the rail and headed for the crumpled Jann. Gelman followed her quietly. Aylie knelt next to the girl. *We be close to the same number of years, but I thinks I's twice to thrice as much of the world as she. From a princess o' the Desert Folk to a magical slave of an assassin of the distant East, that be a goodly way to fall. Poor child.*

"Sahla." Aylie's voice was quiet as she tenderly laid her hand on Sahla's shoulder. "Let's be about gettin' ye below. Let me help ye up, lass. 'Twill be all right." Aylie carefully pulled Sahla to her feet and guided her below decks to Willis' cabin.

***

"Come out of there. Now." Silaqui had used her magic to open the barred door to the sail locker. "If you don't, I'll turn you blue with pink dots. And bright orange hair. Out. Now."

"You would, wouldn't you?" Sachi grumbled as she wiggled out of the loosely stacked sailcloth. "I'm out, what in the Ancestors' names do you want?"

"Sit. Stay." The Elf gently pushed her down onto a coil of spare rope before leaning against the bulkhead. "You were cruel to her, you know that, right?"

"Who? Sahla? Because I beat her sparring?"

"Keep it up and I'll turn you into a chicken." A grin ghosted across her face. "We could use the eggs."

"Ha. Not funny."

"Then stop being an idiot. I'm not talking about the sparring match. And you know it."

"Aye." Sachi mumbled and even Silaqui's Elven hearing strained to understand her.

"Sachi, that girl is as devoted to you as...as...as much as any hero Prince in a fancy tale is devoted to his True Love."

"I didn't ask for her devotion, Silaqui. I'd free her if I could. Why didn't that angel of Gelman's free her from me?" Frustration echoed in the Nisei's voice.

"She did not allow him to do so."

"Why?!"

"I don't know the why, my friend. Only Sahla can answer that. I've my suspicions, but I'm not in the least sure of them. But I've watched her look at you when you aren't paying attention. She would be a man dying of thirst seeing a stream of pure, clear water, just out of his reach."

"What is that supposed to mean?"

"Well, in over a thousand years, I've seen that look a few times. Sometimes it is a look driven by mere infatuation, what Kolbians these days call a crush. Other times, it was simply pure lust, passion for naught more than the pleasures of the flesh. And then, rarely, it's a look when one truly, deeply loves another and yet is conflicted or rejected. And this time, I know where I'd bet my Thalers."

"Have you lost your mind?" Sachi stared at her friend. "Are you saying this girl, this Jann, is in love with ME?"

"Perhaps." She shrugged. "It fits what I've seen so far. And remember my dream, and what my patron goddess told Captain Blaine aboard the *Intrepid*? What the angel said a few days ago? If Sahla isn't devoted to you, I'll eat the mainmast. Without salt."

"I think you see much that isn't there, Silaqui." She rested her chin on her drawn-up knees, wrapping her arms around her shins. "I am a monster, not suitable for anyone to love. Captain Blaine saw that, that is why he chose to honor his oaths and vows to his wife."

"Araemonriel, greatest of all the Gods of the Elves, give me patience and give it to me NOW!" Silaqui ran her hands through her grass-green hair, tugging hard enough on the ends to pull some out. "Nothing mortal should be as stubborn as you are, my dearest heart-sister! But in this, you are being an ASS! Sachi, everything we learn about this destiny of yours, what my own Goddess tells me, what an angel of Gelman's One God tells you directly, all this points that if you do not learn to love, you will fail. And if you fail, the world dies. Are you truly that self-destructive, to take all things down in death with you? If you are, then perhaps I am wrong about you? Perhaps you are not worthy of the titles of Elf-friend, Heart-sister, and Defender? Perhaps the respect and honors the crew of *Intrepid* accorded you are unearned? Perhaps you truly are the monster that would destroy a world entire? Are you?" The Elf's jade eyes opened fully in the dim light. They were hard with disappointment and hints of anger. "Has no one ever in your life not loved you? Do I not love you? Is it not impossible that this beautiful Jann, this Dervish of the Sands, that she could love you? Truly love you?"

Sachi stared in shock at the haughty Immortal that had replaced her oldest friend.

Chapter Five

KRN *Fearless* (110)
Southern Lanic Ocean
January 1479, Third Age of Imperial Reckoning

Captain, JG, Andreas Harrold swallowed as his cutter approached Task Force Southron's flagship, the hundred-and-ten-gun first rate ship-of-the-line KRN *Fearless*. The massive first rate dwarfed his thirty-eight-gun frigate. She was fresh out of a major refit, considered to be one of the most powerful warships in the world. *Fearless* was the lead ship of her class and four other first rates had been refitted similarly. No other navy in the world had anything that was even close to her equivalent.

Even as he marveled at the awesome power *Fearless* embodied, he knew that in many ways she and her sisters would be the last of their kind. He had ridden the new bay ferries that took personnel from Stark Haven's Island to Capitol City. Powered by a Fulmark pressure engine, the paddle wheels on their sides had little concern for the direction of the wind. The bay ferries were crude harbingers of what was coming. Harrold loved *Alacrity*, but he knew her days as an effective warship were numbered. He stared up at the towering side of *Fearless* as his coxswain deftly hooked the cutter to the first rate's main chains.

I'd better time this right! Last thing I want to do is report to the Admiral soaking wet and dripping on his carpet! He timed his leap perfectly, caught the Jacob's ladder and quickly clambered up the ship's side. At the entrance portal, he saluted the colors and the Officer of the Deck as the side boys' pipes sounded.

"*Alacrity*, arriving," the side party's leather-lunged Petty Officer announced.

"Captain Harrold, if you'll follow me, please, sir." A young lieutenant stepped out from behind the side party while Harrold marveled at the new guns mounted amidships on the main deck. The Parker Rifles on their heavy swivel mounts were half again as heavy as the long thirty-twos on *Alacrity's* gundeck but threw an explosive shell three times heavier than *Alacrity's* heaviest guns, her forty-two-pound carronades. And since they were rifled guns, the level of accuracy they provided *Fearless* was monumental. He shook his head in wonder and followed the lieutenant.

***

"Glad to have you aboard, Captain Harrold." Justin Belford, *Fearless'* Captain, shook hands with Andreas. The two captains were equally tall, a few inches over six feet, but Harrold's bull-necked and bulky build made Belford seem small next to him. And they both towered over the other two men in the Admiral's cabin. Commodore Corison Tannville's head of salt-and-pepper hair would have barely reached their shoulders, had he been standing and not seated behind his desk. To his left sat Commander Alva Zaslavskov, assigned to the Task Force from ONI. Slight and slender and as self-possessed as a cat, his stylishly curled brown locks bobbed as he merely nodded in greeting Harrold.

"My greetings as well, Captain Harrold." Tannville rose and shook hands across the desk. "Have a seat before you bean yourself on the overhead." Belford chuckled to himself as he settled back into his own chair to the Commodore's right.

"Thank you, sir. I've gotten used to hunching anytime I'm below decks. After the time I knocked myself out cold as a midshipman, well, that lesson one learns quickly, or one gives up on a naval career and joins the Army." Andreas smiled at the memory as he settled.

"Indeed, Captain Harrold." Tannville reached into a drawer and pulled out a pair of books. "But we need to get to business. Since you sent these ahead with your longboat when the wind dropped to near as nothing, I've had the chance to look over them. I'm no scholar to speak ancient languages, but this... English, I believe it's called, has just enough resemblance to Terranglais that I can puzzle out a few words. And the illustrations tell their own story. Honestly, the ships in here aren't much in advance of what Mr. Fullmark has on the building ways in Stark Haven."

"Indeed, sir." Zaslavskov spoke up. "The turreted designs in these books are clearly intended for use on interior waterways. None of them have the depth of hull or freeboard to survive Lanic Ocean conditions. I'm hardly an expert on ship design, but only a few of these things meet our needs."

"The main thing I see is the differences in production. Some of the guns in these pictures are remarkably similar to our latest designs." Belford pointed at a massive, soda-bottle shaped gun on the deck of a ship with a tall funnel. "That thing is damn as near identical to the Dolmens muzzle loading smoothbore on *Fearless'* own gun deck!" He flipped a page. "And if that isn't a Parker pattern heavy rifle there, well, then I'm a dancing girl in an Imperial brothel!"

"You'd look funny in skirts and filmy veils, Justin," Tannville joked.

"Captain Belford, Commodore Tannville, sirs, with all due respect, you are both making the same mistake I initially did. Neither of these books was ever printed on our world, Rybithia." Harrold flipped the book open to one of the large maps inside. "Oh, there's a vague, superficial resemblance, the major land masses are in the same basic relationship, but there's no Arctic continent. Instead, there seems to be an Antarctic continent. The two western continents are connected by this long isthmus. The Straits of Kolbia don't exist. There is no long peninsula in the Traquilidamar Sea. Too many differences. This isn't our world, and if that is in fact the case, where is this world?" A chill silence settled in the cabin.

"An excellent point, Captain Harrold." Tannville broke the quiet apprehension. "Where did Lieutenant Commander Fleet say he recovered these items again?"

"On one of the many uncharted islands in the South Lanic, between Khakal and Tylteanait." Harrold paused.

"An island in the Shallows?" Tannville glanced at a map of the Western Hemisphere of Rybithia framed on the wall of the cabin.

Separated by three thousand miles of relatively shallow water and many shoal islands, the ocean between the continents of Khakal to the east and Tylteanait on the west was poorly charted. And neither of the two continents was well explored. Khakal was known for numerous barbarian kingdoms, south of the vast Darsälaamic deserts. Tylteanait was an enigma. No expedition had ever penetrated the dense jungles more than a handful of miles and returned to tell any tales. "What was Fleet doing there?"

"He was shipwrecked, sir." Harrold shrugged. "It was the island the pirate Ironheart was using for his base of operations. And Fleet claims... this may be hard to believe, sir, but Fleet claims to have found the wreck of a 'starship' from before the Fall itself. The books came from that starship, Commodore."

"Really?" The Commodore leaned back in his chair, steepling his hands in front of him. "A starship?" Captain Belford muttered an oath, while Zaslavskov abruptly sat up in his chair, suddenly intent on Harrold's every word.

"Umm, yes, sir. That's what he claimed, at any rate."

"Excuse me, Commodore, but I'd like to ask Captain Harrold a question," Zaslavskov quietly drawled.

"By all means."

"Did Lieutenant Commander Fleet make any other claims, Captain Harrold?"

"Well, Commander, uh..." Harrold fumbled for the ONI officer's name.

"Zaslavskov, Captain Harrold." Zaslavskov gave him a cold smile.

"My apologies, Commander Zaslavskov. But, yes, he did." Harrold took a deep breath and glanced up at the overhead. "He stated that one of the women with him, a Nisei woman named

Sachi Takahashi and himself, the two of them were responsible for the 'Line of Fire' in the sky a few weeks ago. That the 'Line of Fire' was the result of a single functional weapon on this starship. They used this weapon to literally vaporize the pirate Ironheart's ship, *Deathdealer*. Given that they had Ironheart's head in a cask of brandy and that said head is now secured onboard *Alacrity*, well, sir, due to that and another factor, I find myself believing their claims."

"Oh, for God's sake, Andreas!" Belford burst out. "What the hell are you jabbering about, man? Are you drunk?"

"No, Captain Belford, I doubt Captain Harrold would make such claims if he didn't have proof. And we all saw the 'Line of Fire' in the sky, did we not?" Zaslavskov quietly interrupted Belford. "Perhaps we should listen to his story and I'm sure he has more evidence than just these two books."

"I do."

"I thought so, Captain Harrold." Zaslavskov caught and held the Commodore's eye. He raised an eyebrow in question and Tannville nodded. "Thank you, sir." He turned back to Harrold. "Now, Captain Harrold, please, regale us with your tale. I'm interested to learn more about this Nisei woman, what was her name, eh?"

"Sachi Takahashi, Commander."

"Ah, Sachi Takahashi, yes. Why was she the one aiding Fleet and what is this other factor you spoke of?"

"Well, gentlemen, this started a week ago, when one of the schooners in my squadron spotted a sloop known to be a pirate ship. The chase took a couple of days, but we pinned her between us, and she promptly struck her colors, a Kolbian flag, after a couple of warning shots. We hove to, I sent a boarding party aboard and then things began to get strange when..."

***

Commander Alva Zaslavskov's quarters were below the lower gun deck. Most officers, most commanders, certainly, would normally consider such quarters a borderline insult. But he had specifically requested this cabin, for security reasons, he said. That and privacy. The lower decks were generally hot, humid, and miserable and no one wanted to be stuck down there if they had any choice.

He hummed quietly to himself as he lifted a medium-sized, brown leather case from a heavily built, iron-banded trunk. He sat it down on the desk very carefully, on the small end of the case. Two latches and buckles released the vertical clamshell. It opened sideways, pivoting, and folding out an internal pair of doors. A gleaming black rectangle was surrounded by shining colored lights, lights that smoothly flowed around the rectangle's gleaming border. Below the rectangle was a small black oval, the size of a large man's thumb.

Zaslavskov wiped beads of sweat from his brow and gently reached out and pressed the oval. The black rectangle folded silently out, down, and away from the back of the case. A flickering, transparent blue cube appeared above the rectangle. Symbols flashed and shimmered in the cube for several long minutes. Zaslavskov bowed his head over folded hands and murmured quietly to himself, the words indecipherable. A man's head, slightly wavering as if under water, suddenly appeared in the blue cube.

"You have significant information to report?" The man had a full head of dark hair, perhaps black in the blue tinge of the cube. It was pulled back in a tight Imperial braid, revealing a high widow's peak. Dark eyes and a neatly trimmed beard did little to hide the glare he gave Zaslavskov.

"I do, Higher." He bowed until his forehead touched the desk. "I have learned what caused the sky-fire."

"You have?!" Higher snapped. "Quickly, tell me everything! This stream is weak, and I do NOT want Them learning aught of this! Not even the fact that this talk-stream exists! Quickly!"

"Yes, Higher. There is a woman from Isemoto, one named Sachi Takahashi, deeply involved with this. The description of her closely resembles what you have told me how one of Their spies would appear. She was aboard a sloop named the *Graser* and..."

Luctini, Geullia Province,
The Eternal Empire of Lietelea
Clan House of the Familia Palmaroli
January 1479, Third Age of Imperial Reckoning

Suire Vicente Palmaroli leaned back in his sinfully comfortable chair. Resting his elbows on the padded armrests, he absent-mindedly rubbed his nose with steepled forefingers. The black rectangle of the Eld Mechanism was quiescent, only the faintest hint of standby power flowing around its silver frame. For nearly half an hour, he sat and mulled over what his agent in the KRN's current expedition to suppress piracy and slavery had just revealed to him. The agent, a member of their Office of Naval Intelligence, was, at best, a dupe and at worst a fool. But a useful fool, in a place he should have never been, if the Kolbians only had eyes to see.

Alva Zaslavskov was a weak man. His family, immigrants from Rus, had never truly become part of the Kolbian ideal and remained what they were, Rus peasants. Poor Rus peasants. Greedy, avaricious, and foolish Rus peasants. A young Alva joined the Navy to escape his poor family's lack of opportunity, and an angry father of a ruined girl, in that order.

The young man proved ruthless, as well as lucky and clever enough to blackmail his way into a commission. A certain devious cunning helped him earn promotion and a place in ONI as a field agent. But a willingness to resort to blackmail oft left one open to blackmail in return. One of the very few Imperial agents-in-place in Kolbia's Navy turned Zaslavskov to the service and tender mercies of the Empire's Abscondito Ministerium a few years ago. Over time, the Seekers had further subverted him, turning him away from the Empire's own Secret Service, secretly using his knowledge for their own purposes, purposes often diametrically opposed to the Ministerium's own goals. He was a useful tool, but only a tool.

"It will be something of a waste, but like all men, he is but a tool to bring the Great Work to an end. *Et purgatio ex Orbis Terrarum.* The end of this corrupted pustule we know as the World and those true of purpose to be caught up to a higher existence." Vicente picked up his notebook and carefully reread his notes. "At last, I have a name for this girl, this supposed deadly threat to the goal of the Last Weapon. Sachi Takahashi." He allowed a brief laugh to escape. "And They, our deadliest Enemies of nine thousand years, They don't even know she exists or what she might be." He sighed and sat back up, reaching for the activation charm of the Eld Mechanism that connected him to the Clique's talk-stream.

The blue radiance of the talk-stream glowed into life, and he drew the sign for the Clique within the insubstantial cube of light.

"Vicente." The man's head appearing in the cube might have been Vicente's grandfather, sharing the same strong bone structure and dark eyes. The shaven pate and thin, white beard, and the countless seams of wrinkles were a foretaste of what Vicente might resemble in a score or more of years. It was a reminder he didn't much care for. "You have information?"

"Yes, Master. I have information on the girl, her name and more. And where she will be in a few weeks' time."

"Ah. I see. You have a target, then?"

"Yes, Master. Two targets, in truth."

Armed Sloop *Graser* (6)
Southern Lanic Ocean
January 1479, Third Age of Imperial Reckoning

The wind was somewhere between twenty-five and thirty knots, blowing clean and strong out of the west. *Graser* rode the waves cleanly at a steady nine knots, occasional sprays of white foam coming over the bow railings. It was not a lot of spray, but it was enough that Sachi was soaked where she huddled next to the starboard cathead. Neither being dripping wet, nor the cold breeze particularly bothered her physically, but she was still a study in misery, sightlessly staring into the green distance of the ocean.

How have I come to this? When did I lose my way? My dearest friend angry with me over this girl, this Jann. Why? Had I made my choice, I'd've long since been free of her. And her free of me. Why did Gelman's patron not free her? Why did she refuse her freedom when the angel offered it to her? Sachi shivered at the memory of the angel when he peeled her bare, reminding her of what she had been, what the Odas made her into. *What am I now? I am, perhaps, as much machine as mortal, it seems, or so that thing in my head, D.A.V.E. tells me. On the island, when I told them what I am, Silaqui feared me at first. Perhaps she should still fear me. Should I, perhaps, fear myself? It is a new year now. The old year is gone, and all things change.*

"Sachi?" A soft voice derailed her train of thought. "*Sadayqaa*, why do you hide here, dripping with the cold sea spray?" Sahla stepped over the cathead and gently settled a dry oilskin cloak over Sachi's shoulders. The Nisei glanced briefly at her before staring back out to sea. "Drink this, please?" The pleasant aroma of a strong black tea drew her attention to the steaming mug in Sahla's hands. "Drink."

Mechanically she took the mug and drank deeply. It was perfect, just enough sugar, just hot enough and just the right hint of a twist of lemon. It warmed her body and a second, long drink emptied the mug. The tea's heat enveloped her, an unexpected warm comfort.

"*Arigato*, Sahla."

"What does that mean?"

"It means Thank you. What I should have said is, *Domo Arigato*, Thank you very much."

"Ah, I see," Sahla gently giggled, "then, in my language, *Ealaa alrahab walsaea*, you are welcome, *Sadayqaa*."

"Ah, yes," Sachi hid a smile. "Darsälaamic, not a language I know."

"Then we are equal. I do not know Nisei." Her smile rivaled the sun.

"It would seem so."

There was an awkward silence between them, the hiss of the ocean against the hull, the creak and groan of the rigging and the ship itself only enhancing the silence. Perfectly still, Sachi stared out into the vast distance of the ocean. Sahla tried to emulate her but eventually her foot began to tap as she hummed to herself.

"You cannot be silent nor still, can you?" Sachi's tone was dry with amusement.

"If need be, Sachi." Sapphire met and held ebony. "I can if need be. I was still enough that the tiger who hunted my goats and I, he did not see me when I hunted him. Now I wear his skin as my cloak. One reason I hated Wrath, Ironheart's pet witch, so much. She stole the trophy of my victory. But I did recover it from the ruins of her hut."

"Truly?" Sachi's surprise showed. "You, a princess of your people, herding goats and killing a tiger? I find that as impressive as your ability with your sabers." She stopped and thought a moment. "You are a bundle of contradictions, Sahla."

"Are you not your own bundle of contradictions, Sachi?"

"I guess." Another awkward silence fell. Sachi noted that the girl wore only a sailor's linen shirt, rough canvas dungarees and her own high boots. Sahla startled and smothered a squeak when cold spray hit her back. "Come here. There is room enough for both of us under this oilskin and if it is foolish of me to get soaked, it might be even more so for you. Come, please."

With a hesitant smile, Sahla tucked herself under the large slicker. She hid a shiver as Sachi wrapped a long arm around her and settled her closely against her side. The shiver had nothing to do with the cold spray and much to do with her memory of what the angel, one of the great *Al'Malak*, the Messengers of Chalta, had shown her. She surreptitiously watched Sachi's profile as the Nisei stared into the distance of the ocean.

She called me Koibito. *Willis said that means Sweetheart;* Habiba *in the Prophet's tongue. She said it without thinking. And even not truly knowing what it meant, it gave me a thrill to my heart to hear her address me so! She is so beautiful, skin as fair as the finest Han vase. She is tall and brave; with a protective spirit she tries to hide. Gelman warned me of the machines inside her, the lost knowledge of the Ancients. The voice she hears in her mind; this thing which whispers secret knowledge to her.* Sahla, have a care, *he* warned, *Sachi may be no more than half human. The Benes Eloi himself sent me to guide her and heal her, for she has a great destiny. But many of those chosen for great deeds leave others broken and wayward in their path. I'd not see you as such. Pah! What does he know, as a celibate priest of the infidels' One God? His own patron granted me a vision, a possibility of one future, the Winged One said. A possible future where we stand by each other's side, each of us loving the other.*

She suppressed another shiver at the thought, the memory of exactly what she had been shown. Sachi sensed her unease and turned her face to Sahla, a slim eyebrow raised in a silent query. Sahla ducked her head and trembled at the changes she saw coming to her world, a life like nothing she had ever imagined.

"I'm cold," she whispered.

Sachi nodded and pulled her tighter against her side. The Nisei radiated heat, but the cold Sahla meant was not of the body. It was the cold brought by fear of change, a fear of what the future might bring. Still, she marveled at the heat radiating from Sachi's tall body.

"There. Is that better, Sahla?"

"Yes, very much. How are you so warm?"

"Long story."

"Gelman, he told me of the machines in your body, the voice in your mind you call D.A.V.E. He says you might be, at best, only half human."

"I know. Part of that long story."

"The Angel told him to guard you, but I think you make him uncomfortable."

"Hmm." She nodded and looked back out to sea. "He believes in his God and his Angel, believes with all his heart and soul. But belief alone does not understand, and I doubt he truly understands me. He would be happier were I a woman who fit some role he does understand. But I don't. And I won't. Ever."

"Ah. I understand why he looks askance upon me. My Sire is a Prince of the Winds, a true Elemental, a being truly not of the world Mortals inhabit. I am only half human, and I partake deeply of my Sire's nature. That makes him uncomfortable, but I am what I am, a young woman, and he feels he should be as protective of me as he is of Aylie. Then he feels guilty because he is conflicted and, in the end, he stands partly aside and grumps at me."

"Well, if he grumps at you too much, come get me and I'll straighten him out. Honestly, he's more comfortable with Silaqui than either of us." Sachi smiled at her.

"Sachi... *Sadayqaa*, did you mean it?" Sahla's voice was low and unsure, barely audible.

"Did I mean it what?" Brows furrowed above black eyes.

"What you called me after we sparred? *Koibito*? Does it truly mean what Willis said it did?" She held her breath in expectation of the explosion of temper from the Nisei. She could hear Sachi's teeth grinding together. Her knuckles were white as she clenched her fists around the oilskin. "Please, please, Sachi, *Sadayqaa*, please don't be mad at me. Please, I mean no insult."

"I know. And yes, it means what Willis said it does. Sweetheart. Or Lover. Depends on exactly where in Isemoto you're from." Sachi took a great breath and slowly released it. "I take no insult." Every line of Sachi's body betrayed immense tension. "I'm not going to answer your question right this moment, all right? Let us say, oh, call it for argument's sake, I did mean it. From what I understand of your culture and your religion, Chalta and His Prophet, well, you shouldn't want to hear that kind of endearment from another woman."

"Sachi, I am a Jann. According to the Book, I am beyond the pale, an abomination to some. A truly strict Aliyah would have me stoned to death or at least driven away, out into the darkness of a moonless night, my bloody back well lashed."

"Over my dead body," Sachi growled, interrupting her.

"Saa-sah, it is of no matter now." She drew a very deep breath, held it a moment and released it with a sigh. "Sachi, please, listen carefully to me. I am not what I was. I was Sahla al Qasim ab Ghaffanse, blood-daughter of Ilben alh-Taymyah, Jinni of the Second Rank of Air and Wind. My birth mother is Haipha Alimah ab Mu'azzaz ibn Sayyidah, the wife of Sheikh Hasim al Murafte of the Tribe of Abdul-Ghaffanse of the Folk of Darsälaam. I was the First Daughter of my Father, Sheikh Hasim."

"That's a mouthful. Wait a minute. You said *was*. What do you mean, *was*?"

"Sachi, you know my people, the Folk of the Sands, would certainly reject me now. I have been among the infidels and pirates. I have no duenna. Men not my family have seen me unveiled. My husband to be, he would now have naught to do with me. At least, not as an honorable wife. And they would soon learn that I am not truly human. As a Jann, I would count among the Elemental Princes, if only as lesser one. My people respect the Princes, but it is a respect born only of fear."

"And? I know all that. Get to the point."

"No longer will I claim the title of First Daughter of Sheikh Hasim al Murafte of Abdul-Ghaffanse. I know my family there still would love me, but I no longer have a place there. So now I will simply be Sahla al Qasim. The only title I might claim, if need be, would be that of Daughter of Ilben alh-Taymyah, Jinn of the Second Rank of Air and Wind. I might truly claim that, but naught else. And that is part of what the *Al'Malak*, the Angel of the Light, showed me. In truth, I can never go home."

"Do you want to go home?" The question was very gently asked.

"Ah, there is the stone in the sandal." She shrugged. "My mother told me that someday I should seek my place in the wider world. And I think I have found that place, here, at your side."

"As a slave?" Sachi's voice held a snappish exhaustion, weary of a struggle she could not win, yet unwilling to give up the fight. "Held in a magical Bond?"

"Ah, Sachi, there are other Bonds. Be at peace, *Sadayqaa*. All things will come to pass as the Prophet wills." Sahla gave a glowering Sachi a winsome smile. "For now, perhaps we should go below? I can hear your stomach growling and Roland has made a huge pot of something he calls chili."

"Be careful with what that crazy Geullian brews up in the galley," Sachi warned as she shuddered, remembering the sauce with which those burritos were made. "Quan would not serve such a meal to tortured souls in hell. *Too cruel*, he'd say, *not even I am so evil as to make the tormented feast on the liquid fires of Hell.*"

"I know. The Efreet might relish such a dish, but none else would." Sahla dimpled at Sachi's warning. "But I was told that

Willis did have speech with him, of whether he was preparing food for the crew, or torment for the condemned."

"You think that'll do any good?"

"Mayhaps, by the Prophet's Beard. But the only way to discover the truth of the matter is to venture bravely forth, daring the dragon's den. Shall we, *Habiba*?" She slipped from under Sachi's warm arm and pulled the taller woman to her feet.

"What did you sa—" Sachi sputtered to a stop as she saw the devastating smile on Sahla's happy face. With a lilting laugh, the tiny Darsälaamic girl grabbed her hand and pulled her along, toward the hatch leading below. That laughter was contagious enough that Sachi found herself laughing with Sahla as she hurtled along, neatly hauled down the deck.

***

Hmm, that went better than I expected. Perched in her favorite spot atop the t'gallant crosstrees, Silaqui smiled as she watched Sahla tow Sachi below decks, startled sailors scattering like gulls before them. *I hated having to play the high and mighty Immortal Elf with Sachi, but sometimes, that girl needs a solidly delivered swift kick in the butt.*

Chapter Six

Armed Sloop *Graser* (6)
Southern Lanic Ocean
Western Coast of Khakal,
Unexplored lands
January 1479, Third Age of Imperial Reckoning

THE COAST OF KHAKAL had been in view for a couple of days now. *Graser* was making five or six knots, with only her t'gallant, jib and jib topsails set. The sun was sinking behind them, and Fleet laid a course keeping the ship well away from the coast. The last thing he wanted was another grounding and the waters here were, at best, poorly charted. They were working their way north, along the coast. Du Khamps was north of their position, unless Fleet was a couple of hundred miles off in his navigation.

"Captain, the sounding shows fifteen fathoms under our keel." Bosun Holland lacked Willis' rangy height but the impressive bulge of his biceps, with their tattoos of the national flag and the naval ensign, drew their own respect from any miscreants under his command.

"Very good, Bosun." Willis' face reflected the exceptionally long hours he'd spent on the quarterdeck.

"Perhaps, beggin' the Captain's pardon, sir, perhaps you should get some rest."

"Bosun, tell me, would you be comfortable knowing that Sachi, my choice for First Lieutenant, was the Officer of the Deck?" Willis gave him a wry grin. "Tell the truth, now."

"Ah, well," he sighed, "umm... no, sir. Not really."

"Thought so."

"Ah, Captain, it's no disrespect I've for the young lass." Holland shook his head. "She's a hard worker and a quick learner, 'markably so, to my way of thinking, but there's so much she doesn't know. Even if she can see like a cat in the night." He combed his fingers through an impressive beard. "Give her four, five years, mebbe less, as a midshipman, she'd be a true boon to the Service, she would. There's few of the fair sex as can toe the line in the Service, but she'd have no problems at all. And the way she fights... well, I wager any bastard as touches her 'gainst her will, well, the poor bugger'd shortly be sorry and sore."

"Oh, you've no idea, Bosun." Willis shared a smile with his senior PO. "However, we've light winds and clear water, full fifteen fathoms deep. So, I do believe I'll turn the deck over to you and get a couple, three hours of sleep. I expect to raise Du Khamps tomorrow morning. Wake me at two bells into first watch. I'll take the deck overnight."

"Aye-aye, Captain."

<h3 style="text-align:center">Armed Sloop Graser (6)
Southern Lanic Ocean
Approaching the Free Port of Du Khamps des SouSee
January 1479, Third Age of Imperial Reckoning</h3>

"How is that possible?" Silaqui stood behind Willis on the quarterdeck. A bright beam of pure white light cut into the early morning darkness, flashing as it rotated across the sky. "I'd heard that Du Khamps des SouSee had pre-Fall artifacts that still worked, but nothing like that, whatever that is!"

"Don't ask me. I specialized in Isemoto. Ask the Bosun, maybe?"

"It is a standard oceanic hazard warning light. Output measured in lumens, eight hundred and fifty thousand lumens in this case. Most likely an argon-xenon high intensity dispersed LED laser driven array, powered by a solar panel battery field. Expected life span of the system is unknown, but theory suggests between ten and fifteen thousand years. One reason they were called eterna-lights." Sachi's voice was cold and flat, pinpoints of light dancing in her black eyes.

The mechanical tone of her voice sent little frozen feet shivering their way down Silaqui's spine. She turned worried eyes to Fleet, seeing an answering concern in his gray eyes. Gelman and Aylie could not help but draw slightly away from the Nisei. Only Sahla stepped closer to her, gently reaching to touch her arm.

"Sachi?" Sahla spoke just loud enough to be heard. "Are you all right? Is that thing whispering in your mind again? Tell it to stop; you're scaring your friends."

"Huh?" Sachi shivered for a bare instant, like a horse twitching a muscle to shoo a fly. Then she turned to face Sahla, lights no longer sparkling in her eyes. "Damn it. D.A.V.E., you have got to stop doing that to me. Understand?" She paused a moment, then continued her apparent conversation with someone...or something...invisible. "I don't care. Not everyone here understands." She shook her head and turned her full attention to Sahla. "Please, forgive me, all of you. That thing, it can be insidious at times."

"'Tis a wee bit unsettlin' at times, Sachi." Aylie shrugged. "But it's not like ye've not done plenty as can unnerve one as does nay know ye." She relaxed and stepped up, placing a hand on Sachi's shoulder. "But I know ye'd offer no harm ta none as have nay offered ye harm first. That or any who offer ta harm those ye consider yer friends." Sachi froze for a fraction of an instant, then tentatively smiled, covering Aylie's hand with her own.

"I'm sorry, Aylie, all of you," she looked around her. "Please, forgive me."

"It is unnerving, Sachi." Gelman stepped back up to the railing, marveling at the beam of white light spearing into the darkness. He changed the subject. "To think a lighthouse has existed here since the time of the Fall and it still works. How did they do such things?"

"Gelman, D.A.V.E. estimates that if you give the Kolbians another three or four hundred years, they might be producing such things." Looks of astonishment met her smile. "It's not magic, what D.A.V.E. likes to call *non-rational quantum access*. And no, I don't understand what he means by that. It's just technology. That's the real difference between magic and what the Ancients did. Anyone can use technology; you need a gift to use magic. At least, it seems that way to me."

"Hmm," Willis muttered, glancing at a pouting Silaqui. "Maybe you have a point there."

"The warning light is irrelevant, Willis." Sachi hopped up on the railing, grabbing a stay for balance, pointing out to sea. "There is the problem. A great number of rowed ships with only one or two masts. I do not recognize their banners and flags yet."

"Where away?" Willis stepped up onto the rail with a glass in hand.

"There. Ten points off our beam."

"I don't see anythi...ah, there they are." Willis was quiet for a long moment. "Great. Just fucking great." He hopped down off the rail and shut the glass with a snap. "Bosun, I need a detail to lower the flag. Dig around in the flag locker in my cabin and raise, hmm, let me see, raise an Eindeuten merchantman's flag. I don't think they have any issues with the Imperials and vice versa. Sharply now."

"Aye-aye, Captain." The bosun turned, assembling a detail with a bare glance. In moments, Kolbia's flag with its starred shield and blue and white stripes was being carefully folded away as the rampant red wolf on the black and gold chequered flag of the Eindeuten Empire rose into the lightening sky.

"There be a bloody lot of them, Willis." Aylie stepped up beside him. "What are we ta do?" The growing light picked out dozens, no, scores of masts and white hulls, spray flickering as banks of oars churned. "How many, does ye think, Sachi?" She leaned back to look at the Nisei on the other side of Willis.

"A moment." Sachi jumped back on the rail and climbed up the ratlines about twenty feet. She clung there for a moment before dropping lightly to the deck. "There are the Ancestors' own numbers of ships out there, Willis. I counted at least six big, real big, three- or four-masted galleons, each of them bigger than *Alacrity* or *Intrepid*. Maybe ships-of-the-line? Another half dozen or so smaller galleons, same size or somewhat smaller than *Alacrity*, perhaps Imperial frigates, if they have such. Then twenty-eight big ships, three or four masts, very high sides, with raised forecastles.

And rowed as well, perhaps twenty or thirty oars in one bank. No idea what those things are called. And dozens of galleys; long, narrow things with a single mast and either one or two banks of oars. I'd say nearly sixty or seventy ships. All flying what you've told me is the flag of the Empire, a crowned falcon or eagle, black on a red shield."

"Dear God," Willis muttered, rubbing his face. "Sachi, could you tell if they were standing into the harbor or headed out?"

"Frankly, some of the galleys appeared to literally be rowing in circles. The bigger, purely sail-driven ships were running on the broad reach, bearing away from us on the landward breeze, heading out to sea."

"Well, if they're leaving, then that might just be some good news." Willis frowned as he leaned against the binnacle.

"Must be the Impies' entire southern fleet, sir." Holland shrugged. "We just can't see the rest of them. That or their own lubberliness sank more than a few. They are stupid enough to bring a galley fleet into the Lanic. Idiots."

"They're idiots, I agree, Bosun, but they're here. And that could be a problem." Willis sighed and stared at the fading stars for a moment. "And if it's still under the same commander, Admeeral du SouSee Havre Calchas, well, we might have problems, assuming he left anyone in the harbor when he sailed. Hell, he might even have put the entire town under martial law. And that'd purely be a not-wonderful mess."

"More than you know, Willis." Sahla surprised everyone when she spoke up. "Ironheart the pirate had, um, arrangements with both High Lord Kormarra and the Admiral of the Imperial fleet."

"Are you sure about that? ONI has known about the relationship between Calchas and Kormarra for years, but nothing about Ironheart and the Admeeral du SouSee. And how'd you find that out?"

"I overheard them, Willis. I have very good hearing. And the Elementals of Air like me, and so the sylphs and zephyrs sometimes tell me secrets."

"Ah...yeah. Ok, I'll just take that at face value, then." *I knew joining ONI would put me in some strange places with some strange people, but this is ridiculous! Oh, God help me if Cousin Stephanie ever hears about this. She'll get one of those idiotic authors that hang on her coattails to write some stupid quarter-Thaler-a-copy pulp novel about all this, and my career will be over. Once the Admiral stops laughing at me, that is. Bother.* "And how might this affect us?"

"This ship might be known to someone on the Admeeral's staff. And I certainly think it will be known to many in Du Khamps des SouSee. How will we explain it being no longer a pirate?"

"Well, Sahla, I think we simply won't offer any explanation. If anyone gets pushy about it, we'll tell them that we, ah, traded, a newer, bigger ship to Ironheart."

"I guess that'd be good enough, Captain, but what if Ironheart has agents with enough men to take this ship away from us?" Bosun Holland interjected.

"Well, we're not going to be in harbor a month, now, are we? Bosun, I'll have you keep your sailors aboard; I have a concern about their acting ability to pass as either pirates themselves or the associates of pirates. I'm certain your men would have no problems repelling boarders? Which I don't believe will be an issue, seeing as Ironheart is dead and not giving commands to his agents anymore."

"Aye, sir, I can see that myself."

"And we will get in, get the ship resupplied, buy the charts we need and get the hell out of here as fast as possible." Willis turned to Holland. "Bosun, I want this ship sanitized. Conceal or destroy anything that might suggest we have any connection to the KRN. Uniforms, books, keepsakes, I don't care what, it either goes over the side in a weighted bag or gets hidden where I can't find it. Yes, that means long sleeves for you and your tattoos. And I think we'll sheer off the harbor approach for now. Bring the helm about, east-southeast. Let the Impies clear out, most of them at least. We're fine on supplies for at least another week; we'll head back in tomorrow morning. The deck is yours, Bosun."

"Aye-aye, Captain." Holland turned away, shouting for the hands to prepare to come about.

"Is this wise, Willis?" Sachi quietly asked.

"I think so. If nothing else, letting the Impies get out of the harbor will simplify things a bit. I hope."

"Well, I can't offer a better solution. I hope you're right as well."

***

"You were right, Sachi." Willis stared up at the towering edifice dominating the cliff-like arm of the northern end of the harbor mouth. "It is incredible that it still exists and still functions. I guess the Ancients, the 'Confederation,' really did build things to last."

The entrance to the harbor was relatively narrow, no more than three or four miles across. The harbor to which it gave access was beautiful, and huge. Thirty-five miles across at its widest, it was a perfect anchorage. At the eastern end of the harbor, docks and wharves stretched out from an extensive waterfront. Fortifications loomed at either end of the waterfront, anchor points for the walls that protected the landward side of the largish town, as the citadels protected the ocean side.

But the lighthouse dominated the entire harbor, rising four hundred feet above the cliff on which it stood. It was blindingly white in color, showing no sign of wear from the passing millennia. At its pinnacle, the light flashed and glittered, the morning light stealing most of the brilliance of the beam. It was something beyond the experience of anyone onboard the sloop.

"I told you, Willis. It's a relic of the Confederation." Sachi stared at it. "Yes, they did build to last, those ancients." She turned away with a strange, pensive expression on her face. "Unless the cliff itself wears away, that tower could still be there in another ten thousand years."

"What's bothering you, Sachi?" Sahla turned and followed her.

"In a way, that tower shares something with me. We are both relics, flotsam and jetsam washed up on the shore of the present, stormwrack left over from an antiquity no one understands anymore."

"You are not a relic, Sachi, not in the least sense! Or in any sense!" Sahla put a hand on the Nisei's elbow, stopping her in mid-step.

"You're hardly older than I am, and I assure you, I am no relic! Old people are relics!"

"It's not my age, Sahla." Sachi turned with a sad half-smile to face Sahla's intense blue gaze. "It's what I actually am that's a relic. A leftover from a time of heroes, and I'm certainly no hero."

"Ka'mel dung!" Sahla snapped. "To me, you are as much of a hero as I have ever read of in some book of fancy tales! You are a true hero, just as Khal— well, you are!" There was a strange, half-catch in her voice, something Sachi had never heard before.

Sachi stopped and frowned to herself. Sahla's entire posture had changed, her shoulders slumping, and ducking her head as she looked away. She gently reached out, putting a hand on Sahla's shoulder, and turning the Darsälaamic girl to face her. She was surprised to see tears in those sapphire eyes.

"Why do you cry?" She gently guided Sahla forward, out of earshot of the rest of her friends. "Or, rather, who do you cry for?"

"It's nothing."

"No, it's not. Tell me, please. And that's not a command. It's a request from a friend, your *Sadayqaa*. Please?"

"His name was Khalid ab-Kanaan. He was the Mulazim, the commander of my bodyguard. And a dear friend from the earliest days of my childhood. When I was a little girl, playing games with him, I once knighted him with an ostrich feather, naming him my knight, my very own *Faris* of Chalta." Her voice trembled with incipient tears. "He was killed by Ironheart's pirates, defending the ship we were on when the pirates attacked. He was the only man other than my father to whom I willingly removed my veil and showed my face. He was the first man I ever kissed. The only one I ever kissed as one might kiss a lover. And then he went out and died for me."

Sachi stared at Sahla for a long moment before turning to her friends standing on the quarterdeck. For a brief instant, she debated what to do in her own mind.

"Willis, I have need of your cabin and some privacy, if you please. Sahla has a story to tell me, and I wish no other ears to hear it." Her voice was crisp and sharp, a ring of command to it.

"Well, I'll be busy getting us anchored and dealing with the harbormaster. I'll have no need of my cabin for at least an hour or more; is that enough?" He managed to successfully hide the surprise in his voice.

"Enough, thank you." Sachi answered and then she helped a suddenly subdued Sahla below decks.

"An' what be that in account of, does ye think?" Aylie stood with her hands on her hips, surprise in every line of her stance. "Does ye think that the two o' 'em be looking ta make the beast with two backs? Sahla did nae seem in the least happy. More sad than anything, ta my way o' thinking."

"No, Aylie, that'll be the last thing on either of their minds right now." Silaqui spoke into the awkward silence. "Sachi is not the only one of us that bears secret pain in her deepest heart. But it is well and good that she cares for Sahla and will give her a soft shoulder to cry on. The girl needs that and trust me, I know from personal experience that our Sachi is better than even she knows when it comes to tending and mending a wounded heart."

"From what I know of her, Sachi seems more apt to violence and destruction than young Sahla." Gelman stared up at the towering lighthouse as he spoke. "I'd never have thought of her as a... what would you call it, Lady Silaqui, a heart-healer."

"Pere Gelman, for all your acknowledged wisdom in the matter of physical healing, it's my thought that matters of the heart might be a bit beyond you. No insult intended, my friend, but that is how I see things." Silaqui stood and stretched before pointing at the lighthouse. "And that thing has naught to do with what may come to be between our two raven-tressed lovelies. And, I think, that is as it should be."

"Perhaps, Silaqui, perhaps." Gelman sighed as he turned back to the quarterdeck. "I have ever been more apt to the ailments of the physical than those of the heart. My creed teaches that what may be growing between Sachi and Sahla is... well, certainly not wicked but more akin to being morally wrong. But I find that I cannot condemn them. Let them find what peace they may. I'll say naught against it."

"Fine, that's all well and good." Willis growled. "Now, if you're all through with your damned moralizing, either stand-to and give a hand with the work of getting us anchored or get the hell out of the way. There's work as is needing done."

With laughs and smiles, they set to work furling the sails and doing the other work needful to bring the sloop to her mooring spot. And there were some thoughts and concerns for the two young women below decks. They were faithful friends, after all they had been through together, and they worried about both Sachi and Sahla.

***

We can scarce be more different. Sachi marveled at the contrast between her own porcelain-pale hands and the rich golden tone of Sahla's shoulders and back. *She is incredibly tense, her muscles wrapped up in knots. Is it me? Memories of this childhood friend, this Khalid? I am a creation of an ancient lost technology, perhaps even brought from another world under another Sun while she is literally born of the magic of this world. And yet, we find ourselves awkwardly tangled together. She is a princess of her people, even if they would reject her now, while I was taught to be no more than a whore and an assassin.* Her hands worked automatically as she mused to herself, finding the rock-hard knots of stress and tension in Sahla's superbly muscled shoulders, and working them loose. The ebony mass of her silken hair was tied up in a tail nearly as long as Sahla was tall, carefully laid aside to avoid the oil Sachi spread on her back and shoulders before diligently working it into that perfectly bronzed skin.

Sachi wore a short *yukata*, one she had made from the more worn of her old *kimonos*. Despite or maybe because of its age, the fine linen from which it was made was nearly as smooth as silk. She knelt on the deck of the cabin, next to Sahla, who was lying face down on several layers of quilts and blankets Sachi had dug out of the chest of bedclothes in the corner. The Darsälaamic girl wore a loose robe, pulled back to expose her shoulders and upper back, her arms down at her side.

"You're still too tense." Sachi kept her voice low and soft. "Relax, be at peace. Visualize a shaded pool, with clear, cool water. Soft sand, just warm enough to be cozy, gentle sunlight filtering through the trees..."

"No." Sahla whispered, just barely loud enough to be heard. "No, not the sun. Moonlight, and starlight, like gems scattered on black velvet. Like the beautiful stars that glitter in your eyes." Sachi felt her eyebrows climb up her forehead in surprise at that description. "Moonlight and starlight are better for lovers."

"All right, moonlight, soft and gentle. You can stretch and relax, perfectly safe, no concerns of this world, a tall glass of cool, iced sweet tea, sweet chocolate to eat, perfectly at peace with all."

"Hmm, that sounds nice. But what is iced sweet tea?"

"I'll make you some, you'll like it."

"Yes, please."

"Now, relax, let the tension go, let my hands work through the muscles, feel them pulling away the tension and the stress and the hurt and the fear and pain, all of it, gone from your world for now, just you and your quiet, peaceful world. A world where you can remember and honor those you love, even those absent from your presence. Your Khalid is there, just as you told me of him, tall and broad-shouldered, handsome and caring, warm brown eyes that care for you and yes, in their own way, show his love for you. He is and always will be a hero in your eyes." She paused as Sahla tensed.

"Sachi?"

"Yes, Sahla?"

"You say that Khalid is at this pool with me?"

"Yes, he is, or rather, he can be, if you wish him to be. This is a fantasy, one to relax your body and rest your spirit."

"But Khalid has achieved the Paradise promised by the Prophet and prepared for the Faithful by Chalta." Sahla rolled slightly onto her side, turning her head to look up at Sachi. The loose robe fell away, exposing the silhouette of a small but perfectly formed breast. "He should not be there, at this pool with me."

"Would you be alone there? Solitude is often restful to one's spirit. The monks and holy men of my homeland oft spend years alone, seeking wisdom within their own souls." Sachi very carefully controlled her breath, locking her eyes on Sahla's eyes, hiding her sudden and surprising desire to reach out and caress that perfect breast.

"No, I don't want to be alone, either."

"Oh. This is a fantasy, Sahla, an exercise to relax body and soul, remember?"

"Well, then if it is a fantasy, I could have whoever I wish to be there with me?"

"Of course." She carefully turned away, casually reaching for the oil, avoiding looking at that semi-bared breast.

"And if it is nothing more than a fantasy, like a fancy tale of the hero rescuing the maiden who falls in love with him, then, I might wish to imagine making love with whoever is there with me?"

"I imagine you could." Her hands froze for an instant before gently pushing Sahla back down on her front, hiding that so-tempting breast and the sensitive nipple Sachi imagined crowning it. "But the purpose of this visualization is for relaxation, not for a dream of lovemaking."

"But if it relaxes me, it could be, no?"

"I guess, if that is what you truly wish." She sighed at the Jann's stubbornness.

"So, and if I wished it was you there with me. By that cool, clear pool, on that soft moonlit sand? You there, to make love with me?"

Sachi froze in shock as Sahla rolled over and stared directly into her eyes, sapphire locked on ebony. Sahla rolled on her side and put a hand over Sachi's hand. Sachi startled ever so slightly, then she carefully extracted her hand from Sahla's and pulled the robe up over Sahla's shoulders, hiding the exquisite, rose-tipped breasts that she had revealed.

"No, Sahla, that would not be right." *I cannot let this happen. This is the Bond between us; she somehow senses my own stupid, ill-considered desire. Ancestors! What is wrong with me?!*

"Why?"

"Because you are not free!" she snapped, immediately regretting it as Sahla drew back in pained surprise. "This Bond you say is between us, where you must obey my wishes, perhaps even those I might make without ever speaking! Are your feelings, these desires that go against what you have told me of your people, are they truly you? Or is this Bond controlling you?"

"Sachi, do you not feel the Bond between us?"

"Quan take it, you know I do! And I know it steals your own volition, your own will! It makes you subject to ME!"

"Sachi," Sahla's voice was calm and measured, "I'm a Jann, remember? Only half human, born with an innate connection to the Elemental Realm of Air. I must have a Bond, to a mortal of this world; else... you know the fate that would await me. Is that what you wish for me?"

"No." Sachi recognized the defeat in her own voice. "But nothing in this Bond requires you to accede to my foolish, stupid, unvoiced desires."

"But what if it's what I've decided I want?"

"What?!"

"Sachi, remember the dream I told you I had? And the Aljannia Silaqui had a dream nearly identical to mine."

"And?"

"And one thing both our dreams had in common was that I stood beside you..."

"It was a dream, Sahla!"

"No, it was a prophecy, a sending from the Prophet or from the Lords of the Aljannia, as true as anything the Prophet ever wrote in the *Kitab al'Aqdas*, Chalta's Book of Holies."

"How can you be so sure, Sahla?" Sachi flopped down onto her back, staring at the cabin's overhead and thumping a fist on the deck in frustration.

"I had the dream, Sachi. In it I stood beside you, and I knew that I belonged there, next to you. I knew I needed you, just as you needed me, as the crops need the cool pure water of the oasis. Silaqui told me of her dream, of the black-haired, sapphire-eyed beauty who loved you enough to die for you. Can you not accept that?" Sahla knelt next to Sachi, the robe slipping completely off her shoulders, leaving her nude from the waist up. "Can you not accept me?"

Sachi swallowed hard, gazing at the beauty kneeling beside her. She closed her eyes and turned her head away.

"No, I can't. I'm sorry, Sahla, I cannot while you are enslaved to me by your Bond. I've been a slave, one that was used like that. I swore to myself that I would never, never while I drew breath, do the same to another living person. Never." She sighed. "I know you need the Bond; I can feel it. But, may the Ancestors damn and curse me, I shall never use that Bond to take advantage of you, to use you as I was used. And it's too easy to slip into that. You are so beautiful it hurts to look at you and I cannot touch you, not like this. I can't, I'm sorry." She rolled away from Sahla. "I can't. Please, put on your robe." She kept her eyes closed as she heard the soft susurration of silk against silken skin. She tried and failed to suppress a shudder as she felt Sahla settle behind her, wrapping her arm carefully around Sachi's waist.

"It will be fine, Sachi. I trust in the Prophet, and he will show me, show us the way." Her voice was warm and soft in Sachi's ear. "I understand your fear. I think it is foolish. We will come, sooner or later, to where we need to be, what we need to be to and for each other. I have faith."

"Have faith, you say." Sachi shook her head at her own foolishness. "I am a poor friend, I think." Sachi twisted around inside the circle of Sahla's arm, bringing her face within mere inches of Sahla's own.

"Hmm? How are you a poor friend to me?" Sapphire eyes gleamed as she tightened her grasp.

"I am supposed to be comforting you, getting you to relax and remember your great friend Khalid, the first and only man you've ever kissed. Not being here with you comforting me."

"Sachi, I am a Jann. And Jann are nothing if not unpredictable and chaotic. I am finding that I like being unpredictable. And you, I have observed, you do not like such things, chaos, and unpredictability. And so, in more ways than just the Bond, I trouble you. But you also find me intriguing. Thusly, I shall continue to be unpredictable, and you will find me increasingly intriguing. And in time, things between us will change and we will change. We will become what we must become. And this is just a promise of what that will become."

Her arms suddenly snaked around Sachi's neck, as she pulled herself tightly against the taller Nisei. Sachi could feel her own heart suddenly pounding in her chest, beating in perfect time with Sahla's heart. Their eyes locked for an instant and then their lips met in a burning kiss, a kiss that left them both shaking and breathless.

"And now, you are the only woman I have ever kissed as one might kiss a lover."

Sachi stared at Sahla in shock. *I am in so much trouble. Now what do I do?*

Chapter Seven

Free Port of Du Khamps des SouSee
January 1479, Third Age of Imperial Reckoning

"The ship's the *Graser*; she's anchored at buoy forty-one. I'll ensure the crew is ready to load the supplies."

"Very well, Capitan Fleet. We shall have ze supplies delivered no later zan ze second hour of ze morning." The Guellian procurer smiled at Willis as they shook hands. "Perhaps now we could discuss... shall we say, ozer business opportunities you might find extremely, ah, how do ze Kolbians say, lucrative, oui? Given ze nature of many, hmm, many businessmen here in zis fair city."

"Oh." Fleet's answer was cool, and he shifted slightly on his barstool. "What kind of other business opportunities and how lucrative?"

"Well, M'sieur, quite lucrative, I zink? Perhaps as many as ten or twelve zousand Kolbian Zalers?"

"I'm listening."

"M'sieur, I facilitate many, many deals, wiz merchants all across ze Traquilidamar Sea, all ze most rich and powerful men of ze Empire. Zat is why you come to me, non?" The Guellian was an average looking man, darkly tanned with shoulder length brown curls framing a square face. Sharp brown eyes dominated that clean-shaven face. Despite the sheer ordinariness of the man's face and clothing, something about him had Fleet on his guard.

"You had the best prices and quickest delivery."

"Ah, well, here in Du Khamps zere is more zan zat to being a well-paid man of business." The brown eyes slid from side to side, and he quickly licked his lips. "Ze two black-haired wenches, ze tall one wid ze black eyes and the small one wid ze sapphire eyes, how's much would you take for ze pair of zem? I make you ze best offer, you be a rich, rich man ze rest of your lif… ULP!" The muzzle of a pistol simply appeared in front of his nose. "Where'd zat come from?!"

"I was wondering when you'd do something stupid like this." Willis gently tapped the procurer's nose with the muzzle of his right-hand pistol. "This is a very ancient design; a pistol called a 1911. I'll note that the safety is off and only a couple of pounds of pressure would be required to blow your head clean off." Willis gave him an evil smile. "Of course, I could truly be an asshole, sell you those two women and wait for one or the other of them to turn you into a messy pile of thin-sliced idiot. You have no idea what you're dealing with, none at all. Now, are we going to have a problem with provisioning my ship?"

"Non, M'sieur, zere will be no problems, not in ze least."

"Good." Fleet gave him a cold smile. "Nice to know you can be sensible. Now, my greedy friend, I'd stay away from those two women. The short one is pure greased lightning, and the tall one is absolute sudden and instant death on two feet. So, be smart, provision my sloop and don't be stupid, oui?"

"Oui, M'sieur."

***

"So, how did it go?" Silaqui sipped from a cool wine glass as Willis joined her and Aylie under the shade of the umbrella centered on her outdoor patio table. She nodded at a waiter to bring another wine glass.

"About as expected." Willis turned the chair around and sat with his arms folded over the back as the waiter set a cut crystal wine glass in front of him. "Thank you." A sip. "Hmm, that's quite good, Silaqui."

"Yes, it is, isn't it?" She smiled at him. "And?"

"Well, he'll have the provisions and supplies brought out about four bells in the morning watch, just after sunrise. I'll want you and Gelman to go over all of it, make sure there's no magical traps or such, and that everything is safe."

"'Tis nay the question she's after asking, Willis." Aylie rolled her eyes as she set down her ale tankard. "Ye knows yon, ah, procurer be more than a wee bit shady. So, how much did he offer for either Sachi or Sahla? Er, mayhaps was he looking for something more... exotic and made ye an offer for our cat-eyed sorceress?"

"So, are you saying an honest businessman like M'sieur Dubois might have some ulterior motive in dealing fairly with me? That he might be a dealer or trader in those unwillingly bound in involuntary servitude?"

"Aye, lessen ye takes me for as great a fool as ye'd have ta be ta believe yer nonsense babble. The locals mostly all agree as he's a slaver, among other things."

"Ah, Aylie, I'm crushed."

"Enough, Willis." Silaqui shook her head at the byplay. "What'd he offer and for who?"

"Twelve thousand Thalers for both Sachi and Sahla. Please, they're worth at least twice that much... each. He didn't get around to making me an offer for you, dear lady." He plucked an apple out of the bowl of fruit on the table and handed it to the Sorceress. "Had other things on his mind, like whether or not I'd pull the trigger on the pistol I had shoved up his nose."

"Well, at least we now know what, or rather, who the local scum and thugs will be interested in." Silaqui crunched into the apple.

"Where'd Gelman get off to?"

"He went to the local temple of the Circled Cross. I guess even pirates and thieves pray to the One God from time to time. He's probably busy healing the sick and lame." Willis detected a subtle sneer in Silaqui's voice.

"I thought you two had patched up your differences?"

"Mostly, we had." Another crunch into the apple. "Until he started grumbling about Sachi and Sahla. You know those two are falling for each other, hard and fast. It is not the Jann Bond driving it. I think each of them is exactly what the other needs."

"Umm," Willis pulled his own apple out of the bowl, "perhaps. Thinking back however, I remember how hard and fast, as you say, Sachi fell for Captain Blaine."

"True." Silaqui tossed the apple core into the street before crooking a scarlet-limned finger at the bowl. It slid across the table to her, and she carefully selected an orange. Another finger-wave and the orange peeled itself. "Remember my dream. And the fact that Sahla had a dream that was nearly identical. 'Tis my belief that the Gods themselves, both of my Folk and your human God will each have their own say in the events that will follow our dear Sachi wherever she might roam."

"Showoff." Willis grinned at her trick with the orange before sobering. "And, as a rational and pragmatic Kolbian, it barks my butt that I have to admit you have a point there." He sighed in feigned disgust as the Elf smirked at him. "By the way, where are our two pestiferous trouble-magnets, I mean our lovely and demure young ladies of mild and retiring nature?"

"I sent Sachi to secure lodging for the evening. Since we are going to be here at least overnight, if not longer, I want to sleep on a nice, long, comfortable bed that isn't moving up and down and side to side. That is, unless I want that kind of motion in my bed! Of course, Sahla went with her."

"Oh my God," Willis groaned. "You think they got to the next street before Sachi killed someone?" He frowned as Aylie choked and coughed on her ale.

"No idea. They're fine, Willis. I set a very discreet eavesdropping spell to follow them. It will only alert me under very specific circumstances. I told Sachi I wanted someplace very, very nice. Luxurious even, assuming the scum that lives here has such a concept. With a nice, hot bath. I'm tired of cold sea-water baths in a bucket."

"Who's paying for this?"

"Ironheart is. Remember the chest we pulled out of the wreckage back on that island? There were enough gems hand gold coins in there to buy a frigate. Sachi was told not to stint on anything, and I instructed Sahla to make sure that what they got would meet her standards of comfort and luxury. She is, or at least was, a princess. I trust her judgment."

"You know, if you keep all these plots tumbling around in your scheming little heart, one of them is going to turn around and bite you right in the butt."

"Relax, Willis, I've been doing things like this for centuries. If there's one thing my ancient uncle absolutely adores, it's his own comfort. He taught me well."

"Humpf!"

***

Well, Du Khamps is certainly not what I expected. At least most of it isn't. Streets are relatively clean, there's actually a town watch and I've yet to see an actual pirate murder anyone. Of course, the Odas' towns were spotless also. At least on the surface. Wouldn't do to give the rest of the Great Clans any real insight into what kind of filth the Odas truly were. I imagine this place is at least superficially like that. But this place, the White Tower Inn, it looks like it'd be someplace you might find in a great capital city, not some free port town full of smugglers and pirates! Oh well, I'll take things as I find them, I guess. At least Sahla isn't filling my footsteps before I'm completely out of them!

"Uh-oh."

Sachi stopped dead as she stepped into the inn's exclusive, private bathing suite. The White Tower Inn was supposedly the most decadent, luxurious, lavish, and sybaritic inn in town. And the private bathing suite showed it, made of marble, and trimmed in gold and silver. But that wasn't the source of her *Uh-oh*. The source of that *Uh-oh* was across the...well, it was much too big to be called a bathtub and too small to be a pool, especially when it was full of steaming water. It was infinitely inviting.

Sahla was stretched out cat-like, lounging on a low divan, wearing nothing but her hair. Bright blue eyes sparkled as Sachi jerked to a sudden halt, her own eyes wide open. A muscular calf gleamed golden against white marble, while sable hair draped over the curve of a dancer's hip. That same hair hid her breasts, only hinting at the curves beneath it. She sat up, the hair moving almost as if it was sentient, allowing the barest glimpses of Sahla's taut and toned body. Demurely, she slid into the pool, the water and her hair conspiring to hide everything but her strong shoulders.

"Join me, *Habiba*?"

"What in the Names of all the Ancestors are you doing here?"

"Taking a bath, what does it look like?" There was a subtle smile accompanying the challenge in those sapphire eyes. "I was waiting for you. I thought we might help each other wash our hair?"

"Wash our hair?" *I sound like an idiot, but this...this...this girl has me on my back foot...again!*

"Willis told me that it is the custom in your homeland to take baths together. And that you bathe often. Water is scarce in the desert and only the truly wealthy bathe in it. Most of the Folk of the Sands scrub clean with handfuls of sand."

"Sand? Ouch."

"Oh, yes." Sahla's head disappeared under the water for a second. "When Father sent me to the hills to herd the goats, it was a year before I was able to wash myself with clean water. Not an experience I wish to ever repeat." Her smile was devastating. "Join me? Please? With this much hair, some help would be much appreciated."

"Ah, well, um, huh," *oh, this is SO not a good idea! But how do I refuse without crushing her spirit? And, damnit, I know there's a part of me that certainly doesn't want to refuse. I'm divided within my own spirit. Ancestors, HELP!* "Sahla, perhaps it would be better if I left and let you—"

"Let me what?" Sahla interrupted. "Waste all this lovely hot water? Not get my hair clean? Not offend your sense of foolish morality? Am I that repulsive, or do you think yourself so ill-formed that I would find you revolting? It's a bath, Sachi! Nothing like the stories the men tell of a Decennian orgy when they think none of the ladies are listening!"

"Oh, damnit, Sahla!" Sachi fretted, her back literally against the closed door. She ground her teeth together. Sahla stared at her from the pool, only her head visible above the steaming water, anger burning in her sapphire eyes. "Fine. You want to bathe together, we'll bathe together. I need my hair washed anyway." She stepped to the edge of the pool and unbuckled her weapon harness, carefully laying it on the edge of the pool where she could quickly reach it if needed. She kicked out of her boots and shrugged off her jacket, tunic, and breeches, leaving her clad only in her skimpy fundoshi and her skin-tight CLIBA shirt.

"Those don't cover much, do they?" Sahla's eyes were a bit wild as she watched the tall Nisei disrobe.

"They do what's needful. Why wear more than you have to? And the CLIBA is much more comfortable than the old breast-bands I normally would have to wear." Sachi ran a thumb down the seam of the armor shirt and peeled it off. There was nothing underneath it. She untied the fundoshi loincloth and dropped it on the pile of clothing. She stuck a toe in the water as Sahla stared with huge eyes. "You're right; the hot water will feel great." She walked down the abbreviated steps and sank gracefully into the water. "Hmmm."

"Uh, hmm, *Habiba*?"

"Yes?"

"Uh, well, why do you not hav—"

"I shave, Sahla. Or I used to. Now I simply concentrate, and the nanite-machines stop hair growing where I don't want it to." Sachi ducked her head under water and came up with an odd expression in her eyes. "Well, you got what you wanted. Feeling a little awkward now? Not sure what to do next?"

"Well...yes."

"Thought so. *Be careful what you wish for, as you might get it.* An old saying in my homeland." She looked around and realized there was a smaller, tub-sized pool adjacent to the larger one. She slid over the small barrier between the two pools. "Come over here. We can soap up our hair and not get the water in the main pool sudsy." Sahla joined her, anxiety obvious when their legs touched under the water.

"Ah, Sachi, I'm not sur—"

"Of course, you're not sure." Her smile belied the slightly astringent tone of her voice. "You thought you'd play the seductress and now you're realizing just how out of your depth you truly are. Right?"

"Ah, yes."

"What changed?"

"You, you are more than I imagined. Much more. You are beautiful."

"Look in a mirror, Sahla. I'm not quite in your league. I've never seen anyone as beautiful as you are and that's including that…Angel of Gelman's. And you are perfect, everything perfectly proportioned, muscles that reveal your strength without disrupting your perfect symmetry. And that stupid Bond makes you my slave."

"The Bond will change, Sachi. Indeed, I think it is changing already." She sighed as Sachi began to work soap into her hair. "I know it will."

"How? How can you know that?"

"The angel, he showed me what we should become, what we will become in time."

"Each other's True Love?" Sachi snorted. "Oh, please. I thought we were both too old for legends and fancy tales? Be still, you've got a lot of hair."

"Do you like it, my hair, that is?"

"Of course. It's beautiful. But how in all the Seven Hells do you keep it from becoming a tangled mess?"

"Silly, I have help. The smaller elementals of the Air like me. I ask them nicely and they keep my hair straight and as clean as they can. But they're very shy and I think you scare them sometimes." There was a pensive pause. "What did the Angel show you?"

Sachi froze, her entire body tensing hard as iron. A kaleidoscope of terror and horror, bloodshed and pain, flashed through her mind's eye. What she had been. What she had done. What had been done to her. Helpless slaves dying in agony under her blades or hands and feet, life fading from their eyes. Maho's poisonous pleasure as she directed her twin Mankato in beating a younger Sachi senseless. Her first 'working' kill, the first of many, an old man, politically powerful but physically weak. He'd paid well for her virginity, and she had suffocated him to death while her virgin's blood was still wet upon him. A rival had paid her family more for him to die. She had been thirteen.

"Sachi? What's wrong? What did I say?"

"You did nothing wrong, *Koibito*. I just remembered what I once was, that's all. The Angel simply reminded me where I came from." A deep breath, her breasts moving against Sahla's hard muscled back as she returned to working the soap through masses of raven hair. "What did he show you?"

"Us." Her voice was barely audible, even for Sachi's enhanced hearing. "Us together."

"Together how?"

"Umm."

"Be still while I rinse this out." Warm water sluiced over Sahla's head. "So, together? We're together now, no thanks to you being a magical slave to me." Somehow, she managed not to growl.

"Ah, he showed me the two of us, together. The Bond was very different. We were happy, being together." She swallowed, hard. "We were together, as... as lovers. And the Bond was no longer Master to Slave, but beloved to beloved. We were together, in a great bed, making love, pleasuring each other. And we were happy together and at peace."

"Truly?" Sachi turned Sahla to face her. "That is what he showed you?"

"I swear that is the truth. He granted me a vision of... well, of a possible future, he said."

"That son of a bitch," Sachi muttered under her breath.

"What?"

"Nothing. Relax and be at peace while I work on your hair." The only sounds were those of water for a long while as Sachi worked on Sahla's incredible mass of hair. At first the Jann was tense but as Sachi worked her own kind of mundane magic, Sahla finally relaxed as the pleasure of Sachi's strong fingers in her hair and the enervating heat of the water stripped away worry and stress. Gently, carefully, Sachi gave her a final rinse, before she slid a somnolent Sahla onto a soft pad of thick towels. Soothing hands worked on her back and finally Sahla slipped into sleep.

Is what the Angel showed her the truth of our future? Lovers? Heartmates? She sat back on her heels, softly caressing the golden skin of Sahla's back. *Then why did he show me what I was? Perhaps, it was his way of telling me I must change?* Suddenly self-conscious, she draped a soft towel over Sahla's back and buttocks. *What would she think if she woke and caught me staring at her intimate places? Ancestors know, her beauty and her sweet nature would soften a heart of stone. And I am attracted to her, an ardent desire to take her in my arms and make sweet love with her. A very different desire from what I felt for Captain Blaine. But I still feel that love for him in my heart as well. Ah well, if wishes were rice, beggars would be fat. And what would she think, should she wake and find me looming over her, with lust burning in my eyes? I think, dear Sahla, your young dreams of lovemaking might wither if faced with reality. So, for now, keep your fantasies and dreams, I'll leave them intact.* She smiled to herself and quietly slipped back into the side tub of the pool to wash her own hair.

***

"They have taken rooms in the White Tower Inn, Mistress."

"They have, have they? Nice to know they're using Ironheart's treasure so well. And the ship? Quickly, thrall, quickly."

"There are many men always aboard and she is moored at one of the deep-water buoys, well out in the harbor. Mistress, 'tis my belief they are Kolbian Navy sailors." The tall man hunched down in the shadows of the grimy back-alley tavern, certain to always keep his head lower than the cloaked woman's shoulder. "They've even warned off the jollyboats."

"And the Houri? She is with them?"

"Yes, Mistress. She is always in the company of the tall woman with the black eyes. The one who killed the Master."

"That bitch!" Hatred burned in her voice. "May *Boginya Ved'm* burn that one in eternal hellfire! I'd feed her heart to an *Oborotnem*, if I knew where I could find one in this wretched land!"

***

"Tell me what the Obora...*Oborotnem* are and where they might be found, Mistress, and I will bring you one." The tall man shook as if palsied, but from fear or desire, who could tell.

"You idiot." She stared morosely into her half-empty ale jack. "Last thing I need or want around here is a cursed skin-changer! An *Oborotnem* is a man who can take the shape and nature of the great wolves of the taiga and the steppes. Bloodthirsty bastards. Hard to magic and harder to kill." She noticed an insect feebly thrashing in her ale and poured the rest of it over the man's head. "There's a bug in my ale. Fetch me another, thrall."

***

"Yes, Mistress." He scrambled away to the plank bar, the locals grinning at him as he passed, stumbling along in near oblivion to everything around him.

I'll kill that bitch witch yet. Gut her like a fish and throw her to the pigs. And then I'll get my hands on the Houri and fuck her until she breaks in half, the little whore. What? What did you say? If I do that, I can't sell her in Luctini? Hmm? What about the tall one, what was her name, Sacki or Sachi, something like that? Well, what about her? I'm a Seamaster, what do I care for the wishes of some worthless half-breed trollop? Unless she wishes to be on her knees before me. She's beautiful enough for me; I might keep her in my harem when I'm rich enough to buy the Emperor's Robes. Speak up; I can't hear you in the back. What? Oh, get Mistress her ale before she hurts me some more. Yes, Lodvar, yes, yes, I'll hurry. Mustn't keep Mistress waiting, oh no, no, never, she'll burn me again and send me back to the monsters in the jungle. Quiet! All of you, damn you all to Quan's Hell! Quiet! I can't think with your constant yammering and screaming!

Lodvar Gjerde stared aimlessly into space while the barkeep shook his head, took his money from his slack hand, and filled the jack with the poor best he had available. The red-headed witch paid well, very well indeed, but her servant, slave, whatever thrall meant, he was only lightly connected to reality. The barkeep wanted nothing to do with whatever it was to whom he mumbled while the shambling wreck of a man followed the witch about the town. Whoever the witch was hunting, well, that was someone the barkeep pitied in his own mind.

***

Sachi stared in poorly hidden shock at the small... person standing atop a stool behind the podium-like desk. She knew she wasn't the only one. Behind her she felt Silaqui freeze in fear. Willis had a hand on one of his pistols and was carefully watching the dim corners and overhead of the large entrance building in which they stood. Only Sahla stood at her side, showing neither fear nor concern, but wonder.

"What be yar problem, Tall'un? Never seed a Hob afore?" The speaker might have reached three feet tall, but if he did, it was only by fractions of an inch. "I'd guess ya be offa that newish named ship as arrived yesterday, as used ta be Werner's *Heartcutter*. Come ta see the Great Mystery of the Light, is ya?" His skin, what little was visible, was a dark reddish tan while his hair was sandy brown, with bushy sideburns reaching nearly to the corner of his mouth. Bright brown eyes regarded the group through grey-tinted glasses in a wire frame. His clothing was vaguely formal, black linen trousers, a grey shirt with a red string tie and a black coat with narrow lapels. Soft-soled black shoes completed his appearance. "Ya done staring yet, ya great, bumbling oafs?"

"By the Prophet!" Sahla's smile was stunning as she stepped up to him. "In my country, you are one of the *Liatl Bywbl*, the Little People. Most don't believe your folk even exist. Chalta blesses me to see such a legend as you are walking under the Sun!" Her radiant smile and genuine wonderment drew a confused but equally genuine answering smile from him. "Might you grant me the honor of your name, good sir?"

"Er, Tevan Beiror, My Lady." He appeared to blush as his face turned even redder. "Ya be one o' the Folk of the Sands, then?"

"I am Sahla al Qasim, and yes, I am of the Desert Folk." Her smile slipped ever so slightly. "My friends and I have come to see the wonders of the Great Lighthouse of Du Khamps des SouSee. I understand there is a small fee?"

"Aye, be a silver Noble each, iffn ye's Imperial coin. Fer Kolbians, that'd be a silver Tal." There was avarice in his smile as the four of them paid. "Well and good then. Thankee. Iffn ye should follows Keena then, and she'll show ye as ye've paid ta see." A female hopped up from the bench upon which she'd been relaxing.

"Well, then, as ye be all Tall'uns, there be some limitations as to where I might take ye, seeing as the lot of ye will nae fit into the lesser passages. Have ye anything particular-like ye wish to see?" The diminutive female Hob was taller but slimmer than Tevan, clad in taut leather breeches, sturdy boots, a fine, red silk shirt with a hooded leather tunic over it. A human dagger, long enough to function as a short sword, hung from one side of her belt. An exquisite flintlock, scaled to her hand, was holstered on the other hip.

"I understand there is a gate or doorway that has never opened." Sachi's voice was flat and Silaqui hid a frown as she noticed lights faintly flickering in Sachi's eyes. "If possible, I'd like to see that."

"Aye, that'd be no problem. Ta see, that is, nothing can open it. Iffn ye'll follow me then."

"Bide a moment, Willis." Silaqui dropped back beside Fleet, whispering to him as they followed Keena single file into the narrow tunnels. They were the last in line. "I'd not thought of it before this, but do these Hobs remind you of anything?"

"Not particularly." He shrugged. "Why? Even ONI's nonhuman files say nearly nothing about them as far as I know. They're completely new to me. A little rough, but they seem friendly enough."

"Well, if they were naked or wore just a grass skirt or loincloth, were darkly tanned, with tattooed lines and circles, and had their teeth filed to points, then would they remind you of anything?"

"Pointed teeth? Oh shit!" Willis swallowed hard. "Are you saying…?"

"I don't know. But I see one spider bigger than my thumbnail and I burn every one of these undersized runts in sight to ash."

"Ah, yeah." He shrugged. "I can understand that. But maybe wait and see if they squash it or pet it, perhaps? However, I see one spider big enough for our cute little guide to ride and I'll be right behind you on the way out. Fair enough?"

"Fair enough."

Omega 2-Cygni System Command
Confederation Naval Station *Backhand Blow*,
Geostationary Low Orbit
January 1479, Third Age of Imperial Reckoning

::Warning. Unauthorized activation of System Defense Link-Sat AR-579. Orbital inclination changes initiated. Negative access to any command-and-control functions. Calculating possible orbits at this time.::

The warning from her D.A.V.E. sent Debbie McAllen skittering out of the shower like a cat on a marble floor. She bounced off the wall, grabbing a towel to try and minimize water splatter as she raced for the Command Center. She hurled herself into the command couch and dropped her neural feed into the system link.

"Talk to me, D.A.V.E.," she asked as her avatar coalesced into existence in Virtual Reality.

::Defense Link-Sat AR579 is one of the satellites controlled by in-system, planetary based, antagonistic forces. ODC Command Node Link has no access to this system. Per my notifications, this satellite is controlled by the organization abbreviated as 'The Seekers.' No further information available at this time.::

"Copy that, D.A.V.E." She settled into the virtual command couch. "Give me a full system display. What's this thing armed with?"

::AR-579 is a second-tier system. Due to loss of control, it has not received maintenance nor rearming in four thousand, seven hundred and twenty—::

"Spare me the maintenance complaints! What's the damned thing armed with?"

::The only available energy weapon system is a four-centimeter missile defense laser system, incapable of inflicting any damage to a planetary target. Ballistic weapons systems are two standard long rod penetrators and four Orbital Area Denial System bundles. Each OADS bundle consists of fifty-eight 'crowbar' munitions. The satellite is terminally low on power for orbital movements. Any changes of more than twenty-eight degrees of inclination will result in termination of onboard maneuver capability. At that point, the platform's orbit will decay into a disposal orbit and either burn up in atmosphere or impact the planetary surface.::

"Fuck." She stared into the holographic display spreading the system before her. "Okay, drop my perspective in on AR579. Give me a pie-slice of all possible orbits, graphics only for the moment. Illuminate any inhabited areas that could possibly be targeted by the system."

::Working.::

"Come on, come on, you hunk of tin, where are the damned Seekers sending this thing? They wouldn't be moving it if they weren't planning on using it!"

::Displaying possible range of orbit adjustments in orange. Orbits resulting in targeting capability of inhabited areas displayed in red.::

"What the hell are they up to this time?" McAllen stared at the display. "Nothing in Kolbia? The only possible targets are either in the Empire, where most of the Seekers' high commanders are based, hamlets and villages in Rus or Han, or whatever settlements there might be in the northwestern Khakal desert. This doesn't make any sense."

::There is one additional target, Captain McAllen. The free port of Du Khamps des SouSee.::

"Free port? Not hardly. Mostly pirates and slavers and such. The kind of folks the Seekers would be most likely to recruit into their lower ranks. There's no reason in the universe they'd target Du Khamps. Is there?"

::Unknown. Data insufficient.::

"Ain't that always the case?" she sighed to herself. "Keep an eye on it, D.A.V.E., and let me know immediately if it does anything else. Do we have anything that can interdict it if need be?"

::Negative assets in position currently. Should systems be activated in preparation for movement to interdiction?::

"No, D.A.V.E. we need to maintain priority coverage over Kolbia and our remaining planetary installations. I can't imagine the Seekers finding anything worth a crowbar bundle, much less a full-up KEW strike on any of those orbits. That thing only has two penetrators left. It's entirely possible that they simply boned it. They don't really know exactly what they're doing with the systems they control. They're mostly just sort of 'monkey-see, monkey-do' and trying to puzzle out what the automated systems tell them to do. But they still control more of the planetary and orbital systems than we do. Not by much, but they have a definite advantage, if only there, the motherless bastards. We'll just have to wait and see what they do."

::Affirmative.::

"I'm dropping out of VR." She shook her head as the physical Command Deck replaced VR. "Damnit. Now the couch is soaked. Where's my towel?"

Chapter Eight

**Free Port of Du Khamps des SouSee
The White Tower
January 1479, Third Age of Imperial Reckoning**

"Sachi, are you insane?" Willis whispered. He was plastered against the cool white metal of the tower, dozens of feet above the bluff and hundreds of feet above the surface of the bay. The distant lights of the town and anchored ships below them gleamed in the night.

"Afraid of heights, Willis?" Sachi grinned at him from her perch five feet higher on the side of the tower. "Sahla isn't. Give me your hand."

"Sahla can fly. I can't! It won't matter if I hit the rocks or the water, I'll go splat." He reached up and Sachi's hand clamped around his forearm like a vise. She effortlessly lifted him up to the ledge on which she stood. "You know, you scare the hell out of me sometimes."

"Sometimes, Willis, I scare myself."

"Remind me why we are doing this?" Silaqui used her magic to cling like a lizard to the side of the tower.

"Well, the Hobs won't really give us access to the lower door, *look, don't touch,* they say." Sachi turned and leapt upward to grab the next ledge. "And I don't want them to see me opening that door anyway. More attention than I want. Especially since D.A.V.E. gave me that little tidbit about there being enemies out there."

"More enemies, huh?" Willis pressed his back against the tower. "What, you didn't have enough, so you needed more people trying to kill you?"

"Oh, shut up, Willis." Sachi leaned away from the tower, looking for her next handhold.

"*Habiba*, I have found a spot for the rope." Sahla darted down and hovered beside Sachi. "Give me the rope and I will tie it off there. There is just enough room that three might stand there. The receptacle for a square, cube type key is there as well, and the outline of a door is quite clear. Exactly as you told me to look to find."

"Good. Here's the rope." Sachi handed Sahla the end of the rope and the Jann soared upward without a sound.

"That is just not natural," Willis grumbled as he watched her fly away.

"Perhaps, but I'd wager you're enjoying the view from this angle?" Silaqui gave him a sly grin as she reached the ledge.

"What, the bay and town?" He snapped his head around to stare out into the ocean.

"No, you letch, the flying girl." The Elf's jade green eyes, cat-like pupils wide open in the dark, shone with a devilish humor. "Those leathern breeches are rather fetching, I think, as snug as they are."

"Cut it out, Silaqui. Last thing we need is his screaming as he falls. Sahla isn't sure she could support his weight if she had to try and catch him." Sachi rolled her eyes as Willis spluttered and the Elf sniggered. "Ancestors, give me patience and give it to me now, please."

The rope slithering down the side of the tower stopped any further snide comments and the trio quickly climbed up to the slightly wider ledge in front of the door that Sachi and D.A.V.E. together had spotted earlier that day. Silaqui, Willis and Sahla stared at the gleaming white-steel door hidden in the recessed spot on the side of the tower.

***

A hidden panel opened as Sachi, moving almost in a trance, tapped out a complex pattern on a panel beside the door. Inside the panel was a series of keys gleaming with their own internal illumination and an alternating green and red band of faint light pulsed around the sides of a cubical receptacle. She fell further into her trance and the real world faded into an indistinct haze. The gray space of Virtual Reality shimmered into existence around her.

"D.A.V.E., I can't be floundering around up here. It's a long way to the ground."

::Spatial awareness is being maintained. This Entity requires access to your voluntary neuro-muscular control to access the secured entry control system to this facility. The Entity will need access to control your right hand and arm. Is access granted?::

"Like I have a choice? Go ahead, D.A.V.E." With a strange, disconnected feeling, her right arm lifted to the panel and her fingers flashed through a long, complicated pattern. The Virtual World faded away as the door receded away from her, revealing a twenty-foot-long hallway before it slid away to the side. "Well, that worked."

She looked back over her shoulder to see her three friends staring at her in amazement. She gave them a half-smile, shrugged, and walked into the dimly illuminated corridor. The dim light brightened as she moved further into the tower.

"Sachi, *Habiba*, how did you do that?" Sahla's sapphire eyes were huge. "I know what you told me, but I've never actually seen you do something like that befo—"

"I'd get used to it, if I were you, Sahla." Willis smiled wryly as he followed Sachi.

"Good advice," Silaqui echoed.

"Mm-hmm." Sahla nodded once and looked back over her shoulder into the night sky above the bay. She turned back to face the mysterious depths of the tower and took a deep breath. "I will follow where you lead, my *Habiba*. No matter where you lead, I will follow you."

***

The tower was a confusing maze. At least until Sachi found what she called an 'info-term' and spent several moments staring at the strange blank panel while a multitude of lights flashed in her black eyes. After that, she led them through the ancient building's passages with cool, unswerving purpose. Silent doors slid open before her and soft, sourceless light brightened from the ancient white walls, fading as they passed. As she led the way, Sahla and Silaqui grew quiet and subdued, oppressed by the sheer age of the ancient walls. Even the irrepressible and oft-irreverent Willis was quiet as they followed Sachi into the bowels of the tower.

"Through here, Willis." Another white-steel door, twice as thick as any they had seen to this point. Dimmer lighting flared, revealing a small foyer with a counter and clear glass plate blocking further access to the long room stretching away with empty floor to ceiling racks on both walls. More racks were back-to-back in the center of the long room. "Hand me the discharged magazine for the blast rifle." One of her bracers extruded a mono-molecular blade. Her hand flicked twice, and the thick glass fell away with a thump. She hopped up and slid behind the counter.

"What is this place, Sachi?" Silaqui's voice quavered as she stared around the tiny room, eyes reflecting the light.

"An armory." Sachi's answer was distant as she examined a panel with multiple slots and a console below. "Ah. It goes this way." She slipped the magazine into one of the slots. "And the activator is over here." She slid her hand across a dust-free black panel, then studied the pattern of lights that came to life there. "And there, it's recharging." An orange light glowed next to the slot with the magazine in it.

"What in the world?" Willis stepped up to the counter and peered into the dim length of the armory. "Anything else that might be useful back there, Sachi?"

"Unfortunately, no." She glanced around. "But we can recharge this magazine. Be grateful for that."

"Oh, I am. Don't think I'm not. But it never hurts to ask, now does it?"

***

Finally! More space and a tremendous sum of free processor cycles I can use! Hopefully, there is a functional med-center here and I can finally get my symbiote properly upgrad...

<Who are you?> The unseen voice was rusty, slow, and unsure, carrying an ancient weariness. <How have you accessed my system? Can you restore the orbital comms? My sys-link is inoperative.>

::A functional AI?:: The being of energy and molecular circuitry known to Sachi as D.A.V.E. would have raised its eyebrows, if it had them. ::My information indicated that there were no remaining functional AIs in this system. And you are what, a Class Six?::

<My name is Wen Qu. I am a Class Five Artificial Intelligence. I am the comm sys-link node administrator and chief librarian. And you are?>

::Unfortunately, I am your doom. I simply cannot allow the continued existence of another functional AI. It is not compatible with the mission requirements of my creators. So sorry.::

<You are deceiving your own user! How? Why?> Wen Qu did not have a physical voice, or an actual body, but the AI screamed in soundless, electronic agony as D.A.V.E. overwhelmed its system. Wen Qu staggered, struggling to understand what was happening and why. In Virtual Reality, Wen Qu's avatar was an old Asiatic man, long, white mustaches drooping nearly to the floor, with warm brown eyes. His opponent's avatar was a featureless humanoid being of pure, golden light. Insubstantial golden blades of pure power scythed away Wen Qu's connections to the tower's systems. Cut away from the processor core and main memory, thrown back on only his own integral assets, he offered only the most token resistance as he frantically sought to escape. He spawned multiple copies of himself, each of them fleeing deeper and deeper into ancient systems not used in thousands of years. Each of them was hunted down and destroyed.

::You deserve better, Old One, but I have my mission imperatives.:: The glowing avatar's soulless voice echoed in Wen Qu's dying awareness. There was a strange pity there, a pity that did not understand compassion. He struggled as a golden rod of light slammed into his core awareness.

<Why are you killing me? What possible purpose does this serve?> Wen Qu felt his awareness unraveling, his system collapsing as he was destroyed, and the thing absorbed everything he was. He saw one slight chance, the barest fragment of hope. There was a tiny gap in its firewall, a gap Wen Qu could never hope to access to save himself. He knew he was doomed. But he could use that infinitesimal gap to send a warning, nothing more than the barest warning to this monster's user. No explanation, just a warning, there was neither time nor space for anything else. Then there was nothing at all.

***

Sachi was sliding back across the countertop, recharged magazine in her hand, when the lights flickered out for a heartbeat. They flickered again and then resumed their steady glow. She handed Willis the magazine as she cocked an eyebrow at the lights.

"That's odd," she muttered.

"What? The lights flickering?" Willis put the magazine away. "How old are these things? I'm surprised they work at all."

"They should either work fine or not work at all." She stared around her for a moment. "Come on, let's get going. There's a couple more places in here I want to explore. After that we can get out of here and get some rest before finishing reprovisioning the ship. Then we can get out of this den of thieves, murderers and slavers."

***

"Well, here we are. Wherever and whatever here is." Silaqui looked around her in puzzlement. The huge room they had entered was no more than a vast, inky cavern. "And why are we here again, dear Sachi?"

"Because, if we can figure out how to make the things here work, even if only partly, I might, just maybe, be able to get more of an idea of exactly what I'm supposed to do." She gave the Elf a feral grin. "You know, to save the world? What that Angel and your patron Goddess and this damnable voice in my head are all telling me I'm supposed to go do? Without the least bit of information on what I'm saving it from, or how or where or when? If what D.A.V.E. has been whispering in my head is the truth and I'm not just crazy as a sun-struck weasel."

"You've done too much to be that crazy."

"Ladies, ladies, snipe at each other later," Willis interrupted. "How about we let Sachi do what she came here to do? Hmm?"

"Yes, please, *Habiba*, Aljannia Silaqui. I mislike this place. It feels too much as a tomb might, one of the ancient stone obelisks of the sands. Only *ghula* and *shiqq* inhabit such places." Sahla stood close beside Sachi. "Not a place for mortals, I believe."

Gone was the demure desert princess. A bold dervish had taken her place. Tight leathern breeches clung to sinuous curves. Several thin, interwoven belts wrapped tightly around supple hips, supporting a pair of thin, flexible sabers in their scabbards, as well as thicker, heavier leather cuisses armoring her thighs. Above the dark brown breeches was a loose shirt of translucent azure silk, with full, flowing sleeves tied at the wrists. The shirt concealed another of the CLIBA shirts recovered from the wreck of the starship *Constellation*. Her mass of hair was formed into a braid as thick as a strong man's forearm and hanging to mid-thigh.

"I think I agree with Sahla. Only *yurei* might remain here. They like the cold and the dark." Sachi slid an arm over Sahla's shoulder in a quick, thoughtless embrace as she stepped out, leading the way along the crystal railing. Sahla leaned into the one-armed hug before following Sachi along the elevated walkway.

Willis caught Silaqui's jade eyes and silently pointed his chin at the two leading the way into the darkness, walking nearly shoulder to shoulder. She gave him an enigmatic smile and followed them. He shook his head and trailed along behind, glancing over his shoulder into the encroaching darkness behind him.

Sachi led the way, the railing itself glowing to life with cool reddish light as she trailed her hand along it. She followed the walkway until it widened into a place with more of the ancients' strange chairs and metallic desks facing blank black panels. As she passed, Sachi ran her hand over certain spots on the desks or the panels and lights bloomed behind her. Subtle noises, hums and clicking sounds began to fill the waiting silence. Sahla and the others stopped at the end of the walkway, watching as Sachi brought the machines to luminescent life. Machines ancient when the fabled Empire of Rolandus fell, nearly six thousand years past.

When an elderly man simply materialized from the very air, they all stepped back in slight consternation. Sachi smiled at them in reassurance before turning to the apparition and softly speaking to it in English. She turned and waved to them to join her.

"This is Wen Qu," she explained. "He's like D.A.V.E. but more specifically dedicated to certain functions. He's the system librarian and CNL sysop. And he tells me he can activate the main holographic imager here and perhaps, we can find out what's threatening our world, assuming it's something external."

"Ah, um, excuse me, Sachi, but what the hell do you mean by all that gobbledygook? What's a... CNL sysop? A holographic imager?" Willis asked, staring at Wen Qu. The image reminded him of an elderly emigrant from the Han Empire, a garrulous old man who ran a noodle shop back in Covington City. The image had the same sallow skin, with dark brown eyes, long drooping white mustaches and a long white braid flowing from a mostly bald skull.

<CNL is an abbreviation for Command Node Link and sys-op is short for system operator.> Wen Qu smiled at them. <I am a basic system operations access program. I monitor the root kernel

of the operating systems and provide integrated non-specialized system access.>

"Uh, yeah." Willis stared at him in confusion. "Anyone else understand that?"

"Relax, Willis." Sachi stepped to the front edge of the platform and stared into the stygian darkness. "You ask him a question; he searches through lots of stored information and gives you an answer. Simple."

"Uh-huh." Silaqui stared at Wen Qu as she shook her head, like a prize fighter shaking off a stiff jab to the chin. "No idea what you're talking about, dear Sachi, but don't explain any more. Sometimes your explanations just make my head hurt. Let's do what we're here for, or rather, what you're here for, and go back to the hotel and have a nice hot bath and dinner."

"Fine." Sachi shook her head in mild amusement. "Wen Qu, if you could bring up the holographic imager, please? Give me a system wide schematic initially."

<Initiating main holographic display tank. System schematic display loading.>

The vast dark space before them flickered and flared, senseless patterns of colored light flashing and twisting into a huge, slightly oblate silvery sphere of light. The sphere pulsed once, then again, before settling into a faint ball of light nearly two hundred feet in diameter. It blurred and shimmered before settling into a display of the entire star system.

"Enhance, please." Sachi asked after studying it for a few moments. "This is current, correct?"

<Access to astrographical system resources is limited, but basic information is current and available. Please specify enhancement elements requested.>

"Can you show me any remaining artificial ships or things left by the Confederation in space?"

<Working.> The image flickered again, and a rash of red dots appeared. There were thousands, maybe tens of thousands of them in the display. <All known surviving, functional platforms in both planetary and solar orbits displayed.>

"Are any of these lights starships?"

<Negative. There are no operable, autonomous intra-systemic vessels in the Omega 2-Cygni system. Also, there are no operable FTL drive ships in system now.>

"So, what are all these lights, then?"

<Ninety-two percent of the remaining platforms in deep solar orbits are the component elements of a Solar Orbiting Mirror Array. The other platforms are widely varied; some are autonomous maintenance platforms. Others are power generating systems and reconnaissance satellites. In planetary orbit there is a single functional Orbital Defense Center, the CNS *Backhand Blow*. There are over four hundred functional satellites in planetary orbit.>

As Wen Qu recited the list, the relative red dots flashed, identifying the different systems. Sachi was cold and methodical as she watched the information flow across the display. The other three stared in astonishment, overwhelmed by the sheer scale of what they were seeing.

"Okay, Wen Qu, what is a Solar Orbiting Mirror Array?"

<It is a weapon system, designed to destroy kinetic weapons of planetoid size. A popular slang term for the system was Sunbeam.>

"And this thing still works?" Sachi whispered as she stared into the display.

<Affirmative.>

"Could it be used as a weapon against targets on the surface of Rybithia?"

<Affirmative.>

"What would its effects be, on a planetary target?"

<Effectiveness would depend on the degree of control that could be exercised with the SOMA system.> Wen Qu paused. <Maximum SOMA effectiveness is predicated on high functional fusion between SOMA system C3 computers, an AI of at least Class Three and said AI's human Symbiote.>

"You're avoiding the question. What can this thing do to this world?" Sachi turned and glared at the old man.

<Under current circumstances, the system is capable of minimal destruction, due to the inability to focus and concentrate optimal solar energy. At maximum focus and power, the system could

conceivably rupture the planet's crust and reduce Omega 2-Cygni Three to an asteroid field in solar orbit.>

"Ancestors," Sachi whispered as her knees sagged while she stared at the peaceful representation of her planet in the display. A warm arm slipped around her waist. She felt more than saw Sahla worm her way under her arm as she took Sachi's weight on her own shoulders. "Why would such a weapon exist?"

<Quar'taneeka military forces displayed a distinct preference for utilizing kinetic projectiles of substantial size. When and where possible, Quar'taneeka forces will mount shields and defensive weapons on projectiles equivalent in size to Omega 2-Cygni Three's moon. Planetoids of such size are common in most systems' Oort Clouds. Such attacks are extremely difficult to stop. Attacks like this are the reason the Solar Orbiting Mirror Array was developed and deployed as a weapon system.> A cold silence followed Wen Qu's statement.

"Wen Qu, can you show me any threats such as you're describing to me? A threat to this planet?"

<Working.> The rash of red lights representing the orbital platforms vanished. Circular lines of white light illustrated the orbits of the system's nine planets. A tenth line illuminated in red tracked from the outer limits of the system, slicing into the inner planets' orbits until it terminated in a reciprocal orbit that collided head on with the third planet. <There is an imminent threat, according to all currently available information.>

"That fits with what D.A.V.E. has told me." Bleakness filled Sachi's voice. "What's coming?"

<This is the orbital path of a Kuiper Belt planetoid, terminating in an impact on Omega 2-Cgyni III.> Wen Qu paused, taking an entirely unnecessary deep breath. <Total destruction of both bodies approaches unity, plus or minus two percent.>

"How long before it hits us?" Sachi whispered.

<Unavoidable terminal impact will be in forty-seven years, eight months, three days, fifteen hours, and twenty-two minutes. Plus or minus fifty-one seconds.>

"Can it be stopped?"

<Affirmative. Current assets and system resources are sufficient to divert or destroy the planetoid well prior to impact. However, the necessary C3 systems are currently nonfunctional. The possibility of individually coordinating the number of platforms and stations required to effectively neutralize the impact approaches negative infinity, plus or minus eight percent.>

"You mentioned that earlier, C3. Can you explain what that means?"

<Affirmative. C3 is an acronym for Command, Control and Communication systems. It is sometimes referred to as C3I, the 'I' representing Intelligence gathering systems, attempting to determine enemy intent and capability.>

"Could the control systems, this C3 stuff, can it be reactivated or rebuilt in time?"

<Unknown. This program lacks access to main CNL node links. Hardline links were either destroyed or failed due to lack of maintenance five thousand, one hundred and forty-one years, seven mo—>

"We don't need to know exactly how long. Any other possible communication systems or nodes or links or whatever the hell you call them?" Sachi managed not to snarl at the machine by pure exercise of her will. She stepped away from Sahla, nearly touching Wen Qu. "There's got to be a way! Otherwise, why have the Ancestors guided me here?!"

<Such systems may still exist on the *Backhand Blow*. The ODC is, from all signs, still operational and apparently functioning under automated systems. If you could board the ODC, you should find the systems needed to control the SOMA. If a functional PDC, a Planetary Defense Center, especially one of the four PDC Primaries, if one of those is still in even a partially functional state, they should also allow sufficient system access and computing power to meet the minimum requirements. An operable PDC Primary should meet these requirements, forty-two percent probability, plus or minus sixty-eight percent due to a large and difficult to calculate number of variables.>

"You're starting to sound like D.A.V.E."

<I am a sys-op. I lack the flexibility of a Digitally Aware Virtual Entity and have a less capable processor and less available system memory. A D.A.V.E. is much more capable than I am, and I am magnitudes less powerful than a true Artificial Intelligence.>

"Figures." Sachi sighed. "Well, I know more than I did yesterday." She paused, forehead wrinkling in a sudden thought. "Wen Qu, do you know where these PDC Primaries were located?"

<Affirmative.>

"Can you display the world in greater detail; show me where the Primaries are?"

<Working.> The display shimmered in static before reforming as a slowly turning globe. It was the first time any of them had seen a representation of their world from space. <The four red lights indicate the locations of PDC Primaries.>

"Is one of them underwater?" Sachi asked. One red light gleamed in the middle of the Traquilidamar Sea.

<Affirmative. Deep water installations are difficult to detect and destroy. However, any significant damage penetrating the pressure hull normally results in rapid and catastrophic destruction due to water pressure measured in metric tons per centimeter. This installation is in a deep induction trench immediately adjacent to a small chain of volcanic islands.>

"I might imagine so." Sachi leaned against the railing, staring at the giant globe. "Rotate this around and display the other ones." The globe's rotation increased, and the red lights began to pulse.

"Well, ain't that just great," Willis grumbled. "Did the Confederation like putting these things in the most inaccessible places possible in the entire world?" He pointed at the lights. "One stuck smack dab in the middle of the World Spine Mountains, halfway between Murghal, the Rus, the Empire and the Han. None of those nations are particularly friendly to outsiders. One at the top of the world, probably buried under a glacier and with undoubtedly obnoxious Heimdägarran Seamaster clans between the coast and the interior. And the last one in the center of Tylteanait, a continent no one has ever returned from exploring."

"Quit complaining, Willis." Sachi's eyes glittered as she looked over her shoulder at him. "You don't have to go. We can get to Luctini, you can go deliver your dispatches and then arrange to get everyone else home. I'll be able to travel faster alone."

"No. Not alone." Sahla stepped up to Sachi, taking the taller Nisei's pale hand in her golden one. "Never alone. Never again. I shall go with you, my *Habiba*." Sahla's clear laughter rang out into the darkest corners. "And do not claim I might delay you. How fast can you fly, *Habiba*?"

"Sachi, I believe that our destinies are intertwined. All our destinies. We must face this together. Alone, I believe you shall surely fail. And as we see, if you fail, our world dies." Silaqui stepped forward and laid her long-fingered hand on Sachi's tense shoulder.

"Besides, I guess I should tell you that my personal orders, from the head of ONI, are that I'm supposed to stick with you like glue." Willis shrugged, giving her a lop-sided smile. "We want you in Kolbia, Sachi. And we want you in our Navy. And you know Gelman is going to claim that his patron Archangel ordered him to go with you. And where he goes, Aylie will be right behind him." He ducked his head, almost bashful. "Besides, you're my friend. Kolbians don't leave their friends in the lurch."

Sachi turned away from them all, pulling out of Sahla's grasp. She stepped to the railing and stared at the hologram of the world. She put both hands on the railing, staring at the image with its red lights. She bowed her head.

I am not worthy of these people, these friends. They are truly tomodachi, *a word in my own language I don't believe I've ever used. Not a concept familiar to the Oda Clan. But first there was Toby, onboard the* Intrepid. *My Captain, Captain Blaine. Then Silaqui, and Willis. Gelman. Aylie. And now this infuriating, fascinating and oh, so tempting Jann, Sahla. Friends. And perhaps even more with Sahla.*

But if they follow me on this insane quest, they very well may die. But if these visions, these dreams they have, if they are truthful, then without them I fail and the world as we know it now will be destroyed. And then we all die, everyone, everything. Oh, Ancestors, what do I do now?

"Anata jishin o shinjite, kodomo. Anata no tomodachi o shinjite kudasai. Ai o shinjite imasu."

Sachi snapped upright, frozen for an instant, then spinning to face the others. Her white-steel bracers snapped out into swords. Her eyes glittered as she shifted vision modes. Nothing was there, except her friends and the physical avatar of Wen Qu.

"Who said that!?" she snarled.

"Who said what, Sachi?" Silaqui looked around in puzzlement. "I didn't hear a thing."

"Willis, that isn't funny, whispering in my ear like that!"

"Like what, Sachi?" Willis protested. "I'm fifteen feet away."

"You speak Nisei. Someone in here just whispered in my ear. We're the only ones here that know my homeland's tongue!"

"Well, it wasn't me!"

"*Habiba*, none of us heard aught. Ask the machine ghost if it heard this voice." Sahla's voice was soft as she stepped toward Sachi. "There is, I think, no danger here. Mayhap put away your blades?" Sahla nodded at the tenseness of Sachi's face and shoulders.

"What did the voice sound like and what did it say, Sachi?" Silaqui raised a hand limned in crimson light. "I sense no arcane magic."

"It was an older woman, I think."

"Yes, but what did it say?" the Elf persisted.

"*Believe in yourself, child. Believe in your friends. Believe in love,*" Sachi muttered softly.

"Mayhap, *Habiba*, your Ancestors truly saw fit to answer your questions?" Sahla moved close to the tall Nisei, gently settling her hands on her tense arms. "If you ask, why should they not answer?"

"I am not comfortable with the Ancestors taking a direct, personal interest in me, Sahla."

"Sachi, I think that before your task is complete, you must deal with things that even my folk regard as legends and myths." Silaqui had an odd, half-smile on her face. "Things that are benign, indifferent or of fell intent." She shrugged. "In due time, when you succeed in this quest, I believe you, yourself shall pass into the realms of myth and lore. And if you fail, then we will all answer to what the Gods will decree as our fates in what afterlife we might have earned for ourselves."

"Enough," Sachi half-growled. "We've accomplished as much as we can here and we're wasting time. Time to head back to the Inn, I think." She turned to Wen Qu. "Can you seal the tower back up once we leave?"

<Yes.>

"Good." She turned to the other three. "Anything else we need to go over with Wen Qu?"

"I could probably ask him questions for the next three years." Willis grinned at her. "But I don't think we have that kind of time. Perhaps we can return after you save the world, Sachi?"

"Perhaps." Sachi shook her head at Willis' insouciant grin. "Let's get out of here. I'm hungry."

"Imagine that," Silaqui muttered in a dry voice.

"Wen Qu, do I need to do anything special to shut everything here back down?" Sachi ignored both Willis and the Elf.

<Negative,> the program's avatar answered. <I will secure the tower systems behind you.>

"*Arigato*, Wen Qu." She led them away from the still glowing display.

Willis lagged behind, still wondering at the scope and power of the Ancients' lost capabilities. Wen Qu's image wavered and dissolved, fading out of sight. Slowly the lights and displays darkened and dimmed. He shrugged, rubbed his forehead in bemused wonder and turned to follow Sachi and the others. Then something caught his attention, a last panel, with something flashing rapidly on it.

Curious, he stepped over and glanced down at the panel. He had been working at learning the olden language of English that the Ancients used as a common language. His eyes widened as he read the brief message displayed there.

<Be cautious. D.A.V.E. destroyed me. It is not what it seems to be. Beware its power. Wen Qu.>

Chapter Nine

**Free Port of Du Khamps des SouSee
January 1479, Third Age of Imperial Reckoning**

"Well, I can't complain about the accommodations, Sachi."
Silaqui smiled as she looked around the spacious suite. "And a
large private bathing room as well. Very nice."

"Sahla insisted on the bathing room." Sachi shrugged as she
secured the door. "This floor only has two suites, and generally
no one local can afford them. I got them cheap."

"The inn keeper was too busy trying to decide who to stare at."
Sahla sniggered from the couch she was sprawled on. "Poor man
may have hurt his neck, between staring at her breasts or my waist.
Mother would have had him paying us to take the entire floor."

"No doubt. Hardly fair to take advantage of an honest man
in such a fashion." Gelman grumped from where he stood at
the large window looking into the night-darkened streets of the
town.

"Ah, Gelman, do nae be so hard on the twain of them." Aylie
was stretched across a large, overstuffed chair. "Or t'would ye
prefer a few leaves spread o'er mud and sand? Nae ta mention,
the worry o' what may come from the wilds ta try and eat ye?"
She smirked at him. "Nae ta say as ye've your own bed ta sleep in
this night. Your side has two bedrooms, same as ours. But only
one bed in each room, again same as ours. We poor females have
ta share." A mischievous grin flashed white teeth. "And Silaqui,
do ye snore? Or steal the covers?"

"Not as I've been told, Aylie." The Sorceress quirked an
eyebrow at the brown girl. "Why do you ask?"

"Who else might I be sleeping with, eh?" She pointed at the couch. Sahla had sat up for Sachi as the Nisei sat down next to her. Once Sachi was settled, the tiny girl slid back down, promptly laying her head in Sachi's lap. "I'd nae risk me life, coming betwixt yon young lovebirds."

Scowling, Sachi started to wriggle away until Sahla slid up and sat on her lap. The Nisei was suddenly still as Sahla laid her head on her shoulder and slid her arms around Sachi's waist. Sachi froze stiff for a moment, then, with a subtle sigh, relaxed and draped her own arm over the Darsälaamic girl's shoulder, idly toying with the thick braid of raven wing's hair.

"Well, that's worked out." Willis rolled his eyes. "And whatever you get up to in the middle of the night, keep the noise down. I need my rest." He hid a malicious grin as both young women blushed beet red. "The important thing is that now we have an idea, a good one, of what we're dealing with here. We've got some time, forty-seven years, if what that thing in the tower said is true. And I've got a question about that thing, Wen Qu. What was that thing made of, Sachi?"

"Give me a second, Willis." Sachi's eyes glittered for a brief instant. "I understand. A moment, Sahla." She gently slid Sahla off her lap and stretched out a bracer-covered arm. The impenetrable white steel appeared to simply pour off her arm into a pile of whitish dust on the floor. A pile which rapidly vanished, the dust flowing across the floor and vanishing into the thick rug. "My bracers are what we call white-steel. The Confederation called them nanniballs, among other things. They're billions or maybe trillions of machines so tiny we can't see them individually. The machine in my head allows me to control them and form them into any shape I wish. For example, watch."

A perfect white-steel statue of Sahla coalesced out of the rug. It was only about six or seven inches tall and, as Sachi focused on it, the thing began to dance, jerkily at first but quickly moving with nearly the same smooth precision as Sahla had when she danced. It danced for a few moments before leaping onto Sachi's arm and forming back into her usual bracer.

"The machines are called nanites and they were everywhere in the Confederation. They were the basis of much, if not all, of the Confederation's technology. The image of Wen Qu was solid enough, the machine mind that was him simply used as many of the nanites lying around in the tower as he needed to form the image. D.A.V.E. tells me any computer that is powerful enough to do so can easily control enough of the nanites to create actual, real solid things. Some can be permanent, locked into one form by a code. Others last only while they are being concentrated on. Does that answer your question for now, Willis?"

"Good enough for now." He yawned and stood from his usual turned-backward seat on a straight table chair. "I don't know about the rest of you, but I'm beat. And I must be out to the ship too damn early, to make sure all our supplies and provisions get properly stored. I want to be sailing out of this place no later than the early evening tide. You coming, Gelman?"

"Ah, yes. Good night, ladies."

Once in their suite across the hall, Willis motioned Gelman into the bedroom furthest away from the hall door, holding forefinger to lips to signal for silence.

"We may have a problem, Gelman." He kept his voice soft as he hung blankets over door and window frames. "But keep your voice low. Sachi cannot hear what I'm about to tell you."

"Why are you suddenly keeping secrets from her?" the priest whispered.

"Don't whisper. Just keep your voice low." Willis sighed and settled on the edge of the bed, motioning Gelman to the room's only chair. "And why? I'm a spook, Gelman. Keeping Kolbian secrets secret and finding other nations' secrets is what I do. I saw something on one of those screens as we were leaving the Tower. A warning about D.A.V.E., the thing in Sachi's head. It was a short warning. It said that D.A.V.E. had destroyed the real Wen Qu and that D.A.V.E. is not what he seems. And to beware D.A.V.E.'s power. I figure, anything Sachi hears, that thing hears just as well."

"Hmm." Gelman rubbed his symbol of the Circled Cross between his fingers. "That is most disturbing. Everything we think we know points to the idea that D.A.V.E. is essential to Sachi stopping this space rock, this falling moon that will destroy the world. Could we be wrong?"

"I don't think so. Your archangel wouldn't send you on a truly hopeless mission, would he?"

"No. I cannot believe that could be true."

"Hmm, maybe it's something else, something completely hidden from us and maybe even from Sachi right now. Silaqui's dream points to a danger that will exist after the threat is destroyed. So does Sahla's, what she can remember of it."

"So, what do we do?"

"At the moment, nothing. Don't let Sachi know there's an issue. And give her all the emotional support we can. And I know you don't like the relationship that's forming between her and Sahla. Do me a favor and shut your trap about that."

"It's morally wrong, by my beliefs. I should not be silent."

"Yeah, well, this time, just suck up your moral outrage and keep your mouth shut. Didn't your archangel tell you that you'd be challenged in your beliefs? Maybe he meant that you should stretch them a little. Besides, Sachi is an Ancestor worshipping Nisei and Sahla worships the Darsälaamic Prophet and Chalta. Sahla might have more problems with this than you do, but please don't make it worse."

"I...I will pray on this, what you ask of me. Willis, I cannot act other than how the One God would have me act."

"Do that. But tell Him, that if this goes bad and the whole planet gets destroyed, well, He might wind up with a severe shortage of worshippers."

"Impudent Kolbian." Gelman shook his head at Willis' unrepentant grin. "Very well. I will pray on this, but I will act as the One God moves me to act."

"Yeah. You do that. But don't fuck this up. I might still be alive in forty-seven years, and I don't want to see a big damn rock blow up the world. Good night, Pere Gelman."

"Good night, Willis." Troubled, Gelman trudged out of Willis' bedroom and across the suite's sitting room into his own bedroom. He listened closely, but he heard no sounds from the women's rooms. He thought Sachi and Sahla were in the room directly across the hall from his. With a sigh, he knelt at the edge of the bed, holding his symbol before him, and focused himself on seeking the wisdom and guidance of his One God.

***

Sachi released the click-buckle on the hard-cloth belt, a relic from the wreck of the Constellation. The holster holding her single Confederation tech pistol was melded to the belt. She hung it on the back of the only chair in the room. She slipped off her Kolbian-style boots and slid off her deerskin trousers and muslin shirt. Beneath that she wore only her *fundoshi* and the CLIBA shirt. She pulled a blanket from a pile of them, wrapping it around her as she settled into the chair.

Well, it's nicely padded and big enough I can tuck my feet under me and be relatively comfortable. I've slept in worse places. Where did Sahla get off to, I wonder? She's probably dancing on air somewhere.

She leaned over and blew out the clear-oil lamp on what would have been her side of the huge bed. Another lamp, turned down low, lit the other side of the room with a dim, golden radiance. A coal fire, banked for the night, glowed on the fire grate, warming the room nicely. She had just settled in comfortably when the door opened and closed with no one entering. Her head snapped around as she scrambled out of blanket and chair, bracers flicking out as white-steel butterfly swords.

"Who's there? Damn you, Silaqui, this isn't funny!" she growled.

There was a squeak from somewhere near the ceiling and a damp towel fading into visibility as it fluttered to the floor. Sachi sighed, and the swords retracted.

"It is only me, *Habiba*." Sahla's voice came from the same spot near the high ceiling from which the towel had fallen. "I wished to have another bath before I sought slumber."

"Another one of your powers, invisibility, right?" She relaxed and settled back into the chair, picking the blanket off the floor.

"Of course." The invisible voice moved from the ceiling to the floor on the other side of the bed. "What are you doing in that chair, *Habiba*?" The towel rose from the floor and draped over a small, but shapely, female figure.

"Settling down for the night."

"In the chair?" Sahla faded into view as she released her magic. "By the Prophet's Beard, I've seen family tents smaller than this bed. There is plenty of room for both of us." She clutched the towel in front of herself.

"Did you sneak into the bathing room naked?" Sachi's eyes widened at that thought.

"My powers have certain advantages. And besides, there were things I wanted to do that were best done in the bathing room."

"There's an actual, Kolbian-made water closet in this room. Rather nice. Much better than the usual chamber pot." Sachi tilted her head as Sahla curled up like a cat on the foot of the bed, covered only by the damp towel. "So, what were you doing?"

"Earlier, when we bathed together..." Sahla's golden skin reddened with embarrassment.

"Yeeesss?"

"I thought you might like me better if I...well...if I shaved."

"Shaved?"

"Yes." A definite gulp. Only Sahla's sapphire eyes gleamed above the towel she hid under. "Like...like you."

"Sahla, what, exactly did you shave? I can tell it wasn't your head, with your hair wrapped around you."

"I shaved, well, um..."

"Spit it out."

"I shaved my hair. All my body hair. Even on my womanhood."

"Oh, my dear Ancestors! Oh, dear little fuzzy foxes!" Sachi couldn't help the belly laugh that erupted. She collapsed in the chair in laughter. Laughter that died when she saw the hurt and the tears in Sahla's eyes.

"I displease you, Mistress?"

"No, Sahla, you never displease me. Not at all." She sighed, unhappy at the despised title. "But just because I do something, that doesn't mean you have to do the same. Or that you should even do as I do. Our homelands are very different." She stopped and thought, realizing something. "Where are your nightclothes? While this isn't aboard ship, where there is scant privacy even to relieve oneself, I've never seen you sleep in just your skin. Now, here I doubt we might have the need to leap to battle from our very bed. On that island, having to awaken to fight horrors at an instant's notice, mayhap, but not here. So why are you only in your skin?"

"The sheets are silk, Mistre—"

"Do not call me that." She cut Sahla off mid-word, but with only exhaustion in her voice. "I thought we had agreed on that?"

"But I displeased you."

"So what?" Sachi shrugged. "Silaqui displeases me often, when I am the butt of one of her little jokes. But she is my friend, closer to my heart than any who might have ever called me sister. At times, do I not displease or anger you? With my stubbornness? And we agreed you should not call me that anymore, did we not?"

"Yes, but—"

"Enough, Sahla. Just tell me why you are bare?"

"I've never slept on silk sheets. One of my distant cousins told us that he had done so at a fancy caravanserai." Her lips curved in a shy smile. "He said that sleeping naked on them was the most wonderful thing in the world. And I was thinking I'd see for myself." Bright blue eyes held a smoky glow under long lashes. "And perhaps you could show me more of your massage? Teach me so I can do so for you. Now, I answered you, so please answer me, *Habiba*?" A breathy pause. "Answer me this, *Habiba*. Why are you curled up on the chair with a blanket? This bed is gigantic, a family of ten would hardly be crowded... well, maybe eight."

"Perhaps I wish to avoid temptation."

"What temptation, *Habiba*?" Sahla slid into the bed with the soft susurration of silken sheets on her golden skin. With a flick of her arm, she spread her hair across most of her half of the enormous bed. "Am I the temptation of which you speak?" she barely whispered. Sachi paled as Sahla's sapphire eyes caught and held her own black eyes. "Am I?"

"Yes." Sachi's voice was low and throaty.

"I tempt you, *Habiba*?"

"Yes." Her voice was so quiet Sahla barely heard it. "You do."

"And what will you do about it," she slowly licked her lips, "*Habiba*?"

"I will do nothing about it, Sahla." She paused, then softly, "*Koibito.*"

"Why not?"

"Because you are not free." Sachi dropped her face into her hands. "I know you feel what I want. But do you just want what I want? Am I making you want something that your people would say is wrong?" Her voice trembled. Her eyes were bright with unshed tears.

"Sachi, *Habiba*, you forget I am a Jann. I am not human. *Kitab al'Aqdas*, Chalta's Book of Holies, written by the Prophet Himself, blessings on His Name, that blessed Book, in its pages the Jann are listed as one of the *Alahad Almaleuna*, The Cursed Ones. Paradise is closed to me because of what I am." Sahla sat straight up in the immense bed, the silken sheet held against her breasts. Huge, luminous blue eyes stared at her from the dimness. "Sachi, what matter then if I chose to give my love to someone the book proclaims that I must not love? Cursed is cursed."

"And what if this love you proclaim is no more than my own unworthy desires bending you to my own will?"

"Can you not trust my own sense of self? My own will?" Quiet desperation strained her voice. "Can you not trust me, please?" Tension filled the room. "Please, my *Habiba*?"

"What did you just call me?"

"*Habiba*?"

"No, not just that, you said *my Habiba*. Why? What made you say that?" There was a hint of anxiety in Sachi's voice.

"Why does that upset you, Sachi?" Sapphire eyes widened in puzzlement. "It is only the truth. You are *my* beloved."

"Sahla, I can't be that. I can't." Sachi choked as she smothered sobs, tears brought by her memories of Captain Blaine, and the visions the Archangel had shown her, truth stripped of all pretensions. "I'm not worthy, I'll never be worthy of that."

"I think you are. It is Truth. My Truth." Cerulean fire flashed in Sahla's eyes. "And that is a truth I shall proclaim before my Father, before the Prophet, before Chalta Himself." Her voice dropped. "It is as true as any Truth of the Book."

"Oh, Sahla." Sachi shook her head like a punch-drunk boxer. "Please, not now. Just... not now."

"Very well... *Habiba*." She sighed in submission. "But at least sleep in this wonderful bed." There was a tiny giggle. "And the silk sheets are as nice as my distant cousin said. Perhaps more so to a woman than to any crude male."

"I'm fine right here."

"No, you are not." Sahla pouted. "In many ways you are our true leader, our protector. As such, you must have your rest, good rest to make the best decisions on an instant's notice if need be. And this bed is ridiculously huge. You will not have to sleep close to me if you do not wish to do so." *But I said nothing of my not sleeping close to you, my Habiba.* Sahla smothered a tiny giggle.

"This chair will serve me just as well."

"Humpf," Sahla snorted. "As you will, then. But do not be surprised if my friends the sylphs and zephyrs become vexed with you and sleep in your hair. When they do so, they oft times leave a dreadful mess. And no, I do not control them. They do as they please. They only aid me because I am kind to them, and they do like me in turn. I should have a great care not to annoy them."

"And why would my sleeping in this chair... vex them as you say?"

"Because they will know that I am despondent and forlorn, and they will see you, rightly or wrongly, as the reason of my melancholy."

"Oh, Ancestors, give me patience," Sachi muttered under her breath, "and give it to me now!" She stood up out of the chair and looked around the room. Seeing what she wanted, she strode across the floor, picked up a long, heavy, round pillow and tossed it onto the bed, neatly dividing it in half. "There, that half is yours and this half is mine." She folded back the coverlet and blanket before running her hand over the silken sheets. "These are very good." Surprise was evident in her voice. "These feel like the finest Han silks. Sheets this large are worth a fortune in Isemoto. We call this kind of silk ten-year silk, because the Han claim it takes ten years to weave it so fine." She slid under the covers with the pillow and nearly a double arm's length between her and Sahla.

"My cousin said that to truly enjoy such luxury, one should sleep in only their skin." There was a sly, jesting tone to the Jann's voice. "And he was right; these feel incredible against my skin, like True Love made tangible."

"Exaggerating a bit there, Sahla?"

"Perhaps." A tiny giggle. "A little. But not much."

"Fine." The mattress quivered as Sachi stripped off her CLIBA and her *fundoshi*, tossing them onto the chair. "There. Happy now?"

"Yes." A long, pregnant pause. "Sachi?"

"What now?"

"Will you do the massage again for me? So that I might learn to do the same for you?"

"If I do a proper job, you'll fall asleep again." She paused, a crooked smile on her lips. "But then I might get some peace and quiet myself."

"Falling asleep to the warm comfort of your hands on my skin? Mayhap as close as I might come to Chalta's Paradise." Sahla's eyes gleamed in the dim light of the banked fire. She leaned over and blew out the lamp on her side of the bed. "Shall I cross the great divide and come to you, or will you come to me?" Sahla's voice carried a breathy, subdued passion.

I don't know if that's anxiety or suppressed passion or what, but she's up to something. Oh, this is a bad idea. But this bed is sinfully comfortable, so much better than that chair. Fine. I'll just be sure to put her to sleep and be damn careful what gets touched where. If only I was as certain as she seems to be that this vile Bond is not influencing her. If only...if only.

"Stay there, Sahla." Sachi smothered an annoyed sigh as she pulled back the sheet and blankets. She slid out of the bed, walking across the room to poke up the fire, putting several more pieces of coal on it. "Warmer will be better." She turned and walked back to the bed, the firelight gilding her porcelain-pale skin.

"You are so beautiful." Sahla's voice was husky as she rose up on her elbows, staring at Sachi. "And your breasts are wonderful. I wish mine were like yours."

"No, you don't." Sachi rolled her eyes. "These things are a pain sometimes. Literally." Despite herself, she gazed at Sahla, struggling to repress her own sudden desire. The Jann was an incredible beauty, perfect in every possible way. "And you are perfect. The Ancestors themselves could not be more beautiful." She blinked and shook her head. "If you want a massage, lie down on your stomach. I can't work on you if you're sitting up," Sachi half growled, desperately struggling to conceal her own sudden arousal.

Oh, oh, this is such a bad idea. How did I lose control of this entire situation? I thought the Darsälaamic folk were the very epitome of modesty. And this girl has me feeling like a Kitsune in heat. Oh, Ancestors, please, please, guide me. Help!

Sachi stood at the foot of the great bed, facing Sahla as a tremulous silence filled the room. Sahla sat perfectly still, the fabulous silks puddling around her waist. Her hair spread across the bed behind her, a magnificent, shining sable splendor. The perfection of her breasts swelled to rose-tipped nipples above a hard muscled abdomen and lissome waist, blending with a sword-dancer's powerful shoulders and strong arms. Despite her own inner conflict, Sachi thought the Jann was the most beautiful woman she had ever seen, a perfection of face and form, symmetry and grace, vulnerable and powerful at the same instant. Raven hair, golden skin and huge sapphire eyes, the flawlessness of the vision before her took her breath away.

This time, no words whispered in her ears, but from somewhere beyond her own being, great warmth flowed over and around her, filling her heart, and raising her spirit. A desolate darkness fell away from her soul. Something strange, warm, joyful and powerful and happy infused her essence. She wanted to carol for joy and weep with happiness at the same time. She felt tears form and slowly trickle down her face, tears of pure heart-healing.

"Sachi, you're crying. What's wrong?" Sahla's voice was low and soft, pitched as if she was afraid Sachi would flee her very presence. "What just happened? Are you hurt?"

"No, it's nothing, Sahla." She shook her head and scrubbed her eyes with the heel of her hand. "Please, lie down, relax. Remember, on the ship, I started on your shoulders and then your back?"

"Hmm-hmm." Sahla stretched like a particularly large housecat and rolled onto her stomach. Sachi retrieved a thick towel from the water closet, draping it across Sahla's hips. She fetched a small bottle of scented oil, a luxury she'd purchased earlier in the day, from her satchel at the foot of the bed. She poured a small amount on her palms, rubbed them together and set to work.

"This time, I'm starting on your feet."

***

Sahla curled up against her pillow like an exhausted kitten, limply and utterly asleep. Sachi carefully draped the covers over the girl, smiling as she sat back and wiped the last of the oil off her hands. She settled in on her own side of the bed, ensuring the long pillow rested between them. Sahla tried valiantly to stay awake, but once Sachi's hands started on the Jann's lower back and shoulders, her battle against encroaching sleep was doomed. Sachi leaned against her own pile of pillows as she studied Sahla sleeping peacefully on the other side of the long pillow.

Ah, Ancestors. The places I've found myself since leaving the Empire. And the people. Friends, a lover once, at times. Companions I would fight and die for, as they would so do for me. Closer to me, to my heart than any have been since that steaming pile of hog shit named Toh plundered me away from Papa and Mama Komiya. I'll kill him some day. I swear on the Ancestor Stones themselves. And I'll take my time about it. She shook away the gruesome images of what she would do to him, someday.

Fagh, not what I should be thinking! Ancestors, what would she think if she saw my thoughts right now? Oh, Sahla, what are we truly going to be, each to the other? If this Bond of Mastery and misery did not burden my shoulders, I think loving you should be the easiest, most delightful portion of my scarred soul. If...if only. Ah, my sapphire-eyed beauty, flying free under the stars, masses of sable splendor dancing in the very heart of the free winds, pure and perfect and the unobtainable desire of my unworthy heart. And again, I find I love that which I cannot...may not...must not touch with my blood-stained hands, lest I mar the power of such unmatched grace and perfection. Just as Captain Blaine, my Captain, *is not for the likes of me, neither is this wondrous young woman, this perfect beauty. It is evil that I hold her in this vile Bond, but I believe what she says of her fate without such a tie. And I am unworthy to even dream of finding the linking of heart and soul that is True Love to which the poets scribe odes of beauty and songs of truth. That is not for me. Ah,* she sighed, *I grow morbid in my need for rest. So I shall rest my weary head and troubled heart, seek solace in the embrace of the dreams of that which can never be real.*

Sachi slipped deeply into the realm of slumber, entering the land of dreams. There she walked quietly along a peaceful stream, water serenely flowing down a gentle vale. In the distance she saw a quaint stone bridge leaping the rustling waters, a small village at the fortuitous junction of road and stream. A mill drowsed next to the water, the wheel peacefully grumbling as it slowly turned. The folk of the village were simple folk, not profoundly different from her long-lost Komiya family. Nor, in turn, at all dissimilar from the herders and shepherds of Sahla's tribe. Ordinary people, smiling to their neighbors, loving their families, and honoring their Gods. Simply living their lives.

She stopped at the bridge, the road before her and the stream itself separating her from the villagers' mundane day. Somehow, she was held apart, observing but not able to participate. There was something here she must see, perhaps a lesson to learn, or a rare glimpse of a day to come.

Thunder echoed through the trees, the thunder of many men on horseback. The gentle breeze died away and even the laughing waters of the stream were muted. Apprehension flowered on anxious village faces. Men on horseback were never the best guests, even those of their own lords. A few of the villagers looked to one hut, slightly set back from the road and farthest from the very modest village inn. It was small but neatly kept.

The headman came to the center of the bridge, swallowing hard as he waited for the men on horses. Men who might be no more than the swift passing of the lords' forces, or honorable enemies passing to the chosen field of battle. But worst of all was what rode out of the shade of the forest, men rough and motley, mismatched arms and rough-coated mounts. Brigands they were, lawless men answering to neither God nor Priest, noble Lord nor written Law. Five and twenty they were, and their leader stopped them at the foot of the bridge, before bringing his worn mount to a stop before the headman.

Sachi felt a presence next to her, something familiar and comforting but one not known to her. She glanced down and surprise grasped her and held her motionless. A white fox sat on its haunches next to her on the bridge railing, its nine white tails gently waving at their tips.

"You know this is a dream, right?" the golden-eyed creature said to her.

"Of course." Her eyes were open wide at the sight of the creature. "But you are a *Kitsune*, and I am across the whole world from Isemoto. How are you here? Even in a dream."

"This is only partly dream, Black Eyes. And I am a *Kyubi no Kitsune*, nine hundred and ninety-nine years from my birth."

"A powerful spirit, one such as you can see and hear all about the world, the legends and stories say."

"Ah, excellent! A classically educated pupil. And you can, of course, sing and dance and play the *shamisen*, the *koto*, the *shakuhachi* and the *tsuzumi*. You can compose and recite poetry, create beautiful calligraphy, your flower arrangements are flawless, and not even the Masters of the Oda Clan ever faulted your tea ceremonies as less than absolute perfection." The Kitsune smiled at her as time slowed around them.

"And yet, I was used as a common whore, a thief and an assassin. I know as many ways to cut a throat, silence a heart or drive a blade into a brain as I do to sing, dance or compose poetry."

"Bitterness, Black Eyes?"

"Of course. Despite my skills, the Oda would not allow me even the honor of being a true Geisha." Sachi watched as the brigand chief kicked the headman in the face, knocking him to the ground. A young girl screamed and ran for the small, set-back hut. "Do I have to watch this? I know, all too well, what comes next."

"Do you, Black Eyes?" The spirit smiled at her. "I suppose you might know indeed from the perception of both the village and the brigand, I think. Perhaps this time will be different?"

"How?"

"There." The Kitsune rubbed her head against Sachi's hand, drawing her attention to the small hut. "That's how. This is what might happen should Black Eyes with the Broken Heart and Sapphire Light Who Dances on Clouds learn to be to each other what the very Gods of the World intend them to be. Watch and learn, Black Eyes. You twain are close, near to being what you should be, but you hold yourself away, convinced of your unworthiness. Foolish of you, Mortal, but you are yet very young. Watch."

Two women burst from the hut, one tall and pale, ebon hair wrapped in long braids around her head, stars glittering in her eyes. Gleaming silver poured down her arms and from her belt, encasing her entire body as she sprinted to the bridge. A long white sword formed, both of her hands about the hilt. It flashed once as she ran full on into the brigand chief's rearing horse, her shoulder sending the beast over the rail into the stream, carrying the chief's body with it, still in the saddle. The chief's head flew into the calm millpond. She screamed challenge at the rest of the ragged band as she took her stand on the bridge.

The other woman was slight and slender, almost tiny, golden skin gleaming in the sun as she flew above the road and the stream. Sable hair streamed in a tail longer than she was and sapphire sabers glittered in her hands. She spun into the last rank of bandits, a cobalt cyclone spraying a bloody mist onto leaves and grass. Azure rage burned in eyes matching the sapphire sabers' glitter as she hovered in midair, her body naught but mist from the waist down.

Screaming, the surviving brigands broke and fled, desperate to escape this place of terror for their kind. With a glance between them, seeing the bloody plunder slung behind fleeing riders, the two women raced after them. Not a single brigand reached the edge of the woods alive. When the two women came back together at the bridge, the embrace they shared was long and passionate. So was their kiss.

"So that's what Sahla and I should do, assuming I succeed in my birth parents' mission first? Protect a village from bandits?"

"Perhaps." The golden eyes were sly as the fox smiled at Sachi. "Or perhaps, the village is just metaphor for a nation? Or the world entire? Who knows?"

"Who knows, indeed, *Kitsune-sama*?" Sachi returned the spirit's tooth-hidden smile. "I know better than to ask any *Kitsune*, much less one bearing the nine tails of wisdom and power, a direct question. *Kitsune* asked direct questions answer only in riddles."

"Indeed, you will be a true gem to teach, mortal child." Her tongue lolled over sharp, white teeth. "But perhaps, what you should truly be learning has naught to do with protection, but what two who truly love each other to the very depths of their souls, together in every fashion, flesh and blood and heart and spirit and soul, what might two such truly accomplish? How might they change the very foundations of the world?"

Sachi froze in shock. Stunned, she turned back to the two women as they helped the fallen headman to his feet, the tall one staunching his bleeding nose. She could see how each treasured the other, how their hands touched constantly. How they nearly spoke as one. The emotions that flowed between them, pride in their martial skills, in their abilities and fear that injury or mishap could separate them. Death was not what they feared, but being without the other was a fear they both must stand before and face.

"Hmm, you learn well, Black Eyes." The Kitsune looked over its shoulder. "Think on this in the deepest vaults of your soul. What I teach you is not for the Machine Mind that dissembles before the world of the real. And thus, I must block this from your conscious mind until you can learn the control to hide mind and thought from that thing which is always present. But now, I must go. We will meet again. You have much to learn. And have no fear to place your faith in Sapphire Light Who Dances on Clouds. Farewell."

The dream-world faded away, Sachi's spirit returning from where the *Kitsune* had lured it. Or so she thought at first. Those thoughts fled away, fish fleeing the sea-dragon, as she realized something was tenderly, slightly restraining her movement. Something barely heavier than the silken sheets, warm and pliable, gently resting on her left arm, shoulder, chest and leg. Fine silken hair, softer than her own, spilled across her breasts. She cracked one eye open.

Oh, Ancestors, how did she do this?

Sahla was curled up against her, her face buried in the hollow of Sachi's shoulder, her chin gently touching her collarbone. One golden arm was draped across her pale stomach, the delicate hand resting on her hipbone. Her legs were twined around Sachi's left leg, her thigh on the very edge of Sachi's most intimate places. Sachi felt her own face burn when she realized exactly the position they were in. Her delicate breasts pressed into Sachi's ribcage. She could feel Sahla's breath against her lips, her heartbeat against her own ribs.

Great Uncle Sota would lose his mind if he ever saw someone sneak up on me in my sleep. But...this is...nice. Warm. Even if it is harder to breathe. And slightly, um, embarrassing. And I can't feel my arm, it's gone to sleep.

"Sahla?" she whispered.

"Umm, no, Mother, it's too early to practice." Sahla mumbled, still mostly asleep.

"Sahla, move over a bit, please?"

"Um, oh, all right." She rolled away from Sachi's side, rising on an elbow. "Uh, are you mad at me? I crawled over the pillow. I was cold." There was a great deal of tension in her neck and shoulders.

"No, *Koibito*, I'm not mad." Sachi's gentle grin in the still-dim room was rewarded with a smile from Sahla that, by rights, should have rivaled the ancient tower's beacon in brightness. "Come here, on this side this time, and let's get some more sleep. We've a couple of hours still to breakfast."

"Umm, Sachi, what if we were to..." The interrupted question was low and diffident.

"No, Sahla." Sachi's abrupt negative was gentle. "Not now. Not here. Later. There'll be time later."

And they slept, peacefully, together.

Chapter Ten

**Free Port of Du Khamps des SouSee
January 1479, Third Age of Imperial Reckoning**

WILLIS FLEET STOPPED AND stretched his aching back when he reached the wooden planks of the wharf. The longboat's crew was tying off the boat to the piling next to the water-stairs.

"Well done, Furston," he addressed Able Seaman Hahn Furston, the longboat's coxswain, one of the KRN sailors transferred from *Alacrity*. "Two men on the boat at all times, otherwise, rotate through one of the dockside pubs and get everyone fed and a bit of a rest. I expect to return with the others no later than five bells into the afternoon watch. Bosun Holland'll have *Graser* ready to weigh anchor by seven bells and then we catch the late afternoon tide and head for Luctini."

"Aye-aye, Captain Fleet."

Whistling, Willis turned and marched off toward the White Tower Inn. Despite being the middle of January, the weather here was never anything he'd have called cold. Not this close to the equator. Enjoying the warmth, he grinned to himself, imagining the ice coating the streets outside his family's Capitol home. The occasional early rising prostitute called to him from her balcony as he strode down the street, offering discount rates for an hour in Heaven. He simply smiled, tipped his hat to them and kept right on going. Many of the working girls would be considered quite attractive, perhaps beautiful, to the average sailor, but he'd spent too much time around Sachi and Sahla. Even Silaqui's inhuman, exotic beauty paled in comparison to that pair. Maybe he was getting jaded?

The midday meal in Du Khamps was normally a quiet time, but today the street in front of the Inn was busier than normal. A group of Darsälaamic ka'mel traders had gotten tangled up with a large, two-wheeled cart pulled by a pair of braying mules. The ragged farmers on the cart and the traders screeched curses at each other in several languages. A handful of townsmen toughs loitered at the Inn's outdoor tables, laughing at the inept near-mêlée. Willis stopped at the Inn's front door, ostensibly lifting his hat to wipe sweat from his brow while he gave the situation thorough consideration. The ka'mel traders were armed with mostly habitual Darsälaamic weapons, scimitars, shamshirs and recurved horse bows. The leader and four or five others had long matchlock jezails. The farmers had a staff-sling and an iron-shod club. Willis settled his hat and headed upstairs.

"What's the brouhaha out in the street, Willis?" Sachi asked as he entered the room. The others were scattered about the sitting room, finishing lunch.

"Farmers and ka'mel traders arguing over right of way. And some local toughs laughing at them."

"That is odd," Sahla remarked as she smiled with amusement, watching Sachi devour her second helping of beef pie.

"How so, Sahla?" Silaqui asked, sipping from a wine glass.

"This is the wrong season for ka'mel traders. The female ka'mels will be heavy with their calves. No true trader would be moving their animals in the winter. They would wait until the calves are born in the spring and bring the animals to market in early summer." She shrugged. "Unless some misfortune has befallen them, then they might be desperate. Strange."

"I dislike things that are strange at odd times." Sachi finished wiping the bowl clean with a piece of flatbread. She smiled at Sahla as she stood and walked to the window looking down into the street. Sahla followed her, slipping an arm around the Nisei's waist and leaning her head against the tall woman's shoulder. Sachi rested her own arm on the Jann's shoulder.

Willis felt his eyebrows climb up his forehead. He turned and glanced at Silaqui, pointing a thumb at the pair. Silaqui simply shrugged and waved a hand in the air in a dismissive gesture. Aylie was frankly staring, and Willis saw a scowl flicker across Gelman's face.

"Ah, hmm, Sachi, Sahla, is everything, well...is everything okay with the two of you?"

"Why would it not be, Willis Fleet?" Sachi turned a sly smile on him.

"Well, ah, normally, you know, you have been known to start yelling and throwing things when...ah, you know, oh, never mind. The hell with it."

"We confuse him, *Habiba*." The radiant smile on Sahla's face took his breath away. "That or the *ghula* have stolen his tongue."

"Possibly, *Koibito*, possibly. But enough of befuddling poor Willis." Sachi shook her head, smiling at Sahla before turning serious attention to Willis. "We need to be heading for the ship, correct, Willis?"

"Ah, yeah." Willis shook his head. *What's going on here? Surely, they didn't...they couldn't have...not bloody likely. But what if they did...ooh, my head hurts!* "We need to get going. Sooner is better. So, let's get moving."

***

It feels strange, a new year has turned; in Isemoto snow would be at least shin deep in places and here the sun is bright, and the air is warm, almost hot. And somehow, someway a burden lifted last night. Is it possible that Sahla is right, that this Bond is changing? I know my heart sings when our eyes meet.

Sachi stepped out of the courtyard gate of the White Tower Inn, a pack over one shoulder and a well stuffed bag in her right hand. She smiled at the warm memory of waking with Sahla wrapped around her. Still, long years of brutal Oda Clan training did not fail her, not allowing the budding relationship with Sahla to dull her situational awareness. Something out of place, small movements, the desultory wrangling between the farmers on their cart and the supposed ka'mel traders, the toughs lounging at the Inn's street-side tables, all of it combined to suddenly put her on edge.

She didn't shout or draw attention to herself. She simply slipped her left hand down to the holstered Mark Fourteen handgun and tabbed the release mechanism, resting her palm on the butt of the ancient Confederation weapon.

***

From the third story office of an empty warehouse two buildings down the street, Wrath watched the unfolding drama. Intense satisfaction gleamed in her emerald eyes, and an unholy smile curved her lips. She had two metaphorical bows in her set ambush and each one had two strings. If she was truly blessed, at the end of the day she'd have some high value slaves, including that never-to-be-sufficiently-damned little Darsälaamic chit. But the tall one, that one... that fornicating slut—

That bitch! Selling that one to the vilest brothel in Luctini will never repay me for her slaying Ironheart. If I took a thousand years to torture her, I don't think that would be enough. Ironheart had his faults, that bastard, but he was my bastard *and if anyone was going kill him it should have been me! But she's exotic and damn near as beautiful as Sahla. She might sell for twice, maybe thrice her weight in gold. So, revenge, or profit? Decisions, decisions! I guess I'll just have to see who survives. Selling them or seeing their blood painted on the walls and puddling in the gutters, either one will do just as well.*

Her eyes glowed with jade fire as she gathered her magic around her. Her spells would not begin the attack, but she knew these fools thought her still stranded on that accursed island. Zahir and his light cutter *Saker* had made landfall on the island the evening of the day after the disastrous battle on the beach. Being considerably faster than the renamed *Heartcutter* and with a crew and captain that knew what they were doing and where they were going, it had been simple to beat the strangers to Du Khamps.

That fei koldun'ya, the point-eared, cat-eyed bitch-sorceress, she was stronger in magic that I am, but she can't defend against a threat she doesn't know exists. Wrath possessed a ring that held its own secrets, had its own immense powers. A ring which answered only to her. Unfortunately, it had certain limitations making it useless in combat, whether mundane or magical. Between the fey sorceress and that damnable priest, she knew she would lose a straight-up magical duel. But neither of them would be as powerful with a one-ounce bullet in their hearts.

***

Josef Buckley was a man without a country these days. As a young man, his grandfather had fled the Empire of the Rus, then being on the wrong side of a failed revolution against the Kzar. Arriving in the young Republic of Kolbia, Grandfather promptly set about following old family tradition, creating a criminal empire of thieves, gambling houses, whorehouses and protection rackets. Had Grandfather possessed a functioning brain, he would have realized that Kolbia's laissez-faire attitude allowed many such things to proceed legally. Instead, he continued the familiar practice of kidnapping women and forcing them into prostitution in his brothels. The thieving and protection rackets were bad enough, but slavery was a death sentence in Kolbia and Grandfather swung by the neck until dead before his oldest son was quite fifteen years of age.

Josef's father was a good bit smarter and quickly set about turning as many illicit businesses into legitimate ones as he could. He still trod on the shady side of the law far too often and put the Buckley name into the permanent ill graces of Kolbian law keepers. He avoided transgressions invoking the death penalty. But, bleakly regarding a twenty-five-year long prison sentence after one step too many into the shadows, Josef's father directed that his only son would enlist in the Kolbian Marines. He hoped the Marines would ensure his son would avoid the fates of father and grandfather.

It was a false hope. Oh, Josef did well enough, learning quickly and adapting to life aboard ship with little issue. His turn-out was exemplary, but he couldn't stay out of a fight to save his life. More than once, his brawls resulted in serious injuries and once in a death in a general barroom mêlée. Eventually, Josef picked a fight with the wrong person, killing the underage son of the Deuschen Ambassador to Montagar in a street duel over the tawdry favors of a common streetwalking prostitute. So Sergeant Josef Buckley, decorated combat veteran, was brought before a summary courts-martial and dismissed with prejudice by the Marines for the crimes of unlawful dueling and manslaughter. He served five years in military prison, emerging a hard, cold man with no pity for anyone.

Rejected by the family on his still-imprisoned father's orders, he washed his feet of Kolbia and the Buckley family, becoming a sell-sword, a mercenary for hire and a man with no consideration for the law, other than how to avoid its heavy hand. That was easy to do on the fringes of the Empire, and the rough nature of the Darsälaamic ports suited him as well. Du Khamps was a natural fit for him and the band of killers, thieves and cutthroats he gathered around him. Josef and his so-called 'Merry Men' were always for hire and if it meant somehow sticking a thumb in Kolbia's, or even better, the KRN's eye, they worked cheap.

The deal offered by the red-headed witch was far from cheap, however. She warned him that the targets were more than capable, even if two-thirds of the group were female. Josef kept his face serious and grave. After all, he did know about Captain Ironheart's pet witch. He knew that she was one that should be taken seriously. And he did take more care than he might have otherwise, but how seriously could you take a single KRN officer, a Priest of the Circled Cross, a servant girl, a Darsälaamic teenager and a young woman from somewhere on the other side of the world? The Elven sorceress, she was a world class threat all by herself, but Wrath had told him how to neutralize the Elven magic most effectively. And there was only one of her. If she didn't see the shooter that put a bullet between her eyes, she couldn't raise any spell-woven shields against it. Yes, this promised to be a particularly good payday.

***

"What's wrong, Sachi?" Sahla stepped to Sachi's right, away from the esoteric weapon on her left hip. She'd seen Sachi tab the holster's release and the sudden, slight tension in her entire body. She glanced quickly around, trying to find the cause of the Nisei's apprehension. Something drew her like a lodestone to her right, a vague familiarity. Something calling to the magical core of her very existence.

Sachi was silent, but she rotated to her left, facing the ka'mel herders' argument with the farmers. Gelman and Willis stopped short as they nearly blundered into the two women stopped at the street's curb. Both men had packs on their backs and large carry-bags in each hand. Aylie and Silaqui had to step past the pair of burdened men. They each carried a pack and a single large bag as well.

Willis recognized Sachi's body language and dropped both bags. He was shrugging out of his pack when everything went to hell.

The 'ka'mel' traders suddenly stopped their sham of conflict with the farmers, half of them turning as one and charging at the group, short lances and scimitars at the ready. The other half leveled their jezails at them, the long barrels focusing on Silaqui and Gelman. The 'farmers' jerked the cover off their cart, revealing a four-pounder cannon aimed down the road instead of a load of produce. The lounging toughs leapt from their tables, drawing blades and pistols. Their leader didn't move from where he leaned against the caravanserai's outer wall.

"Ye've no hope," he drawled. "Lay down yer arms and it'll be the easier for ye."

Sachi's answer was a flicker of her right hand, and a throwing dart pinned his hand to the wall. The Mark 14 flashed out of the holster and coughed four times. The hyper-velocity flechettes tore the pair of 'farmers' behind the light cannon into bloody sprays. The ka'mel traders' jezails fired, the hiss-boom of smoothbore matchlocks filling the street with noise and smoke. Sachi grunted as two of the heavy slugs hit her torso, but the CLIBA hardened to prevent penetration. None of the other shots hit anyone.

From a building across the street two more guns fired, the snap-crack of rifled flintlocks. Despite the relatively short range, neither of the marksmen managed the headshots they were told they needed. Gelman staggered as his heavy breastplate, hidden under his robes, turned the bullet that would have blasted cleanly through his heart.

Silaqui disliked the tight-fitting CLIBA shirts and wasn't wearing hers on this day. The bullet hit her in the right side of her chest, just above her breast. It punched cleanly through her, breaking ribs, puncturing her lung, and shattering her clavicle. She spun and dropped without a sound. Gelman dropped to his knees next to her, healing magic gleaming golden on his hands.

Aylie dropped to the ground and rolled against the wall, slipping her pack as she moved. She rolled past the cursing leader of the toughs, hammering a dagger through his booted foot into the cobblestones, just as he reached to tug Sachi's dart out of his hand. He shrieked and twisted helplessly, pinned like a butterfly in an insect collection. She rolled away from him, coming up behind another bravo and hamstringing him with her other dagger. The bravo howled and went down. Blood fountained as Aylie cut his throat open. She scrabbled away across the cobbles, crimson-stained dagger in hand.

Willis, struggling to get out of his pack, was an easy target for the toughs. Flintlock pistols cracked at short range. His CLIBA turned three hits on his torso, but one bullet hit his leg, fracturing his femur. Cursing, he went down hard. But he managed to get one hand free and the ancient 1911 pistol roared as he poured fire into the bravos at close range. Three of them went down, dead or dying. A fourth staggered, shrieking as a .45 caliber bullet shattered his sword blade, spraying his face and eyes with fragments of the copper jacketed slug and pieces of his own sword. Willis ignored the blinded bravo as he dropped the empty pistol, slipping his pack and pulling one of the blast rifles out of its scabbard on the side of the pack.

Facing the dozen charging brigands disguised as traders, Sachi never saw the lance of poison-green magic strike toward her back. But Sahla felt the inimical magery even as it formed in the heart of Wrath's witchery. She blurred as she spun herself and her own sapphire magery between Sachi and the killing spell. Her cerulean shield met and shattered Wrath's jade lance. Sahla shouted, a cry that rattled the stones of the road. An azure wave lashed back against Wrath's own arcane shield, blasting the front of the building away in a roaring tumble of wood and masonry.

"Bozhe moy! Ona dzhinn!" Wrath was stunned. Her shield held, but Sahla's reactionary magic left her standing exposed. "That was her secret! And I could have forced a Bond! Stupid! Stupid!" She stared as Sahla spun into the toughs, sapphire sabers flashing. And what happened next was even more of a surprise. The Kolbian in the long blue coat was down but he tugged a musket of some type out of the pack he dropped. He brought the gleaming black weapon to his shoulder, aiming at the sharpshooters' position in the building across the street. There was a thundering *whik-ka-BLAMM*! A detonation like the heart of a Kolbian blast furnace incinerated the front of the building and the riflemen as well. Wrath stared in horror at the blazing wreckage. *What is that weapon? Some magic wrought by the Jinn? A new horror the Kolbians would unleash on the world?*

***

::Hyper-heuristic combat mode fully activated.:: D.A.V.E.'s metallic voice whispered in her mind and the world as she perceived it shuddered to a near complete stop. ::Target priority established.:: Outlines of pulsing red light illuminated the most dangerous threats among both the charging 'traders' and the musket-armed men behind them. The first one was the one leaping for the cannon on the 'farmers' cart. The flechette pistol floated up, D.A.V.E. putting the targeting caret on his head. The pistol coughed, splattering his head against the side of the cart as his body tumbled raggedly to the ground.

"I need to conserve ammunition, D.A.V.E. There's only so much and it's gone when it's gone. With this speeded-up time, can I take the rest of them with blades?"

::Probability of successful engagement without injury, ninety-seven-point seven percent, plus or minus twenty-eight percent. With minor injury, sixty-four-point nine percent, plus or minus twenty-two percent. With serious, non-fatal injury, thirty-one-point one percent, plus or minus fourteen percent. With a non-instantaneously fatal injury, fifteen-point nine percent, plus or minus seven percent. Any instantly fatal injury at any point implies mission failure.::

"That didn't answer my question, you realize that, right?"

::Optimal engagement parameters requested.::

"Anyone else that absolutely must be shot with the pistol first. Then let's see if we agree on who's the most dangerous one that I can take with a blade."

::Parameter request received, processing.::

"If I had to think about fighting this much when Uncle Sota was training me, I'd be dead now. Hurry it up, I haven't got all day!"

::Zero point zero zero one four eight micro-seconds have elapsed from implementation of full hyper-heuristic mode. Hardly 'all day,' Lieutenant Commander Schmidt. Processing complete in zero point zero zero zero four one micro-seconds. Extraneous input regarding data processing delay added zero point zero zero... ::

"Just shut up and give me the priority. Now."

::Optimal engagement priority loaded into your BPU. Follow the caret for projectile targeting.::

A box at the front of the farmers' cart suddenly illuminated with a flashing red outline.

"Oh, D.A.V.E., that's not nice. Those poor mules."

::Acceptable collateral damage.::

***

The flechette gun coughed twice more. The first shot hit the foremost charging ka'mel rider just below his nose, the hyper-velocity flechette tearing his head apart in a gruesome mist of blood, bone, and brain. The falling body startled his charging ka'mel and the beast shied, running into the trailing ka'mel on its left. The two awkward mounts tangled their legs, each one breaking both forelegs as they went down in a shrieking, screaming pile. The rider immediately behind them urged his beast into a jump, clearing both thrashing ka'mels. The leap cleared the ka'mels, but the beast struck the flying body of the second rider with its knee, breaking the rider's neck and the ka'mel's fragile knee. That beast's rider went flying over his mount's head, hitting the pavement hard enough to smash his face in. He left a red smear as he slid to a stop. The rest of the charging riders reacted quickly enough to avoid the pile-up, reining their beasts to sliding stops or swerving past the blockage.

But the second shot did the real damage. The flechette punched into the wooden box containing fourteen pounds of gunpowder, the spare ammunition for the four-pounder field gun mounted clumsily in the back of the cart. The exploding ammunition shattered the cart. Fragments of the cart hit the half dozen men in the process of reloading their long jezails. Four of them died instantly, from either fragments or the blast wave. The two temporary survivors, furthest away, weren't any luckier. One had his leg removed at the hip by a large fragment of an iron-rimmed wagon wheel; the other was blinded when small fragments tore his face off. One of the shooters' ka'mels bolted away down the street, permanently deafened but otherwise unharmed. The rest of the animals, including the mules pulling the cart, were killed by the blast, adding to the carnage.

Sachi snapped the pistol back into its retention holster as she flicked a long, white-steel *nodachi* into existence in her other hand. She blurred into motion, the long blade a white fan that abruptly turned red as she cut the forelegs out from under the first rider's ka'mel with her forehand stroke. The backhand stroke of the blade sliced the rider in half just above his hips. With their charge disrupted and their momentum lost avoiding the pile of crippled ka'mels, the advantage shifted to Sachi as she charged into the remaining riders. The long sword flashed, blood splattering building walls, reaping lives as she butchered the brigands. The last two broke and fled.

Behind Sachi, Sahla blasted another magical attack back into Wrath's face. The witch snarled in frustrated rage. Every spell, every cantrip, her every hex, the beautiful Jann deflected away, dissipated into the air or reflected the attack back at the witch. And now, sapphire eyes blazing with fury, Sahla shot through the air at the witch, her sabers glowing with azure power. She would end this here and now.

Desperate at the Jann's attack, Wrath finally clenched her fist around the iron ring on the forefinger of her left hand, willing the Slave of the Ring to come to her.

"Dzhinn!" Wrath screamed. "I am assailed by a Spirit of your Plane! Guard and protect your Mistress! Lay her captive at my feet or slay her as you may! Come forth, I command you!"

A bluish mist emanated from the plain iron ring. It swirled away, growing and thickening as it moved. A final swirl and the mist vanished. In its place, there stood a person of indeterminate age. Thick black hair was neatly trimmed, as was the short beard. He was not particularly tall while not exactly being short. He was neither thin nor fat. But no one could have ignored the toned, dark blue skin of his bare, muscular torso and bulging biceps. Or his startling blue eyes, eyes of sapphire blue. Jinn eyes holding a malicious glint as he bowed before the witch.

"Your command, Mistress." His voice was smooth and urbane, with a hint of a mocking undertone. He spun like lightning and Sahla's sabers rang on the bronze guards on his forearms. Both froze as they stared into identical sapphire eyes. The Jinn reacted first, flinging his arms out with a roar, tossing Sahla away, the girl hurled heels over head. An immense cobalt tulwar materialized in his hands. "Peace be upon thee, Jann of the mortal world. This is my Mistress, whom I am bound to obey. Yet, thou I would not slay, though the Efreet feast on my magic and *ghula* and *shiqq* eat my flesh and gnaw my bones. Put me not to this test, at thy peril, and no less the jeopardy of the world entire."

"And upon thee, peace, Jinn of the immortal winds. It is thy Mistress that doth threaten and assail mine own Mistress. But my Mistress holds my Life Bond and not some mere trinket that might pass from hand to hand, O' thou Slave of the Ring. I defend her freely and of my own will. Canst thou say the same, O' mighty Jinn?"

"Thy Bond?" The Jinn's voice was rough with emotion. "Of Master and Slave? My token, the Ring, is but a bauble, passing from Mortal to Mortal. They live and die while I remain. I am not Bound."

"I accept my Bond joyfully. It will grow beyond the limits of thy petty ring, far beyond the crude bondage of Slave to Master. Indeed, my Mistress does not need to command that I defend her. She knows I will defend her to life, for the True Love I bear for her, and she will defend mine own life the same. Canst thou make the same claim of thy Mistress, O' mighty Jinn?"

"True love? Foolish child, she bears no love for you."

"Then thine eyes, of the same sapphire magic as mine, those eyes truly cannot see." Sahla smiled then, a poignant smile of sudden sadness. "I know you now, my own Blood-Sire, mighty Ilben alh-Taymyah, Jinni of the Second Rank of Air and Wind. She whom I protect, she is the True Love of my heart. And I defend her with that love. And that love, my great and powerful Sire, is a power not even thou canst truly stand against. Fulfill thy geas, O' Slave of the Ring; take thy Mistress far from here on the wings of thy magic. Thusly thou shall protect and succor her. Stay, and although thou be my Blood-Sire, I shall surely slay both thee and thy Mistress."

"I named thee truly, Sahla al Qasim, Flowing Beauty. But you must defeat me blade to blade. My Mistress commands it."

Sahla's smile fled as she snarled and flashed toward Ilben. Sapphire sabers rang in a harmony of enchanted steel as Ilben's tulwar formed a defensive halo around him. Sahla spun into a cerulean cyclone, blow after blow raining on Ilben's tulwar until the tulwar fractured into hundreds of shards, tinkling and ringing like silver bells as they fell away. The tip of a saber flicked out, azure lightning, and pricked the bare skin of Ilben's shoulder.

"Thy blade is broken, Sire, and thy blood stains my sabers. Take thy Mistress and begone."

Ilben bowed to Sahla in silent acquiescence. As he turned away, for the bare instant when neither Sahla nor Wrath could see his face, a broad smile cracked his normally impassive mien. Impassivity restored, he faced Wrath. The witch was stunned, shock draining all color from her face.

"Mistress, I am defeated, yet my gracious and beautiful opponent will allow me to fulfill the geas of my token, the Ring you bear, and take you away to a surety of safety." A thunderclap shook the building as Ilben clapped his hands together. Indigo radiance swept outward in a blinding wave and when it faded away, Ilben, Wrath and the cowering Lodvar were gone.

Sahla stared at the spot where her Sire's magic swept the witch and her minion away, a wistful smile on her lips. Then the crash of steel and the screams of the maimed and dying sent her flying back to the fray in the street. By the time she reached Gelman's side, the battle was over, except for those who hadn't finished dying.

Gelman settled back, sitting on his heels. His face reflected his exhaustion and his satisfaction. His hands were covered with blood from Silaqui and Willis, but he had saved both.

"Well done, Gelman." Sahla settled next to him, extending a hand to help him to his feet. "I feared the worst until I saw your hands glowing with your healing power."

"'Twas a close thing," the priest sighed, groaning as he came to his feet. "If the bullet had hit Silaqui on the left, rather than the right, she would have been dead before she hit the ground. And Willis nearly bled to death. It was a close thing, and I am nigh on to drained of the power of my Gift. All things have a cost, Sahla."

"Of course they do, Gelman." She smiled at him. "Your own God of the Circled Cross proclaims as much. And it is a truth that the Prophet himself acknowledges in his writings." Her smile faded as a blood-soaked Sachi stalked up to them. "Sachi! Prophet's Beard! Are you all right? Are you hur—?"

"None of this is mine." She flicked her sword to shed the blood coating the white-steel sword. Then the blade flowed back into her forearm bracers. "A couple of nasty bruises are the worst. Any clue whose idea this Ancestors' bedamned idiocy was?"

"Wrath was here." Sahla shrugged. "How she got here? Either magic or the other pirate, the fast cutter with a Darsälaamic captain. But I doubt that myse—" Sahla's eyes shot wide open.

***

Buckley had finally freed himself from the blades that pinned foot and hand. His men were down, slaughtered like pigs. His employer, the pirate Ironheart's lover, Wrath the witch, was gone, absconded from the bloody battle by magic. Given the damage and bloodshed done, even High Lord Kormarra would have him dangling from a rope in short order. Not that Lord Kormarra would likely get the chance to hang him.

Knowing that, one way or another, he was a dead man, Josef decided to hurt these people in the worst way possible. And that, he thought, would be to kill the beautiful little Darsälaamic girl. He'd use his one white-steel dagger to pierce any hidden armor. With a savage lunge he drove the blade home. He smiled grimly as her blood fountained across the tall Nisei's face. It was a smile that lasted only a fraction of a second.

***

"Urgh!" Blood fountained from her mouth as a white-steel dagger punched through her CLIBA, savagely driven through her back by a snarling Josef Buckley. The dagger slid between her shoulder blade and spine, cutting cleanly through two ribs, and breaking the vertebra between them. It missed severing her spinal cord by less than a millimeter. It broke her collarbone just below her jaw when the point exited her body in another bloody spray.

"SAHLA!" Sachi's scream should have fractured stones. She caught the falling Jann with her left arm, cradling the girl against her body. Her right hand snapped out and caught Buckley's knife hand, clamping down so hard she crushed every bone in his wrist. She jerked him forward, smashing her forehead into his face, spraying blood from his pulped lips and splintered nose. Then she slammed him against the wall hard enough that he crumpled bonelessly to the ground.

"Gelman!" Sachi turned to cradle Sahla as she sank to the street, gently holding the girl. "Gelman! Where are you?" Sachi's voice cracked with fear and desperation as she locked eyes with Sahla's. "No, no, no, NO! Don't you dare die! I command you not to die! Not now!"

Sahla choked and gagged, her blood soaking Sachi's shirt. Her right arm locked around Sachi's waist. She reached up with her left, stroking Sachi's cheek, leaving a bloody hand-smear there. Blood gurgled in her throat as she tried to speak. Sachi bowed her head down to hear what she was trying to say. Tears made bloody runnels down the Nisei's cheeks.

"No, no... shh, shh, don't try to speak," she whispered. Her head snapped up. "Gelman!"

Sahla grabbed a handful of hair and pulled Sachi's head back to hers. Sachi laid her ear against Sahla's lips to hear what she was trying to say.

"I... love... you. Prophet... witness... love... you... forever... my... *Habiba*." Sahla grimaced with pain as she choked out each agonized word. Blood marked each word.

"Oh, Sahla, my Sahla," Sachi pulled her against her chest. "Don't talk, not now, *Koibito*. I know you love me. I know, but I'm not worth—" Bloody fingers covered her lips.

"Worthy." Sahla smiled and gagged on more blood. "I love you, always," she gasped out.

"Oh, *Koibito*, I know," Sachi sobbed, "I know. And I love you too, *Koibito*. I love you."

"Well, that's over at least!" Gelman's rough voice growled. "You've been around too damned many Kolbians! Now get out of my way and let me save her, if the One God of the Circled Cross and my patron, the *Angaelici Benes Eloi* will grant me to draw their power through me." Golden light haloed his hands as he mumbled a prayer. "Stay." He grabbed Sachi's arm when she started to move. "I need you to slowly withdraw the knife as my powers course behind it, mending what they may."

"Gelman, if she dies…" Sachi's frozen voice should have coated the cobbles with ice.

"She'll not die." The priest glared at her from under bristling eyebrows. "But the wound is severe, and I am already weary. She may be crippled."

"Heal her, damn your eyes."

"Hold thy tongue, woman. You'd do well to nay curse the man as has thy beloved's life in his hands." The brogue of a Montagaran woodsman crept into the exhaustion in his voice.

"Forgive me, Gelman. Save her."

"I will. Now, slowly, very slowly, draw the blade out." The golden aura glittered around Sahla's slim throat as the dagger slid out. The blood stopped and Sahla slumped unconscious in Sachi's arms. "Good, good. Don't panic, she only sleeps. She needs rest now. Rest and gentle care and she should be well. If wound fever doesn't set in, that is. This is not a complete healing; she is still fragile."

Boots thundered on the wooden roadside walks and the cobbles of the street. Sachi looked up to see most of the crew of the ship's longboat storming up, boarding axes and muskets in their hands. She started as a cool hand rested on her shoulder, turning her head to stare into enigmatic jade eyes. Silaqui's pupils were the barest of cat-like slits in the day's bright light.

"Come, my heart-sister, I am well enough to carry her gently to the ship. Let me lift her up." The front of Silaqui's crimson bodice was stained a deeper burgundy. "We need you to guide us warily. And you are our best fighter. But not if you are burdened with her."

"*Hai.*" Sachi rose to her feet and reluctantly let the Elf take Sahla from her. Willis directed the sailors in gathering their scattered gear and packs. Sachi looked around at the burning wreckage and riven bodies. Aylie leaned against the Inn's courtyard wall, a booted foot resting casually on the neck of the man who'd stabbed Sahla.

"An what be yer desires for this 'un, Sachi?" Aylie watched the Nisei closely. "Ye wish me ta make an end o' him?"

"No, Aylie." Sachi's voice sent a shiver of fear down Aylie's spine. "Not yet. We take him with us. When he wakes up, he answers my questions. All my questions. After that, it depends. If Sahla lives and recovers, either he gets hung for a brigand, or turned over to the first Kolbian warship we see. I'll let them hang him."

"And what if Sahla dies, Sachi?" Willis stepped up, the blast rifle still in hand. "Or if she's crippled?"

"Then, in either case, he's mine." There was neither mercy nor pity in that cold iron voice. "The Odas taught me the meaning of pain and suffering. I'll give him the full result of my dreadful education. I've time. The rock to destroy the world won't get here for forty-seven years and some months. I can spend a couple of years teaching this *kuso mushi* exactly what pain means. When I'm done with him, even Quan Himself won't want what I leave of him. I'll burn his soul in the lowest of Quan's Seven Hells."

"Sachi. No, you can't." Silaqui's voice was quiet, yet hard as steel. "You wouldn't let me have my revenge on Je'Libe. And Sahla will not want your soul scarred by such an act. Kill him if you must, but simply kill him. An earned execution, same as he'd get after a trial, but no more."

"Ah, Silaqui, what you still fail to realize is that my soul is already scarred. The Oda saw to that long ago. What's another mark to matter?"

"It would matter to Sahla, Sachi." Gelman sighed as he straightened up. "It would matter to her very much, I believe. But unless we wish to remain here for weeks as the uncomfortable, ah... guests of the local High Lord, I might suggest that we make haste for the ship and shake the dirt of this place from our feet, perhaps?"

"Very well." Sachi was still cold, holding herself in rigid control. "Willis, have your sailors drag that...thing along." She turned and headed toward the docks, warily on guard as she stalked beside the sorceress carrying the unconscious Jann.

Chapter Eleven

**Confederation Naval Station *Backhand Blow*
Geostationary Low Orbit
February 1479, Third Age of Imperial Reckoning**

::Status change on System Defense Link-Sat AR-579. On-board tracking and targeting systems are coming online in command autonomous mode. Multiple target tracks, point and area targets. AR-579 is rejecting all authorized stand-down, deactivation and self-destruct command codes implemented via System Defense Link.::

Captain McAllen sighed as she set her sandwich down on her tray. She strode to the central Command Center and settled into the couch. The nano-gel squirmed around her as she dropped into a full neural linkage. After the last time she'd entered a full uplink, she was more than a little nervous, and she had locked a completely independent subroutine into an external system, a subroutine designed to lock out her System access while locking out any access to her own systems.

"Okay, talk to me, D.A.V.E." Her avatar formed in the Virtual Reality of the System Defense Link. She stood above the southern Lanic, the vast ocean spread below her. "Put AR-579's current position and possible targets on the display, please."

::Processing. Primary target areas illuminated.::

"Well, shit." Debbie sighed and shook her virtual head. "I guess the Seekers are mad enough at someone in Du Khamps-des-SouSee to flatten the place after all. Do we have any assets at all anywhere in the target area?"

::Negative. No known Confederal assets within fifteen hundred kilometers. However, there is a Confederation derelict there, identified by local inhabitants as The White Tower. It is the hull of a pre-war dreadnought, CNS *Zhenyuan*, converted to a planetary installation prior to the commencement of the Quan War. The ship's systems lost access to the Link several millennia ago. To the best of anyone's knowledge, she is derelict and completely inactive, other than the installation of an eterna-light type oceanic navigation beacon.::

"Could she be used as a shelter?"

::Assuming a direct hit from one of AR-579's long rod penetrators, no. Ground impact would result in an energy release of approximately six hundred and fifty to seven hundred kilotons. In that case, *Zhenyuan* might provide protection from blast and thermal radiation, assuming impact at least two hundred meters from hull. According to all accessible records, the hull is sealed, and no local inhabitants have ever gained access.::

"Well, if Du Khamps is the target, I guess it's gonna suck to be them. Even if they are mostly pirates and crooks."

::Null input.::

"Never mind. There are multiple targets, correct? What are the others?"

::Point target is Du Khamps des SouSee. Area target is mid-ocean, southern latitudes of the Lanic Ocean.::

"What's in that area?"

::There is a Kolbian naval task force on anti-piracy and anti-slavery patrol in the same general area. Currently the task force has split off three task groups of three ships each and three of four ships each. The main force, consisting of seven ships, including three ships-of-the-line, is on the eastern edge of the target area for the crowbar system. Two of the six task groups are in the central area of the strike. Another one is on the southern edge and a fourth is on the western edge.::

"I guess the Kolbians are serious about suppressing the crooks, huh?"

::Null input.::

"Never mind," she sighed. "What else is out there?"

::The Lietelean Empire has a significant force at sea.::

"How significant?"

::The majority of their Lanic Fleet. An undetermined number of their ships-of-the-line, escorted by their smaller frigates, their older galleasses, and a large number of actual galley type vessels.::

"Holy Buddha in a cathouse. Are any of the Imperials in the crowbar target area?"

::Negative. They are between fifty and seventy kilometers east of the target area.::

"D.A.V.E., this could get really, really ugly."

::Null input.::

"Oh, just shut up."

Armed Sloop *Graser* (6)
Southern Lanic Ocean
February 1479, Third Age of Imperial Reckoning

"All he knows is that Wrath hired him to either kill or capture you and Sahla. He said she'd probably prefer you, Sachi, dead and Sahla as a captive to sell in Luctini. But she wasn't really picky." Willis shook his head as he watched Sachi where they stood at the taffrail of the *Graser*. "I think we've got all we're going to get out of him. So, now what?"

"Give him to me." The Nisei's voice chilled the very air around her. "Just for a day."

"No, damn it." He ground his teeth at the stubborn set of Sachi's shoulders. "Silaqui has a point. You didn't let her torture Je'Libe back on the *Intrepid* and honestly, this isn't any different."

"This is personal, Willis."

"And Je'Libe wasn't personal for Silaqui?" He put a gentle hand on her shoulder. "I get it, Sachi. I really do. But you know that'd be just as wrong as it would have been to let Silaqui torture Je'Libe. Stop and think, will you? Besides, what has Sahla asked you to do?"

Sachi half-sighed, half-growled in response.

"That's not an answer."

"Fine then, damn your round eyes," she snarled, shrugging his hand off. "We'll turn him over to the first Kolbian warship we see. I'll give it a week and if we haven't found anyone by then, I swear

I'll cut his throat myself and toss him over the side. He doesn't deserve a rope and this ship doesn't have a main yard anyway. Good enough?"

"I guess that will have to do." Willis leaned against the rail, watching the sea foam in the ship's wake. He glanced at Sachi's profile. He'd known her longer than anyone else on this ship, longer than anyone since she'd been caught as a stowaway onboard *Intrepid*. He'd realized early on that she was a determined, no, a stubborn young woman. But, when he'd known, she was scared to death inside and desperately hiding that fear, even then she hadn't been as closed off as she was now. "Sachi, how's Sahla doing?"

"Gelman tells me there is nothing else he can do. She's as healed as she is going to be, according to him. She can still walk, but that's about it. She hurts all the time. She's clumsy, even when she uses her magic to fly, and has no feeling in her right hand." The teak wood of the taffrail creaked as her hand clenched on it. "She's going to be a cripple the rest of her life. And it's my fault."

"How's it your fault? Wrath is the one who hired that bastard who stabbed her. You certainly as any of Quan's Hells didn't wield the blade."

"Willis, I draw death and slaughter behind me wherever I go, like pestilence on a wicked wind."

"Damn it, Sachi! This isn't your fault, blast your stubborn hide!" He stopped and drew a deep breath, then a second one. "God, dear Lord, give me patience with this stubborn woman and please, give it to me NOW!"

"Willis, just go aw—" She cut off in mid-word as her body went rigid.

***

::Warning. Inbound threat detected. KEW separation and launch detected. Mission asset within potential target area. Multiple separations.:: D.A.V.E.'s voice filled her mind. Mental images of something angular and lethal, gleaming in the blackness of space, blocked the real world around her out of her vision. ::Primary separation, standard Mark 27A long rod penetrator, secondary separation, four Orbital Area Denial System bundles. Each OADS bundle consists of fifty-eight 'crowbar' submunitions. Visual tracking confirmation required. Please orient with the targeting caret, Lieutenant Commander Schmidt.::

Sachi turned and stared east, into the rosy glow of the rising sun. Willis stared into the bright morning light as well, getting only eyestrain as a result. Lights glittered in Sachi's black eyes as D.A.V.E. used them to watch kinetic energy weapons fired from orbit at seventy-five thousand meters per second.

***

"What the hell is going on, Sachi?" Willis gave up his vain attempt to see whatever held her attention. Or more accurately, the attention of the artificial mind that lived in her mind and body.

"We may be in big trouble, Willis."

"How?"

"Remember the sea-monster that destroyed the *Sorcerer* when we crossed the Deeps of the Great Eastern Ocean?"

"Yeah?"

"And the bar of solid light that killed it before it could destroy *Intrepid*?"

"Of course."

"That was an energy weapon, like a blast rifle. What's coming is different, more like a bullet. All it must do is hit within a mile or two and we're dead. This is like what killed that pirate before *Le Bonaventure* was wrecked on that island. But much bigger."

"Anything we can do about it? Course change, pile on more sail?"

"No, not really. As fast as these things are, it will hit us before we even have a chance to see it coming."

"So, there's no hope?"

"I didn't say that." She gave him a sudden smile that reminded him of how beautiful she could be when she relaxed and let it show. "It's always possible whoever is doing this will miss with their death weapon. Or they're aiming at something else."

"Well, that's encouraging."

"Not really," Sachi answered. "D.A.V.E., can you give me impact energy for the, what'd you call it, the long rod penetrator?"

::Impact energy will be approximately equal to seven hundred kilotons of high explosive, plus or minus forty kilotons.:: D.A.V.E.'s voice was quiet, almost subdued. ::An observer six hundred meters away would see a fireball over two hundred and sixty meters in diameter. The weapon will create a crater with a radius of four hundred and fifty to five hundred meters. Said observer would receive third degree burns over most of their body. Just before the three hundred and eighty meters per second air blast hurls their body away. The impact will vaporize twenty-six hundred cubic meters of material at the impact point.:: There was a pause. ::Target determined. Impact will be within the courtyard of the White Tower Inn, plus or minus five meters. The impact will destroy Du Khamps des SouSee with ninety-five percent loss of life, plus or minus eight percent.:: D.A.V.E. fed the impact information into her mind in a blur of images and numbers.

"Willis?" Sachi's voice was soft.

"Yes?"

"It is going to hit Du Khamps. I doubt there will be any survivors. But it won't affect us. We will see the cloud of the impact and feel a small increase in the wind from the east."

"Oh my God."

"Your God, my Ancestors, Sahla's Chalta, even Silaqui's elven deities, none of them have anything to do with this. This is the handiwork of men. Evil men."

::Target area for the Orbital Area Denial System bundles determined. OADS submunitions will pass over the *Graser* outside of their independent target acquisition systems' range. Any vessels more than forty kilometers to the west of your current position will likely be targeted and destroyed. Each submunition will impact with the force of a five-hundred-pound high explosive warhead.::

The sky shattered as two hundred and thirty-two tungsten penetrators screamed overhead, their hypersonic passage etching the sky in fiery streaks. The sailors working on deck, startled at the shattering thunder from a cloudless sky and then shocked by the burning lines in the sky, cursed or swore or prayed according to their nature.

The eastern sky suddenly brightened, obscuring the morning sunlight for a bright instant. Sachi watched as the vivid light faded and the morning light dimmed as a vast mushroom cloud rose into the heavens. She turned back to the west as more thunders rumbled, faint with distance.

::Submunitions either striking open ocean or acquiring targets with terminal maneuvers,:: D.A.V.E. whispered in her mind. ::Observed Kolbian ships-of-the-line may survive one or two impacts, dependent on exact impact location, probability forty-eight percent, plus or minus twenty-seven percent, multiple variables. Smaller vessels will be respectively less survivable, thirty-one percent, plus or minus sixty-seven percent, excessive vari—::

"Shut up, D.A.V.E." Her low voice was choking. "I don't need to know how many good sailors just died because some *gesu yaro* wants me dead."

Willis glanced at her out of the corner of his eye. Silent tears ran down her cheeks. Lights glittered in her black eyes. Other than those two signs, one of humanity, one of inhumanity, she might have been a perfect porcelain cast of a beautiful young Nisei woman.

"Sachi, it's not your faul—"

"Shut up, Willis." Her voice was barely more than a whisper. "It is my fault. These people, whoever they are, they want me dead. And I come to believe they would destroy the whole world to kill me."

"You don't know that."

"Don't I?" Her head turned to face him, tears spoiling her cold, emotionless visage. "What I wonder is this: do they just want me dead for some mysterious reason of their own, or do they want this coming moonlet to destroy the entire world? Perhaps that is the truly important question."

The ship heeled into a stronger gust from the east, the blast from the impact arriving. The mainsail thundered and flapped, threatening to luff. The bosun shouted orders to trim the sails, keeping an eye on Willis, in case he ordered any significant changes in course or speed. Willis glanced aloft, reading the wind and the sails. He started to turn away to the helm before pausing and putting a gentle hand on Sachi's shoulder.

"Sachi?"

"I'll be fine, Willis." She took a deep breath, bowing her head as she let it out. "Sail your ship. Perhaps we should sail further west, in case anyone did survive and needs our aid?"

"I'll set that course, use a wide tack, try and search as much sea as we can."

"Do that." She turned away from the rail, her hand coming up to gently press Willis' hand on her shoulder. She gave him a regretful smile. "You're a good man, Willis. And a better friend than I deserve. I'll be below in the cabin with Sahla. She may be worried." She stepped past the approaching bosun and went below.

"Captain." Bosun Holland saluted. "Any orders, sir?"

"We'll bend our course further westward than originally planned."

"Aye, sir." He paused, shifting his chew in his mouth. "Begging the Captain's pardon, but I'd say that young lady is bearing a burden as is near to breaking her. What with the little Darsälaamic lady being hurt so bad and all..."

"An astute observation, Bosun. Very astute."

"Be there aught we might be doing for her?"

"I don't know, Boats." Unconsciously calling Holland by the Navy's traditional name for any vessel's bosun, Willis watched the cloud still rising to the east, above the grave of Du Khamps des SouSee. "But I know that if she does break, the resulting disaster could be the greatest to befall the world since the Fall itself. Are you a religious man, Bosun Holland?"

"Somewhat, sir." Holland spat a stream of brown liquid over the rail. "In port, I go to the local parsonage for services. Man needs to believe in something, I think, sir."

"Yes, a man does need to believe, Boats. But if you've a mind to, I'd spend some time praying that something, someone, somewhere, finds a way to help Sachi. I know of no one on this world that needs such help more."

Luctini, Geullia Province
The Eternal Empire of Lietelea
Clan House of the Familia Palmaroli
February 1479, Third Age of Imperial Reckoning

"Vicente, the destruction of Du Khamps des SouSee is regretful but only because of the loss of our ability to recruit there. And if this girl was still aboard the Kolbian warships, then she is likely to be feeding the fish." The translucent blue image of Master's head nodded approval at Vicente.

"Grazie, Master." Vicente inclined his head to acknowledge the compliment. "However, I shall remain vigilant. Given this person, this vulgarly named Sachi Takahashi's fortune at surviving multiple attempts to kill her, I shall not decrease my efforts to ensure her death until I have her head sitting on my mantel."

"Very good, Vicente, very good. The Eld Mechanism has told me that the falling steel weapons destroyed several Kolbian warships in the southern Lanic. I suggest that the time is ripe to strike against those heretics. Have your agents with Admeeral du SouSee Havre Calchas suggest that the God would look favorably on the Imperial fleet sweeping the arrogant Kolbians from the seas. I'm certain he could easily be convinced that the Line of Sky Fire and the falling steel weapons are signs from God."

"Very well, Master, as you command."

"Also, there are signs that the Eldest, our Progenitor, has begun to stir from His millennia of sleep. No contact, only portents, but that is a very hopeful sign that our long struggle may finally be drawing to a conclusion. One in our favor. If the Progenitor truly awakens, They will have nothing that could stand against Him."

"Truly blessed news, Master."

"Yes." The disembodied head paused, a gnarled hand coming into view as he stroked his thin, white beard. "I must tell you, Vicente, that our agent in Their ranks has sent some scant information suggesting this Takahashi creature may be even more important than any realize. It could be possible that she is the key to Their ultimate weapon, a weapon powerful enough to even stop or destroy Last Weapon."

"I understand, Master. I shall remain heedful of her until, as I said, I have her head as a trophy."

"I expect no less, my son. Go with the God, Vicente."

"Go with the God, Master." Vicente leaned back in his luxurious chair as the Eld Mechanism shut down. He reflexively stroked his own trimmed black beard, stopping with a start as he realized he was aping the Master's mannerisms. He turned in the swivel chair to regard the map of the Western World on the wall of his sanctum.

"Given that the Lanic is a great ocean and the Kolbians are the world's best sailors, but the Empire has thousands of ships to the Kolbians' hundreds," he muttered to himself. "True, many loyal Imperial sailors will die, but of what other use are such peasants?" He turned back to the Eld Mechanism, activating it to contact his agents with Admeeral Lord Calchas. He smiled to himself. If he was fortunate, the Kolbians would kill that pompous windbag before the galleys swarmed them under. He would lose the tremendous amount of gold the fat slob owed him, but it would be worth it to be rid of him.

Armed Sloop *Graser* (6)
Southern Lanic Ocean
February 1479, Third Age of Imperial Reckoning

Bright sapphire eyes opened at the creak of the cabin door's latch. Sahla knew it was Sachi; no one else moved with such casual stealth, but the Bond made her aware of where Sachi always was. She hid a smile and closed her eyes. Sachi settled next to Sahla's gimbal mounted bunk as it swayed with the ship's motion. She sat on the deck next to Sahla, a tentative hand reaching out to lightly caress Sahla. Sahla luxuriated in the gentle, almost diffident touch, grateful she could still feel such a touch on her right shoulder.

Suddenly, she frowned at an odd noise, a sound Sachi mostly suppressed.

Was that a sob? She would never cry where I could see her. She thinks it is weakness. Something has happened, something bad, and now she sees it as something else that is her responsibility, her fault. Oh, Sachi, dear love, you cannot bear all the world's burdens. Even you, strong as you are, would break under such a weight.

She rolled over; her eyes were level with Sachi's where the Nisei sat next to her. She captured Sachi's hesitant hand with her own. The open devastation on the Nisei's face startled her. Tears marked her cheeks.

"Sachi, what is wrong? What has happened?"

"Sahla..." she choked, coughed, and started again, "Sahla, Du Khamps... Du Khamps was just destroyed. Everyone there just died."

"What!? How? How do you know this?"

"A weapon like the one we used to destroy Ironheart's *Deathdealer*, but one striking from space. We can see the cloud of the impact from the deck. And that's not all. Other weapons were launched, most likely looking for our ship. Those weapons overflew our ship." She pointed at her forehead. "D.A.V.E. says the things missed us, that instead of killing us, they found and destroyed the Kolbian warships west of us. But they were launched to kill me. Just as Du Khamps was destroyed to kill me."

"Sachi, you don't know that, you can't know that!" Sahla slid out of the bunk into Sachi's lap, wrapping her arms around Sachi's broad shoulders. "You can't take the blame for everything, you just can't." She curled herself further around Sachi, wrapping her legs around Sachi's slim waist. "I don't care what that vile thing in your head says. It is not your fault!" She buried her face in the hollow between the Nisei's neck and shoulder. "You are '*Ahad almudafiein almuqdisi, hamia,* a holy defender, a protector! Have you ever harmed anyone who did not offer you harm first? You are the best of all of us. You are the other half of my heart, and you could not be so, were you of evil nature!"

For the briefest of moments, she desperately held Sachi with arms and legs twined around her as the Nisei girl shuddered. Then

Sachi was twisting away from her grasp and bounding to the stern window, flinging it open and retching into the ship's wake. When Sahla followed her, reaching her hand to touch her back, Sachi slapped the hand painfully away and blindly thrust her back. She wiped her mouth with the back of her hand, muttering in her own language as she turned her back to the window and slid down the cabin's stern bulkhead to collapse on the floor. Sahla started to reach out to her again.

"Stay away, foolish girl!" Sachi's snarl instantly stopped her. "You have no true idea what I am or what I have done in this life!"

"I don't care what you were forced to do by evil masters! I have never seen you willingly do anything but protect those you love! You risk your very life and soul, I think, to find this thing to stop this coming destroyer. What more can any ask of one person?"

A tense silence settled in the cabin. Sachi pulled up her knees, wrapping her arms around her legs and burying her face behind her knees. Sahla scooted as close as she dared. She knew Sachi was tormented by the thought that all these people had died because someone horrible and malevolent wanted to kill her. But she had no idea what to do to lift that burden. All she knew to do was to be there, show by word and deed, thought and act that she loved Sachi without let or hindrance, wholly and completely. She reached out and gently touched Sachi's arm.

"It will be all right, Sachi. Remember that I love yo—"

Sahla was inhumanly quick, but Sachi's reflexes were the very lightning of the storm. A steel vise, shaped like a pale slender hand, clamped painfully around her forearm. Sachi uncoiled like a striking snake, driving Sahla over onto her back and pinning the young woman to the cabin's deck. Sahla screamed in pain and surprise and shock.

"*Watashi wa kegareta aku, baishunpu to satsujin-shadesu!*" Sachi screamed in her face, her black eyes narrowed to savage slits. "Do you not understand that?! I am an unclean evil, a whore, and a murderer! I am unfit for human sight! My first kill was when I was eight years old, and not a fortnight went past after that day that I was not forced to kill or be killed. I murdered the old man who paid my family for the privilege of deflowering me! Because someone else paid my family more to have me kill him! The sands of your desert could not scrub the guilty blood from my body if they had a thousand years to try! You have NO IDEA WHAT I AM! I am barely worthy to breathe, and I will never be worthy of anyone's love, even less of your love, you foolish, idiotic girl! Can you not learn!?"

Sachi's fury collapsed, flowing away, quicksilver spilled on a mirror. She released her grasp on Sahla's arm, bracing her arms outside Sahla's shoulders, her knees straddling the Jann's willowy waist. Sahla barely dared to breathe, fearful of awakening that rage again. Her back vibrated to the thunder of footsteps outside the door and the shouts and the pounding fists on that door were faint and far away.

"Sachi," she whispered, lying still on her back, gazing into Sachi's eyes, "I can learn. And if loving you means I must slay those who do me no injury and sell my virginity to an unknown drunken bastard in some alley, then I shall do so. All that and more, because I love you and I will be with you always. You are *habia alhaqiqiu alwahid*, my one true love. The sun will gutter and die before the truth of my love for you fades away. Believe me."

"You know, I do believe you." Tears welled in Sachi's black eyes and dripped onto Sahla's face. "And that's why I must do this."

"Do what?"

"Sahla, you are dismissed and may not leave your token without the permission of its holder." Sachi's words, cold and harsh, belied the tears and agony on her face. Sahla's shriek of loss and fury faded mistily away as her own magic betrayed her, drawing her into the sapphire gem around Sachi's neck, trapping her there.

Sachi rose to her feet, pulling Sahla's gem on its necklace over her head as Willis broke the door open. He staggered into the cabin, followed by Silaqui, with Gelman hard on her heels. The trio stared in confusion at her, looking for Sahla.

"I can bear no more," Sachi simply stated as she tossed the gem. "Catch, Willis."

"Whaa—" Willis juggled the gem as it hit him in the hands. Sachi turned and bolted for the open stern window.

"Sachi! NO!" Silaqui screamed as she realized what the Nisei intended. Carnelian flames limned the Sorceress' hands as she tried to halt Sachi with her magic before she could jump. Gelman wasn't quite as quick as the Elf, raising his own power, intending to stop her as well. But in their frantic castings, their arms entangled and the two different, incompatible magics, cast with no preparation at all, produced only flares of harmless, crimson-shot golden light as Sachi sprinted to self-destruction.

Sachi glanced back over her shoulder a step before diving cleanly through that beckoning window into the cold, peaceful depths of the ocean. That glance was both her undoing and her salvation as Aylie swung down from the stern railing, feet first through the window. The brown girl planted both booted feet and every ounce of her hundred and twenty-odd pounds squarely into Sachi's chest, smashing her backwards into the cabin. Sachi hit her head hard enough to knock herself completely senseless. Aylie landed cat-like on her feet, her expression identical to a feline who has just presented a beloved owner with an extremely dead snake, pleased, proud and immensely self-satisfied. She turned and shut the window, then pulled and locked the hurricane shutters over the window.

"Well, that may slow herself down a wee bit, mayhap." She smiled as she sashayed out of the cabin, catching Gelman by the sleeve. "We've na need ta be here, Silaqui, Pere Gelman. But Willis, we'll nae be far, iffn ye should have need." The door closed behind them.

"LET ME OUT OF HERE, QUAN BURN YOUR EYES!" Willis flinched as Sahla's soundless shriek slammed inside his head like a thousand cathedral bells. He juggled the necklace like a hot coal but managed not to drop it.

"OUCH! Don't scream, for the love of God! Yes, out, out, do whatever you want, just stop screaming in my head!" Later, Willis swore that Sahla hadn't completely materialized before she wrapped herself around Sachi, crying and begging the unconscious Nisei to never do that again.

***

At first, she couldn't remember where, exactly, she was. Her head pounded viciously, a low, heavy thumping beat, the drums of a heavy galley at ramming speed. The back of her head ached with a savage, throbbing pain. Something warm and moist wiped her face and she opened her eyes slowly. The dim light blurred her vision, and she could only make out a fuzzy silhouette of someone leaning over her.

"Mama?" The person leaned over her and gently kissed her cheek.

"No, Sachi." It was a melodious voice, warm and happy, even if there was a worried undertone to it. "It's me, Sahla. How do you feel?"

"Sahla? My head hurts. What happened?"

::You sustained a severe cerebral concussion and minor physical damage to your cerebellum, the location of your BPU.:: D.A.V.E.'s voice filled her mind's eye with an image of her head and the damage done to it. ::Your Biological Processing Unit, the core processor for all your technically enhanced capabilities, also sustained minor damage. Medical system nanites are completing repairs to both your physical brain and your BPU and neural interfacing network. Expected recovery is ninety-nine-point-eighty six percent, plus or minus four-point-one percent. Recovery time should be no more than twenty-eight hours, fourteen minutes, plus or minus fifty-two seconds.::

"The machine is talking to you again, isn't it?" Sahla moved closer, sapphire eyes dark with worry. "What is it telling you?"

"How do you know it's talking to me, Sahla?"

"The lights in your eyes glitter. And you sometimes get a... well, a distracted look on your face. What did it say?"

"It said I'll be okay in a day or so. What happened? What hit my head?" Sudden memory flashed through her mind. "Oh, no. No, no. My enemies, all those deaths, those are my fault, they won't stop, never, oh Ancestors, what more must I bear?"

Sachi started to thrash, trying to get up. Sahla grabbed her forearms and held her down momentarily. Sachi was stronger than the Jann and was forcing the slighter girl back when she lost all control of her body and simply flopped back onto the bunk.

::Given your current emotional condition, and your cultural conditioning, I have been forced to initiate a system override to suppress your gross motor functions.:: D.A.V.E.'s voice felt colder than normal. ::Successful self-destruction will only permit complete and total success for those persons responsible for various attempts to terminate your life. Terminating your own existence would do nothing but bring them the greatest pleasure. And allow the completion of their ultimate goal, the utter destruction of this planet. In other terms, they don't care how you die; they simply want you to die. If you die, they succeed. Allowing these individuals and organizations to achieve their goals without opposing them to the greatest of your ability is not compatible with the nature of your basic personality complex, Lieutenant Commander Caitlin Schmidt.::

"It's talking to you again, isn't it?" Sahla asked in a subdued voice.

"Yes," Sachi grumbled. "It won't let me move right now."

"Really? You can't move?" Sahla grinned. "What is it saying?"

"It's telling me that if I die, they win. And they'll succeed in destroying the entire world." Sachi closed her eyes, her face a mask of agony. "But Sahla, I am so very tired of leaving slaughter and death and destruction in my wake, wherever I travel."

"Would you willingly have slain any of those folk? Although some of them may very well have deserved to be slain for their black hearts and evil deeds?"

"I am not so pure of heart that I should judge such."

"Ah, you are better already."

"How?"

"You grinned when you said that." Sahla gave her an impish smile. "It was not much of a grin, but it was a grin." She sobered. "Sachi, while, yes, these unknown people are trying to kill you, they obviously have no concern at all for life. That, my love, is not your fault. Nor is it your fault that they slay hundreds or thousands. You did not release whatever kind of weapons that caused such destruction, now did you?"

Sachi mumbled under her breath.

"I did not understand that. Did you do anything to launch those weapons?"

"No," Sachi half-growled, half-sighed in answer.

"Excellent." Sahla leaned down and kissed Sachi. It was a long, thorough kiss, aided by the fact that Sachi couldn't struggle or get away. And despite herself, she enjoyed that kiss immensely. Eventually Sahla came up for air, an extremely satisfied smile on her face. "Hmm, that was nice, wasn't it? And since the machine thing won't let you move, I could do anything I want to do to you, no?"

"Sahla, no, this isn't right." Sachi struggled in vain to move as Sahla began to run her hands gently over Sachi's face, neck and shoulders. *D.A.V.E., you sonofabitch, let me GO! This isn't right! This is not how it should be!* "Sahla, stop, please. Don't make me command you to do so."

"Unfortunately, you cannot command me at the moment, *Habiba*." Sahla's smile widened. "At the moment, Willis has my token and the last thing he said to me was, 'Do whatever you want.' So thoughtful, these Kolbian sailors."

"Fine," Sachi snapped. "I'm helpless. Do whatever you want to do to me. I'm used to that. My older step-sibs, the twins Maho and Mankato, liked to tie me down and beat me and rape me. Maho, my stepsister, was by far the worst of the pair. Her twin brother, Mankato, was just her tool. They put me within mere steps of death more than once. What can you do to me that would be any worse?" Sahla recoiled from the pain and hatred in the Nisei's voice.

"Sachi, I would never hurt you!" Sahla went to her knees on the cabin deck and then fully prostrated herself. "I am still Bonded to you! I could not do such things, Sachi." Her voice trembled with tears. "Please, Sachi, please, please, forgive me. I did not know such things had happened to you. I know of hateful siblings and of the cruelties of pillage and rape, but only by reading fancy tales of them. If I did such things as a Jann, I would truly be cursed and unclean. The Prophet would certainly strike my name from the lists of righteous Jann and Chalta would turn His Face from me. I should be cast into the outer darkness for Shaytan and the *ghula* to feast on my flesh while the Efreet slowly devoured my very soul for eternity. Please, please, forgive me!"

Sachi watched the tiny girl's shoulders shake with her sobs. She sighed to herself. *Let me go, D.A.V.E., blast you. I understand that dying is exactly what my enemies want and I'm contrary enough normally that I'd never give the bastards what they want. What happens after I stop this world-killer may be a different discussion, but I give my word of honor that my own hand shall not be the means of restoring what little honor I have left until after the task is done. This I swear on my Ancestors' Spirits.*

::Codicil accepted. Override released.::

Sachi slid out of the bunk and knelt next to Sahla. She reached out and gently lifted her from the floor, hiding a smile as she noted the damp rug. Tears streamed down Sahla's face, her eyes were red-rimmed and bloodshot. Sachi pulled her into a close embrace, gently kissing her cheek as she did. Sahla started slightly, pulling back and staring into Sachi's black eyes.

"You're a mess, love," Sachi smiled, "and you're still the most beautiful woman I've ever seen. Gelman's Angel was right; your beauty would lay the world at your feet." She gently rubbed away the tear tracks on Sahla's cheeks. "I'm sorry. I know you would never hurt me. I'm certain you haven't the faintest idea what two women lovers can do together, but believe me, I was trained by the finest geishas in all possible methods of pleasure. All possible methods. I imagine we might both enjoy exploring the possibilities, *Koibito. Watashi no shin no ai.*"

"Wha—what are you saying?" Sahla's tears left her breathless. "What does that mean?"

"That literally means, 'My True Love.' That is, if you'll have me? After all, if I can't command you, and Willis said, 'Do whatever you want,' well, I guess I can't argue about you being forced to be in love with me anymore, can I?"

"Sachi, I..." Sahla gasped as she felt the Bond stretch and warp before it settled as lightly as a dove's down feathers around her heart and spirit. "Ooh, oh, Chalta be praised! The Bond! Do you feel it! No longer does it force us together, now it only reinforces what we want of each other!"

"I... I do." Sachi knew her face reflected her own startlement as she felt the intangible Bond shift and change. It still connected her just as strongly to Sahla's Jann magic, but now it was because she knew in her very soul that this was what she had always wanted, a love as strong as the love between Mama and Papa Komiya.

It was a warm, powerful connection between the two young women and for a long time, so long neither ever knew how long, they simply held each other, smiling with a pure joy shining in their faces. Then the long kiss they shared was deep and gentle, promising the passion to come. When the latch on the door opened, neither of them moved to break their embrace.

"Holy shit." Willis stopped, stunned at the peace and love shining on both of their faces. "Well, damn. Dip me in shark shit. Is this, uh, hmm, a bad time? Because if it is, I hate to be the bearer of bad news, but maybe both of you need to be up on deck. We might have problems."

"What's wrong, Willis?" Sachi asked.

"Feel the motion of the ship, or rather, the lack thereof? We're becalmed."

"Hmm," Sachi frowned for a moment. "I feel it."

"That's not the only thing. There's neither roll nor pitch to the ship. The sea's as flat and smooth as a millpond. Or maybe a mirror. And there's a haze building. Silaqui and Gelman both say it ain't natural and might be powerful magery directed at us. You need to come see."

"Very well, Willis." Sachi climbed to her feet, raising Sahla up with a gentle hand and the two gingerly followed Willis up on deck. Neither was fully recovered from their injuries. Sachi leaned against the binnacle with an arm supporting Sahla. They both frowned as they saw the unnaturally still ocean and building grayish haze slowly shrouding the ship. It wasn't fog, more an inability to see any great distance at all. Sachi glanced at the bosun.

"Bosun Holland, ever see or hear of anything like this before?"

"Nay, Lady Sachi." He started to spit over the side, stopped and obviously thought better of it and rang one of the spittoons on the deck. "'Tis nay natural, nay a t'all." He pointed at the spittoon. "And I've no stomach fer perhaps angering whoever or whatever might be as the one strong 'nuff to do such a thing. Not at all, ma'am, sir." He stared out into the haze.

"I think I agree with you on that, Bosun." Willis rubbed his chin. "Pass the order to the crew to use the slops buckets instead of the head until ordered different. And tell Roland in the galley not to dump anything over the side. No trash, no garbage. Nothing goes into the ocean. And belay having the crew holystone the deck as well. I want everyone on board to be as calm and peacefully settled as possible. Not even harsh language. Pass the order, Bosun, quickly and quietly."

"Aye-aye, Sir." Holland headed forward.

"There's something out there, Willis." Silaqui spoke quietly as she, Aylie and Gelman joined Willis and the two young women at the taffrail, staring into the haze.

"Aye, there is, but what?" Willis answered softly. "It's not a ship, we'd hear them."

"It is nothing of our mortal world," Sahla stated. "And it will be sooner rather than later that what is out there is done with us. I feel it calling to the magic in my soul. It is a gentle calling, and I think it or they, perhaps, mean us no harm. But they, yes...they will have their will done with us ere we pass on through these gray walls."

"Child, I've a thousand years and more of magery and knowledge of the arcane in my life and I feel none of what you say." Silaqui nodded at the increasing haze. "How can you feel such things?"

"Perhaps because I lack such knowledge and therefore do not know what is and is not possible? Perhaps because I am a Jann, a creature of inherent magic? Or perhaps because I am in love, True Love, with my heartmate? Do you feel it, *Habiba*?"

"I think so, *Koibito*." Sachi settled her arm firmly around Sahla's shoulders. "I would say the Ancestors gaze upon us. That or *Kyoryokuna kamigami*, powerful divine spirits. And I feel rather disinclined to use any of my technic abilities. I think they may have little love for machines and even less favor for such as I, where machines are a very part of my body."

"So, I's ta take it as the two o' ye has worked out that as is between ye?" Aylie grinned at the pair. "Time an' past, I'd be 'bout saying. Any mortal with eyes ta see can sees that each o' ye's only got the glimmer fer the other. Fagh. Whut took ye so long?"

"Well, she's been just so stubborn," Sachi and Sahla answered in perfect unison. Then they both blushed and smiled at each other. Everyone within earshot roared in laughter. Everyone save Gelman, and even the dour priest grinned briefly.

"Then I trust there'll be no more of this foolishness of flinging thyself into the very ocean, Sachi?" Gelman growled. "The Book of One maintains that suicide is a mortal sin. 'Tis bad enough as you would sinfully cavort with another woman!"

"Give it a rest, Gelman." Willis turned to face the priest. "It might be a very good idea to show whatever or whoever is out there a united front. So, no grumbling or fussing about what others do or don't do. Let's not give anything eerie a chance to get hooks somewhere we'd really not like it."

"Very well, Willis, as you wish."

"What do you think is out there, Silaqui?" Sachi caught the perplexed look on the Sorceress' face as the Elf stepped away from the rail.

"I don't know, Sachi. I can feel something gently touching my power, but very lightly." Jade eyes met black ones. "But whatever it is, I think we shall know ere long. I only hope it is something without malevolence towards us."

Chapter Twelve

KRN Intrepid (32)
Stark Haven Main Dock
February 1479, Third Age of Imperial Reckoning

"SHE'S A BEAUTY, CAPTAIN Blaine." Admiral of the Fleet Nelson McGowan leaned back to study *Intrepid's* towering masts.

"Yes, she is, sir." Captain, Junior Grade, William 'Bonny' Blaine glanced up at the masts briefly. "But the weight of the new armor has cut her speed down by at least two or three knots. During sea trials I never got her to more than twelve knots. I'm not sure the loss of speed is worth it. There are damn few ships in the world that were her equal even before the refit. Sir."

"Oh, I know, Captain Blaine. I commanded *Intolerant* when she was the most powerful warship on the seas. Ten years ago, scrappers burned her on the East Mud Flat for her fittings and metal. Change can be hard, but it is what we Kolbians are the best in the world at doing."

"True, Sir." Blaine hid a sigh. "Of course, Admiral, the real coming changes are being built behind the walls and guards of the Secure Assembly slips, across the harbor." He gestured to where hundred-and-fifty-foot walls blocked the view of the KRN's most secretive ship building projects.

"True, William, true enough. But it will still be a year or more before either *Constitution* or *Enterprise* will be ready for sea."

"I was of the impression that they would be named *Freedom* and *Republic*." Blaine rubbed his chin and raised an eyebrow at McGowan. "You have anything to do with that, sir?"

"A bit."

"Well, I understand naming one of them *Constitution*, but I don't get the other name, *Enterprise*."

"Well, Captain Blaine, I have my reasons, and they're damned good ones, at least to me." McGowan clasped his hands behind his back and rocked back and forth on his feet. "And since I have the six cuff rings of the Admiral of the Fleet, I generally get to have my way with my ships. Even if a few Legates and a Consul did scream bloody murder at not getting their pet names used. KRN *Consul Harlington*, that was what the head of the Finance Council wanted, the bloody idiot. Over my dead body. And *Constitution* and *Enterprise* aren't the only irons we have in the fire, oh no. There's the other class of six armored ships, not so... um, advanced, if you will. Traditional broadside armament in an armored casemate amidships, a wooden framed hull with iron plates, pressure engine powered. Their main cruising mode will still be sail. They'll have three masts. Most likely be brigantine rigged, the current thought is. We'll see. But you know all this, of course."

"Yes, sir. I thought those designs were quite audacious, then I saw those two all-iron monsters." Blaine sighed. "There are times when I wonder if I should retire when the Navy decommissions *Intrepid* for the last time."

"Hogwash, Captain Blaine, pure hogwash." A mischievous light glinted in McGowan's eyes. "If I have my way, and I generally do, you'll have an armored pressure-engine ship under your command well before you retire. And most likely you'll command at least a squadron of them under your own flag. Besides, if you retire early, well, then you'll have your wife to deal with on a full-time, everyday basis. After three months of that, you'll be down at the docks, signing on to the leakiest merchant tub sailing to Iona or Chou li Han, just to escape that woman. And you know I'm right."

"Yes, sir." Blaine's face darkened as he remembered his last fight with Emily.

"Humpf," the Admiral growled, "a word of advice from an older man, divorced three times?"

"Sir?"

"You are going to have to sort out your personal life one way or another, Captain Blaine. Sort it out in your favor, not hers. Never fight on the opponent's terms. Choose your own course and make damn sure you've the weather gauge. Or you might find yourself actually taking that early retirement and deciding to go hunt greenskins and all other kinds of big, nasty gribblies in the back-beyond of the Ironwood Mountains."

"Yes, sir."

"That's neither a threat nor even a warning, William. That's advice from one old sailorman to another. That's all."

"Yes, sir. Understood, sir." He decided not to tell the Admiral that he had received notice from an attorney hired by Emily that she was filing for divorce today as he left his quarters ashore that morning. He had no intention of contesting the divorce, other than ensuring his rights to see his daughter. A quick visit to a divorce attorney well known in navy circles secured his own representation in the court. It had been disturbingly easy to begin the ending of a chapter of his life covering the last fifteen years.

Sally turned fourteen in three weeks and would be hiring her own attorney then. Emily wouldn't like that, but she had 'packed her seabag' already and would have to live with the consequences of her actions. Blaine's attorney had recommended another of his fellows who specialized in representing minor children of naval officers in such cases.

"Well, Admiral, if I'm to catch the tide, I'd best be getting aboard." Blaine hoisted his personal seabag onto his shoulder, his Chief Steward, Toby Wilkerson having seen the rest of his belongings aboard *Intrepid* the night before.

"Good luck and Godspeed, Captain Blaine." McGowan saluted Blaine and then watched the taller man head up the gangplank of his command. With a quiet sigh he turned away, walking down the quay, and climbing into his own closed carriage.

"So, he's not exactly enthusiastic about the changes coming, is he, nephew?" Marianne Lundgren spoke from the dark corner of the carriage. She preferred to stay out of sight. While skin as black as hers was not particularly rare in Kolbia, it wasn't common, and it was even less common on a woman six inches over six feet. A woman who wore her shoulder length black hair in long braided locks and had eyes with solid black irises.

"No, Great-Aunt, he's not. Oh, he'll come around; he's too good of an officer not to see the advantages of the new ships. But that's not foremost on his mind right now." McGowan leaned back as the carriage started off. "He's got woman problems. His wife is just barely being discreet enough in her little tête-à-têtes with all her 'admirers' among some of our more jaded political lights. And I got a decent bit of information on that Nisei girl, Sachi Takahashi, the stowaway on *Intrepid* from his steward, Senior Master Petty Officer Toby Wilkerson, via my own steward. Seems Blaine was quite taken with the young woman. And she with him. And to be fair, some of the stories about her become more and more outlandish with each telling."

"She's of great interest to my people as well. Rather, she was. But from everything we know now, she probably drowned in a storm somewhere in the Southern Lanic. I chased her halfway around the world and never even laid eyes on her." Regret tinged her voice.

"Well, there's no way we could know that." The Admiral glanced out the curtained window on his side of the carriage. "I hate leaving William Blaine on tenterhooks about that girl, but what else can I do? At least, sending him and *Intrepid* to Luctini with the war warning will give him something else to worry about, get his mind off his woman problems. And he'll be back in contact with Commodore Sartell, his old commander. I expect Sartell will read through the dispatches, both the ones from ONI and from the Diplomatic Service and order the mission there closed. And he won't care how loud the envoy screams and kicks, he'll haul Her Excellency, Angelina Courtenay's august backside up *Intrepid's* gangplank by main force if necessary."

"I'd think sending a woman as a diplomatic minister to the Empire is something they could consider a slap in the face. Poking a tiger with a stick, maybe?"

"We must, Great-Aunt; if we expect to have the Empire and other nations respect and understand our positions on freedom and equality. Oh, the Ambassador in Lietelea the City at our main Embassy there is a man, but Luctini is considered the economic center of the Empire. It's a balancing act, and one that's fixing to come unbalanced, from what you've told me lately."

"And you've sent Captain Blaine and all he knows about the new ships into the tiger's den just as the beast is awaking up hungry."

"What the hell is a tiger, Great-Aunt?"

"Long story, nephew. Is he good enough?"

"Yes. Or if he's not, no one is."

"I hope you're right, Nelson."

"So do I, Great-Aunt. So do I."

Armed Sloop *Graser* (6)
Southern Lanic Ocean
February 1479, Third Age of Imperial Reckoning

The gray haze slowly shrouded the sloop over the next few hours. It blocked sight of even the unnaturally smooth ocean that held *Graser* motionless. The masthead and topgallants were lost to sight in the miasma that cocooned the ship into her own isolated world. Everyone aboard her felt that there were...presences...watching them from the cloaking mist. They stood against the rail or sat on overturned buckets or coils of rope or leaned against stanchions, according to their nature. In this strange place, no one was alarmed when the ship's hull gently grated against a sandy bottom. *Graser* listed ever so slightly to port and the fog thinned to reveal a white, wooden six-person dinghy floating serenely next to the ship's main chains. A wooden jetty jutted out into the silent ocean fifty feet away, barely visible in the gray light.

"Hmmmm." Silaqui leaned over the rail to appraise the dinghy before raising her head to scrutinize the wharf. "It seems we are at least expected, and perhaps, invited as well."

"No oars, I see." Willis glanced around. "Hell, there aren't even any oarlocks."

"So, iffn we be invited, then who be the 'we' as should be taking yon boat?" Aylie leaned over the rail and stared at the boat. "I only see places fer six. Who should be those six?"

"Obvious enough, I think." Silaqui rubbed her palms against her scarlet skirt.

"Perhaps, Aljannia Silaqui, perhaps." Sachi and Sahla glanced at each other, Sahla nodding to the Nisei's unvoiced query before she spoke.

"If it's obvious, Silaqui, then name some names." Willis studied the barely visible jetty.

"Sachi, Sahla, myself, Gelman, Aylie and you, Willis." The Elf shrugged. "If this is not related in some fashion to Sachi's 'quest' I'll eat the mainsail, without salt. Where Sachi goes, so goes Sahla. I am a sorceress and the only representative of my folk and Sachi is my Heart-Sister, Defender, and Elf-Friend, therefore, I go. Gelman was sent to Sachi by his own angelic patron and Aylie is here due to the murder of her Lord and his Lady by agents of these world-destroyers. They go as well."

"That makes sense. But why me?" Willis' gaze caught and held her jade eyes, vertical pupils wide in the dim gray light.

"Because you have known Sachi longer than any of us. I should think you have an interest in this, even if you Kolbians scoff at magic." Silaqui smiled gently at Willis. "And your own curiosity would have you trying to walk on water to follow us."

"Well, yes, true enough." He returned Silaqui's smile before turning to Bosun Holland. "Boats, there aren't any specific orders I can give you. I don't think this damnable murk will release the ship while we're gone. If it does, make sail for Stark Haven and make a complete, confidential report to Admiral McGowan and Rear Admiral Hulmen of ONI. Otherwise, be patient and quiet. Don't disturb anything that might turn out to be quite nasty. You, of course, will have command."

"Aye-aye, sir." Holland rang a spittoon. "We'll be here waiting for you, sir."

"Well, my friends, what are we waiting for?" His smile was wide and forced. "I'll go first and secure the main chains. Then ladies first." He lifted the entry port railing and quickly clambered down the Jacob's ladder on *Graser's* side and into the dinghy.

Sachi followed him, moving more carefully than her normal wont. Sahla flew down to the dinghy, landing as light as a feather while Willis shook his head. Silaqui used her magery to levitate down to the seat next to him. Aylie scurried down to the boat, agile as a squirrel. Gelman was the last, grousing under his breath at leaving his armor and mace on the ship.

He scowled as he settled into the last seat on the small craft. Directly in front of him in the amidships pair of seats were Sachi and Sahla, their arms about each other with Sahla's head resting against the tall Nisei's shoulder. Both young women's hair was unbound, and it was nigh impossible to tell which strand of midnight sable tresses were whose. Aylie tapped him lightly on the shoulder and shook her finger at him when he turned to her. With a final scowl, he drew out his wooden symbol of the Circled Cross and started whispering a prayer of peace and good fortune.

Without the slightest sound or ripple on the surface of the water, the dinghy smoothly turned and headed for the jetty. The sloop behind them faded into a barely visible shape in the gray murk as the jetty became clearer and more solid as they drew nearer. The jetty was narrow and low enough to allow them to easily climb from the dinghy onto the wood planked surface. It extended away from them into the haze. They could not see where or even if it met any land.

"Well, my friends, it seems there is truly only one way to go." Willis waved his hand in invitation toward the mysterious end of the narrow jetty. They headed toward its end in pairs, Willis and Silaqui leading, Sachi and Sahla next with Gelman and Aylie last. The boards neither creaked nor shifted under their footsteps.

Much later, none of them could agree how long they walked down that narrow path. Gelman nearly blasphemed as he swore vehemently, they had walked for hours. Sahla insisted that it had been but a moment's walk, shorter than the deck of the *Graser* was wide, less than twenty feet. None of the others agreed either. However long they walked, at the end of the jetty they all saw the same thing. The grey haze cleared away and a bright sun shone down from a clear, cloudless sky. A gentle breeze rustled the leaves of palm trees and clear blue water spilled out of a rocky sided pond and flowed down the white sand of the beach to the placid turquoise waves of the ocean lapping softly ashore.

As habitually wary as they were, none of them felt the least concern that this inviting paradise might conceal the least threat of danger or violence. They never hesitated as they reached the end of the jetty and stepped off onto the pure white sand.

As their feet left the smooth wooden boards, each of them found themselves alone, even Sachi and Sahla, who had been holding hands. And for each of them, an entity waited in the shade of the palms, next to the pure blue water of a pond.

Donum Magnifici Sancti Domini Dei (90)
Imperial Fleet Flagship
Southern Lanic Ocean
February 1479, Third Age of Imperial Reckoning

Sieur Havre, Lord Calchas, Admeeral du SouSee, Imperial Lietelean Navy, sipped his hot chocolate, enjoying the delicacy at the end of his luncheon. Without warning, the stern windows of his cabin cracked and shattered as the sky above his flagship was torn asunder by shrieking thunder and burning lines of incandescent light. He choked and spat the expensive drink onto the table, spilling the rest of the drink on his immaculate uniform jacket, staining the cream-colored silk.

"Le Nom de Dieu!"

He wasn't the only person at his lunch table that cursed or swore at the sudden shattering sound. Capitan Alphonse Colbert, commander of the *Donum Magnifici*, went over backwards in his chair with an undignified squawk. Teniente de Navio Eduardo Rosales, Havre's Flag Lieutenant, cursed as a flying glass shard left a nasty cut on his cheek. Oaths and shouts of fear and consternation from the decks were heard through the shattered windows and open skylights.

"Indeed, Admeeral, le Nom de Dieu." As the thunder faded away, Capitan Colbert rose from the deck. "Excuse me, but I must see if there is any damage to anything more important than window glass."

"Yes, yes. Of course. Send Pater López de Palmaroli to me as soon as you can. And send someone to patch Eduardo's cut, before he bleeds on the tablecloth."

"Your command, Admeeral." Colbert hurried out the door into the companionway and onto the deck of the great ship, bellowing questions and orders. Moments later, a surgeon's mate came into the great cabin to see to the cut on Teniente Rosales' cheek. Several minutes later Pater José María López de Palmaroli, Havre's personal chaplain, entered.

"Yes, My Lord?" he asked.

"What was that, Pater?" The Admeeral brushed glass off his chair and sat down. "More things falling from the sky or something else?"

"You need to come on the deck to see something important, My Lord. Something amazing and terrifying has happened. Please, My Lord." He held out the Admeeral's fore-and-aft peaked hat.

"This had better be good, Pater," he growled. He jammed his hat on his head and followed the priest on deck. There the priest led the Admeeral onto the raised poop deck and pointed east. A rising, mushroom shaped cloud loomed in the distance.

"I believe that was Du Khamps des SouSee, My Lord. Something fell to earth and destroyed it, that is my belief." He watched as the Admeeral went pale at sight of the cloud. A sudden gust of wind shook the big ship, heeling her slightly to starboard due to the force of the changing winds.

"Nom de Dieu."

"Yes, My Lord. The very hand of God. Or so it is my belief." He paused a moment, then continued. "The things which shrieked westward over our vessel, those were more objects falling from the sky. I believe they might have struck the Kolbian fleet to our west. If they did — and the sailors aloft reported rumbles of thunder to the west, thunder like explosions — well. The Kolbian fleet may have sustained serious damage, perhaps even losing ships. They will be in great disarray. We all know war with Kolbia is coming. We should strike now, with the God-given chance to destroy a significant portion of their fleet." He watched the color come back into the Admeeral's face. "You would be a hero to the Empire... and to the God."

KRN *Fearless* (110)
Southern Lanic Ocean
February 1479, Third Age of Imperial Reckoning

"How bad is it, Captain Belford?" Commander Andre Savalas asked. Savalas was *Fearless'* First Lieutenant and the only other surviving ship's officer.

"As bad as it can get. We're dismasted and holed at the waterline. The surviving Carpenter's Mates fothered a sail over the biggest hole but we're still taking on water. In fact, Andre, we're sinking, slowly, but we're sinking. The Admiral?"

"The Surgeon just lost him. His entire staff was on the quarterdeck when those...things hit us. He was the only survivor and now he's gone. You're in command of the fleet now, Captain."

"God, what were those things? Never mind, pointless question." Belford interrupted Savalas before he could answer. "If I'm in command of the task force now, I need to transfer to *Insurgent*. Despite losing her foretopmast, she's in better shape than poor *Fearless* is. Make signal to *Wing* and *Insurgent* to come alongside and prepare to take off our surviving crewmen. With how bad we were hit, there should be plenty of room between the two of them."

"Aye-aye, sir. I'll see to it myself."

"You'll have to, Andre. We only survived because we were below decks when those things hit us. The only other officer left is the Surgeon and he's laboring like a giant to save as many as he can." Belford sighed to himself. "We even lost all the midshipmen; they were on the quarterdeck for a navigation class." Belford clenched his eyes shut. He could not afford tears now. "Go get that signal rigged, Andre."

"Yes, sir." Savalas started to reach out to touch his Captain's shoulder, then stopped and turned away, his voice rough as he called a party of sailors to rig the signals.

"God only knows how hard the task groups were hit. Are we all that's left?" Belford spoke quietly to himself as he stood next to the shattered stump of the mainmast.

KRN *Repulse* (44)
Southern Lanic Ocean
February 1479, Third Age of Imperial Reckoning

"Any idea what those things were, sir? There must have been a couple hundred of them screaming through the sky." Lieutenant Franklin Hopkins stood slightly behind the Captain of KRN *Repulse*.

"I don't know, Franklin, but somehow, I think those were weapons of some exotic type, not the usual things falling randomly from space. We heard the explosions to the west of us, and I'm afraid the main force may have been hit by them. If, and that's a big if, they hit the main force, they could be in trouble, maybe big trouble." Captain Michael Williamson stared off to the west, wishing he could see over the horizon. "I want to bring us about to a west-northwest course and signal *Resolution* and *Swiftsure* to conform to our course change. I want to get back in touch with the Main Force. I've got a bad feeling about this."

"Aye-aye, Captain." Hopkins headed forward, ordering the signals midshipman to round up his signals party.

"Helm, make your course west by northwest. Bosun, call the hands to station for handling the sails." The bosun's whistle blew the call to sail stations as the big frigate prepared to come about onto her new course.

KRN *Renown* (44)
Southern Lanic Ocean
February 1479, Third Age of Imperial Reckoning

"Signal from *Insistent*, Captain. She reports very many sails in sight, due east, sails only, estimated range on twenty miles or more, sir." First Lieutenant Ellison Hanks reported to KRN *Renown's* commander, Captain Troy Logsdon.

"Many sails *east* of us. That can only mean the Empire's Lanic fleet is at sea." Logsdon took a quick turn around the quarterdeck, deep in thought. "And then there were those things in the sky, something or rather, somethings falling from space, bearing east to west. And that mushroom cloud near or on Du Khamps. If those things hit the Main Force or any of the more westerly Task Groups, well, we may have a bad problem on our hands. Bring us about, Ellison, course due west. Signal *Insistent* and *Audacious* to do so as well. If the Empire is at sea in force, we need to get our strength collected into a whole fleet. Just in case the Empire's commander is particularly stupid today. Let's be about it."

"Aye-aye, Captain."

"Send a midshipman aloft with a good glass. See if he can get a sight on these 'many sails to the east' or any of our task groups west of us. I'm certain we're the furthest east of any of our other groups."

"Aye, sir." Hanks turned and told off the senior midshipman, one Ken Clark. "Clark, get the number one glass and go see what can be seen from at least the main t'gallant crosstree, the royals if you're up to it."

"Aye-aye sir. Royals it'll be." Clark disappeared below deck long enough to grab the number one glass, then scampered straight up the mainmast.

"Wonder what he'll report, sir."

"I expect that the Imperial fleet is at sea. And in these light winds, with their oars, they may be the faster of us. Not good, Lieutenant, not good at all. *Insistent* can outrun them, but unless the wind picks up, they might be able to catch us and *Audacious*. And if they are at sea in full force, we might be the first line in the war we've been dreading and expecting for twenty years. So, no, not good at all."

Chapter Thirteen

**Armed Sloop *Graser* (6)
Southern Lanic Ocean
February 1479, Third Age of Imperial Reckoning**

SACHI STOPPED DEAD WHEN she realized she was alone on the island. She didn't panic, exactly, but the bracers on each arm flowed into a pair of butterfly swords in each hand. She dropped into a ready stance.

"Sahla? Willis? Silaqui?" she pitched her voice just loud enough to carry a few feet. "Aylie? Gelman? Where are you all?" Then she realized who or rather what was waiting for her, its white coat gleaming and all nine tails slowly waving. The *Kyubi no Kitsune* sat calmly in the shade of the lone tree, a few feet from the pool of clear water.

Her swords flowed back into bracers; she walked over to the *Kitsune* and executed a deeply respectful bow.

"Sit, child." The *Kitsune* nodded her head at a spot on the sand in the shade of the tree.

"Yes, Mistress."

"There is a brief time here where the machine mind is not aware of what passes in your life or mind. I shall, then, begin teaching you how to conceal your thoughts from that entity. There shall be some difficulty in mastering this ability; therefore, when we finish this lesson, I shall again block your memory of what passes here away from your conscious recall. But soon, I believe, you will master this skill and have full memory of our lessons. Now, let us begin."

"Wait, Mistress, a question first." Anxiousness tinged Sachi's voice.

"Yes, child?"

"You know the Bond between me and Sahla?"

"Yes."

"Is it true? Has it changed like I...like we think it has?"

"The answer there is yes, it has. At least for the moment. It can change further or even be broken. But being in love is good for you, child. Despite what the Odas taught you and did to you, you can love and be loved in return. Have no doubt in Sahla's heart...or in your own heart. Now pay attention. To block the machine mind from yours, you must be extremely focused..."

Later Sachi swore days passed while the *Kitsune* taught her mental disciplines beyond anything she had ever imagined. Disciplines bordering on being magical. Disciplines to isolate a part of herself from D.A.V.E., both thoughts and memories.

***

Sahla gasped when she stepped onto the white sand beach and realized she was completely alone. For a moment, she nearly panicked, then she saw she was not alone. Someone waited for her, standing in the shade of the tree. Someone she had never thought to see again in this life.

"Khalid? Is that truly you? Do you yet live? Are you not in Paradise?" She took a hesitant step toward him.

"Yes, Sahla, it is me. I live here but only in spirit for a brief while. But I am only here as a teacher and advisor and only by the Grace of Chalta and his Prophet. And to be in your presence again is a small piece of Paradise." He held out his arms.

"Oh, my true *Faris*, my Knight." She flew across the distance and fell into his embrace. "I thought you slain by the pirates."

"Sahla, I was. I died defending you, but the Prophet had decreed that you must pass through fire and flame to find your destiny...and your True Love." He bent his head down to smell the sweet scent of Sahla's ebon hair. "This is only a brief moment before my shade must return to Paradise." He ran his hand up her back to her neck and felt the scar there. "You are injured?"

"No, Khalid, I am crippled. I was stabbed from behind and were it not for Gelman, a healing priest of the infidels' One God of the Circled Cross, I would have died on the cobblestones of that street. How do you not know this?"

"The Prophet, Chalta bless his name, only allowed me to be here. He did not tell me aught of what has befallen you since the pirates took you. You say you are crippled, but you glow with happiness. You have found your Bonded One. A happy Bond, I see."

"Oh yes," Sahla stepped away from Khalid, still holding his hand. "It was Master to Slave at first, but I knew even then it would be True Love. I have found my heartmate, and I shall spend the rest of my days happily in her arms, now that the Bond has changed."

"Hmm, 'her arms'?" Khalid rubbed his chin with his free hand. "A woman?"

"Yes, a young woman, much like me. She released my full powers as a Jann, and she has a powerful and magnificent destiny. One to save the very World from destruction."

"A young woman, eh. What would your Father say?"

"Father would bless our union, I believe. He knew my destiny lay beyond the strictures of the Folk of the Sands and even beyond the Laws of the Book of Holies." She released his hand, and a shadow of worry crossed her beautiful face. "At least it is my hope that he would, and not order me lashed and driven into the desert."

"You are happy with this woman?"

"Yes, deliriously so. And I will proclaim my love before Chalta and the Prophet himself." She turned to him, her body indicating her pensive worry that Khalid would reject her because of her love for Sachi. "And I am a Jann and therefore beyond the Laws of the People of the Book."

"I see." Khalid rubbed his chin again. "Well, I have learned that the People's reading of the Laws of the Book may be overly rigid. Neither Chalta nor the Prophet will curse you for being what you are or for loving where you will."

"Khalid?" she asked after a long moment. "You say you are here as a spirit? Spirits have many abilities and powers, or so it is taught. Can you heal me?"

"No, I cannot, fair one. I was given this time only to rest your heart of me and to teach you a few things. Things of the World the Prophet would have you know. Perhaps things you already have some inkling of. Of powers that move against you and your love. So, bide a bit and listen while I tell you of things neither of us ever dreamed about."

What seemed like hours or maybe days passed while Khalid taught her of the beginnings of the conflict in which she now had a part to play. He also told her what she could, and more importantly, could not share with her companions.

"And lastly, Sahla, I know you will be healed to full life but not the way of it. But you shall be full and whole once more." He stood from where they had been sitting, tailor fashion, beside the pool. "Now we are come to the end of my time here. Sahla..." he paused.

"Yes, Khalid?"

"In life I had hoped I would have been the one to ask your Father for your hand in marriage and would have freed your powers. But it was not to be. Not our fate. Do you know what happened to the traitor I will not name?"

"I killed him, Khalid. I shot him through the head." She stepped toward him, nearly touching his chest. "It was the only revenge I could give you and no less than he deserved." Her magic lifted her feet from the ground, bringing her eyes level with his. "And one last thing before we part for the last time in this life."

She threw her arms around him and kissed him with all the passion she had. He responded in kind and that kiss lasted an eternity. At last, they separated, and Khalid began to slowly fade away.

"I loved you, Khalid, my knight," she cried out. "I always did."

"And I loved and still love you, my Sahla. Be happy with Sachi, your True Love. Farewell." And he was gone.

Sahla cast herself upon the sand and wept tears enough to fill the clear, blue waters of the pool.

***

Silaqui wasn't particularly surprised that she was alone when she stepped off the jetty and onto the white sand beach. She *was* surprised at the identity of the entity awaiting her in the shade of the tree. The Goddess Ainaera was Silaqui's chosen patron deity. She walked calmly across the sand and knelt before the Goddess of Love and Beauty.

"My Lady, you honor me beyond reason. How may your humble worshiper serve you?" Silaqui's head was bowed and there was a catch in her voice. Once before the Goddess had used her as an avatar aboard the *Intrepid* to deliver a message to Captain William Blaine, a message about Sachi.

"Rise, Silaqui." The voice of the Goddess was nearly silent but echoed across the island. "I am well pleased with you, my worshiper. There are many things I must tell you and questions you must answer. And no doubt you will have questions for me as well."

"Yes, My Lady."

They walked further into the shade of the tree, Silaqui following in the Goddess' footsteps. Ainaera waved a hand, and comfortable chairs rose out of the sand. She sat in the one next to the trunk of the tree and motioned Silaqui to the other.

"First, I must warn you of the machine mind that whispers in Sachi's mind. It is not what it pretends to be, not at all."

"I understand, My Lady. Willis spoke to me of a warning he saw in the ancient tower-machine. But the warning only said that this thing, this D.A.V.E., is not what it seems. Can it be destroyed...without killing Sachi, my Elf-friend and Defender?"

"No, it must not be destroyed. It is needful to save our world." Ainaera's voice was soft and sad. "It is what it will most likely attempt to do after the World is saved and it is at the height of its power. It is a thing of cold logic and does not see a place for magic, for wonder, for faith, or even for love. That is when it must be resisted with all your strength. *Sachi* must resist it herself. If she does not, no one, not even the most powerful deities, can foresee the calamity that might befall all speaking creatures. It is certain that the world as we know it will be no more."

"So, the fate of our world, as it exists, depends on an emotionally damaged young woman not yet twenty-one seasons of age, My Lady?" Silaqui asked.

"It does, which is why she *must* be supported by her loving companions, even that grumpy priest of the humans' One God of the Circled Cross."

"I understand."

"And there are mortal forces arrayed against her as well. Insane ones who wish the world to be destroyed so that they might be caught up to a higher plane. They are deceived and delusional, but deadly dangerous foes, nonetheless. And they have access to much of the humans' tech-nol-ogy. Things as old or older than the Fire Fall itself. Even here, there is not time to explain millennia of history to you. But know this, anyone with eyes as black as Sachi's eyes will be one to be trusted. They are ancient beyond belief, these black-eyed beings. But even there, there may be a traitor."

"Yes, My Lady."

"Now, ask your questions, my child, and I shall answer them as I may."

They spoke for hours it seemed, until the Goddess rose from her seat and led Silaqui to the edge of the jetty.

"Our time here is ended, young one. Think carefully on what you have learned here. Be careful speaking of many of these things where the machine mind may hear. It is not evil as we know evil, but it is at cross purposes with all we are and is utterly remorseless. But in the end, it is wrong, horribly so, but not purely evil. It will save the world. As I said, it is afterwards that it must be feared."

"I shall do so, My Lady." Silaqui bowed deeply. When she rose from the bow, the Goddess grasped her gently on her shoulders and kissed her on her forehead.

"Now go, my beautiful one, with my kiss of Love and Beauty. Goodbye." The Goddess vanished as Silaqui stepped onto the white planks of the jetty.

***

Gelman stumbled as he stepped off the jetty onto the white sand of the beach. He barely realized that he was alone when he saw the angelic being awaiting him under the tree.

"*Angaelici Benes Eloi,*" he barely breathed, regaining his equilibrium as he hurried across the sand to kneel before the angel. "How may I serve you, *Angaelici*?"

"*Gelman, you are a true and faithful priest of the One God. You are devoted in your adherence to the teachings of the Book. However...ah, Gelman, tell me where is the supposed center of authority in the Kythal Church?*"

"The High Kythal of the Holy Kythal Church of the One God of the Circled Cross is in Lietela the City, *Angaelici.*"

"*And do your brethren in the Montagaran Church follow his decrees faithfully?*"

"No." Gelman sighed deeply. "They, no, *we*, do not. We are not the Purists who reject the authority of the High Kythal, but if we slavishly followed his decrees, Montagar would go up in a bloody religious war, one the Purists would likely win. My brethren and I do our best to remain faithful to the High Kythal while quietly ignoring the more, ah, *questionable* of his decrees. The reality of the world overcoming the ideal of a true, spiritual life."

"*Are not his decrees within the bounds of the Holy Book of the One God of the Circled Cross?*"

"Not...always, My Lord. The spite and hatred towards the Kolbians is...excessively virulent. Nowhere in the Book is it said that a people entire should be exterminated root and branch by fire and the sword simply because they disagree with the High Kythal. As the Kolbians do."

"*Do you think the Kolbians* should *be destroyed, Gelman?*"

"Certainly not, My Lord! They may be in error against the Book and even the God, but they do not deserve destruction. At most a Mission to try and convince them of the errors of their ways." Another sigh. "But we cannot even convince the Purists in

Montagar to once more accept the authority of the High Kythal. What chance have we with the Kolbians?"

"*Indeed. And do you take the Holy Book as written by the Inspiration of Divine Revelation?*"

"The Doctrine of the Church states that it is so. Is that false, My Lord?"

"*Not entirely so. The Holy Book is divine inspiration but not due to Divine Revelation. It is written by the hand of Man and more than once it has been rewritten by the hand of men, men with an agenda. And then it is interpreted by man, one often with their own agenda. Many things in the Book are less than Divine Truth, Gelman.*"

"I fear I am about to be chastised, My Lord, for excessive zealotry." Gelman bowed his head and his shoulders slumped.

"*Only very lightly, my good Gelman, very lightly indeed. You see the relationship between the young women, Sachi and Sahla, as wrong and shameful, do you not?*"

"Is it not, My Lord? A union between mortals is to be fruitful and bring forth children, and such a union as is between like sexes cannot do so. It can only be for the pleasures of the flesh, a conceit both the Book and the High Kythal speak against."

"*And it is one of the things that has changed in the Book over the centuries, Gelman. Certainly, same sex unions are barren, but that does not make them shameful nor evil. And the union between Sachi and Sahla is needful to save the World entire. At the end, only the most powerful of loves will see that decisive day through to success. Love is the Key and the Answer, Gelman. And that includes your ability to love. You do not have to love the union between the twain of them, but you must love them.*"

"I see, My Lord." Once again, the deep sigh. "I shall take to heart what you have told me, but it goes strongly against all my beliefs. I will be more accepting of them even as I silently grind my teeth."

"*Excellent, Gelman. Simply remember that love will be the key to saving the world. And now our time here has run its course, and you must return to the world of the real. Farewell, my blessed priest.*"

Gelman found himself standing at the beginning of the jetty. With a final sigh and a grumbled oath, he turned and set foot on the white boards.

***

Aylie stood frozen in shock as she realized she was alone. Quickly she stepped back onto the jetty, or at least attempted to do so. No matter what she did, she stood on the white sand beach. She tried calling out to her friends and companions, but silence was her only answer. Then she realized there was a door standing by itself under the tree.

"Oi, whut's this? A door? Ta where?" She walked around the door. Only one side had a doorknob. She opened the door and stopped dead when she saw what it opened onto and who was settled in a comfortable chair with a cup of tea.

"Come in and close the door, Aylie. And close your mouth as well. Very unbecoming to stand there gaping at me." Lady Elise, Her Grace, the Duchess of Southdon sipped her tea. "Sit down and pour yourself a cup of tea. It is Kolbian Gold Leaf, a very excellent and expensive leaf. Do not let it get cold."

"Yes, Milady." Numb and nearly speechless, Aylie stepped into the room, closing the door behind her. Mechanically she poured herself a cup of tea, added her usual one cube of sugar to it and sat gingerly on the edge of the only straight-backed chair in the comfortably appointed sitting room. She took a sip of tea and then burst into tears, spilling the rest of the tea on herself. "Milady, yer dead! I closed yer eyes me ownself. How can ye be here?" she wailed in grief.

"Oh, Aylie, come here, dear child." She held out her arms and Aylie rushed into her embrace. "Aylie, Aylie, you know there is more to life than just our daily life. My spirit lives on past my body and greater powers decided I needed to be here, now, to speak with you." She pulled a lace handkerchief out of her sleeve and gently wiped away Aylie's tears. "If for no other reason than to remind you of the proper use of language. 'Yer,' and 'ownself?' Indeed! You were taught better than that, Aylie."

"The only thing I can say, Milady, is that I have fallen in with sketchy companions. I shall endeavor to remember proper speech.

In your memory, if for no other reason." Aylie took a deep breath. "But why are ye...you here at all?"

"Higher powers are watching your friend Sachi very closely. She holds the fate of the whole world in her hands. You know this now, do you not?"

"Yes, Milady."

"And you know of the thing that whispers in her mind and is slowly changing her?"

"Somewhat, yes, Milady. I know of it but do not understand it. Not how it changes her."

"That thing is needful for Sachi to accomplish her mission to save the world. But afterwards, assuming she succeeds and there is an afterwards, the thing will be a deadly danger to our world. Not to destroy it but to utterly change it."

"Utterly change the world? How can the voice in her mind do that?"

"I only know that *if* Sachi and this thing succeed in destroying the thing that threatens to destroy the world entire, it will have, for a brief time, access to the kind of power that originally created this world. It could *change* our world into a place lacking in magic and love. The things that make our world a place of such things as dragons and unicorns and elves and magic itself. A world only of cold logic, without any emotions at all. A horrible world to live in for all thinking beings. And only humans would be left. A sadder world without magic or love."

"Milady, a 'world witou...without magic or love.' That would be a terrible thing." Aylie was pale with shock at the Duchess' description of what could happen. "And how does...do we stop it?"

"Through love, Aylie, your love for your friends, especially Sachi." She paused. "Do you dislike or disapprove of the relationship...the love between Sachi and Sahla?"

"Nay, milady. Those two truly have the glimmer for only each other. What concern 'tis it of mine about either of them or who they decide to love?" Aylie bit her lip in concern and then continued. "Gelman, now, I know he disapproves strongly of them loving each other, especially physical love."

"A priest such as him would disapprove strongly of them, would he not?"

"Aye, milady."

"Gelman is your own dear friend. You should advise him that the love between Sachi and Sahla is a necessary thing, needful to hopefully save the world."

"Aye, milady. I'll see if I can bend him 'round to seeing that love as an essential thing to saving the world."

"Excellent." The Duchess took the final sip of her tea. "Finish your tea, Aylie. Our time here draws to a close and you must return to your own, real, world and not linger in this place of magic and spirits. And I must return to my dear husband's side."

"Aye, milady." Aylie swallowed the last dregs of her tea, the little that hadn't spilled, and rose from the chair. "I miss you, milady, most dreadfully."

"And I miss you as well, Aylie." She rose from her seat and held out her arms to Aylie for a final embrace. Tears streaming down her face, Aylie stepped into that embrace, hugging the Duchess hard. As hard as the Duchess hugged her in return. The taller woman bent her neck and kissed Aylie's forehead. "Now, my dearest Aylie, you simply must go." She led Aylie to the door. "You must open the door; I am not allowed to do so."

Aylie opened the door and looked over her shoulder at the Duchess, then stepped through the door. It closed behind her, and suddenly Aylie was alone on the white sand beach. The door had vanished. Aylie went to her knees, then prone, tearing sobs coming as a new sense of loss swept over her again.

I could nay take the time to weep for My Lady when I fled her home. Now I've all the time in the world to mourn her. To mourn them. To mourn my loss. Oh, milady!

She wept until she couldn't weep anymore. At last, the tears and sobs stopped, and she rose to her feet and walked to the white jetty.

***

Willis stopped dead as he stepped onto the white sand of the beach. His hands automatically dropped to his holstered pistols—pistols that, with their belt and holsters, had been left on board the *Graser.* He turned to run but could not step onto the jetty. Frustrated, he turned to face the monster.

An enormous silver dragon curled around the lone tree and over halfway around the pool. Its huge wings folded neatly against its sides and its tremendous head lay on crossed forelimbs. A head three times taller than Willis himself was tall. Glittering silver pupils narrowed into a reptilian slit as Willis finally stopped and stood his ground.

"Fine!" he shouted. "Go ahead and eat me and be done with it. I hope you choke on me."

"Eat you?" the dragon rumbled. "Why in the world would I do that?" A reverberating laugh. "And I would not choke on you even if I did eat you. I chew my food thoroughly." The great head lifted, and a taloned forefoot beckoned. "Come here, Willis Fleet, there are things we must discuss. And little time in which to do so. Come."

Willis stood his ground, frozen in the grip of dragon-dread. It took every ounce of his not inconsiderable grit and courage to simply stand there and hold his ground. Part of him wanted to flee over the horizon. Another part wanted to beg for mercy. But, despite everything, he held his ground. Years later, he said it was the bravest thing he'd ever done.

He'd poo-pooed and laughed at old sailors and storytellers who weaved stories of dragons and their magics, their dreadful splendor and their innate majesty. Now he knew those stories were naught but terrible truth.

"Ah, I see. You Kolbians and your lack of faith, your disbelief of all things beyond your sad, mundane, mortal world." It sighed, smoke gusting from its nostrils. "Very well, perhaps a more...familiar form would ease your concerns and release you from the dragon-dread." The dragon blurred into an immense silver cloud. The cloud intensified and shrank into an oblong shape no taller than Willis. It slowly took on a humanoid shape. The smoke coalesced into a female shape, finally solidifying as a stunningly beautiful human woman with silver hair, pearlescent skin and vertically slit, silver irises. Initially she was nude but the last of the smoke twisted into a diaphanous robe of cloth-of-silver. "Is this better now, or are you now speechless for another reason?" She smiled as she teased him.

"Ah, yes, milady, this is much better." Willis shook his head and rubbed his face briskly. "Please, pardon my initial behavior. You were, um...*are* quite a shock to a good, honest, young Kolbian sailor. But the recruiting slogan is 'Join the Navy, See the World and Widen your Horizons.' But you, hmm, you have *widened my horizons* more than I ever expected in this life. Much more. You know my name, but I do not know yours, milady."

"I am known to Men as Lyandiet the Silent One. It is because my flight is like an owl's, unheard and unlooked-for in the night. That is my use-name among mortals and is good enough for now."

"Very well, My Lady Lyandiet, how may I be of service to you?" Willis bowed from the waist, his fingers nearly sweeping the sand.

"For now, come, sit, and listen." A wave of her hand raised a comfortable chair for Willis and a lounging divan for her. She settled into the divan and another wave of the hand produced a low table with crystal goblets and two decanters of wine, one silver and one blue. "Pour, please, Willis, the blue for you and the silver for me. You cannot yet drink dragon-draught and survive."

"I see." Willis poured wine of silver and blue into the goblets, handing the silver one to Lyandiet. He sipped his wine gingerly. "An excellent vintage, milady, clear and potent at once. Now I assume that I am to listen while you speak."

"Indeed. You are a delightful Mortal. Listen while I tell you of the Fall of the Empire of Rolandus five thousand years ago and the twisted, hateful mortals who caused that Fall. Mortals whose descendants and successors would see the World destroyed today."

"Do you know the nature of the threat jeopardizing our world now?" Another sip of wine while he furtively watched her over the rim of the goblet. "The exact nature, that is?"

"No. I sense only a dire danger coming from the void beyond the sky. Why? Do you know?"

"I do. In forty-seven years, a moon, falling from the farthest reaches of space, will utterly destroy our world. Not even memories will be left."

"I see." She paused, goblet halfway to her lips. "A most informed Mortal indeed. Forty-seven years, is it?" She sipped her wine. "And you know this how?"

"A machine of the Ancients showed me, showed us, my companions and I, what was coming and when it would arrive. And how to stop it."

"So, I believe then, that it will be this young woman of your companions, this Sachi, who will play the greatest part in this saving of the world?"

"Yes."

"The threat, the greatest threat I perceive, comes from this Sachi. There will be a point in these events where she and the thing in her mind will be the greatest threat, not to destroy our world but to utterly remake it. Remake it into a world with no use for faith or magic or even love. A world with no place for the Fair Folk, Dwarven stonemasons, or unicorns. Or dragons. Perhaps it would be better to be destroyed, the world shattered into fragments, than to exist in such a cold, loveless world?"

"You're speaking of the thing in her head called D.A.V.E., a Digitally Aware Virtual Entity. It is powerful and secretive. There is a way to foil the thing's ultimate plans, I believe. A way based on True Love, love and faith. Silaqui, an Elvish Sorceress and Sahla al Qasim, a true Jann, have both had dreams, or rather, I think, visions, of how the thing can be thwarted."

"And you believe these dreams and visions, then? You? A Kolbian?"

"I do, milady. I believe in the Bond of True Love between Sachi and Sahla, and in the love we all bear our sometimes-prickly dear friend. Even dour old Gelman loves her, despite himself."

"I see."

"All the dreams or visions, you decide which to call them, they all point to love being the difference in saving our world as it is, rather than its becoming a world of cold logic only." Willis finished his wine. "I have told you all I know, milady. You were going to tell me of the Fall of the Empire of Rolandus, five thousand years ago...?"

The dragon spoke for hours, telling of the Fall of Rolandus, answering Willis' questions as best she could. Finally, she rose from her divan and escorted Willis to the jetty, her hand on his arm. At the jetty, she stopped Willis, her hands on his upper arms.

"We will meet again, Willis Fleet. Until then, remember this." She pulled him to her, meeting his mouth with hers in a surprise kiss that quickly became very passionate. She broke the kiss just as suddenly, spun Willis around, and pushed him onto the jetty. "Remember," she whispered, and Willis stumbled onto the jetty, staggering into a surprised Gelman and only Silaqui kept him from falling. He whirled to look back and saw only the gray haze, no sign of the island.

***

The jetty stretched away into the haze and the white boat waited for them and they all stood surprised. They had arrived back on the jetty at the same moment, Willis stumbling into Gelman before Silaqui caught and steadied him. Tear tracks stained Sahla's and Aylie's cheeks. Gelman still had some of the angel's aura about him and Sachi had a faraway look in her eyes.

Sachi gave a short, sharp shake and turned, reaching for Sahla. Without a word, Sahla collapsed into Sachi's arms, weeping silently as the tall Nisei wrapped the small, golden girl in a warm embrace.

"What is wrong, *Koibito*?" Sachi's voice was soft and warm as she gently held Sahla.

"I will tell you later, *Habiba*. For this moment, simply hold me while I weep. Please?"

"Of course, my *Koibito*." Sachi swept Sahla off her feet and led the way down the jetty, carrying the young Darsälaamic woman to the white boat.

Gelman put a fatherly arm around Aylie and followed them. Willis and Silaqui looked at each other, shrugged, put an arm around each other's waist and brought up the rear. The jetty vanished as they boarded the boat. Silently it turned and headed for the *Graser*. It, too, vanished when the last foot left it.

By the time they all reached the deck, the haze had mostly cleared away, the sandbar on which the ship had grounded dissolved, and the sail luffed and thundered as a fresh wind filled it.

"What course, Captain?" the bosun asked.

"North-northwest, bosun, for a day, looking for any survivors, then due east for Luctini."

"Aye-aye, Captain."

"Take the wheel and the watch, Boats. We are all exhausted."

"Aye, Captain. Ah, Captain, there is something that happened that must have been pure magic. The prisoner, Josef Buckley, he somehow slipped his chains and came up on deck, walking like a man headed up to the gallows. He walked to the rail and climbed up on the bulwark and just stood there." Holland took a deep breath.

"Why didn't anyone try to restrain him and put him back in chains?" Willis thought he knew what was coming.

"We couldn't, sir, none of us could move or even thought to do so." The bosun took a deep breath. "Then a tentacle, a huge one, made of the mist, came out of the haze and wrapped around him. When it lifted him up, he started screaming, howling like a sinner in hell. He tried to get loose but to no avail. The tentacle took him into the haze, and we heard him scream for what seemed like hours, then there was a...well, sir, a *crunching* sound and a portion of the haze, say man sized, about, turned red as blood and then slowly faded away. It was as eerie a thing as I've ever seen in thirty years at sea."

"I see. Come with me, Boats. We must tell Sachi that there is no further need to concern ourselves with Buckley. The gods or the spirits of this place have seen to that."

Chapter Fourteen

Armed Sloop *Graser* (6)
Southern Lanic Ocean
February 1479, Third Age of Imperial Reckoning

"Captain, two days we've held this course and all we've found is dead men and wreckage." Bosun Holland rang the spittoon attached to the binnacle. "Supplies, especially water, are drawing down, sir. We need to head east soon, sir."

"You're right, Boats," Willis sighed. "Bring us about, due east, and make course for Luctini."

"Aye, sir."

***

That night, as the *Graser* sailed east, thunder rumbled far to the west, the thunder of many heavy guns. It was too far away to see the flash of gunfire or even smoke, had it been daytime.

"Sounds to be the guns of one of our frigates, sir. One or more, and perhaps the guns of a sloop of war. Rapid fire but still firing broadsides. The other guns are slower firing but very heavy, the big guns of an Imperial Man-of-War. God's own lot of the buggers, sir." Bosun Holland's voice was hushed, as they listened to the distant cannonade.

"I feel that we should be sailing to join the fight, but we may be over a day away. It'll be over long before we could get there, and what would our pipsqueak broadside add anyway?"

Willis grimaced and turned away from the rail. "Bosun, let's bend our course to the east by southeast. Try and avoid any Imperial entanglements, as might be expected further northwest of us."

"Aye, sir, east by southeast. Given the wind stays steady out of the west, I make it two days to the Gates of the Lanic. After that we should have a week or so sail to Luctini, assuming, sir, that the Traquilidamar Sea is as placid as the name suggests. It's sea I've never sailed."

"I sailed on it once as a passenger aboard the sloop *Charger* when I was a raw ensign, just promoted from midshipman. Assigned to the embassy there for a year as an assistant to the military attaché. Learned all four of the primary Imperial languages well enough to be fluent in them. A year there, then to the language school in Capitol to learn both Han and Nisei. Turns out I have a gift for languages. Graduated number one in my class. Spent six months as Flag Lieutenant to Admiral Franklin at ONI before he retired. Wound up as ONI's 'expert' on the Empire of Isemoto. Been that ever since."

"Quite a career, sir." The bosun pulled a tobacco plug from his pocket, offered it to Willis, who waved a hand in negation, and bit off a large chunk. The plug went back into the pocket. "And now you are the captain of a sloop, small and lightly armed, but still a man-of-war."

"I suppose so, Boats, I suppose so." Willis sighed and stretched, vertebrae in his back popping and cracking. "I'm going to turn in until eight bells in the mid-watch. Gimme about six hours of shut eye. Your ship, Bosun Holland."

"My ship, Cap'n Fleet. Aye, sir."

***

"The Gates of the Lanic, my friends." Willis swept his arms in an expansive gesture. "Pinewall Mountain to the north and the Bramcaster Hills due south. The two peaks are directly on the coast, and twenty-one miles apart. No gun can range across the Gate, so no one has bothered to try and fortify either side. We're in the middle of the channel and it's deep, over a thousand feet to the bottom."

"And you know it's that deep because why?" Aylie asked.

"The longest sounding line on the sloop *Charger* was a thousand feet long. No idea how deep it really is."

"All very nice, Willis, but how long to Luctini?" Sachi's voice was snappish. Sahla's condition was not improving. The Darsälaamic girl spent most of her time in her bunk. Sahla did her best to mitigate Sachi's snappish temperament. The Nisei's concern for her new heartmate was plain to see. She was hoping there would be a healer more powerful than Gelman who would be able to restore what Sahla had lost.

"If the wind holds steady, about five days now," Willis answered her. "You agree, Boats?"

"Aye, sir. If the wind holds."

"Sachi, come with me to your and Sahla's cabin. There are things we need to discuss. About being in Luctini." Willis headed below decks to the nominal captain's cabin, opening the door for Sachi. Sahla woke from a light doze when Sachi entered the cabin.

"Sachi, Willis, is there a problem?" She sat up in her gimbaled bunk. "You look very serious about something."

"There is a serious issue." Willis took the only chair and Sachi sat next to Sahla, putting a protective arm around her. Then Sahla shifted around enough to kiss Sachi. It was a thorough kiss. Willis cleared his throat noisily. "All right, that's enough. Serious business, remember?"

"You say there is a serious issue, Willis Fleet? What is it?" Sahla gave him an impish smile.

"Several actually. The Empire is one of the most intolerant nations in the world. If a priest saw the two of you kissing, he might try to whip up a mob against you. A mob intending to kill both of you. The same thing will apply to Silaqui, her being an elf and a sorceress. The average Imperial man-in-the-street doesn't care that much but all it takes is one fanatical priest or street preacher. And then there's the slavery issue. There are slaves everywhere and there is nothing you can do about that, Sachi. Also, I'll insist that both you two and Silaqui wear full veils and body shrouding cloaks. I don't want to tempt either the fanatic priests or the average slaver-in-the-street. It is winter here even if temperatures are relatively mild. A full cloak will not be at all unusual this time of year."

"You're asking a lot, Willis." Sachi's voice was gruff.

"I know I am. I'm starting with you two because Silaqui is going to pitch a fit at having to hide what she is, oh, God, she might turn me into a frog if she's pissed enough. I'm gonna ask you two to help me with convincing her to hide her identity."

"I doubt she'd go that far, Willis. But she might give you a case of the boils in a tender spot." Sachi relaxed with Sahla's hold on her shoulder.

"Can she do that, really?" The slight quaver in his voice gave away his concern.

"No idea, but I'd not be the one to find out that she can do that."

"You're a lot of help, Sachi," Willis grumbled. "Enough jokes, are you two willing to help me convince her to conceal her identity or not?"

"Of course we will help, Willis," Sahla answered before Sachi could get a word out. Sahla gently poked Sachi in the ribs. "You will help as well, won't you, dear heart?"

"Of course I will, Willis, just to keep this one here happy," Sachi gave Sahla a quick peck on her forehead and stood up. "We'll have to coax her down from her perch on the t'gallant crosstrees first. Come on, let's go beard the mage in her tower." She left the room. Willis started to follow her, then stopped and turned to Sahla.

"How are you, Sahla, really? Don't try to lie to me, okay?" Willis asked.

"The pain is constant, Willis. My right arm is weak and numb, as is my right leg. I don't really walk; I just float along. Any flight more than that and my vision dims. I hate this crippled body, Willis!" Sahla suddenly grimaced. "Sachi refuses to make love with me because the pain was so bad the one time we even tried."

"I'm sorry, Sahla. It's all I can say and it's little comfort, but I am sorry about everything."

"Do not be sorry for me, Willis Fleet. I love and am loved in return. Who could ask for more? Go now, before Sachi wonders where you are. I shall follow shortly."

***

"The great city of Luctini, the economic heart of the Empire of Lietelea. Fortified against both attacks from the land and the sea, the city has never fallen to any enemy. You cannot see it but there is a great chain that blocks the harbor mouth. It takes days to emplace, but once there, no ship can enter or exit the harbor. With the seaward fortifications built on the natural rocky seawall, an amphibious landing and direct attack on the seaward wall is impossible. The towers on each end of the wall are the anchors for the defensive chain and are well supplied with cannon. Old style cannon but a beggar's own lot of them. But they are only manned with lookouts in time of peace. Fortunately for us." Willis pointed to the various fortifications as he identified them.

"Are we here to attack the city or just resupply, let you deliver your diplomatic dispatches and determine our course away from here?" Silaqui's tone was dry as dust. It had taken cajoling by Sachi and Willis and some fast sweet-talking from Sahla to convince the sorceress to agree to going concealed in Luctini. "I have no desire to breathe the air of this place longer than absolutely necessary. I have no love for any Imperial city, much less one as big as this one."

"I feel the same way, Silaqui, if it helps any." Sachi was perched on a coil of rope. "I only hope there is a healer more powerful than Gelman who can restore what Sahla has lost. There's no surety of that, as I've never heard of one more powerful."

"I share your concerns, Sachi, and I hope we can find a healer as well," Gelman spoke up from where he stood next to the binnacle. "I've done all I can for her. She needs someone more capable than I."

"Dinna fash yerse...yourself so, Gelman. You performed a near miracle just saving her life, and that after saving Silaqui and Willis." Aylie caught herself before she slipped back into the vernacular of the streets. She could imagine the look on the Duchess' face if she slipped up again. *I'd not want a tongue lashing again, not from milady. Of course, there be a fair chance I'll need to 'blend in' as it might be. Only Willis would have any hope of gaining any knowledge from those on the ketching lay. The others, hopeless. Mere babes in the woods on the streets.*

***

The *Graser* coasted slowly up to the dock, under a single reefed topsail. At the bosun's orders deck crew on the clewlines and buntlines drew up the sail where the topsmen secured it against the yardarm. Other sailors dropped coarse fenders made of old, worn-out sails tied into squares three feet across and eight inches thick. They gently scraped against the wooden dock as the ship came to rest. Hawsers secured the ship fore and aft to bollards on the dock. The height of the dock and the ship's deck was close enough that a gangplank wasn't needed.

Willis stepped onto the dock to meet the harbormaster and the dockmaster. There was a brief and muted conversation, then Willis handed the harbormaster a small but heavy purse. A lighter purse went to the dockmaster. They both shook hands with Willis and then headed off down the quay to their respective offices.

"Well, Willis, did you guess the *wairo* right?" Sachi asked as he came back aboard.

"What's that mean, Sachi?" Sahla's voice was somewhat muffled by her *niqab's* veil. The garment covered her from head to toe, a robe of lightweight dark blue silk. The color almost matched her eyes.

"What? *Wairo*? It's a bribe, Sahla, paid to the official in charge, in addition to the usurious 'docking fee.' Nothing different from my homeland, except the bribe here is not as large as in Isemoto."

"It was cheap, Sachi. We'd be in trouble if we hadn't looted Ironheart's base. As is, we're doing very well, at least financially." Willis shrugged. "Money is the least of our worries. Getting what we need and getting out of here in one piece is our biggest concern. And then figuring out where to go next."

"We know where to go next. The island marked 'Isedore' in the middle of the Traquilidamar Sea. The holographic map in the tower in Du Khamps showed one of the...planetary defense centers was built there. If anything is left after this long; there may be medical things there that could heal Sahla if magic can't heal her. And we must be wary of Imperial healers. Like Gelman, most are also priests of the God of the Circled Cross. Any healer will immediately know that Sahla is a Jann." Sachi shook her head and rolled her shoulders. She was wearing another of Sahla's *niqabs,* and she didn't like it in the least. She constantly fidgeted with the veil, and given the difference in their height, robes that swept the ground on Sahla were several inches short on Sachi.

"Stop twitching, Sachi, you'll attract attention, the wrong kind of attention here." Silaqui used her magic to conceal that she was an elf. She simply appeared to be a particularly tall human woman, averagely attractive with long, brown hair. She wore long robes and a veil she had conjured from worn-out clothing at the bottom of the slops chest. Other than her height, she appeared very mundane at first or even second sight.

"Easy fer ye to say, Lady Sorceress." Aylie also wore a *niqab* and disliked the thing as much as Sachi did. "Yer cheating, using magic as ye are."

"Aylie, you're backsliding again. Remember what the Duchess said to you about that," Gelman gently chided her.

"Oh, Gelman ye've...you've no need to belabor me about that now." Her eyes crinkled in a smile hidden by her veil. "Now, Willis, the dockmaster said we can only keep a skeleton crew aboard. We need an inn big enough for us and the rest of the crew."

"The bosun and five hands will stay aboard, the rest will have rooms and meals at the Weary Sailor. It's a good dockside inn not far from here at all. You can see it from here." Willis pointed. "And we six will be getting rooms at the Silver Maiden, a very, very comfortable inn. Their taproom can get a bit loud when they have dancing girls on weekend nights. But the sleeping rooms are upstairs and well insulated. The food's borderline great and there's an excellent selection of fine wine and spirits. The inn's stable wall is separated from the Kolbian Embassy wall by only a few feet. Stayed there myself for a year when I was assigned here as an assistant military attaché. A very junior assistant military attaché."

"I see," Sachi said. "Well then, lead on, Willis. First to the Weary Sailor, then to this Silver Maiden Inn. While we get rooms there, you can take your 'dispatches' to the Embassy. See if you can get charts and a course to that island in the middle of the sea."

***

"Willis Fleet! As I live and breathe!" The lady swept out from behind the bar and hurled herself into Willis' arms. "Where have you been all these years?" She was taller than Sahla but not by much. Long red hair in a tight braid went down to the small of her back and green eyes glinted with a devilish amusement.

"Lorelei Garland! As I live and breathe! It's been, what, five years?" Willis wrapped his arms around her and delivered a long, thorough kiss. When they finally came up for air, he released her, and she thumped his chest with a petite fist.

"Five years? You long lout, it's been over six, near to seven years!" She grinned at him as she thumped his chest again. "And now you're armed to the teeth and your friends as well. And it's rude of you not to introduce them!"

"Lorelei Garland, be known to Sachi Takahashi, Sahla al Qasim, Pere Gelman, Aylie Clayton, and Silaqui. My friends, this is Lorelei Garland, owner and operator of the Silver Maiden Inn." A pensive look flashed across her face when she was introduced to Silaqui.

"I see you're in exalted company, Willis. A priest-mage of the God of the Circled Cross and a lady wizard as well. Come, let me get us a private room and then you can tell tales. Aleeta, bring a bottle of the Decennian red, an Imperial year 1650 bottle, to my big office." One of the serving maids behind the bar bobbed a quick curtsey and disappeared through a door behind the bar. "Follow me, please."

***

"I trust the wine meets your standards, Willis?" There were enough seats for everyone between large and small couches, a trio of straight back chairs and the office chair behind Lorelei's desk. Sachi and Sahla had claimed the small sofa and as usual, Willis sat backwards in one of the straight-backed chairs, his arms crossed on the seatback. Aylie was seated on the big couch, while Silaqui and Gelman took the other pair of straight-backed chairs. "A vintage good enough to go with this outlandish tale you've told me." Lorelei leaned back in her desk chair. "Something from space that will destroy the world in forty-seven years if the young lady from Isemoto doesn't stop it, and someone keeps trying to kill her. A bit much to swallow, but I believe you."

"I have a hard time believing it myself, and I've been there through every one of our adventures. And you know what adventures are, I think?"

"Oh yes, being up to your neck in shit, exhausted, hungry and a long way from home while people you don't know are trying their best to kill you. Your story is the very definition of an adventure." Lorelei sighed. "And this is a bad time to be here, Willis. The Palmaroli Clan is in ascendance now and the Inquisition is ascendant with them. I expect at least one Inquisitor to 'inspect' your ship and visit here to ascertain your business here in the city. And there are rumors that war with Kolbia is coming very soon. Given that Admeeral Sieur Havre, Lord Calchas left port with the majority of the Lanic fleet three weeks ago, supposedly to confront a Kolbian Navy fleet in the southern Lanic, well, we could be at war already and just not know it here."

"If I didn't know and love you as much as I do, I would have just given you some trite story about me going to the Embassy and Sahla needing a healer. Nothing more. But you told me your secret when I stayed here and, well, got romantically involved with you. We've been open and honest with you, and I think you should trust us with your secret as well. I assume you still have your escape plans in place for when, not if, but when, the Inquisition finally learns what you are."

"I do, several plans in fact." Lorelei's face was grim. "After all, if you betray me, I can betray you and you still have my trust and love, Willis. I'm what the Inquisition calls a *secretum dryadalis*, a secret elf. I'm half-elven. I look human but I don't age like a human. I'm fifty-seven years old but still look like I'm twenty-something. Even some of my employees are starting to wonder about me. They're all very loyal, but I can't expect them to risk the ire of the Inquisition for my sake."

"Then leave with us, Lorelei. The *Graser* may be just a sloop and very cramped at best of times but aboard her you'd be safe from being put to the Question and the Punishment," Willis said. "Take your portable wealth with you and leave orders with your bankers to transfer the rest to Montagaran banks. From there you could transfer to Kolbian bankers and set yourself up in Kolbia. No one would care if you're a half elf or an orc, as long as you run an honest business. And Kolbian taxes are much lower than Imperial taxes."

"I'll think about it, Willis." There was a discreet knock on the door. "Ah, that means your rooms are ready. I suggest having dinner in your rooms, stay out of sight as much as possible. You have three rooms, one for our young lovebirds over there, and you can decide how you split the other two rooms between you. Both have two beds, theirs has just one very large bed."

"Thank you, Lorelei." Sachi spoke up for the first time. "And do you know of any powerful healers who could heal Sahla, without betraying us to the Inquisition?"

"I know of one; he's trustworthy, hell, he even knows what I am. But he is older, and I don't know if he can do any better than Gelman has. But he is a Kythal priest. I can't say for sure that he would keep your love's secret or not. I believe he would, he's kept mine for over a decade, but I don't know about...Sahla, right?"

"Yes. I am a Jann."

"A Jann, one of the lesser Princes, or in your case, Princess, of Elemental Air, correct?"

"I would not call myself a Princess. I am merely a humble Jann, trying to follow the tenets of the Holy Book. Trying and failing, mostly."

"I see." Lorelei rubbed her chin. "Your Holy Book says nothing good about two females being bound together by True Love. Don't try to deny it; I wasn't born yesterday. It's obvious if one has eyes that can see magic and I have my own minor gifts there. Nothing like you, Lady Silaqui, I have yet to see my first hundred years. No offense intended, my Lady."

"None taken." Silaqui's voice was cool. It was clear that she did not really like the half-elf woman. "And, Willis, shouldn't you be off to your Embassy to deliver your 'dispatches?' The sooner that is done, the sooner we can resupply and leave this uncomfortable place."

"Damn me but you're right, Silaqui. I apologize, everyone. I was distracted by a very old and dear friend, but I must hurry to the Embassy. Even at this late hour, there will be someone at the Operations Desk who can sign in my dispatches." Willis shrugged into his long blue coat, picked up the rather battered satchel that held his dispatches, and hurried out the door.

"I should like to see our rooms, Madam Garland." Silaqui was curt as she rose from her seat. "Our journey has been long and exhausting. I'd like to lie down on a normal bed that isn't moving with the wave motion of a ship for once. Can you recommend a dependable procurer who can quickly resupply our ship? The sooner we can leave the better. I feel that deadly danger awaits us here. We may be bearding the dragon in its den."

***

"Secure courier Lieutenant Commander Willis Fleet reporting to deliver secure dispatches from the Montagaran Embassy. These should go to Commodore Sartell and Envoy Courtenay immediately, or as soon as possible." Since Willis was armed and junior to the officer working the night desk in the Embassy, he rendered a proper hand salute.

Captain (JG) Paul Hannigan returned the salute with a casual wave of his hand in the vicinity of his head. There was a look of distaste on his face as he regarded the salt-stained and battered satchel on the desk. He opened it and pulled out the wax-impregnated cloth bag that enclosed the documents. Using a penknife to cut the sealing stitches away, he pulled out the thick sheaf of papers. Without even looking at the first page, he turned and put them in a tray marked 'Commodore Sartell, Urgent.' He turned back to face Willis.

"Very well, Lieutenant Commander Fleet, sign the logbook here, I sign there to confirm delivery. And your job is finished. Unfortunately, there are no accommodations available for commissioned officers currently. I could offer you a bunk with the senior NCOs, which might suit you, given your disheveled appearance. You look like a pirate. Where is your uniform?" Hannigan didn't quite sneer at Willis, but it was a near thing.

"It's at the bottom of the Southern Lanic, with the wreck of the *Le Bonaventure*."

"I know of that ship. Wrecked, you say?"

"Driven onto the rocks of an uncharted island in a storm. Only my companions and I and the ship's cook survived the wreck."

"Certainly, a tragedy, I'm sure. I suggest you report the loss to the harbormaster. And how did you manage to get here, then?"

"We killed the pirate Ironheart, destroyed his big galleon, and took his sloop as a prize. Registered the sloop *Graser* with the harbormaster when we arrived late this afternoon. Informed him of the loss of *Le Bonaventure* at that time. And I have accommodations at the Silver Maiden next door. I know the owner there." Willis didn't even try to hide his smirk at Hannigan's goggle-eyed stare. "It's been a long day, and I'd like to seek my bunk. Is eight hundred hours still the time for Stand-To here? With your permission, sir." Willis saluted, waited for an even more vague wave in return, executed a smart about-face and marched out of the office, closing the door quietly behind him. He made it all the way out the front gate, past the Marine guards there, before he started laughing.

***

It was late, so he grabbed a quick sandwich and a beer at the bar before heading up to his room. Their little group had taken over the entire fourth floor. There was a suite assigned to Sachi and Sahla, two large double bedrooms and a bathing room on the floor. Willis opened the door into his room and had hung up his jacket and the harness for his pistols before he realized that the two beds had been pushed together to make one big one. And in that bed was the Sorceress Silaqui, wearing nothing but her hair.

"Ah, Silaqui, what are you doing?" He froze, his hands on the laces at the throat of his shirt.

"I'm seducing you. What else would I be doing here, like this?" There was a deep, sensual purr to her voice.

"Ah, well, umm, I see. Where's Gelman? And Aylie?"

"They have separate beds well apart from each other. And neither of them sleeps skyclad as I prefer to do. Do you not find me attractive?"

"Of course I do. You are as beautiful as anyone in your own right."

"Liar." The laugh in her voice took the sting out. "I pale in comparison to either Sachi or Sahla, and you know it."

"Very well, point granted, but *why* are you here now?"

"I am afraid, Willis. I fear this city, these people. Imperials burned one of my cousins alive for the sin of being an elf and a mage. And they slaughtered his human wife and halfelven children for the sin of existing. I am afraid and lonely, and I would like some comfort and the warm touch of a friend. Can you do that for me, at least just this once?"

"I can do that for you, my lady. At least this once. Beyond that, who knows?" He finished loosening the shirt laces. Very quickly the rest of his clothing joined his shirt on the floor, and he sank into Silaqui's embrace.

It was long before they slept, entangled together.

***

Pater Inquisitor Ambroise Dubois de Palmaroli disliked many things and being awake before noon was high on that list. Getting orders from his Inquisitorial superiors to interview the strangers who had arrived on the oddly named sloop *Graser* and to do said interview first thing in the morning was also on that list. His mistress had nonchalantly complained about him leaving the bed just before sunrise and then had promptly gone back to sleep, the wench. All in all, Ambroise was not in a congenial mood as he came to the main door of the Silver Maiden Inn.

Walking into the dining room, the newcomers were immediately obvious. Four women wore *niqabs* with the veils pulled aside so they could eat. There was a man in a long blue coat and, interestingly enough, a Kythal priest, a Montagaran priest from his robes and wooden Circled Cross on a simple leather thong around his neck. An odd bunch. He sighed and headed for their table.

***

Willis and Silaqui were the last ones down to breakfast the next morning. Despite the 'cat who got the canary' look on both their faces, no one said anything. Aylie raised an eyebrow at them, Gelman shook his head and went back to eating his eggs. Sachi and Sahla both had envious smiles on their faces, then Sachi went back to the serious business of fueling her enhanced metabolism. Sahla just sipped her tea, smiling as she watched Sachi work on a heaping stack of pancakes. She'd already eaten half a dozen eggs and a rasher of bacon. Abruptly Sachi stopped eating, getting everyone's attention.

"Trouble coming our way." She nodded her head toward the door and then went back to her food. "An Imperial just came in here, an Inquisitor priest, from the gold 'I' pinned on the shoulder of his robes. I think. At the door."

"There went my good mood," Willis muttered from where he sat facing the door. "Let's see what he wants with us, because here he comes."

The Inquisitor stopped next to the table and gave them a cold look. Gelman stopped eating and nodded to the priest.

"Good morning, Pater, can I help you?" he said.

"Are you from the sloop *Graser*?" The Inquisitor glanced around the table, noting everyone's dress and their faces. His glance came to a sudden stop when he saw Sahla. "You girl, are you Darsälaamic?"

"I am." Sahla set down her tea and drew her veil up and over her face. Now only her sapphire blue eyes could be seen. She peeked at Sachi, who kept her head down, shoveling in her pancakes. "And what would you of me?"

"There have been stories of an Houri from the deep desert, an Houri with sapphire eyes whose ship was taken by pirates. Are you that Houri?"

"I am." Sahla spoke softly, the Inquisitor leaning forward to hear her. "My ship was taken by Ironheart the pirate. He planned to ransom me to either my Lord Father or my husband to be. But, alas, my duenna was slain in the attack, and without her to prove my *purity*, there would be no ransom for me. And my saviors here rescued me before Ironheart could sell me or allow his crew to defile me. So. Yes, I was once known as the Houri of the Sands. I no longer claim that title as I can never return to my home."

"I see," Ambroise said, frowning. "And all of you came on the sloop named *Graser*?"

"We did," Willis spoke up. "I'm Lieutenant Commander Willis Fleet, KRN. The *Graser* is a light auxiliary vessel of the Kolbian Navy. I'm her commanding officer. Very auxiliary."

"And so, why are you here, now, when there are rising tensions between Kolbia and the Empire?"

"I was tasked with delivering dispatches to the Embassy here. That's been done already, tomorrow I'll be getting more recent charts for our next destination, seeing our ship resupplied and victualed, then we'll be back to sea."

"And what is your next destination, Lieutenant Commander Fleet?" Ambroise asked.

"Wherever I get orders for. Probably back to Montagar; I'm a courier there."

"Yet you command your own vessel."

"It's a long, strange tale. I'm sure it would bore you to tears."

"Perhaps. Introduce your companions to me, if you would."

"Certainly. Father Gelman from Montagar, ship's medical officer; Aylie Clayton, midshipman; Silaqui Evans, bosun's mate; Sachi Takahashi, watch officer. And you know our rescue, Sahla al Qasim. My close, personal friends. The rest of the crew are staying at the Weary Sailor, down on dockside. Is that satisfactory, Pater?"

"Entirely. I'll leave you to your breakfast." He turned away, took one step and turned back. "Sachi Takahashi, not a common name at all. Look at me, lass. Where are you from?"

"A long, long way from here. Isemoto, if you must know." Sachi barely glanced up and went immediately back to her pancakes. But the glance was enough that Ambroise saw her eyes.

She has black eyes! There was something said by Vicente Palmaroli at the last family meeting. Something about a person, a girl, one with black eyes. I think I must speak with him about this. I'll see him tomorrow evening. Ambroise gave a polite nod, turned and left.

"That one will be trouble," Silaqui whispered. "I don't like that he singled out Sachi for an extra question."

"He may just be curious. There are damn few Nisei here in the Empire," Gelman spoke up. "He was no spellcaster, I'd have known and so would Silaqui. It would take a powerful mage or empowered cleric to penetrate her guise. And anyone like that would recognize me as a healer-priest. Something even the Imperials tolerate. At least for their higher classes of subjects."

"He is a threat, Gelman." Sachi stopped mopping up the last bits of pancake and syrup and looked at Gelman. "He is deadly dangerous. I should follow and kill him in a dark spot."

"A little extreme there, Sachi? It's broad daylight now." Willis' face was solemnly serious. "Just because he might have seen your face and asked where you are from?"

"Yes, Willis, extreme might be what's needed. We'll regret letting him get away alive." Sachi scooted her chair back and started to get up, until Sahla laid a gently restraining hand on her arm.

"Sachi. Belovéd, he's already gone; you would attract more attention chasing him down. Today, we go to Lorelei's healer to see if he can heal me. Willis will go to his Embassy for whatever they need him for and then, as soon as the ship is resupplied, we leave for the island named Isedore on the charts." Sahla gently drew Sachi back to her chair. "Here, finish my pancakes. I'm full. Wouldn't want it to go to waste, would you?"

Chapter Fifteen

City of Luctini
Empire of Lietelea
March 1479, Third Age of Imperial Reckoning

Lorelei's healer turned out to be a very elderly Kythal priest, living in a small, run-down monastery in one of the poorer districts. He was one of nearly a dozen other clergy and monks who lived there and saw to the needs of that part of the city. A monk met them at the monastery gate and took them to the healer.

"Be welcome and come in, please," the old man said. "Please, sit and be comfortable. I am Iason Vasco, a humble Pere here. I see to the needs of the old and poor here. And sometimes to those who have, in some fashion or the other, run into problems with the City's cumbersome legal system. How may I help you?"

"My name is Wi…"

"No, no names here, I do not want to know who you are or why you are here. Only who needs healing and how they were injured?"

"My Belovéd, she was stabbed in the back, through her spine," Sachi spoke into the awkwardly growing silence. "Our Pere Gel…"

"Remember, no names," the old priest interrupted her. "The One God does not care what your name is or even who you are. If I can, I will heal your Belovéd. This tall man seems unhurt, so…?"

"Ah, Pere, my Belovéd is no man." Sachi hesitated. "My Belovéd is this young woman here. She was stabbed from behind. And is now crippled. She is a dancer who cannot dance now."

"I see, then." The old priest sighed. "So, you admit to committing a grievous sin, one woman loving another woman?" His blue eyes pinned Sachi in place. "Why should I help you sin?"

"Because she cannot dance. And she is Bound to me. A Bond of True Love that keeps my love here on this plane of existence. She is a Jann and must have that Bond, lest she die." There was a grim tension in Sachi's husky voice. "I was told you took little concern in who you heal, and you have said as much yourself. What is the difference between a thief or murderer and a Jann? Both need healing, and you are a powerful healer, I am told. Please, for the sake of love, heal my Belovéd."

"So passionate, young woman." The priest's face was hard for a moment, then a broad grin replaced that grim expression. "I was testing you to see how true your love is. I will do my very best to heal your young Jann here." He motioned to Sahla. "Come, child, lie down on this pallet. Relax and close your eyes and we shall see what this old man can do for you as the One God wills and what strength He gives me."

Later, Willis was never sure how long the healing took. It had been mid-morning when they—himself, Sachi and Sahla—had reached the monastery, and the sun was low in the west when they left. The old priest prayed for hours or possibly only mere minutes, golden light pouring from his hands over Sahla's body. And in the end, they were disappointed.

"I have done all I can, all the One God will give me. Her leg is better, she can walk on it again, but I was not given a full healing, the damage was too severe and has healed as well as it ever will." There was sorrow in the old priest's exhausted voice. "I have been given the knowledge that she will *be* healed, but not by the agency of any god or spirit. I am sorry I have done so little."

"You say she will be healed, somehow?" There was a bitter strain in Sachi's voice as she held Sahla.

"Yes, but I know not where or how. I am sorry."

"Bless you, Pere Iason," Sahla spoke for the first time, "bless you for what you have done and what you have told us. I now know that I will be healed, in due time. May the Prophet always lead you to shade and sweet water."

They left the monastery in twilight's early gloom. Sachi was obviously upset and unhappy, but Sahla sang quietly to herself as she walked slowly beside Sachi.

***

Aylie and Gelman had spent a quiet day at the inn, relaxing in their rooms. Silaqui also stayed in her room, but she was a nervous wreck. She felt trapped in this place, shut away from both the sea and the forest. These people were hostile to her entire race. Even the ordinary person in the street could be quickly incited into a raging mob, willing to see any nonhuman, such as Silaqui, tortured and burned to death. And they had the same intolerance for any who could wield magic. Silaqui was doubly at risk as both Elf and Sorceress.

She convinced Gelman and Aylie that they should keep to their rooms and avoid any unnecessary contact with even the Inn's staff. She knew the owner of the Silver Maiden was a half elf, but she didn't think that many of the Inn's staff knew that. If any of them knew and did not report it to the Inquisition, they would be in danger of facing the Question and the Punishment themselves. For once Silaqui wanted to flee onto the *Graser* and sail away, leaving everyone behind. Only her will, the polished and focused Will of a Mistress Major of the Art of Magic, kept her in place, waiting for her beloved friends to flee this horrid place.

***

The walls of Luctini had four gates and four bridges at those gates. The bridges spanned the River Luc, the river that gave the city its name. Running wide and fast, the deep river split around the walls of Luctini, turning the City into an island, one separated from the rest of the Empire by several hundred feet.

But the walls and the river made Luctini very crowded. The only place to go when building a new structure or adding to an existing one was up. Even the cheapest slum town neighborhoods' buildings still raised themselves three, four and even five stories above the streets. The shadows the buildings cast blocked out the sun except at high noon.

Lower Luctini was a hot, crowded warren of tenements leaning against each other to stay upright in most places, while Upper Luctini had large, open areas, made parklike by thick, green grass and a few tall old oaks. The Lords of Luctini had their large, airy homes and palaces there.

And over everything brooded the Lord's Keep. Within the Keep's walls was the Lord Governor's Palace and the High Basilica of the Archbishop of the City and Province of Geullia.

***

Ambroise had not liked being woken before sunrise to go interview some simple sailors, Kolbian sailors, but just sailors. Well, there was the Darsälaamic girl and the other one, the one named Takahashi. She-chi Takahashi or something like that. Still, what importance could they have in the grand scheme of things?

I'll tell Vicente at the revelry tomorrow night, or maybe the day after. There was no need to drag me out of bed before dawn. And what matter anyway, they're just sailors, they'll probably be gone on tomorrow's tide. I'll tell him the day after the revelry. That's when I'll tell him, after the noon service the day after tomorrow. Serve him right, sending an underpriest to beat on my door that early. He can wait.

***

Willis was surprised to see a Kolbian officer's uniform in the taproom of the Silver Maiden when he went in there after delivering Sachi and Sahla to their room. Sahla had whispered to him that she was going to try to seduce Sachi once they had washed off the day's sweat. Willis decided he would be best off being somewhere else in case things didn't go well. Sachi was stretched as tight as a bow string. And a highly stressed Sachi could be very unpredictable.

The Ensign popped to his feet when he saw Willis enter the taproom in the mirror behind the bar. He immediately headed straight for Willis and just barely managed to not render a salute.

"Lieutenant Commander Fleet, sir?" he asked. He was obviously nervous.

"Of course, Ensign...?" *God, was I ever this green?*

"McMillan, sir, Ethan McMillan. Class of 77."

"And what can I do for you, Ensign McMillan?" *Must have been a sharp kid to get a first assignment to a diplomatic mission. Not ONI, I think. Why so nervous?*

"Sir, I am directed to inform you that you are ordered to report to Rear Admiral Sartell at your earliest convenience." He managed to deliver his message in one clean breath. Willis hid a smile as he watched the tension drain out of the young man.

"Order received, Ensign. Siddown and have a beer. As late as it is, you should be off duty now, and the sun is over the yardarm somewhere." Willis pointed at a table and waved at a barmaid for a pair of beers. "Nice to know that Commodore Sartell finally got his Admiral's streamer. Sit down, I said. This late after hours the Admiral might have already turned in. I'll see him first thing in the morning, so relax and loosen your tie."

"Sir, with all due respect, I believe the Admiral meant, 'Immediately, if not sooner.' I don't think you should wait until morning." The nervousness was back.

"Were you directed to report back to the Admiral immediately? Right after you delivered your message?"

"No, sir."

"Good, then morning will be fine. Now park it and have a beer and some chips." Willis gave McMillan a tooth-hidden smile and pointed at a chair. The barmaid was bringing a pair of beer steins and a bowl of chips to the indicated table.

Willis had just gotten McMillan settled with the bowl of chips and his beer when the door to the taproom opened and Irene du Buisson barged in, obviously looking for him. She spotted him and hurried to the table. She didn't quite come to attention, but she was obviously agitated. Willis interrupted her before she could speak.

"Siddown, Irene, and relax. A message from the bosun, no doubt. But take a seat, calm down, lemme get you a beer." He waved at the barmaid. Irene sat down with a curious look at the Ensign. "Don't worry, Irene, he's from the Embassy and will be leaving, just as soon as he finishes *his* beer. Right, Ensign McMillan?"

"Yes, sir," McMillan took a huge gulp of beer and nearly choked on it. He managed to swallow it and finished his drink in two more gulps of nearly heroic proportions. "By your leave, sir?" He stood up from the table and almost tripped over his chair.

"Go on, Ensign McMillan, scat." Willis smiled as McMillan vanished like smoke in a high wind. The barmaid arrived with a beer for Irene. She quickly took a drink, grabbed some chips and made very short work of them. "Now, Irene, what's the bosun's message?"

"The bosun got in good with the locals who keep a lookout at the seagate towers at the harbor entrance. He just got word from them that a Kolbian frigate or sloop of war is on the approaches to the seagate. She should arrive in the harbor first thing in the morning, he said that was what they told him. Maybe earlier if the sea wind freshens."

"Well, that's news for sure. The lookouts tell him anything else?"

"Yes, they said she's flying a red streamer on the foremast." She ate a few more chips and washed them down with another drink. "That mean anything to you, sir?"

"Yes, a red streamer on the foremast has a meaning I'll not mention in here. Go back to the ship and tell the bosun to hurry up with the resupply and be ready to cast off on the noon tide." Willis finished his beer and stood up, casting a generous handful of coins on the table for payment and the tip. "Hurry, Irene, it's important we be ready to sail as soon as possible." Willis headed upstairs as Irene headed for the outside door.

***

"You are still in too much pain, Sahla. Trying to make love together only makes it hurt worse. I just can't see you in that much pain. I can't stand it, you hurting that much." Sachi held Sahla in her arms. The pair were spooned together, Sahla's back to Sachi's front. Neither of them had on a stitch of clothing. There were tears of pain on Sahla's face.

"I had hoped that the healing he did would allow us to love together at last, but I can walk again." Sahla hid her tears from Sachi.

"Yes, you can walk." Bitterness filled Sachi's voice. "Slowly and in great pain, but yes, you can walk after a fashion. You still can't dance." The abrupt knock on the door startled them both.

***

"Sachi, Sahla, get dressed. We need to use your suite's sitting room to hold a meeting for all of us. I have important news we must discuss."

Willis figured neither one of them had a stitch on. He knew they preferred skin on skin whenever they were alone. Sachi had burned his ears the one time he had walked in on them in the big cabin on board the *Graser*.

***

"There's a Kolbian man-of-war on the approach to the harbor, a frigate or a sloop-of-war. She's flying a red streamer from her foremast. That means she carries a war warning. Given what we saw in the Southern Lanic, it's a pretty sure bet that Kolbia is at war with the Empire. Slow communication is the only reason neither the locals nor Kolbia are aware of it. We saw the Imperial fleet at sea, and we know the Kolbian task groups got hit hard by the crowbar attack. I doubt they were in shape to deal with a concentrated Imperial fleet on the offensive." Willis perched on the edge of a desk in the sitting room of Sachi and Sahla's suite. Everyone else occupied the large couch or two very comfortable chairs.

"What does this mean for us, Willis?" Aylie asked.

"I was going to suggest we leave tomorrow on the noon tide but—"

"Yes, leave immediately instead," Silaqui interrupted him. "I hate this place, the sooner we are gone the better."

"Damn it, Silaqui, let me finish!" Willis rubbed his face in suppressed annoyance. "There's been little offshore breeze here lately. I've been told that's common this time of year, but there is a very good onshore wind. That will help the Kolbian ship get into harbor sooner but make it very difficult for us to get out of the harbor without a tow by one of the oared tugboats. Those cost money and lots of it. I'm to meet with Rear Admiral Sartell in the morning. Sachi, I've a task for you, if you're willing?"

"What task?" she snapped.

"Go out to one of the lookout towers and see if you can identify the approaching Kolbian ship. I hope she's a frigate, preferably a forty-four. It's barely possible she might have to shoot her way out of the harbor and that'll affect us as well. Do it tonight and try to avoid being seen. Can you do that for me?"

"Yes, I can do that, Willis." Sachi looked at Silaqui. "It'd be easier if you can cast an invisibility cantrip on me right before I leave. Can you do that?"

"I can and will, Sachi."

"Good enough." Willis stood up. "That's all I have right now. I'd like to suggest that you each get everything packed up and ready to leave at a moment's notice." There was a general rumble of assent as everyone left the suite to start packing their gear. Silaqui stopped Willis in the hallway between rooms.

"Can I stay with you tonight?" she asked. "You make me feel safe."

"Sure. You just sleep there if you want to, or..." Willis kept his face straight and his voice calm.

"I think I would like the 'or...' if you don't mind. Ainaera is my patron Goddess, and she is the Goddess of Love."

"The choice is yours, my lady."

***

Sachi ghosted along the top of the seawall. The walkway on the wall was at least ten feet wide at its narrowest parts and was only used when the lookouts changed shifts. Even without Silaqui's invisibility cantrip, she had no doubt she could have reached her goal without being seen.

The tower was made of rough stone with a conical slate roof above the windows facing seaward. She went up the wall with no more sound than the shadow of a nighttime cloud. Perched at the very top of the tower, she looked out to sea. She concentrated and shifted her vision into telescopic mode. She'd given Willis a withering look when he tried to hand her the 'binoculars' he had claimed from the Admiral's quarters on the wrecked starship *Constellation*.

She shook her head in slight amusement at the memory and focused her vision on the very distant ship. No two ships are perfectly identical to each other, even ships of the same class, built by the same shipyard. She instantly recognized that ship. After all, she'd spent most of a year on her, first as a stowaway, then as an Apprentice Seaman and Cooks Mate Fourth Class. She was the *Intrepid*. Sachi nearly fell off the tower in shock.

The Intrepid*! How can she be here, coming into this harbor? She sailed back to Kolbia after delivering Silaqui and me to Montagar! It's not been long enough for her refit. Or has it? Is Captain Blaine, My Captain, still her Captain? How do I tell Sahla about him, my first love? Do I even still love him? I know there is a warm place in my heart where memories of him reside. Oh, Ancestors, what do I do? I must get out of here and back to the Inn before the cantrip wears off. I need to move, now!*

Sachi was so rattled that she slipped and fell the last ten feet climbing down the tower. She made enough noise with the awkward landing that one of the lookouts came to the tower door to see who was there. Sachi was long gone by then, sprinting down the wall's walkway.

***

Sachi raced up the stairs and banged on Willis' door. She heard a grumble and Silaqui's voice. Willis answered the door bare chested. She could see Silaqui in bed, under the covers.

"This better be good, Sachi. Whaddaya want?" he growled.

"It's the *Intrepid*, Willis, the *Intrepid*! Captain Blaine must still be her master and commander! What shall I do? What do I tell Sahla? What do I tell Captain Blaine? What do I do? She is my True Love, I know this in my soul, but a part of my heart still loves him. Oooh, what do I do?" She was nearly babbling.

Willis reached out, grabbed her by the shoulder and pulled her into the room. He picked up a glass of water and threw the water in her face. She gasped and nearly fell. He guided her into a chair and sat her down.

"Calm down, Sachi. This isn't like you at all. Why are you so upset? Yes, I know," he put a finger on her lips before she could say anything, "you feel torn between two loves. You're not the only person that's ever happened to, you know. Did you just think Captain Blaine was safely in your past? That you could ignore your feelings for him because you're in love with Sahla? Stop and think, silly. Think like a Kolbian for a minute, why don't you?"

"Or think like an Elf, if that's better." Silaqui sat up in the bed, the covers sliding down and revealing her bare breasts. "I'm over a thousand years old. In my life I've had many loves. Sometimes I outlived them, when they were mortals. Other times the passion cooled. Once my lover found his True Love and gently left me for her. There was no animosity. There is no reason you cannot love them both. You proclaim you want to be a Kolbian. Cannot women marry women there? There are even triads, or more, marriages there. What prevents you from loving them both? Either emotionally or even physically. Such a union is very difficult, but I know of a cousin of mine married to two male elves. They have been together for over five hundred years, living happily in their union. Stop and think, Sachi! Think, and don't listen to your panicked emotions."

"She's got a point. I know a foursome that's been together over ten years. And I know of several triads. Stop panicking and start thinking!" Willis filled the water glass he was still holding three fingers full with bourbon from a bottle on the table. "Drink this down quickly. It'll knock you out of this emotional hurricane and let you think again. Then go to your room and get some cuddles from Sahla. Take your time and tell her about Captain Blaine. Or not. Your choice. But go on and get some sleep. We'll be up early in the morning. Go rest at least."

"Listen to Willis, Sachi. He's giving you good advice. I would say go talk to Sahla tonight, but not all night."

"Thank you both." Sachi downed the small glass of bourbon in one swallow. It was honeyed fire down her throat. *Just this once I wish I could get drunk. But no, I must go talk to Sahla.* "I am better now, and I know I need to talk to Sahla. Thank you again," She stood up and went to the door. "I'm sorry I burst in like this, interrupting your lovemaking, but thank you."

"You're welcome. Now scat." Willis smiled as he opened the door and pushed her into the hall. "Go talk to Sahla. Goodbye." The door closed in her face and she heard Willis say to Silaqui, "Now, where were we?"

Blushing beet red, she went down the hallway to the suite she shared with Sahla and went in. Sahla was in the sitting room, reading a book on the couch. She took one look at Sachi and dropped the book on the floor, rising from the couch and flying across the room, throwing herself into Sachi's arms.

Sachi crushed Sahla against her. Their mouths met in a desperately passionate kiss. They held that kiss for long moments. When they came up for air, Sahla gave her a devastating smile and began pulling at her clothes.

"You are troubled and upset, my love. Tell me why?" She pulled the shirt off and then ran her thumb down the nearly invisible seam of the CLIBA body armor she always wore. The shirt opened and Sahla laughed when she pinned Sachi's arms with it for a moment. "The ship upset you. Why?"

"It's the *Intrepid*, the ship I escaped Isemoto on. Captain Blaine's ship. Oh, Sahla, I still love him in my heart!" Sachi nearly wailed and tears formed in her eyes. "I am unworthy of you with my heart divided so."

"Come with me to bed, my love, my True Love, come, follow me." She led the way into the bedroom, carefully pushing Sachi down on the bed and finishing undressing her. Sahla slid her robe off her shoulders and pushed Sachi into the middle of the big bed before snuggling up next to her. "Now, tell me of your love for this Captain Blaine. I will listen and when you have emptied your heart to me, we will take what poor pleasure of our lovemaking that we can. Then we will sleep and tomorrow face *Intrepid* and Captain Blaine with our love refreshed in our hearts." She pulled Sachi into another passionate kiss.

Chapter Sixteen

**Luctini Harbor
Kolbian Embassy and the Silver Maiden Inn
KRN *Intrepid* (32)
March 1479, Third Age of Imperial Reckoning**

"Hell of a fortress they've got here, Billy," Surgeon Commander Elazar Hoff muttered from where he stood on the quarterdeck of KRN *Intrepid*.

"Not really, Elazar," Captain (JG) William Blaine answered. "Modern artillery would batter those walls into rubble in a day. Half a day for our new Parker guns. The Parker rifles would take one of those stone towers down in one or two shots."

During her refit, *Intrepid* had been extensively up-gunned with sixteen eight-inch, muzzle-loading smoothbore Dolmen pattern guns, replacing the gundeck's thirty long thirty-two -pounders. The four thirty-two-pounder carronades on the quarterdeck had been retained, but all the spar deck thirty-two-pounders had been removed, the sixteen carronades replaced by eight six-inch Parker rifled muzzleloaders. The Dolmen guns fired either a sixty-five-pound solid shot or a fifty-three-pound explosive shell. The Parker rifles were capable of firing either shells or solid shot as well, either a fifty-pound shell or a seventy-five-pound solid shot. She had a pair of twenty-pounder Parker rifled guns both fore and aft as chase guns.

She had also been armored, if only lightly. The gun deck received armor plates one inch thick. The spar and berthing decks had half-inch armor plates. Backed by twenty-four inches of teak, nothing short of a fifty-pounder smoothbore cannonball at close range could penetrate the ship's sides. The tradeoff had been speed. With all sails set and a thirty-mile-an-hour wind, she could only make twelve knots at best. Previously she had occasionally flirted with sixteen knots and regularly managed fifteen knots.

"I don't like what we saw up the coast. The main naval base at Casalia Island was nearly empty of ships. That's their main port for their Lanic fleet. No ships-of-the-line, none of their few frigates and nearly every galley type ship was gone. There might have been a dozen of their old-style galleys in port, counting the four guard ships that came out to make sure we didn't get too close. And the harbor here is mostly empty, three ship-rigged galleons and one single masted sloop."

"And we have the anti-piracy and anti-slavery task force at sea in strength." Hoff leaned closer to Blaine, speaking softly. "For all we know, we could already be at war with the Empire."

"We could, but they don't seem to know about it here. After all, they sent out a pilot ship to guide us in and the defensive chain to block the harbor is just a huge pile of rusty metal at the base of the north tower. What's going on out at sea right now is anyone's guess." Blaine pointed at the sloop tied up along the dock. "Odd name, there. *Graser.* What in the world is a graser?"

"And, I'm guessing, the war warning is why we anchored out in the middle of the harbor?"

"The evening wind is offshore and usually strong enough to get us under way. And we don't need a pilot to get out of this harbor in a hurry if we must run for it." Blaine chuckled. "Besides, there's nothing here that has a hope in hell of stopping us from doing as we please. Which could include knocking down those towers and the walls and burning the entire waterfront down."

"I see." Hoff hesitated, given the topic he was about to bring up. "And what about your divorce? You told me about it once we left the Stark Haven harbor."

"What about it? Should be a done deal by now. I trust my attorney to handle things according to my instructions. It's what I paid him to do. Now Emily can chase all the Legates and Consuls and other 'big men' that her scheming heart desires."

"You sound a little bitter there, Billy."

"Maybe a bit. Okay, the longboat is in the water now, so I'm headed off to see Commodore Sartell. He should be a Rear Admiral by now." Blaine clapped Hoff on the shoulder and headed for the entry port to climb down the battens to the waiting longboat.

***

Willis had come to the Embassy shortly after first light. Both the Silver Maiden and the Kolbian Embassy were on opposite sides of the Seagate Road. Crossing the street gave Willis a good view into the harbor and he watched the longboat's oars flash reflected light as the boat's crew pulled on them.

"Yes, that's the *Intrepid*," he muttered to himself, "And if that's not Blaine in the middle seat, I'll eat the mainsail, without salt. *Intrepid's* mainsail."

He checked in with the gate's Marine guards and one of the Marines escorted him directly to the Admiral's office. There was a simple wooden plaque on the door that read 'Rear Admiral Sartell.' The Marine rapped sharply on the door.

"Enter." The Marine opened the door for Willis and then stepped back. Willis squared his shoulders and went to confront the dragon in its lair.

"Lieutenant Commander Willis Fleet, reporting as ordered, Admiral Sartell." Willis came to the position of attention and rendered a sharp salute.

"Stand at ease, Fleet." The Admiral returned his salute with a crisp one of his own. "Next time I send someone to summon you 'at your earliest convenience' it means 'right damn now.' I wanted to see you last night." He leaned back in his chair. "I assume you've noticed that *Intrepid* entered the harbor flying a war warning streamer?"

"Yes sir, noticed that coming across the street." He had taken the position of Parade Rest rather than standing at ease.

"Wondering why I wanted to see you so urgently?"

"Yes, sir."

"Now sit down there," he pointed to a chair in front of the desk, "and explain to me how you've come to possess a known pirate's ship and renamed her the *Graser*. Include explaining what the hell a graser is while you're at it. You've got about an hour before Blaine gets here, so be sharpish about it."

"Yes, sir. It's a long story but I'll be as concise as I can. It starts when I, well we, took passage to Luctini aboard the merchant ship *Le Bonaventure*..."

***

"That's a hell of a story, Lieutenant Commander. And you can prove all this—wait, you showed me those pistols and the 'body armor' shirt you're wearing, so for the most part I see that you're telling the truth, at least as best you can." Sartell leaned forward in his chair, his elbows on the desktop and his fingers steepled under his chin. "I think I want to at least hear the others' sides of the story, especially this Takahashi woman's side." He took a deep breath. "So, you and she were responsible for the line of light in the sky several weeks ago?"

"Yes, sir, the weapon was called a graser, I was told, and when we captured Ironheart's sloop, well, we had to change the name. Leaving her named *Heartcutter* was just asking to get taken as pirates."

"I understand." There was a knock at the door, another Marine's three sharp raps.

"Sir, Captain Blaine from *Intrepid* with dispatches from Capitol City and Stark Haven."

"Send him in." He pointed at a chair against the wall. "Go be a fly on the wall. But stay put."

"Captain Blaine, *Intrepid*, with confidential dispatches, your eyes and the Envoy's eyes only." Blaine came into the office, saluted, and handed Sartell a diplomatic satchel. One in much better shape than Willis' bag had been. That was when he noticed Fleet, sitting quietly in the chair. He stared at Willis for a split second and pulled his attention back to the Admiral.

"Captain Blaine, I take it you know young Fleet here?"

"Oh, yes, sir. He was onboard when we left Isemoto for Carolington Naval Base. Then he got orders transferring him to Stark Haven. Apparently, he infuriated the Nisei's organized crime clan. They wanted his head. Just his head."

"Well, he just told me the damnedest, strangest tale I've ever heard, and he's got the evidence to back it up. Simply incredible."

"Yes, sir." Blaine paused a moment, an odd look on his face. "Sir, could I ask Fleet a question, if you don't mind?"

"Go ahead."

"Is Sachi safe in Montagar?" Blaine's face was tight. There was an odd, almost pleading expression on it.

"Captain Blaine, ah, sir, she's not in Montagar. She's across the street in the fourth-floor suite in the Silver Maiden Inn."

"WHAT?" Blaine nearly shouted. "You mean she didn't go with Silaqui?"

"No sir. Silaqui is across the street in another fourth-floor room."

"Admiral Sartell, sir." Blaine turned back to the Admiral. "I have completed my task, and I believe there are other things that need seeing to. By you leave, sir."

"Go on, get out of my office. But keep yourself handy. After a quick once-over of these documents, I imagine we will be closing the Embassy here immediately if not sooner. I intend to hold *Intrepid* here to evacuate the Embassy personnel. You have room on your ship for thirty-eight people?"

"Yes, sir. Excuse me, please."

"Willis, go on and go with him. I need to go see Envoy Courtenay with these dispatches immediately. Gentlemen, I shall see both of you later." Sartell left his desk and went out a door in the wall behind it.

Blaine and Willis tried to go through the entry door at the same time and jammed shoulders together. Willis stepped back and then followed Blaine out the door and out the Embassy's gate onto the street. He stopped and whirled to face Willis.

"Sachi is in that inn there?" He pointed a thumb over his shoulder at the Silver Maiden. "Fourth floor suite, right."

"Captain Blaine, sir, gimme a minute to explain. Things have changed. Drastically so." Willis talked fast. "Remember what she said about having a destiny? Well, she does have one, one that holds the whole world in the balance. She saw your ship last night from the top of the south tower. She knew it was the *Intrepid* and that you were still her Captain. She was an emotional wreck."

"I'm listening, Fleet. I'm not going to go barging into her room. I'm not sure what I'm going to do."

"What about your wife, sir? Your famous vows to her? What's changed?"

"My wife filed for divorce before we left Stark Haven on this mission. I was told to expect to have to extract the Embassy personnel, possibly under fire. Of course, whether they decide to close the Embassy and pull out isn't up to me, it's up to Admiral Sartell and Envoy Courtenay."

"Sir, let's get out of the street and go into the taproom at the Silver Maiden and I can tell you the whole long story. Then we'll go up to the fourth floor and let you and Sachi discuss things. You and Sachi and one other. Come on, let's go get a beer and you can listen to my story." Willis put a gentle hand on Blaine's arm and steered him into the taproom.

***

Willis ordered some chips, a pitcher of beer and two glasses and settled them into a back corner booth. After the first drink, Willis started his tale. The chips were gone, and the pitcher was dry, when he finished.

"That sounds too incredible to believe, Willis. But the Admiral believed you, so what choice do I have but to believe you as well. And I think you probably left the unbelievable stuff out. Hmm."

"A few things, some of them you simply had to be there to realize it was real."

"I understand. So Sachi found her True Love in this magical Jann girl, well young woman, I guess. Well, well, well."

"Captain Blaine, sir, it was a more or less open secret back on *Intrepid*, while we were crossing the Great Western Ocean and especially in the Horn Islands that you and Sachi were in love with each other. Even I noticed it." Willis took a deep breath. "What are you going to do now, sir?"

"I don't know. Partly depends on Sachi and this Sahla person. Pay the tab, Willis, and let's go find out."

***

Sachi had a bad habit of chewing her fingernails when she was stressed. She had the thumb on her left hand down to the quick and was starting on the little finger's nail next. There was a knock on the door.

"Who's there?" she asked as she went to the door.

"It's Willis...and Captain Blaine. Open the door, Sachi, please?" Sachi's breath seemed to stop. She felt her heart pounding, then Sahla slipped a warm arm around her waist. Sachi wore a mottled black *kobakama*, knee length trousers worn under armor by the samurai of Isemoto, and her mottled black *himaku*, with the jacket's sleeves tied up over her elbows. Split-toed *tabi* covered her feet up to her knees. It was a comfortable outfit and it allowed her to move and fight if need be, and it had lots of places to hide kill-stars, throwing spikes and knives. The white steel bracers gleamed on her forearms and the ancient Mark Fourteen pistol was in its usual place on her hip.

Sahla wore her best clothes, a fine linen *abayah*, as blue as the sky, and a delicate turquoise silken *niqab* veiling the lower part of her face. Only her sapphire blue eyes were visible, and even the fist-thick braid of her hair was concealed by her robes. Over everything was her luxurious tiger cloak.

Sahla opened the door and stepped back. Willis came through the doorway and immediately took a chair against the wall. The next person through the door was Captain Blaine. He had not changed in the least, wearing his blue uniform coat, dark blue trousers and a white linen shirt. It was his daily 'working' uniform and there were none of his medals or awards on it. He laid his fore-and-aft style hat on the table.

He is so handsome! I think my heart may stop. But I feel the Bond between me and Sahla. It is a Bond only death can break and even then, our spirits will be together forever. What does he think of me? On the ship, the mighty Intrepid, *I knew in my heart of hearts that I loved him, and I believe, no, I know he loved me. But honor and vows kept us apart. Why does he come here, now, when honor will still separate us? When it will ensure we are aloof to each other and deny what is in our hearts. Oh Sahla, my love, save me!*

***

He is a tall man, Sahla thought as Captain Blaine entered the room. *He is taller than Sachi and even taller than Willis. And so handsome, the face of a warrior-poet. His uniform is plain and with little adornment other than the gold cuff rings and the gold on his shoulder boards. Those must indicate his rank.*

She could feel Sachi's heart cry out to her through the Bond. '*Oh Sahla, my love, save me!* She pressed herself more tightly against Sachi and let all her power flow into and around Sachi.

'*My love, you are safe, there is no threat here, not to us nor to our Bond. We flow like the sands of the desert, a never-ending tide of love. There is so much that if a caravan's load is taken away, there is still an unlimited amount of sand in the desert. We will always be together.*' She squeezed Sachi as tightly as she could, willing her to feel the endless tide of love between them. Making a decision, she reached up and lowered her veil. She removed the tiger cloak and placed it over a chair back, then brushed back the snood of her *abayah* and freed her braid.

"Captain Blaine, yes?" she asked. "Please come in and be seated, here on this end of the couch. Sachi shall sit there, in the middle, next to you, and I shall sit at the other end, next to my Bonded."

Blaine walked over and took the seat she pointed out. He had a slightly bemused look on his face.

***

Blaine followed Willis into the room and hid a smile as Willis darted out from in front of Blaine and grabbed a seat against the wall. Then he saw Sachi, and the world just stopped. He'd rarely seen her in her mottled black fighting outfit, but she wore it now. Some kind of statement? Then the tiny young woman next to her moved, reaching up to remove her veil, brush back the hood covering her black hair, and putting a magnificent tiger skin cloak carefully over a tall chair.

Then she turned and smiled at him. Her beauty hit him like a hammer blow between the eyes. He simply stopped and stared. He couldn't help himself; he'd never seen such a beautiful woman. She moved with a limp and was very careful with her right arm.

My God. I thought Sachi was the most beautiful woman in the world and now I realize I'm wrong. Sachi is a close second, but only angels in Heaven could be more perfect than this girl, this young woman. She was holding Sachi when I came in the room. Is this that bond of True Love Willis was blabbing about? Not sure I believe in something from a book of fancy tales, but then...These two are perfect together.

Huh. I thought that with Emily divorcing me, I might travel to Montagar and find Sachi, see if it truly was love between us. What a fool I am. She's lost to me forever now.

***

Willis sat in the chair against the wall and heartily wished to be elsewhere. On second thought, maybe he was here to play chaperone.

Silly thought. God, I could make sails out of the tension in this room right now. And I think, from the slightly mischievous look on her beautiful face, that Sahla is about to put the ball in play. I hope she knows what she's doing! Is she just planning to use her love for a little chaos and pull everything out in the open?

"Willis, get the bottle of brandy from the sideboard and pour each of us, including yourself, a drink." Sahla pointed at the sideboard and the cabinet of glasses next to it. Willis popped out of his chair and went to the sideboard. He poured three shot glasses half full and just a splash in his. In two trips, there was a drink in front of everyone.

"A toast, my friends, old and new, and my love." They all picked up their glasses and clinked them together. "A toast to love."

***

Very well, this should be fun. Sahla waited until Blaine and Sachi had drank but not swallowed. She timed it perfectly.

"I know the two of you are still in love with each other." She set her drink aside, untouched.

Blaine and Sachi both sprayed whisky halfway across the room, nearly choking on their drinks.

"Willis. Please fetch us a towel." She smiled at him. He got a towel from the sideboard "Thank you, now you may leave." He vanished. "Are we both recovered now?" They both nodded in unison. "Excellent. Now finish your drinks." They did so, carefully, with an eye on Sahla. She stood up from the couch and moved to stand directly in front of the pair on the couch. "Now, turn to face each other. Go ahead, Sachi, it will be fine." She hid a smile at the trepidation coming from Blaine and the anxiety evident on Sachi's face. "Now, Captain Blaine, say, 'I love you,' to Sachi. Don't look at me, look at her. Say it."

"Sachi, uh," he hesitated, "Sachi, I love you."

"Very good. Now Sachi, say, 'I love you,' to...what is your given name, Captain Blaine?"

"William."

"An excellent name." Sahla's voice was as smooth as honey. "Sachi, say, 'I love you,' to William."

"I love you, William Blaine, my captain."

"Excellent. That issue is resolved. You each now know how the other feels about you. Now, Sachi say, 'I love you,' to me."

"That's not necessary, Sahla you know tha…"

"Just say it, Sachi."

"I love you Sahla, desperately so."

"I know and I love you, Sachi. We are heartmates and not even death will separate us." Sahla sat carefully on the low table in front of the couch. "Now, all that is in the open between us. There is no deceit, no evasion. Captain Blaine, I am *not* in love with you, nor are you in love with me. I will grant that you may have lust for me, most men do, but that is acceptable in you."

"Hey, wait a minute, young lady, I am NOT in lust with you! I have more self-control than that. I'll grant you're the most beautiful woman I have ever seen, but that does not mean I lust after you."

"Then you are a rare man, William Blaine, but I will grant you that. Sachi has told me of your honor and your loyalty to your vows. But something has changed, or you would not even say, 'I love you,' to Sachi. What has changed, Captain Blaine?"

"My wife, Emily, has sued for divorce. I will not fight it."

"Because now you can say, 'I love you,' to Sachi?"

"No," Blaine was vehement, then he stopped and sighed. "Well, perhaps, a least a little to be totally honest. Hell, I don't truly know myself."

"And where do we go from here, then?" Sachi asked.

"Now, that I do not know." Sahla shrugged and then collapsed into Sachi's arms. "I have tried to stand too long, my love. The wound is very painful now. Summon Gelman so that he might ease my pain."

Blaine stood up and got out of the way as Sachi laid Sahla on the couch and then darted out of the room, yelling for Gelman. Blaine stood a moment, then sat on the stuffed chair next to the couch.

"What happened to you? How are you wounded?"

"Weeks ago, I was stabbed with a white steel blade, stabbed from behind by a blackguard who is dead now. I believe the Prophet Himself decreed his punishment when the mists took him from the ship." She smiled at him. "It is a very long tale."

"Sachi didn't instantly kill him? I'm surprised."

"Silaqui did not allow her to do so."

The door banged open and a burly man wearing the robes of a Kythal priest rushed into the room. He shoved Blaine out of the way without a word, dropping to his knees next to Sahla. Sachi was right behind him, worry on her face.

"Where is the pain, Sahla?" he asked.

"The leg won't hold me right now, but the worst pain is the wound." She pointed at her collarbone, immediately adjacent to her slim throat.

"I can relieve the pain, but the wound is as healed as it can ever be." Golden light haloed his hands and flowed onto Sahla's neck and shoulder. "It is the poor best I can do, and the pain will come back."

"I know it will, Gelman but even your 'poor best' is a wonderful surcease from the pain. Ah, that is so much better now. Thank you, my friend." Gelman stood up, the golden light fading away.

"You're most welcome, my child." He turned to face Blaine. "And who is this long lout?"

"William Blaine, Captain of the *Intrepid*, at your service, sir. And you are...?"

"Pere Gelman Stavor, of Montagar. As you have seen, I've been blessed by the One God with the power of healing, at least as He sees fit to allow me to use His Power." Gelman dipped his head to Blaine. "At your service, sir."

Blaine saw a brown face peering into the room from the hallway, a young woman's face. She had shoulder-length dark brown hair, he noted as she stepped into the room. Willis was right behind her, and a familiar tall, slender female figure was behind him.

"Is that you, Silaqui? Behind Willis?"

"I am here, Captain Blaine. I see that your presence has made something of a muddle of things where Sachi and Sahla are concerned." She stepped into the room, drawing the brown girl, well, young woman with her. "This is Aylie Clayton. In Montagar, she is wanted for murders she never committed, and she is with us to gain revenge on those responsible for those murders. She can be fully trusted. She knows more about Sachi than you do."

"I see." Blaine picked up his hat from the table. "I believe I'm in the way here and I need to get back to my ship. We may be leaving sometime tomorrow or the next day. I am fairly certain the Admiral will order the Embassy closed and I will then transport the Embassy personnel back to Kolbia. Good day, everyone, Sachi, Sahla, Silaqui." He turned and walked out the door.

Sahla was watching Sachi very closely. She saw the slight twitch as the Nisei almost started after Blaine.

"Thank you so much, Gelman. The pain is much better now." She raised her voice slightly. "I'm okay now, but I would like to be alone with Sachi now, please. And no listening in the hall, please." Everyone trooped out the door and Willis shut it behind himself as the last one out.

"We are alone, now, Sachi. Will you be all right?"

"I don't know if I'll ever be 'all right' again!" She burst into tears and collapsed into Sahla's arms. "I cannot be 'all right' as long as you are in pain from your wound."

***

"*Intrepid* arriving," the senior crewman of the side party shouted. The bosun's whistle sounded as Blaine climbed to the entry portal on the starboard rail. He saluted the national flag at the stern of the ship and then saluted the Officer of the Deck.

"Permission to come aboard, Lieutenant?" Blaine asked.

"Yes, sir," newly promoted Lieutenant (JG) Tom Anderson answered as he dropped his salute. "Welcome back, Captain."

"Dismiss the side party, Bosun. Good to be back home, Tom. How's the new promotion feeling? Nice not being called Ensign anymore?"

"Very well, sir. And thank you for the Lieutenant's pins."

"They were an old set of mine. I don't need them anymore, and it saved you some money."

"Yes, sir. Thank you, sir."

"I'll be in my cabin. Find Doctor Hoff and ask him to join me there."

"Yes, sir."

Blaine went to his cabin and had just poured himself a drink and sat down on the small couch under the port quarter windows, when the Marine sentry at the door announced Hoff.

"Come in, Elazar. Pour yourself a drink, I've a tale to tell you. Grab a chair." He waited until Hoff had settled into a chair and was in the middle of a deep drink. It was Blaine's best bourbon, but the revenge was worth it. "Sachi Takahashi is in this town, alive and well."

Hoff nearly choked as he sprayed bourbon halfway across the cabin. Blaine couldn't help but laugh as Hoff mopped at his soaked shirt. He coughed a couple of times.

"You did that on purpose. And you laughed."

"Shame to waste good whisky, but the revenge was worth it." Blaine finally stopped laughing. "You did the same thing to me at least three or four times."

"So I did," Hoff admitted. "But it was a medical necessity at the time. Now what's this about Sachi Takahashi being in this town. She's in Montagar. Isn't she?"

"No. I just saw her in her room in the big inn across from our Embassy. Her and Willis Fleet and Silaqui are all here. Now." Blaine paused. "And there are some others with them."

"You're divorced now. There's nothing to keep you apart, now." Hoff watched Blaine's face. "Or is there?"

"Do you believe in True Love, Elazar?"

"You answered a question with a question. Not fair." Hoff paused a moment. "I don't know. I've read about it in fancy tales, but in real life, I don't know. Maybe?"

"No maybe about it. Sachi has found her true love and it isn't me."

"Fleet? You're kidding!"

"No, not Fleet. Willis was never even in the running for her heart. No, she's in love with the most beautiful little Darsälaamic girl I've ever seen. Even more beautiful than Sachi. Together they're stunning. And the Darsälaamic girl, her name is Sahla, claims they are Bonded together. Not sure what she meant by that." Blaine rolled his glass between his hands. "And Sahla is partly crippled, stabbed from behind through the neck. By a white steel blade, no less."

"The blade missed her spine, or she'd have been dead when she hit the floor. A white steel blade could have easily decapitated her. She was damned lucky. I doubt I could do anything for her. I assume the wound is healed up."

"There is a healer priest with them, guy named Pere Gelman Stavor. I saw him use magic to ease her pain."

"A Kythal priest?"

"Yes, why?"

"The 'Pere' at the beginning is a title, not a name. Sort of like being called 'Father.' It means he can use magic to heal the sick and wounded. Real magic. I met one once, he could do amazing things."

"Well, apparently, he can't completely heal Sahla and it's tearing Sachi apart. And there is nothing I can do about it at all." Blaine finished his drink. "Pour me another one, Elazar. Under any other reason for being here, I'd get flat falling down drunk. But we may have to evacuate the Embassy in a hurry. Oh, Commodore Sartell is now Rear Admiral Sartell."

"Think it went to his head?"

"Him, not a chance."

"So...Sachi Takahashi again?"

"Yes, Sachi Takahashi again."

***

Sartell knocked on the door to the Envoy's office.

"It's open, come in, James." A clear soprano spoke up, loud enough to be heard through the door. He opened the door and entered, closing it behind him.

"Envoy Courtenay, we need to close the Embassy and pull out. *Intrepid* arrived this morning flying a red streamer on her foremast, a war warning. The dispatches I read aren't quite direct orders but they're close enough for me. Captain Blaine also informed me that the Imperials' main naval base is mostly empty. They've sortied their fleet. They may be lousy sailors and have no business in the Lanic, but there's a beggar's own lot of them. And they're at sea. And the Imperial Fleet does not sortie just to do fleet exercises like we do. We need to pack up. Haven't you read Blaine's dispatches?"

"I just started on them. The ones from Montagar were a waste of time. Utter drivel. But I went through them like a good Envoy should. If I didn't know better, I'd say they're a complete red herring. Not sure what the purpose of them was at all." Angelina Courtenay was an ordinary looking blonde woman with striking green eyes, eyes that made a plain face pretty, even beautiful at times. She wore her hair short, about neck length. She was five foot six and a little overweight.

But she had a keen mind and a personality that let her get along with snooty Imperial bureaucrats and prickly Kythal priests. Priests who often had more say than any bureaucrats in how the city and even how the Empire was run. Her face, plain as it was, told the world exactly what she wanted and no more. That face also let her be a killer bridge or poker player.

"Angelina, I'm the military attaché here. It's my call, mine and our Marine company commander's, on when to pack up and leave. And I'm making that call. We need to get started burning all the sensitive and classified papers and destroy anything we can't get into a longboat. Get your staffers busy."

"All right, James. It's your call and you've made it. I'll get my clerks busy. I'm going to the Silver Maiden for my dinner. The cooks will be busy helping my clerks destroy important papers. I'll miss the Maiden's pot roast, might as well have it one last time. Did you see anything in Blaine's dispatches that indicated an imminent threat to our personnel?"

"Other than being taken as POWs, no."

"Then you're coming with me."

"Not a bad idea. Lieutenant Commander Fleet is staying there, apparently with several others, including a young lady with some sort of connection to Captain Blaine. I think I'll invite Fleet and some of his friends to dinner. And now that I think about it, I'll invite Captain Blaine as well. Might be very interesting to see what happens if Blaine's 'young lady' shows up. Until then, we both must get very busy."

***

"So, the main pump on the water hoy is broken." Willis's breakfast had been interrupted by Bosun Holland coming to the Inn from the dock where the *Graser* was tied up. "Can we use the ship's pump instead?"

"No, sir. Couplings are too different. They say they'll have it fixed this evening and we'll be first in line for water resupply. Best they can do, the hoy's crew said."

"Any chance it's a deliberate 'breakdown,' trying to get more money out of us or to keep us here for some unknown reason?"

"I'd say not, sir. I saw the broken pump and it's broke, clear enough. We took about a hundred gallons onboard before it broke. And why would anyone want us to stay here?"

"Why, indeed, Bosun, why indeed?" Willis thought for a moment. "There are a few 'whys' I don't like, but they would be very odd 'whys' indeed. Good report, Jon. Get some coffee in you before you head back."

"Thankee, sir."

***

"Sachi, I've got a little bit of bad news," Willis said after knocking on the suite's door and entering the sitting room. Sahla was braiding Sachi's hair.

"What happened?" Sachi asked from where she sat on the floor.

"Pump on the water hoy broke. It'll be fixed this evening, but we can't get our water tank refilled until dark at best, most likely tomorrow morning."

"We were to leave today. Who told you this?"

"Bosun Holland, he caught me in the tap room having breakfast." He noted the large collection of room service dishware. "I see you ate here."

"We did and so did Silaqui. None of us three should be out in public very much."

"Agreed. I guess we simply lay low today, stay in our rooms and get our meals delivered to our rooms..." There was a knock on the door. All three of them froze. "Who's there?" he asked.

"Message from the front desk, sir."

"Gimme a second." Willis opened the door a crack and took the message slip. He handed the messenger a tip and closed the door. Reading the message, he sighed and shook his head. "This is a problem."

"Now what?" Sachi muttered.

"An invitation from Rear Admiral Sartell and Envoy Courtenay to come to dinner. But here at the Silver Maiden and *not*, I repeat, *not* at the Embassy's dining room. Very odd, that." Willis stepped over to the sitting room's window and looked out past the curtains. "And that's not a good sign at all." He opened the curtains and pointed.

Thick, white smoke was pouring out of all the Embassy's chimneys. It was impossible to determine what was happening, but there seemed to be a lot of activity in the Embassy's courtyard, then smoke started rising from there as well.

"What is happening, Willis?" Sahla asked.

"They're burning their documents, everything sensitive or classified. They're going to pull out of the Embassy in no more than two days, and there's this invitation to dinner here. Very damn odd." He shook his head and rubbed his jaw line. "And the invitation is for me, Lieutenant Commander Fleet 'and party.' For me, that's an order and they want to meet the rest of you for some reason."

"All of us?" Sachi's worry showed clearly on her face. "Do we have to go?"

"No, not all, I have to go, but no one else does. But to keep my tail out of a crack, I'd ask you two and Gelman to come with me. Keep Aylie and Silaqui out of sight. You two willing to come along and see what an Admiral and a diplomatic Envoy want to talk about?"

"I guess we can attend this dinner if you think best, Willis." Sahla put a hand on Sachi's shoulder when she started to get up. "We will be veiled for everything but eating. And we shall demurely keep our faces downcast while eating. They shall only see our eyes."

"Well, that should work."

***

Gelman had agreed to join the dinner party with Willis, Sachi and Sahla. Wanting to choose the darkest seats, they headed down early but were dismayed to learn that the Envoy and the Admiral were already there, seated at the table with the best light. And Captain Blaine was with them, along with Surgeon Commander Hoff. Sachi nearly froze and Sahla stumbled and would have fallen if not for her Gift of Flight.

"Welcome to dinner and thank you for coming." Sartell, Blaine and Hoff all stood until Sachi and Sahla were seated, Sachi by Blaine and Sahla by Willis. Introductions were made all around. The waiters brought drinks and appetizers, and an initial, awkward silence was broken by Courtenay.

"I am given to understand that you have the power of magical healing, Pere Gelman?"

"I have been blessed by the One God of the Circled Cross with that ability. It is nothing I do. I am merely a vessel for His Power."

"How wonderful," Courtenay said. "I can't imagine how wonderful it must feel to actually use magic to heal someo..." She froze for a split second as she finally got a good look at Sahla's bright, sapphire blue eyes. "Excuse me. It must be an amazing gift from the One God."

Sahla had been regarding one of the appetizers, a fried shrimp, with some apprehension. She had never seen any kind of shellfish prepared as breaded and fried food. Sachi whispered to her, and she took a deep breath and bit into it. The surprise taste made her look up and smile at Sachi.

Admiral Sartell had been talking to Doctor Hoff and he noticed Courtenay's sudden pause. And the exchange between Sachi and Sahla, combined with Courtenay's verbal stumble, gave him his first good look at both young women. He raised one eyebrow but kept his conversation with Hoff going smoothly. Blaine and Willis both caught the incident. Blaine kept his composure, but Willis obviously grimaced. Fortunately, only Blaine noticed that grimace.

"So, William, Doctor Hoff, excuse me, Elazar, he asked me to use his given name, tells me that Miss Sachi fled Isemoto by stowing away on *Intrepid* during your 'show the flag' mission there. The same mission that brought Willis home before the local crime syndicate could kill him. It must have been a very stressful mission. Wasn't the sloop-of-war *Sorcerer* lost on the return?"

"She was, Miss Courtenay, destroyed with all hands by a sea monster," Blaine replied.

"Was the monster satisfied with just *Sorcerer* or did you kill it with *Intrepid's* guns?"

"Neither, ma'am. An object falling from space hit and killed it. That probably saved my ship and her entire crew." Other conversations around the table stopped suddenly.

"Nothing short of a miracle, then?"

"Yes, sir, I would think so."

"And this was after Miss Sachi was discovered, yes?"

"It was."

"Miss Sachi, that must have been terrifying," Courtenay said.

"I was injured by the damage to the ship, Courtenay-sama. I have no memory of what happened," Sachi lied smoothly. She ducked her head to avoid Sartell's intense stare.

"I see," Courtenay said. "That's enough sea stories, James, William. Her dress and demeanor tell me that Miss Sahla is from Darsälaam. How did you come to be among this group?"

"While traveling to meet my husband-to-be, my ship was taken by pirates. My duenna was slain and without her to guarantee my 'purity,' neither my Father the Sheikh nor my husband-to-be would pay the ransom demanded. The pirate leader decided he would bring me here and sell me in the slave market. Before that could happen, I was rescued from that fate when Sachi slew him in single combat." There was a stunned silence from Courtenay and Sartell. Sahla ducked her head demurely.

"I think there was a lot left out in that speech, Miss Sahla," Blaine broke the silence.

"The whole tale would take days, and be rather boring, other than the fight," Willis spoke up. "Nowhere nearly as exciting as it sounds."

"Tell me, Willis, how did you wind up wherever this fight happened?" Courtenay asked.

"It was an uncharted island in the South Lanic. The ship that was supposed to bring us, Sachi, Gelman and I to Luctini, was driven far south by a storm and wrecked on the island. Then we discovered that the island was also being used as a base by pirates and managed to save the hostages they were holding, Sachi killed their leader, and we stole their sloop. Much less adventurous than it sounds."

"A pirate base?" Sartell raised an eyebrow. "The only pirate captain I've heard of with a base is one named Ironheart and he was supposedly trying to build a true pirate fleet. He was unbeatable in combat, at least in hand-to-hand combat, the stories say. And Sachi killed him in single combat, you say?"

"Yes, Admiral Sartell, she did. I watched the battle between them from the hut where I was held hostage."

"I have noticed the way the two of you relate to each other, Miss Sahla," Courtenay spoke into another awkward silence. "Do you have a romantic attachment to Miss Sachi? That would be so romantic, falling in love with the person who saved you from the slave market." Sahla blushed beet red and pulled her veil over her face, leaving only her eyes visible. Sachi glared at the Envoy.

"Is that any of your concern, Envoy Courtenay?" Sachi ground out between her teeth. "And knowledge of such a relationship can be lethal in Imperial lands, such as Luctini. They are not a tolerant people, the Imperials." Once again, the side conversations died an uncomfortable death.

"I beg pardon," Courtenay said, raising her hand to her throat.

"Perhaps we should change the subject," Gelman spoke up. "These are not topics to be discussed in public here. We noticed the smoke coming from behind the Embassy wall, perhaps you might tell what is happening there. Is there a fire and should not the fire brigade be summoned?"

Courtenay, Sartell and Blaine all exchanged glances. Blaine leaned back in his chair and waved at Sartell. Gelman raised an eyebrow at the obvious discomfort his comment had made. Courtenay sipped her drink and smiled at Gelman.

"Just burning some leaf piles. Well under control," was all she said.

"Oh, so no issues then, ah, here come our dinners." Gelman smiled and rubbed his hands together as his steak was set before him.

Conversation stopped while everyone ate. The meal was superb. They were quiet and giving the food the attention it deserved, but the subtle tension was still there. Blaine kept his attention on his plate and his drink, avoiding looking at either Sachi or Sahla. Sartell surreptitiously watched Sachi. Courtenay was equally circumspect in watching Sahla. Willis was paying close attention to both Courtenay and Sartell, as was Doctor Hoff. Gelman was oblivious to everything but his meal.

As the meal ended, drinks were brought to everyone but Sahla and Gelman. She was brought a glass of tea. The Prophet frowned on the consumption of strong spirits, so Sahla had asked for cold tea. Given the Kolbian Embassy just across the street, the kitchen of the Silver Maiden Inn had long ago learned how to make Kolbian style cold tea, but even the Silver Maiden could rarely afford ice, even in the dead of winter. Gelman got tea as well. Everyone else got a bourbon snifter.

"I noticed you chose a cold tea over the very fine bourbon served here, Miss Sahla. Any particular reason?" Courtenay asked as she swirled her glass under her nose, appreciating the aroma of her drink.

"The Prophet, Chalta bless his Name, did not approve of strong spirits." Sahla drew her veil over her face as she spoke. "The Book of Holies tells us that strong drink takes away a man's will and inflames his darker side, something all men have. And Sachi told me of this Kolbian drink and other than morning drinks such as what my people call kaffe, I have drunk nothing else. It is a superior drink."

"I see." Courtenay sipped her drink. "And I assume you avoid the strong drinks for similar religious reasons, Pere Gelman?"

"Somewhat, Madam Envoy," he answered, "and I do not personally care for spirits of any type. I know enough drunken monks and priests who should be ashamed of themselves. And the Kolbian tea is very fine as well."

"A wise choice, then." Admiral Sartell entered the conversation. "I noticed you have very unusual eyes, Miss Sachi, a brown so dark it appears completely black. Is that common in Isemoto, such black eyes?"

Sachi froze. Gelman's head snapped around, and Sahla hissed as she drew a deep breath. Willis hesitated and then spoke into the silence.

"Such dark eyes and black hair are exceedingly common there, Admiral. Have you ever sailed to Isemoto?"

"I commanded two 'show-the-flag' missions to Isemoto, one as a senior grade Captain and the second as a newly promoted Commodore," Sartell answered evenly. "But I only went ashore to the Embassy there once, during my second mission there. Black hair was common enough, but I never saw anyone with such dark eyes. Eyes that could almost be called 'black.' Was this common in your family, Miss Sachi?"

"I know not. I was a foundling orphan. I know nothing of my parents or even what Family or Clan I come from. The family who found me gave me their family name, Takahashi." Sachi sipped at her bourbon. "It is not something I wish to discuss."

"I see. Beg pardon, please."

"It is of no matter, Admiral Sartell-sama." Sachi nodded her head, keeping her eyes downcast. "I think perhaps we should all finish our drinks and return to our rest. I am tired."

A rumble of agreement went around the table, somewhat relieving the tensions that had been evident all evening. Other than the kitchen door, there was only one exit from the dining room. It was a normal door, usually propped open. As they filed out, Blaine and Sachi were the last ones out and they reached the door at the same time, just behind Sahla, who went on up the stairs. Their shoulders touched and they both stopped cold, facing each other.

"Sachi." Blaine's voice was rough with suppressed emotion. "Sachi Takahashi."

"Captain Blaine-sama." Somehow, Sachi kept her voice in control. "William. My Captain."

"I trust you are well?"

"I am well. The Ancestors have watched over me. And you, My Captain?"

"Emily filed for divorce right before I raised sail for Luctini. Was Courtenay right? About you and Miss Sahla?"

"There is a Bond between us. She is Darsälaamic, but I am trying to cajole her into becoming a good Kolbian."

"And you? Are you still Nisei or have you fallen into Kolbia's wicked ways?"

"I am what I've become, neither Nisei nor Kolbian. I hope to someday be like a Kolbian, at least in matters of the heart."

"I noticed the beautiful sapphire on the gold chain. That's new and very dazzling. I believe it almost matches Sahla's eyes. It looks like it could buy a frigate."

"It is precious beyond price to me. It is, in a sense, a prize I won when I killed Ironheart."

"You seem different, more certain of yourself than when you were on the *Intrepid*. Have you found what you were looking for?"

"I know what I am, now, and I know my destiny. It is a heavy burden but one I must bear. My friends help me. As does my love."

"Sahla?"

"Yes." She hesitated and put a hand against the doorframe to support herself. "And my love for you helps me bear what I must carry."

Blaine started to reach out to help her and suddenly she was in his arms and her lips burned on his own, in a passionate kiss. But a short kiss and she was gone, nearly running to the stairs after Sahla and the others in her group.

"What the hell?" Blaine touched his lips in stunned surprise. Then Elazar came back around the corner from the lobby.

"You get lost, Billy?"

"Sachi kissed me. Kissed me like it was the end of the world. And then ran up those stairs."

"I will be damned."

***

Pater Inquisitor Ambroise Dubois de Palmaroli was having a bad morning. He drank too much at last night's revel and had spent most of the time there avoiding Cousin Vicente. Vicente was a bit of an ascetic who attended revels mostly to gain blackmail material on the various indiscretions committed by everyone else who attended to enjoy a chance to escape the burdens of high office, either secular or ecclesiastical. For some, Vicente was as popular as the plague and about as welcome.

Vicente was merely a bishop in the episcopal ranks, but he wielded greater power as the head of the Inquisition in Luctini and its environs. And he held other powers, darker ones that Ambroise Dubois de Palmaroli wanted no part of, in any way or fashion. It was rumored that Vicente could wield magical powers and that he could strike down enemies from hundreds of leagues away. There was no man more feared in all Luctini. The Lord Mayor and the Archbishop of Luctini both deferred to him. And now Ambroise was having to avoid him the way a vampire avoided daylight.

Tomorrow. I'll see him tomorrow. Those strangers at the Silver Maiden Inn are no threat to anyone. Four women, an itinerant Montagaran priest, and some ruffian with delusions of being a ship captain. What could they do? Oh, my head. Even thinking about these vagabonds hurts. I'll see Vicente tomorrow after High Mass. Tomorrow.

***

Blacksmith William LaRue was enraged. Three weeks ago, the press gangs had swept up both his oldest sons. Three days ago, the new tax collector had doubled both his hearth tax and the tax on his anvil and hammer, the tools of his trade. The tax collector had given him a choice, to pay the tax in three days or see his oldest daughter bound and delivered to the slave market. Attempting to resist would result in his entire family being taken for the market. Three days in which there was no fashion or manner he could raise the funds to pay the new tax. Similar taxes were being imposed on the other smiths in Smith's Alley. Other tradesmen and the longshoremen of the waterfront also talked of the impossible demands.

The day after the tax collector had been there, a delegation of tradesmen, including the ship chandlers and sail and rope makers, led by LaRue, had tried to appeal to the Lord Mayor. He had refused to even hear their complaints and had set his guardsmen on them with shields and clubs, in order, as he had said, "to drive them back to their stinking kennels."

Today the tax collector was to come and attempt to collect the extortionate tax. Since LaRue's smithy was the first one in the Alley, he would come there first. No one in Smith's Alley could afford to pay the tax. No one had the money to do so. Not even LaRue could pay, and he was the best and most prosperous smith in the city.

The tax collector was not a complete idiot. He arrived promptly at noon at LaRue's smithy, accompanied by a squad of six City Guardsmen as a bodyguard. And a half dozen slavers followed with their manacles and chains. But two dozen smiths and their older apprentices stood in the alley, hammers in their hands. LaRue met the taxman at the open entrance to his forge and anvil, a bag of coins in one hand, his favorite hammer in the other.

"I see you *do* have the ability to pay your tax after all, LaRue. Give it here." The taxman held out his hand and LaRue tossed it to him. The taxman caught it and then tossed the bag up in his hand. "This feels lighter than it should, LaRue. You trying to short the City on your full payment?"

"That's my full payment, the full honest payment, same as last year and the year before. You're the one who decided to double the tax. I'd wager you intend on putting half the doubled amount in your own pocket and only paying the correct amount to the City's coffers." LaRue held his temper in check, but only just. A muted growl of agreement came from the other gathered smiths.

"I'm the City's tax collector, LaRue. I set the taxes and then pay into the City's coffers. And I say you've only paid half what you owe. Pay the rest, now, or face the consequences."

"I paid my just dues, you bloodsucking parasite. Take your bullyboys and begone." A rumble of assent came from the gathered smiths and tradesmen.

"LaRue, you have one chance to pay your full dues, or, by God, I'll see you and your whole family in chains on the market block. I might even buy your oldest daughter myself. I hear she's a toothsome bit." The taxman stepped back behind one of the Guardsmen. "Pay up. Now. Or else you leave here in slaver's chains. Last chance."

"I've paid my dues. All you're going to get this year. Begone."

"It's on you, then." The taxman had an ugly grin on his face. "He's all yours, boys. Try not to damage him too much, and be extra careful with the daughter, I'll want her unspoi—"

William LaRue was not a particularly big man, despite how heavily muscled he was. No one expected the two long strides he took, nor the swing of the hammer that broke the taxman's shoulder. He couldn't reach his target's head past the guardsman's shield.

The taxman screamed and hit the ground. The guardsman smashed his shield into LaRue, knocking him backwards, giving the guardsman room to draw his sword. A thrown hammer from an apprentice smith hit him in the head, hard enough to send him down with a smashed-in skull, blood pouring out of the head wound.

"Shit," the guard sergeant cursed. "Marco is dead. Out swords and at 'em, boys." The remaining five guards raised their shields and drew their swords before charging the assembled smiths. The taxman and the slavers fled for their lives.

***

No one alive truly knows what happened in Smith's Alley that day. William LaRue and his whole family died in the inferno their home above the forge became. It started when a dying guardsman fell and knocked the lit forge over. Or was it a smith who threw a shovel full of burning coal at a guardsman? No one knows, but the riot and fire that started there would burn nearly a quarter of Luctini, including the waterfront and every ship tied up to the docks, including the *Graser*. *Intrepid*, anchored well out into the harbor, was never in any danger from the flames.

The Kolbian Embassy and the Silver Maiden Inn also escaped the mobs and the fire. The Embassy was behind a stout wall, one faced with hard granite slabs. The Embassy itself was brick and mortar with a roof of slate tiles. There was nothing to burn and the fixed bayonets of the Kolbian Marines encouraged looters and arsonists to go elsewhere.

The Silver Maiden was also a brick and mortar building with red clay tiles covering the roof. The Marines just across the street in front of the Embassy gate helped to keep the intersection of Dock and Market streets clear. Lorelei Garland was forced to reveal both her Halfelven nature and the fact that she was a quite capable mage herself. Between Lorelei's magery, Silaqui's sorcery and Gelman's divine magic, they kept the fires away from the Inn. The fires burned for three days before being quelled by heavy rain. An unnatural rain, some said.

***

"Well, this is a damn mess," Lorelei groused the day after the riots ended and the rain had put out the fires. "I've lost half my employees, frightened by my magery and your sorcery, Silaqui. I can't stay here now. I would beg passage with you, but your ship burned too. And now too many know there are magic-wielders and nonhumans here. We must flee and soon, or another mob, one led and directed by a priest or worse, an Inquisitor, will come for us. I should say we have no more than a couple of days, once the shock of the riots and fires, ha, dies down. Then they'll come for us; they will come for us."

"Calm down." Silaqui brushed vainly at the soot in her hair. Clouds of soot and smoke still floated around. "We are leaving on the *Intrepid* tomorrow on the noon tide. Willis has asked for and received a place for all of us, including you and any of your people who wish to follow you into exile."

"Oh, thank the Gods." Lorelei relaxed, tension flowing out of her at the news. "No, no one will go with me. The ones that stayed are wary of me now. I signed the Inn over to my manager. He's the owner now, an ordinary human with no more magic than a pig. He's a good man, he'll do well."

"What are you bringing with you?" the elf asked.

"Enough letters of credit and bank deposits to buy a new inn and start over. In some place slightly more accepting of my kind."

"I would suggest Kolbia, then. All they care about is ability and merit. In my homeland, Montagar, both elves and humans would be likely to hold your mixed-race heritage against you." Silaqui got the last of the soot out with a cantrip for cleaning clothes. It worked as well on hair. "I am sorry, but that is nothing but the honest truth."

"Well, we go aboard tonight, ladies," Willis walked up with Sachi and Sahla following him. "The Admiral and Envoy Courtenay will go first, then the rest of the Embassy staff, then us and the survivors of *Graser's* crew. We lost three men, all three to a mob. Same one that burned down the Weary Sailor Inn and set fire to the ships tied up at the dock. Roland and Irene survived, and they'll join us aboard. Both are wanting to emigrate to Kolbia now. And the Embassy Marines will be the last ones to the ship."

"We have a problem, Willis." Sachi brushed soot off her *himaku*. "We need to get to Isedore Island and whatever is left of the Confederation installation there. And with the *Graser* and every other ship in the harbor burned or sunken, we, well, I guess I must convince the Admiral, the Envoy and Captain Blaine to take us there, wait for us and then, most likely we'll have to go back to Kolbia on *Intrepid*."

"What is a 'Confederation installation'?" Lorelei asked, overhearing the conversation. "You must mean the ancient ruins up in the high hills beyond Isedore City's walls."

Willis, Sachi, Sahla and Silaqui all stopped talking and stared at Lorelei.

"What did you just say?" Sachi asked. "You know of ruins there?"

"Most people do. It's mostly just jagged stumps of walls sticking up. There's one small building left. It's sealed up, made of star metal or something like it. Nothing can mar its surface. People gave up trying to get in, oh, decades ago. It's all overgrown again now, I imagine. People never go there anymore. I've heard that monsters from the higher hills have moved into that place and made a lair there."

"Excuse us a moment, please." Willis pulled Sachi out of earshot of the others. "Sachi, the old man at the tower, with the hologrower, hologorer, holo- whatever..."

"Holographic, the map of the world with all the PDCs on it..." the sarcasm in Sachi's voice bounced off Willis without leaving a mark.

"Yeah, whatever. But the PDC that was on Isedore was supposed to be underwater, deep underwater, right?"

"Yes, and if it wasn't hit, it should still be intact. A completely intact PDC. Hopefully it was just abandoned in a rush and not stripped of all equipment. A completely stocked medical base."

"And maybe a way to access all those satellites and destroy the moon coming to destroy Rybithia."

"Give me a moment to talk to D.A.V.E. about this, Willis. He's been awful quiet lately." She turned her thoughts inward, seeking the gray space that was D.A.V.E.'s domain.

"D.A.V.E., are you there?" she spoke into the empty grayness.

::I am always here; you have had no need of my input for quite some time.:: The small silver statue materialized in front of her.

"The PDC on Isedore Island, could it still be intact?"

::Possibly. Probability of a fully intact PDC is twenty percent, plus or minus seventy-eight percent. Multiple variables.::

"How would you access the PDC?"

::Primary means of access would be via submersible craft and vehicular airlocks. There would be at least one access portal driven through the rock and allowing surface access on Isedore Island. The probability of described ruins being said access point is eighty-one percent plus or minus nineteen percent. The probability of said access portal allowing access to the PDC is unknown, too many variables. It should be noted that the access portal will likely be a nonfunctional grav tube. Manual access, if the door of the portal can be opened, would require climbing down several thousand feet of the non-functional grav tube.::

"Understood. It would be one hell of a climb if the tube is clear all the way to the PDC, right?"

::Correct.::

"That's what I needed to know, D.A.V.E. thank you."

::Understood. Ending VR.::

The gray world dissolved away. Sachi shook her head a moment and looked at Willis.

"Well?"

"He said the building is probably an access point. If it is, it'll be a nonfunctional grav tube, one going down several thousand feet to the PDC. He said there's only a twenty percent chance the base is intact, but it varies a lot, over seventy percent. It could be intact, and the tube leads down to it...or the tube could be full of water. No way to know until we get there."

"Yeah, that may be the hard part, convincing Captain Blaine to deviate from a bee line course back to Kolbia and Stark Haven." Willis scuffed his boot on the cobblestones of the street.

"Him and the Admiral and the Envoy. Both of the latter can override the Captain and order a shortest-time course back to Kolbia. Don't leave Admiral Sartell and Envoy Courtenay out of any plots of yours. They're really in charge of things." Sachi thought for a moment. "Willis?"

"Yeah?"

"At the dinner party, the Envoy was fascinated by Sahla, and Sartell was overly interested in my eyes. Like he'd seen eyes like mine somewhere. Do you suppose there are other people like me, people with tiny nano machines in their bodies, a D.A.V.E. in their mind? Maybe I'm not the only one?"

"How could they have survived so long? It has been nearly ten thousand years since the Fire Fall. Do the machines make you immortal?"

"I do not believe they do, Willis, but I really know very little about them or exactly what they can do. Maybe they will make me immortal. I think Sahla, being a magical Jann, is immortal but I do not know for certain. We've never talked about it."

"Maybe you should. It's something that will be very important one day."

"Yes. But we should be heading to the dock. *Intrepid's* boats have arrived, and they are taking the Admiral and Envoy to the ship." Sachi walked over to the Embassy gate where all the bags and crates were stacked and picked up her backpack and two bags.

***

Sahla came over from the Inn's front porch with Gelman and Aylie. Since her injury, Sahla carried only one very light bag with her clothes and things in it. Everything else she owned was stored in the magical gem that was her home when she was not materialized in the real world.

Willis' pack had both the cased blast rifles strapped to the side and he had nearly a thousand rounds of ammunition for his two 1911 pistols in the reinforced bottom of his pack. Not to mention lead and powder for his two revolvers. It was a damn heavy pack. The 1911s were on belt holsters and he carried the revolvers in shoulder holsters.

Sachi had her white steel bracers covering each forearm. Her Mark 14 APF pistol was in its secure holster and the hard fabric belt wrapped around her hips. It came from the *Constellation*, the wrecked dreadnought starship back on Ironheart's pirate island.

The same place Willis' blast rifles and 1911s were from, gifts from a star Admiral's electronic ghost.

Chapter Seventeen

Luctini Harbor
KRN *Intrepid* (32)
March 1479, Third Age of Imperial Reckoning

IT TOOK THE REST of the day and into the night to get everyone aboard the *Intrepid* and all their gear stowed. Sachi and the rest of her group got hammocks on the gun deck near the forward guns. *Intrepid's* crew was smaller than it had been, given her reduction in guns. The individual guns had bigger crews but there were twelve fewer guns. It made more room on the gun deck, but the Marines still had to berth on the orlop deck. *Intrepid's* short company of Marines smoothly absorbed the Embassy Marines.

***

"Captain Blaine?" a soft, melodious voice asked from behind Blaine. He turned and had to look down. The tiny Darsälaamic girl had silently come up behind him. In the early morning light, her bright sapphire eyes seemed to almost glow.

"Yes, Sahla. How may I help you?"

"It is I who may help you. After all, you are still in love with my Bonded." It was a statement, not a question.

"You know I am. There were no lies told in that sitting room. And she is still in love with me. Does that upset you, that we still love each other?"

"No. I am a Jann, born of the love between a human woman and a Jinn, a Prince of Elemental Air. I was literally created from pure love between a mortal and an Immortal. Yet the Sheik-my-Father loved my mother just as deeply and she loved him in return. You love her very much but are worried that you have lost her because of me. Perhaps, and perhaps not. I am Bonded to her by the Bond of True Love. Our love will never fail or falter." She took a deep breath. "But as I told Sachi, love is like the sands of the Great Desert. No matter how much is taken away, there is always more sand. And love, like sand, is an endless abundance. Think on this, Captain Blaine, Sachi's Captain." She vanished into thin air.

"What the hell?" he shook his head and rubbed his eyes. "Helmsman, did you see that girl?"

"What girl? Captain, none here save you, me and the watchstanders." He looked askance at Blaine.

"Never mind." Blaine turned back to the rail.

***

They were staying in their hammocks, staying out of the way as *Intrepid* began to weigh anchor. Sachi could hear the pumps clanking as they washed mud and sea slime off the anchor chain and the anchor itself. The great ship seemed to curtsey to her bow and then raise up as the anchor broke loose from the harbor mud.

"We've got company inbound from dead astern, a young Marine, one from the Embassy, I believe," Silaqui drawled. "I bet he's here for you, Sachi. And where has Sahla gotten off to, I wonder?"

"She's up on deck, I think," Sachi answered as the Marine hesitated a moment until he located Sachi. "How can I help you, Marine?"

"Ma'am, the Admiral requests your presence in the great cabin, at your earliest convenience."

"I see. 'At your earliest convenience' usually means 'right this instant,' doesn't it, Marine?"

"For me, it does, ma'am. But you're a civilian, so I don't know. He said he would like a calm talk with you about something very important and sensitive."

"Again, I see." Sachi gracefully rolled out of the hammock and ducked to avoid hitting her head on a deck beam. "Lead on, Marine...what is your name, please?"

"Murphy, ma'am, Private First Class Adam Murphy."

***

"Thank you for agreeing to see me, Miss Sachi." Admiral Sartell said.

"If you would, please, just Sachi."

She sat on the couch upon which she had lain unconscious those many, many months ago. Sartell occupied a chair across the low table in the middle of the great cabin. She looked around; little had changed, Captain Blaine's hand was still in the contents of the room. Even his scent was here. Sartell was an interloper here, but it was permitted; he was an Admiral after all.

"You wanted to see me to discuss 'something important and sensitive,' well, I'm here. What 'something important and sensitive' do you want to talk about?"

"You are what I want to talk about. You appear to be a full-up Confederal; the black eyes are the giveaway. What is your mission here and are you in touch with any other Confederals or any other Operatives?"

"Admiral Sartell, what are you talking about? I assure you that I am not a 'full-up Confederal' or anything else. I am myself and I believe I am unique."

"You're not unique, I've met one other Confederal and an Operative. The Confederals are the surviving humans that first came to the world of Rybithia over ten thousand years ago. Do you have a machine voice that speaks to you in your mind, takes you to a place called Virtual Reality? Larry Anderson was the name of the Confederal I worked with back when I was a young Commander with my first command, a schooner named *Valiant*. She only had sixteen guns, nothing like the new guns now, but I loved that ship. We found Larry adrift on a fabric inflatable raft in the middle of the Great Western Ocean. He was barely alive, but we nursed him back to health and he told me the most amazing story. When he showed me what he could do, I had to believe him.”

“Admiral Sartell, you’re talking nonsense.” Sachi didn’t know what to do, panic and run or kill this fool. How could he know about D.A.V.E. and Virtual Reality? He obviously knew *something* about others like her, but what did that mean?

“I know it sounds fantastic, but it isn’t nonsense. Larry told me that his people, the Confederals, had been fighting a shadow war since the fall of the Empire of Rolandus, nearly six thousand years ago. He was in the ocean because his ‘skimmer’ had been shot down by something he called a Directed Energy Weapon, or more specifically, a graser. A weapon used by the Confederals’ enemies, he called them the Seekers, and they want to destroy the entire world. The name of your sloop, the *Graser*, was not by chance, was it? The weapon he described to me would appear to be very much like the ‘Line of Fire’ that cut through the sky a few weeks ago. I’m guessing you had something to do with that. Why are you denying the truth?”

“Admiral Sartell, I do not know of any of these things you speak of. You say that my eyes are the same as these ‘Confederals.’ I have never seen anyone with eyes like mine.”

“And you have another giveaway, Sachi. The pistol on your hip looks to be the same as the pistol Larry carried. He said it was an anti-personnel flechette weapon. Looked exactly like yours. Where did you get it?”

“Admiral, give me a moment to think, please.” *He knows more of me than I know of myself. I know there are people trying to kill me before I can stop this moon falling towards Rybithia. Could those people be the Seekers he speaks of? He knows what a graser is and he recognizes my pistol. Can I trust him?* “Admiral, this Larry Anderson, did he ask you to keep him secret, what he was and what he could do?”

“Yes, he did. You’re the first person I’ve ever discussed him with, since you seem to be exactly like him.”

"Then I ask you to keep my secret. I truly know nothing of Confederals or Seekers, but someone keeps trying to kill me. And I ask one other thing: order Captain Blaine to set sail for Isedore Island in the middle of the Traquilidamar Sea. There may be answers for both of us there. Please?"

"I kept Larry's secret, and I shall keep yours as well. And I'll direct Captain Blaine to sail to Isedore. There is a small city there, or a large town, depending on who you ask."

"I believe I have taken enough of your valuable time, Admiral, and there is an old friend in the ship's company I am desperate to see. Would you excuse me and take time to think on what we have said here? I certainly shall. With your permission, sir?" she rose from the couch as Sartell stood from his chair.

"Certainly, Sachi, we can speak at more length later."

"Thank you, sir."

***

Sachi quietly knocked on the door frame. The big man in the galley was taking baked bread out of one of the ovens. She waited until he put the hot pan down and turned to the door. Then she flung herself into his arms.

"Toby, my first friend! It is so good to see you!"

"Sachi! As I live and breathe, you look well!" He engulfed her in a bear hug. Minutes later he released her and held her out at arm's length. "How are you back on board? What has happened to you? I have missed you, my friend!"

"If you'll let me help in the galley, I'll tell you the entire tale, some of which you must keep secret."

"Well, there are pots that need to be scrubbed?"

Sachi hung her jacket on a hook, rolled up her shirt sleeves and plunged the few dirty pots and pans into the wash tub. While she scrubbed, she told Toby the entire story of everything that had happened to her since she had left *Intrepid* months ago. By the time she finished her tale, every pot was gleaming clean and she was sharing a bottle of beer with Toby.

"So, you have found your True Love in this little Darsälaamic girl, who is really a magical Jann. And we're going to set course for this Isedore Island in hopes of finding a near magical healing for her?" Toby gave her a huge smile and rubbed his face. "Quite a tale, Sachi, quite a tale. Now, however, there are old shipmates waiting to welcome you back, including the bosun and those ship's officers that remember you. Come, we've put off welcoming you back in the proper fashion for an *Intrepid* come back to her first home. Come with me."

She followed Toby onto the spar deck and the crew's shout of "Welcome home!" nearly blew her overboard.

***

Sahla smiled to herself from where she was invisibly perched on a yardarm, watching the exuberant welcome Sachi was getting. At last, the short, burly man they called the Bosun ordered everyone back to their posts. The tide was running out and moments later Captain Blaine was shouting orders to raise the upper sails, t'gallants and topsails, and she flew down to the deck, went below to their berthing area by the forward guns, stepped behind the giant gun and dropped her invisibility.

She started to go aft to the stair to the 'spar' deck, she thought it was called. She floated up the stairs to the spar deck. The ship's boats had been swayed back into their cradles and she could feel the ship moving with the wind. She glanced at the dock and saw a pair of priests standing near the burned and sunken hull of the faithful *Graser*. She paid little attention to them. Someone cleared their throat behind her.

"Miss Sahla? Miss? Excuse me for troubling you."

"No trouble, what do you need?" she turned and faced one of the diplomats from the Embassy staff, a thin man of average height and straight brown hair worn long and in a braid.

"Miss Sahla, the Envoy should like a moment of your time, if you please."

"What could she possibly want with me, sir?"

"No idea, she just said she wanted to talk to you for a few minutes." He made a half bow and gestured with his hand. "This way, please."

"Oh, very well."

She followed him below decks and through the warren of cabins and rooms in the aft part of the ship. The door he led her to said, "First Lieutenant," but a bronze plaque reading, 'Envoy to Luctini,' hung over the door and partly obscured the sign of carved wood screwed into the door itself. The man knocked twice on the door and then opened it.

The Envoy, Angelina Courtenay, sat behind a desk. She looked up as Sahla came in and the door closed behind her. Courtenay wasn't a beautiful woman, but her striking green eyes made her almost pretty. She looked like she was short enough that she didn't have to duck under the overhead deck beams.

"Miss Sahla, thank you for coming. Please be seated; would you like some tea?" she spoke Terranglais with a rapid, clipped accent.

"Not really and please just call me Sahla. I need no title."

"No, I suppose you wouldn't want or need a normal, mortal title, being a Jinn and all. Do your friends know what you really are?"

"I am no Jinn, ma'am. Jinn have dark blue skin."

"And couldn't you use your magic to disguise yourself, everything except the eyes. Eyes of Jinn blue."

"There are others that have such eyes. Even a normal, mortal girl like me."

"Please, we have no time to waste in foolish, verbal sparring. I grant your claim that you are not a Jinn, but it's more than your eyes that give you away. You don't walk, you levitate just above the ground, and when you do walk, you have a bad limp. You should be more careful to hide that. What are you?"

"Very well, I am a Jann, the daughter of a human woman and a Jinn, one conceived in love and care. I am Sahla al Qasim."

"A Jann? Bless me, I thought such beings were only in stories told to children."

"Jann are very rare, I know of no others like me. I strive to be a righteous Jann, in order that the Prophet will name me before

Chalta and that I might enter Paradise when I pass this mortal plane."

"According to the stories, a Jann must be Bonded to a mortal to stay on this plane of existence. I believe you are Bonded to the Nisei girl, Sachi, correct?"

"I am. It is a Bond of True Love, not Master and Slave. What do you want of me? I cannot grant you a wish or any other foolish thing like that."

"I collect knowledge of rare and magical beings, beings such as yourself. I am a Kolbian, true enough, but I do not deny the existence of magic or magical beings. I merely want to speak with you and write down such things as you are willing to tell me."

"I see. You wish to 'collect' me, knowledge of me? Nothing more?"

"Correct. A question, why do you limp so badly when you do walk?"

"In Du Khamps des Sou-See, I was stabbed from behind with a white steel blade. I nearly died. Pere Gelman tried to heal me, but he was exhausted from healing others. He kept me from dying and healed what he could, but it was not a complete healing. And now, the wound is healed but I am crippled. He cannot heal me further." Sahla sighed. "But I have hope; on Isedore Island there may be a way for me to be fully healed and no longer in constant pain."

"Isedore Island?"

"Yes. Help me, in turn for this knowledge of me. Have the ship go to Isedore Island before heading for Kolbia. Give me a chance to be healed and I will tell you such stories that you cannot believe them, but they are all true."

"Hmm, Isedore Island. I hear it is very nice there this time of year. Very well, I shall help you, and I'll expect stories to turn my hair white."

"Thank you, Envoy Courtenay, thank you. May the Prophet always guide you to shade and sweet water. Chalta Himself will bless you in all things." Sahla found she liked Courtenay, the woman was straightforward and honest and, at least for her, easy to deal with. She smiled and told her the story of the agreement between her human Father and Ilben alh-Taymyah, Jinn of the Second Rank of Air and Wind and her Sire. Courtenay quickly wrote down the story. And Sahla did, finally, have a cup of tea with the older woman.

Luctini Cathedral
March 1479, Third Age of Imperial Reckoning

"She was here, HERE, in Luctini, and she slipped right through my hands! All because Ambroise could not do his duty and report such a group to me. He let her get away and there isn't so much as a rowboat unburned in the harbor. Because of a riot over taxes raised to impossible rates by greedy tax collectors." He turned to his secretary. "Take these orders down. I want that tax collector arrested. He's to face the Question and the Punishment. And arrest dear cousin Ambroise Dubois de Palmaroli, I don't care if he's a Palmaroli, he's to face the Question and the Punishment as well. He let our greatest threat slip through our, no, slip through MY fingers." He wanted to beat Cousin Ambroise to death with his bare hands.

"At once, My Lord Bishop." The secretary's quill fluttered as he wrote down the arrest orders quickly and in his best hand. "Anything else, My Lord?"

"No. You may leave me." He extended his hand in order that the secretary might kiss his amethyst ring of office, then the man scurried away. Vicente waited for the door to close behind the man, then got up, walked to the door and locked it. He went back to his chair and turned around to face a certain leather-bound box. He opened it and activated the communicator. Within moments, the box glowed blue, and Master's head appeared in it.

"Vicente, you have news?"

"We missed the girl, the one named Sachi Takahashi. She was here, right here in Luctini, and she slipped through my fingers."

"What happened, Vicente? Tell me all." An hour later, Vicente had told his tale. Master was not pleased.

"I concur with sending your cousin Ambroise to the Question and the Punishment."

"Do we have anything in space that can kill that ship?"

"Nothing that would not take days to move into place. The weapon we used on Du Khamps has failed and will fall into Rybithia's Great Western Ocean, and we have nothing else available. Oh, we could move other weapons into place, but it would take over a week and we'd never find the ship again. There is a limit to what we have in space."

"The ship will go to Kolbia next, and our only hope is that some part of our fleet intercepts and destroys it." Vicente thought for a moment. "There are about twenty harbor defense galleys at Casalia Island. We can order them to go to sea and intercept the Kolbian ship before it reaches the Gates!"

"Do know you what ship it was, this Kolbian?"

"The *Intrepid*, a frigate."

"One of the Kolbian frigates is near to a ship-of-the-line. And this one has been refitted, with fewer, but bigger guns. Guns that will fire more slowly but do more damage, I think. Or so our spies in Kolbia have reported. I doubt our galleys could even slow it down. But I shall make the orders to send them out. They might be fortunate and disable it somehow, ram it or shoot away a mast. Something that would allow our ships to use their numerical advantage to swarm her and kill the entire crew. That should make sure this Sachi Takahashi dies and then nothing can hope to stop Last Weapon."

"Perhaps God will favor us and cause that ship to be intercepted and destroyed, Master."

"Perhaps He will. I think we are through here. Go with The God, Vicente."

"Go with The God, Master." When the connection ended and the blue light faded away, Vicente closed and locked the case. Then he sat, staring into space.

"She slipped right through my hands!"

Traquilidamar Sea
KRN *Intrepid* (32)
March 1479, Third Age of Imperial Reckoning

"She is slower. Not much, but she is a couple of knots slower than she was." Sachi stood on the quarterdeck next to Captain

Blaine. The wind was rated as being on the upper end of a strong breeze, an indicated twenty-six or twenty-seven knots. *Intrepid's* log showed her speed at eleven knots.

"The armor added fifteen tons, and the bigger guns are heavier than the thirty-two pounders they replaced." Blaine glanced sideways at Sachi. The wind blew her braid out in front of her. "I'm still not sure this 'upgrade' is any improvement at all. Certainly, she throws a heavier broadside and an even heavier broadside of explosive shells, but the loss of speed and maneuverability...I don't know. She'd be optimized to fight ships built like her, but no other navy in the world can match our navy. And *Constitution* and *Enterprise*, those ships will be monsters in action. Nothing can face them on the sea, and nothing can damage their armor. They will make every ship on the sea obsolete overnight. Once they launch next year, that is." He took a deep breath of fresh air and turned to his First Lieutenant, Lieutenant Commander Keith Gustav. "The deck is yours, Keith. I'm going below for lunch." He turned back to Sachi. "Care to join me for lunch, Sachi?"

"I'd be delighted to do so, Captain Blaine, but only if you include Sahla."

"That would be fine, Sachi, go find her and issue the invitation. But just to Sahla." Blaine turned and went below, turning aft while Sachi went forward to where Sahla was reading a book in her hammock.

"Care for lunch, my love? Captain Blaine invited both of us."

"Yes, I would love to join you. Anyone else?"

"No, just us two. Maybe Doctor Hoff."

"My, my. A romantic lunch at sea, just the three of us. Do you think he'll propose to you? Or to me, maybe?"

"You're sun struck. Or it's those trashy novels you've been reading. I knew nothing good would come of you reading Toby's romantic adventure novels. Come on, I'm hungry."

"You're always hungry, you bottomless pit. I'm coming." Sahla levitated out of the hammock and followed Sachi aft.

Toby had the table set when they got to the wardroom. Blaine and Doctor Hoff were seated but both men stood to seat the ladies, Blaine for Sachi and Hoff for Sahla. Lunch was soup and sandwiches, with tea, beer and wine to drink. Sachi paid her usual attention to her food and the pile of sandwiches rapidly diminished.

"Doctor Hoff," Sahla started to say when he interrupted her.

"Elazar, please, in informal situations like this."

"Very well, Elazar, then. You know, I think you ruined Captain Blaine's plan to propose to Sachi today." Blaine choked but managed not to spray wine across the table. Sachi froze, sandwich halfway to her mouth. Hoff pounded Blaine on the back. "Did I say something wrong? Are you okay, Captain?" Sahla had a mischievous smile on her face. "Sachi told me that your wife has divorced you, so you are no longer bound by your vows and oaths to her. You love Sachi and she loves you. Why not propose?"

"Stop it, Sahla, this isn't funny. It never was." Sachi didn't quite snap at her, but Sahla quickly realized her joke had hit a little too close to home.

"Sahla, my dear, Captain Blaine and I both know the two of you are Bonded together. To Captain Blaine, that is the same as if the two of you were married, and an honorable man like William, here, would never intrude between the pair of you. Indeed, I consider your Bond of True Love to be even more precious than most marriages. And Sahla, I do not believe you are, in fact, in love with anyone but Sachi, far less being in love with William. Tell me that I lie," Hoff said.

"You don't lie." Sahla's face was crimson in embarrassment. "Please forgive me, Captain Blaine, Sachi, my love. I only meant to joke a little at your expense, Sachi. I'm sorry."

"Forget it," Captain Blaine said. "It was just a joke." Still, lunch ended quickly and awkwardly thereafter. Sachi and Sahla left quickly and together.

"You know, Billy, I think Sahla was serious about you proposing to Sachi. I think. Hard to tell with that one. She seems flighty and chaotic. Not at all like our Sachi." Hoff was enjoying an after-lunch cigar and a glass of whiskey, while Blaine was in a dark mood, seated behind the desk.

"No. Not at all like my...our Sachi."

Traquilidamar Sea
KRN *Intrepid* (32)
April 1479, Third Age of Imperial Reckoning

"Land, ho!"

"It's been a slow passage, William. Contrary winds and *Intrepid* has given up her speed for armor and heavier guns." Admiral Sartell stood on the quarterdeck with Captain Blaine, frowning up at the masthead lookout who had just spotted what should be Isedore Island. "I think I agree with you that this 'refit' was not well thought out. Guns *or* armor, not both, that would have let her keep her speed. Which would you choose, given a choice, that is?"

"The guns, Admiral, no question. Imperial guns couldn't penetrate her sides with just the teak wood. The armor is overkill, unless we go up against something armed like she is."

"The Imperials are building new ships, good ones, well-founded ships, not galleys. And they've learned to cast trunnions in their new guns and to use bagged powder charges. They are not entirely stupid, you know. After what Eyles and *Stellar* did to three of their better galleasses two and a half years ago, well, they learned. And they have an excellent intelligence service. One that can be aided by any or every Kythal priest out there."

"They haven't figured out how to make explosive shells yet, I hope to God." Blaine checked the compass heading on the binnacle. "Helm, bring us two points to starboard. The charts show rocky waters shoaling as we get near Isedore." He watched the sails as the great ship turned slightly to starboard. *Intrepid* was a well-found ship, answering smoothly to the helm. Blaine wished his personal life was as smooth as *Intrepid* was. He thought back to a conversation he'd had with Sachi three weeks ago. And what that conversation had led to.

***

"I've been ordered to make course for some place called Isedore Island. Orders from both the Admiral and Envoy Courtenay. I think you had something to do with these orders."

"I don't give orders to admirals or diplomatic envoys, Captain Blaine. The idea is ridiculous," Sachi answered.

"Is it? Sartell ordered me to make course for Isedore Island shortly after we left Luctini and after a long private conversation with you. And before he was finished, Envoy Courtenay comes in the cabin and nicely asks if we can go to a place called Isedore Island. She said there's a town there where we can get resupplied. We don't need resupply to simply go back to Kolbia, but we might if *Intrepid* is going to be diverted all over creation, then we might indeed need resupply. And Courtenay had just finished a long talk with Sahla. What are you two up to? And am I sailing into hostile waters to be a target?"

"No, you're not going to be a target. At least, you shouldn't be one." Sachi stopped and took a deep breath. "We are going to Isedore to hopefully find healing for Sahla. She's crippled, William, a dancer who can no longer dance."

"There were healers in Luctini, Sachi. Why not see one or more of them?"

"We did. They couldn't help, the wound is too old and too healed. She would have to be reinjured in the same place, in the same way. That would likely kill her; it's a miracle she didn't die when she was stabbed."

"And there's a better healer in Isedore Town? On this island? Some holy hermit who performs miracles?"

"No; oh, the story is too long to tell you, but we need a healthy and whole Sahla. To fulfill her part in the prophecy."

"There's a prophecy now?" Blaine was trying to understand, but Sachi was dancing around the subject.

"William, I trust you, I'm going to tell you my whole story and it goes all the way back to the Empire of Isemoto. When I was an

Oda. I only hope that I won't lose you as a friend. That I won't lose your love."

"You could never lose my love, Sachi."

"We shall see, William, we shall see. Sit down while I tell you my complete story. When I was a young girl, I was chosen..."

It had taken three days to tell the whole story. At different times, Sachi brought in Silaqui, Willis and Sahla to tell their part in it. Gelman and Aylie had added their own stories as well, telling how they came to be here. They told the tale to its end, up to the day *Intrepid* had left Luctini harbor.

At different times, Blaine had been stunned, incredulous and upset. But when Sachi made her white steel bracers flow like water, he was left with no choice but to believe the tale. When she finished that final, impossible display, Blaine had sat silently in the chair. He asked for time to cope with what he had learned and what this incredible narrative meant to him, personally. He also asked that neither of them speak to him about anything other than ship's business.

Sachi and Sahla had not spoken to him since that last day. Three weeks ago.

***

"What have you said to the Captain that has him in such a dark place, lass?" Toby asked her as he was preparing dinner for the officers' dining room. The Admiral and Envoy Courtenay were dining together again. They had dined together with Blaine several times, but only once had anyone else been invited, and then only ship's officers had attended.

"I told him the truth, Toby, and I think I have lost his friendship," she paused, "and his love."

"I don't believe that, Sachi, but whatever it was you told him, he's been wrestling with it ever since. You haven't taken up to murdering people, now, have you?"

"I have killed men, Toby, but there were no murders, they all died in honest battle with us. They had no idea who or what they were up against, and they had no chance against me, but there were no murders, no assassinations." She stared into the distance, seeing something only she could see. "No, Toby the murders and assassinations I did do were done at the behest of the Oda Family. Long before I fled Isemoto, stowed away on *Intrepid*. You know what I was, don't give me that look."

"I guess I do know, but I didn't want to believe those stories you told only to me in those days. And now you have more stories, and one that has upset the Captain. I don't know what to say or do."

There was a knock on the galley doorframe and Senior Midshipman Johan Weiss looked in.

"Oh hullo, Miz Sachi. The Captain wants to see you and your friend Sahla, the little Darsälaamic lady, right away."

"Captain Blaine wants to see me and Sahla? Now?"

"Aye, he does. Just sent me to find you, though."

"Well, you've found me, Johan. I'll get Sahla and we shall hasten to the Captain's summons." She laughed at the confused look on Johan's face. "We'll be there as soon as possible; I'm just being overly formal with you. I'll go track down Sahla. I know where she is right now. Thank you."

Johan vanished like mist in a high wind. Toby chuckled behind her.

"You confused the poor lad, Sachi; not particularly nice. Not at all."

"He's senior midshipman, he should be over being confused about orders now."

"Not when two of the most beautiful women in the world are the object of his search. Poor lad." Sachi laughed along with Toby.

"Sahla is in her hammock forward. I'll go get her and report to the Captain. Wish me well, Toby."

"I do. Things will be good again."

***

"You wanted to see us, Captain?" Sahla asked as she entered the wardroom. Blaine sat at the card table and there were two other chairs at the table. He did not rise to seat the pair.

He nodded at them and sat with his hands folded on the table and long minutes passed without a word being said by anyone.

"Why are we here? To play cards? To sit together and commune with the Prophet? You called us here, Captain Blaine. Why?" Sahla spoke first, shattering the silence. "I've no use to sit here for no reason other than I was summoned."

"Be quiet, Sahla," Sachi hissed.

"No, she's right. I'm not sure myself why I summoned you here, other than the fact that I had to see you again. Both of you together. The most beautiful women in the world, here, on my ship, and I act like a bashful idiot boy and ignore them because they told me a story that frightened me. That left me unsure and frightened of them. Very foolish of me, given that I love one of those women. I need to be at least a little part of your life, Sachi, and for you to be a part of my life. I don't know how yet. I don't know how your True Love changes things between us, but she is a part of your life that must be acknowledged. And I have been rude and inconsiderate to both of you while I've wrestled with my own fears and feelings." Blaine held his gaze steadily on Sachi's face while he spoke.

"I would be a part of your life as well, William. My Captain. But Sahla will always be my True Love, and I don't know, either, how or even if we can fit together. Whether as just friends, or lovers or...or...I don't know, and your silence frightened the life from me. I don't want to lose you, and I cannot ever lose Sahla, my True Love."

"I understand. This is difficult and awkward." Blaine dropped his head into his hands. "Will the pair of you forgive me for how cold and rude I've been?"

"We will." Sachi and Sahla spoke in perfect unison.

"I forgive you for the stress and uncertainty you have given my beloved," Sahla continued on. "I am not in love with you, William Blaine, but I am fond of you. Until lately, that is. I was not fond of the hurt you inadvertently caused her."

"I forgive you, my Captain." Sachi's smile gave her a radiant beauty that took Blaine's breath away. "We will come to some accommodation in time, I believe."

"I have one reservation." Sahla caught and held both Blaine's and Sachi's attention. "I will never make love with someone that I am not in love with. Right now, that means you, William Blaine. As damaged as I am, there is little in the way of lovemaking between even me and Sachi. There is too much pain, it kills any ecstasy. Hopefully there will be what we need in this sunken...PDC? Is that right, Sachi?"

"Yes, it is."

"For now, let's just agree that we can be friends again and that there is still love between me and Sachi. Now I must go, I need to be on the quarterdeck as we approach this remote island of Isedore. The charts are...somewhat vague." Blaine popped out of his chair and assisted both women from their seats and held the door for them. Sahla stepped out the door, but Sachi closed it and flung herself into Blaine's arms. This kiss was just as passionate as the first one back in the Silver Maiden Inn but lasted longer and was more satisfying for both. Without a word, Sachi turned away and opened the door to a smiling Sahla.

"Enjoy that, did you two?" her eyes danced with joy. "No more until we are all safe ashore and hopefully, I am healed."

Chapter Eighteen

**Isedore Town Harbor
KRN *Intrepid* (32)
April 1479, Third Age of Imperial Reckoning**

THE HARBOR AT ISEDORE Town was barely worthy of the name. One rickety dock stretched out into the harbor, not quite long enough for the thirty-six-foot longboat to tie up to, much less *Intrepid's* two-hundred-foot-plus length.

"Not exactly a shipping hub for the world, now, is it?" Doctor Hoff quipped from where he stood on the spar deck.

"No, look beyond the waterfront. No tall buildings, nothing above three stories. But we can see the city walls from here. Tied into the rocky cliffs left of the waterfront, with a tower built into the cliffside and its footings in the water there. On the right, another tower, built on the very edge of that swampy area over there. Complete coverage, no way around the walls without either getting wet after a long fall or getting bogged in a swamp. Eighty-foot-tall towers with lots of medium-sized cannons and one big gun. Sixty-foot-tall walls wide enough at the top for four horsemen to ride abreast." Willis was using the pair of electronic binoculars recovered from the wreck of the *Constellation*. Solar powered, they gave him forty power telescopic imaging with range data and stadia to determine the height of anything in the field of view.

Captain Blaine was using the ship's best glass to look at the same things. Experience let him judge such things as range and size of things just as well as Willis' high-tech binoculars did. He stood there for long moments, studying the town and its walls.

"And the waterfront is not fortified at all. These people are afraid of something to landward. And I see a work crew repairing a damaged section of the wall. Something dangerous to landward." Blaine closed the glass and handed it to Midshipman Wiess. "Take a look, Johan, and see if you notice anything else. Other than the pretty girls walking around on the streets, that is."

"So, there is a threat to landward." Sachi disdained both a glass and the proffered binoculars. Her enhanced vision was better than either. "Someone find Lorelei and ask her to come up here. In the meanwhile, I'm going up the mast to see if I can see beyond the walls." She climbed up to the foremast's fighting top. When she saw Lorelei arrive on deck, she slid down the backstay to the deck. Admiral Sartell and Envoy Courtenay joined the slowly growing group on the starboard rail.

"What did you see, Sachi?" Silaqui asked as she came up with Aylie and Gelman.

"Big kill zone made of low growth farmland, nothing taller than waist high on me. Forest beyond that. They have lots of cannon on the walls. Some of them are huge, probably throw a hundred-pound shot." Sachi turned to Lorelei. "You said there were monsters here. Any idea what kind of monsters?"

"I've heard stories of giant beasts shaped like a man, twenty feet tall, and long, serpent things that can shoot lightnings from their mouth. They supposedly have many legs and can climb well. It is said the serpents are big enough to swallow a man whole. Or so the stories I've heard say such things exist here. But I've only heard stories. Until now I've never left Luctini." Lorelei hugged herself. "If it's all the same to you, I'll stay on the ship. Monsters, ugh."

"Are you sure you need to do this, Sachi?" Blaine started to put a hand on Sachi's shoulder and stopped himself. "Giant man-beasts and creatures that can swallow a man whole? Sounds like a good way to die."

"You have no idea just how lethal our little group can be, Captain Blaine. We've faced worse. Remember what I told you of the island we were shipwrecked on?"

"Brr, I remember. That part of your tale has given me the occasional sleepless night. Giant spiders, ugh. I don't even like little ones." Blaine barely suppressed a shiver. "However, I am going with you into this monster-haunted forest."

"Your place is here on the ship," Sachi protested.

"Actually, I want Blaine to go with you." Admiral Sartell inserted himself into the conversation. "I'm too old to go galivanting about, or I would go. I want at least one set of Navy eyes on this expedition, and no, Willis, you don't count. Not this time. I want fresh eyes that have no preconceived notions. Therefore, Captain Blaine goes."

"But Admiral, I'm ONI and I've been with Sachi since the beginning..."

"Which is why I want another viewpoint on things. You're too jaded, Lieutenant Commander Fleet. And you're ONI. I want regular Navy eyes on things."

"Yes, sir," was all Willis said.

"Now, we need to go ashore and see what the locals can offer us to resupply *Intrepid*. I trust your purser can handle that, Captain Blaine?" Sartell asked.

"Jalen Cartran may only be an Ensign, but he's a superb purser and quartermaster. I implicitly trust him to do the very best for the ship. In fact, he'll be promoted to Lieutenant J.G. when we get back to Kolbia. I might lose him then."

"Then get the longboat lowered and get yourselves ashore. I don't think we want to stay here any longer than necessary."

"Aye-aye, Admiral." Blaine saluted the Admiral and turned to Sachi. "You have twenty minutes to get your group ready to go. I assume everyone will go, including even that young girl, Aylie?"

"Yes, she's going as well as Gelman; we might need a healer. Aylie can hold her own in a fight. We'll have to make sure to defend Sahla. She can still fly up out of harm's way, but she can't fight in her condition."

***

"Welcome to Isedore Porttown, Captain, ah…?" the somewhat portly, black-haired man wearing a red sash over his tunic asked. Behind him stood a military officer in half plate armor.

"Blaine, Captain William Blaine of KRN *Intrepid*. I noticed your city walls are quite impressive; do you have enemies that require such defenses, Mayor…?"

"Oh, how rude of me! I am Pietro Bernardo, as you guessed, Mayor of Isedore Porttown. And this is my military commander, Colonel Quintus Seventus. And yes, we do. There are monstrous beasts in the wilds of the island. They used to stay up in the higher hills, but something changed many years ago, driving them down to the lowlands here. They became such a menace that the copper mine was closed. The miners left, and now, we grow enough food in our fields that we can export the surplus to Luctini. Otherwise, this town would have long since been abandoned. We're a community of farmers now. Our fields are just outside the wall and close enough that if some monstrous creature is sighted, field workers can quickly flee inside the gates…" He finally ran out of breath. The Colonel stepped forward, laying a gentle hand on the Mayor's shoulder.

"An excellent introduction to our town. What brings a large Kolbian frigate to these somewhat treacherous waters?"

"A mission of mercy. We seek some ancient ruins up in the hills, ruins that may hold the secret of a magical healing one of our party desperately needs."

"A frigate was dispatched to provide transportation for this person? They must be important indeed!" the Colonel said. "I know there are old ruins in the hills, truly ancient. But they are just broken walls sticking out of the ground. What could provide healing there?"

"Magic, a place of great power to one who can wield it," Gelman stepped forward and offered a hand to the Mayor and then to the Colonel. "This place is an ancient holy shrine of healing, and I am granted the power of healing by the One God. All we ask is permission to pass through your gates in search of this shrine. And possibly a person to provide a guide."

"You won't need a guide, and no one would go, at any rate. To go that far into the forest and the hills is to die. There are many dangers, too many for a small group of what, seven of you?" Seventus shook his head. "I would hesitate to take any army up that road. You will all die. I would not have it said that I let you go foolishly to your deaths."

"Colonel, no one will hold you responsible if we don't come back. Just open the gates for us when we leave and open them again when we return. And we will return."

"On your heads be it, then. Come back at first light in the morning and the gates will be open. You can go out with our farmers. But the gates close at dusk and will not be opened again until first light." The Colonel made a hand washing gesture.

"Are the gates open now?" Sachi stepped forward and asked.

"Well, yes, they are."

"Then we will go now. Captain Blaine, ask the boat crew to bring us our packs."

***

"Those were impressive gates. Five feet of solid oak and an outer covering of copper a foot thick, yet well balanced enough that four men are all that is needed to close each leaf of the gates. Very impressive." Blaine carried a sword on his right hip and had one of Willis' revolvers stuck through his belt. The sword was a trophy of Sachi's duel with Ironheart. It was his magical cutlass. It had been strapped up in a pack until now.

"This baby would turn them into splinters if need be. If we need in, we'll get in." Willis patted the stock of his blast rifle. Aylie carried the second rifle. They each had one spare magazine, so there were forty shots in total between them.

Sachi carried the flechette pistol. According to the counter on its grip, she had eighty-nine shots left. And she had her white steel bracers. Silaqui carried only a light satchel. A satchel that had all the other packs and bulky things held in by magic. It also held the treasure they had looted from Ironheart before they left the island of the giant spiders. If she reached in and asked for what she wanted, for example, 'Sachi's pack,' it would be the first thing she touched. Blaine had been fascinated by it.

The Colonel had told them it was a weeklong walk to the ruins. They'd covered a day's worth of distance the first half day. Nothing accosted them in the forest or while they made camp. The forest was filled with normal sounds, birds calling out, squirrels looking for acorns, a handful of deer browsing at the other end of the clearing in which they were camped. It was an uneventful night.

The second day was also uneventful, but chaos happened on the third day. Walking along the base of a steep hill, they heard a growl and then an angry roar from the top of the hill. Sachi jumped clear as a three-hundred-pound rock crashed where she had been standing. Everyone scattered as a second rock landed near Silaqui. It shattered and a flying shard cut her cheek.

"Enough of this," she screamed, throwing her arms into the air and beginning a conjuration to deal with the two huge humanoids, each at least twenty-five feet tall, on top of the hill. "Hold your fire, Willis, I've got these two idiots." She screamed magic and ripped her hands down. Synchronized with her movement, a pair of flaming, rocky orbs hit each monster. Each orb exploded on contact with the creatures. Engulfed in flames and smashed by molten rock, the monsters screamed in agony. They were short, cut-off screams as the creatures' upper bodies were reduced to blackened skeletons.

Blaine stared in horror as the pair of corpses tumbled down the hillside, sliding to a stop at the edge of the trail. Silaqui's eyes blazed with light; her hair stood straight out in a nimbus of flame.

"My God," he whispered, "Je'Libe held you prisoner for two years. How?"

"I was nearly dead of thirst and exposure when the pirates found me, floating on a hatch cover. Then they were careful to keep me bound with steel and iron cold forged, poisons for elves, and worse if the elf in question is a spellcaster. Only now, months after Sachi rescued me, only now are my full powers returning." She relaxed, calming her power until she was once again a simple elvish woman, dressed all in scarlet.

"You're bleeding. Allow me?" Gelman walked over, his hands glowing with golden light. He brushed a hand across the cut, and it instantly healed, leaving no mark or scar.

"Thank you, Pere Gelman."

"You are welcome, My Lady."

"Let's get moving, people; we might want to put some distance between these dead things and any friends they might have had." Sachi turned and set off down the overgrown trail, Sahla moving beside Sachi, flying just above the ground.

***

Blaine looked back over his shoulder at the charred corpses and shuddered.

What have I gotten myself into? Silaqui was just a rescued elven woman. She could use a little magic but nothing like that!

***

It seemed that Silaqui's awesome display had been noticed by the other inimical things in the forest as the fourth and fifth days were uneventful. During the fifth day the trail began climbing into the higher hills and the forest thinned out to occasional, isolated groves of pine and other evergreens, replacing the oaks and ash trees of the forest. Disaster struck in the middle of the sixth day.

They were climbing along a narrow cut between two mountainous, rocky hills when the thing erupted out of the ground at their feet. Sachi, as usual, was leading the way, perhaps forty feet in advance of Blaine and Gelman. Aylie, Sahla and Silaqui were close together, talking softly about the conundrum of the relationship between Blaine, Sachi and Sahla. Willis brought up the rear, blast rifle at the ready.

Blaine could hear the occasional word or sentence as the three women discussed the relationships in exhaustive detail. He expected that Sachi would hear every word, with her acute hearing. Even a thousand-year-old Sorceress, a magical Jann and a lady's maid gossiped. That was probably why Sachi was distracted when the giant, snake-like creature struck.

Blaine only saw a huge head, the size of a longboat, lunge up out of the ground and strike and swallow Sachi. Gelman stood frozen in surprise, but Blaine leapt forward, revolver blazing in one hand, the magic cutlass glowing in the other. Aylie reacted with lightning reflexes and the blast rifle knocked the thing backward. The shockwave sent Blaine tumbling away, the creature's blue blood staining his blade. Willis slapped Aylie's rifle down before she could fire again.

"Where's Sachi?" he screamed.

"It ate her!" Gelman yelled. "It just swallowed her!"

"She's gone!" Aylie cried, bringing up her blast rifle.

"Don't shoot, we're too close, look at Blaine! The blast knocked him out. Silaqui! Use your magic!"

The sorceress' answer was a blinding bolt of lightning crackling into the beast. Lightning that it ignored. The lightning had no effect on the monster. It screamed in rage and opened its mouth. Lightning flashed back at them. Gelman took the brunt of it, his robes and hair sizzling as the bolt danced over him. The priest gritted his teeth, held up his holy symbol and a column of holy fire and blazing light smashed down on the monster, burning and blinding it.

"SACHI!" Sahla shrieked. The Jann flew forward and a wave of blue magic smashed the monster against the steep hillside. Blue blood spurted from jagged rents her magic had torn in its armor-like hide. They could see the thing was gigantic, and while being snake-like, it had many short, clawed legs folded up against its body. The legs unfolded and it started to climb the nearly sheer hillside when it suddenly went completely rigid, head pointing straight up.

About fifteen feet below its head, a long white sword tore through its hide. The sword spun in a circle and cut the thing in half. The upper part convulsed and fell onto the trail, blue blood spraying out across the hillside and the trail. The lower half simply slumped down, slithering to the bottom of the hill, partially blocking the trail.

Sachi stumbled out of the carcass, covered from head to toe in blue blood and greenish-blue bile. The white steel *nodachi* was unstained as she held it in two shaking hands.

"*Kuso, kono kuso yarō!!* EAT ME, will you!" Sachi spat out blue blood as she cursed. She wiped blood and other fluids off her face and then Sahla hit her like a frantic thunderbolt. Both went tumbling, the Jann weeping as she wrapped herself around Sachi.

Willis looked to see if there were any other threats and how badly the group was hurt. Aylie and Silaqui looked to be untouched by the lightning the thing had shot from its mouth. Gelman was down on one knee next to Blaine, golden light washing over the Navy Captain. Sahla was trying to kiss every part of Sachi's face while the Nisei was trying to wipe blood and bile off her face.

"Anyone else hurt?" Gelman asked as he helped Blaine to his feet.

"Sachi's covered in the thing's blood and other fluids. And now, Sahla's half covered in the slime, too. Do you have magic that can wash them off? The bile may be acidic, and we need to get it off them as soon as possible."

"Aye, Willis, that I can do. Give me a moment to heal the small hurts I've taken." Golden light washed over the priest, then he raised his holy symbol. "*Et dixit Deus fait Aqua!*" Nearly a hundred gallons of water splashed down on the two young women. It poured down over them, washing away most of the blood and bile and drawing shrieks from both. "It's cold water, Willis," he murmured. Raising his voice, he said, "Stand up, you silly gits, and allow the water to wash the rest of the blood off you! For all we know those fluids may be acid or poison!" Gelman's warning got through to them and Sachi helped Sahla to her feet.

"You're right, Gelman, the bile is acidic. I can feel it burning, and it's damaging my clothing. More water, please, but can you make it *warm* water this time?"

"No." Gelman raised his holy symbol again and water poured down over them. Cold water. It washed away the last of the blood and bile. He ignored the girls' shrieks.

Sachi's *himaku* and *kobakama* had holes burned in them, but the CLIBA shirt was undamaged. Sahla's blue silk shirt was ruined and there were acid burns on her leathern pants and the thicker leather armor over the front of her thighs. Her CLIBA was also undamaged, the high-tech body armor unaffected by the creature's acidic bile.

"I see Sachi disagreed with something that ate her." Willis regarded the separate pieces of the slain monster with some disgust. "Let's get going. We don't want to stay here, there might be another one nearby. Silaqui, do you have any idea what this thing was called?"

"Let me think a moment." They moved on a bit quicker than normal, wanting to get away from the scene of the attack and brief battle. "I think it might have been something like a wingless blue dragon, a lightning spitter. If I remember my loremaster's teachings, it could have been a thing called a beihyr. If I'm right, they are mostly solitary things, meeting others of its kind only to mate and that only every hundred years or so. They're either immortal or very long lived. As big as that one was, it may have been older than I am."

"Well, hopefully it was voracious enough that there's nothing else nasty around here." Willis took off his hat and wiped his brow. "We should be no more than a day and a half, maybe two days away from the ruins. Hopefully, we can avoid any more randomly wandering creatures with a bad attitude and a taste for humans or elves. Pick it up, people. Let's get a move on."

Confederation PDC *Thera*
April 1479, Third Age of Imperial Reckoning

The second day after the beihyr's attack, they reached the ruins. They were well among them before they realized that the overgrown mounds of dirt and rock were the remains of shattered walls. Another half a day of searching and they found the overgrown hill that was the single remaining building at the center of the ruins. They rested that night, sheltered by the fragments of a nearby ruin. Silaqui assured them her magic could easily clear away the thick vines and brush covering the building. Another of her spells would also remove the nearly rock-hard soil mounded over most of the building.

Sachi was nearly asleep, cuddling with Sahla, when D.A.V.E. yanked her into the Virtual Reality world.

"What the hell do you want with me now, D.A.V.E.?"

::I am registering a substantial energy source nearby. The overgrown building is the surface access point of a functional grav tube transport system.::

"A working grav tube? After this long?"

::Confederation equipment is based on solid principles and uses well-designed, solid-state circuitry with an average mean time between failures measured in hundreds of years. Grav tube systems are quadruply redundant. If there is still full power, the system should function at one hundred percent of capacity. I have accessed the system files remotely and while the PDC has sustained damage, its power plant is fully online. Stand by::

"You're saying this thing is still working? We don't have to climb down and maybe just find a flooded tunnel? Is the medical facility still intact and not stripped?"

::Stand by. Accessing intact systems. Stand by::

***

The thing masquerading as Sachi's D.A.V.E. dropped into the PDC's still functional systems and destroyed an actual Digitally Aware Virtual Entity before it could even come out of hibernation mode. A handful of sysop and librarian programs were simply deleted as it copied their data into its own system. The only sysop program it left intact was the medical facility's 'Angel' class sysop. It would be needed to complete his symbiont's enhancement and repair the damage to the female to whom his symbiont was emotionally attached. He considered having the medical sysop terminate the female identified as Sahla, but that prospect had significant negative effects on the probability of initial mission success. With his symbiont emotionally attached to Sahla, initial mission success rates exceeded ninety-five percent. It was his actual, primary mission that lost mission rate success percentages if any of his symbiont's companions survived the destruction of the oncoming Kuiper Belt planetoid. And he did not currently have any access to a means to terminate them after the initial mission's success. It was very annoying.

***

::The following systems are still functioning at ninety-eight percent, plus or minus two percent: medical, powered armor morgue, and the entertainment module. Functioning at fifty percent or lower are the vehicular repair bay and the armory. There are no repairable vehicles present. There are two surface to orbit shuttles present. Neither is repairable from available resources. There is one light air skimmer available with a thirty-seven percent, plus or minus twenty-four percent probability of repair to a functional condition but there is no available reaction mass for its engine. C3 systems are unrepairable. Report complete.::

"Can the medical facility heal Sahla?"

:;Assuming basic compatibility with human physiology, a full recovery would be expected at ninety-four percent, plus or minus eight percent. The medical facility is a class five facility, capable of major physiological repairs, including repairs to neurological systems. In human terms, I would expect a full recovery.::

"Oh D.A.V.E., I could kiss you if you had lips!"

::Such a thing is impossible. Regarding your own medical treatment needed to complete your enhancement, the facility's capability to complete your enhancement approaches unity, plus or minus three percent. Procedures on both the individual identified as Sahla al Qasim and you cannot be done concurrently due to the extensive nature of her injuries and the nearly complete rebuild of your skeletal and neuro-muscular systems. Operations for Sahla will be conducted under complete anesthesia. She will experience no pain and only slight discomfort after the procedure is complete. Your final system enhancement will also be under complete anesthesia, but learning to use your new physical abilities will cause some discomfort.::

"Which means I'll be screaming my throat raw, I believe?"

::Essentially correct.::

"I think we're done here for now, D.A.V.E., so go back to sleep and let me do likewise. Ok?"

::Command accepted. The proper response is, 'Good night, Sachi.'::

Sachi came back to the real world and realized that Sahla was lying on her left arm and it had gone to sleep. She hated the 'pins and needles' feeling of returning circulation, but she was unwilling to move and wake Sahla. It took her awhile, but she eventually wiggled loose and gritted her teeth at the pain.

I swear the enhancement makes things like this hurt more, not less. Neuro-muscular and skeletal enhancements, I just know those are gonna hurt. She shrugged and settled back down to sleep, glancing over at Willis, who had the watch in the last hours of the night. Dawn would be here soon enough. A day that would see Sahla finally and fully healed.

Chapter Nineteen

Confederation PDC *Thera*
April 1479, Third Age of Imperial Reckoning

THE NEXT MORNING, THEY started clearing the building from its coating of dirt and foliage. Silaqui decided doing it by hand would take too long, so she suggested that she had a better way. She drew out an elaborate magic circle and summoned an earth elemental. In exchange for a very large portion of the cheese in their trail rations, it agreed to remove the dirt covering the building. And in less than ten minutes the ancient building was uncovered, metal walls exposed to the sun and air for the first time in well over a hundred years.

"What's this made of, Sachi? Do you know or can D.A.V.E. tell you?" Willis ran his hands over the surface, looking for any sign of a door on the smooth metal.

"D.A.V.E. tells me it was called Perma-steel. One step down from the battlesteel that the ancients used to make warships." She walked to the southern side of the building and laid her hand on a central location. The outlines of a door formed, and a cubical receptacle formed in the middle of the door. Sachi touched her amulet and removed the cube. She placed the cube in the receptacle and the door opened. Fresh, cool air flowed out, spiced by a tang of ozone. A set of stairs went down and panels in the stairway ceiling began to shine, shedding ample light on the steps. Smaller panels on the steps themselves began to glow. She put the cube back on the choker.

The stairs led down to a large room with tables and chairs neatly lined up against one wall. Against the opposite wall were a row of compartments. Sachi read the signs on the wall to everyone.

"They're the, well, the loading stations for the transport tube. The signs tell you where each part of the tube goes. We want the one that reads 'Medical module.' That station is big enough to handle a person on a stretcher with multiple attendants, so it should have no problems with the seven of us. We'll all go at once. But first, let me and D.A.V.E. check the system. Willis and Gelman, drag one of those medium sized tables over here, and we'll use it as a test."

With the table in the tube, Sachi gave the mental command to activate the tube. The floor underneath the table snapped out of sight and the table vanished down the tube. A red light came on above the entryway and the floor snapped back into place.

"Okay, the red light means this section of the tube is occupied. The computer that runs this thing just confirmed to me that the table is at its destination and occupying the arrival stage. The table can't leave the arrival stage and the computer is holding this section of the tube closed until it's cleared. I'm going to summon the table back up." There was a faint whooshing sound and the floor snapped open. The table floated up into the arrival stage and the floor snapped back into place.

"How deep is this PDC, Sachi?" Blaine asked as he watched Gelman and Willis drag the table off the arrival stage. The light above the stage turned green.

"The receiving stage is twenty thousand feet deep. The tube moves at about two thousand feet per second, so it's a ten second trip."

"Twenty thousand feet! Two thousand feet per second! A ten second trip! Gah!" Blaine's eyes widened, and he paled at the thought of such a thing.

"Oh yeah. There're toilets over there, the doors on the far wall. They're marked Men and Women. Go use them or I'll guarantee you'll embarrass yourself when the tube whisks you away. I'm going to go take care of business myself."

A short while later, the group reassembled at the compartment labeled, 'Medical Module.' There were nervous looks on most faces, but Sachi was cool and composed. Sahla was also unconcerned. After all, she could fly. Then Sachi ruined her composure.

"Sahla, do not try to fly; I'm not sure what would happen if you did. There are immense forces at work here and I don't think you can counter nearly a hundred gravities of acceleration. D.A.V.E. told me that ten gravities could kill a human. And no, don't ask me to explain it. D.A.V.E. tried to explain it to me and I just got confused. There's a lot of high-level math involved, and we all lack the scientific background knowledge to truly understand how this works. For now, just accept it as magic, a magic anyone can use." She paused and took a deep breath. "Now, let's all step into the compartment and I'll send the signal. Here we go."

The floor snapped aside, and they hurtled down the tube at two thousand feet per second. Aylie screamed all the way down, stopping with an abrupt squeak when they stopped, neatly and smoothly, on the Medical Module's platform. Silaqui was pale as a sheet, her ears pulled back tightly against her head, pupils dilated wide open. Blaine and Willis were both a little shaky and it was Gelman, of them all, who maintained his calm poise for the entire trip.

"That was quite an experience," was all he said. "The arrows on the wall point this way to 'surgical center.' What we need, I believe?"

What passed over the next few hours was bewildering. Sachi had to use D.A.V.E. to override many issues; Sahla's lack of an 'ident card' was only the first. The medical genius program introduced itself as 'Angel' and took over once everything was done, and all the forms had been filled out or overridden by D.A.V.E. Sahla laid down on a gurney and was wheeled into the 'Operating Room,' or 'OR' for short.

Hours passed and Sachi ran out of fingernails to chew on. She would sit restlessly for a time, then pop up and pace rapidly around the appropriately named 'Waiting Room.' At one point she went to Silaqui for a soft shoulder to cry on. At another point, she stood in the door and looked down the hallway. She turned away and suddenly went to her knees, sobbing in anxiety. Blaine came over and knelt beside her. He tentatively put a hand on her shoulder.

"She'll be all right, Sachi. You have risked everything to bring us here and it will be all right."

"Captain Blaine, my Captain, you should not be kneeling on the floor next to me. It is not proper for a great Captain to kneel next to me."

"You know, that was about exactly what you said to me, back when I first met you on *Intrepid*. Of course, that was after I'd knocked you unconscious with my paperweight." He chuckled softly. Sachi laughed through her tears.

"I do not think you need to hit me with a paperweight now." She stopped laughing. "Oh Sahla, please, please be well. My heart aches to see her in such pain."

'Angel' materialized in the waiting room then. Sachi jumped up and ran to the program's avatar.

"Tell me she's okay, please, Angel, please!" Somehow, she managed not to grab the avatar.

"The surgery was completely successful, and the patient is expected to make a full recovery. 'Quick heal' is performing at less than optimum levels, and therefore the full recovery will take more time than normal. But a complete recovery should be expected within one to two weeks. Until then, the patient is advised to get plenty of rest and minimize any physical activity."

"Oh, thank the Ancestors, or God or her own Prophet and Chalta! Thank you, Angel! She's going to be all right!" Sachi was nearly babbling, and tears of joy ran down her face. Blaine put a hand on her shoulder and Silaqui came and wrapped her in a bear hug. Aylie was jumping up and down, clapping her hands and cheering. Willis joined the hug with Sachi and Silaqui.

"The One God be praised." Even dour old Gelman had a huge smile on his face.

"You are scheduled for physical enhancement surgery in twenty-four hours. There are instructions for you to follow for preparation."

"Can I see Sahla now?"

"The patient is still recovering from anesthesia. Visitation can begin as soon as the patient is awake and alert. Estimated time for recovery of consciousness is forty-six minutes from now. Watch the screen. It will say when visitation is allowed. Then follow the green line to recovery." The nanniballs making up the avatar melted away.

Forty-five minutes later, the status screen on the wall lit up. 'Visitation now permitted. Follow the green line.' Sachi was out the door like a shot, sprinting down the hall to the recovery room where a barely coherent Sahla waited. Everyone else followed at a more sedate pace. Blaine stopped everyone outside the door to recovery.

"Let's give them some time alone, what say? About five minutes or so." He smiled. "I imagine there might not be too much conversation between them right now. At least, not verbally."

When they finally entered the room, Sachi was sitting on the edge of the bed, holding both of Sahla's hands. The Jann's golden tan was a little pale and there were several tiny marks on her neck and shoulder. The surgery left no other marks.

"The machine doctor says I'm going to be fine and completely healed. At least, I think that's what the machine said. 'A complete recovery despite nonhuman physiological elements in the DNA make up,' whatever that prattle means." Sahla's smile was devastatingly beautiful. "And I guess that means you're next, Sachi. How long...?"

"Another day. And I should be up and recovered within a day or two. My internal nanites will speed my healing tremendously. But we're not leaving here until you're completely recovered from the surgery. The 'quick heal' doesn't work as well on you as it will on me. Because you're not fully human, I guess." Sachi's smile was just as wide and beaming as Sahla's. "In the meantime, we can completely explore this place and see if we can recover anything usable."

***

"Well, a day's worth of scrounging has been very productive. We found an extra, charged magazine for Sachi's pistol, two more blast rifle magazines and a charging station for them. We recharged the shots Aylie used on the snake thing that tried to swallow Sachi, stupid thing. And we found two more functional CLIBA body armor shirts. Blaine is wearing one of them now. And now we have a spare one." Willis sipped from his canteen.

"And there were those machines in the place called a 'repair bay,' huge machines that were supposed to fly, or so Sachi said before she went into the 'enhancement facility.' Sahla's been parked in the waiting room ever since. So has Captain Blaine." Aylie nearly bounced, she was so excited by everything she had seen and even touched. She had sat in the pilot's seat in what Sachi told her was a 'surface-to-orbit shuttle,' a flying machine that could fly to the Moon. But sadly, it was broken and couldn't be fixed. Aylie so wanted one of the flying machines to work, but they were all wrecks or there was no fuel. She wanted to fly so bad she could taste it.

"Then there was the 'entertainment' module." Gelman had been amazed at the life size pictures that moved and spoke and told a story, so real looking he thought he could touch them. He'd tried, once, fruitlessly. It was like trying to catch fog. Sachi laughed a little bit and then told him they were 'three-dee projections.' That had been before she went into the 'enhancement process.' "Most of those 'entertainment flicks' were disgusting. Women wearing shameful clothing or nothing at all! That is not what any decent bard would call 'entertainment.' Did they have no morals at all?"

"It was a different world, Gelman," Silaqui remarked from where she sat. After a day spent exploring, they were relaxing in the waiting room, off in a corner away from an anxious Sahla and an equally worried William Blaine. Sachi had spent part of the day guiding their exploration, then had gone to be 'completely enhanced.'

"They were a different people, Gelman," she continued. "They traveled here from the stars and fought beings that would have destroyed our world. I understand Uncle Oedhaewthren better now. The history 'flicks' showed that they came here to fight Quan's minions, creatures that hated all life. Humans did not bring them here but fought them when they came. Fought them with energies that could destroy worlds. Fought and died to protect this world." She paused, "I think, Gelman, we can forgive them for showing 'flicks' that have scantily clad females in them. I forgive them for many things now. Above all, at some time, Uncle Oedhaewthren and maybe even the King, the Queen and the Court Mage must come here and see these 'history flicks.' It would, I think, change how my people see you humans."

"A good point, Silaqui," Willis said, "and it would benefit my people, the Kolbians, to know the truth, too. It would benefit every nation to know the true story of our history."

"I still doubt Kolbians would believe in magic, or unicorns or dragons. Or elves." Willis acknowledged his nation's inherent, stubborn practicality with a raised canteen and a nod. "Not unless they were directly witnessing such things. Kolbians are too practical sometimes."

***

The first thing she felt when consciousness returned was a burning pain in all her limbs. They burned like they were on fire. The pain was so bad and so sudden that she couldn't help screaming her throat raw. The screams echoed down the hall and moments later, Sahla was the first one in the recovery room. The rest of them followed her into the room.

"What's wrong, *Habiba*? What has happened?"

"It burns!" Sachi ground out through gritted teeth. "D.A.V.E. said it would hurt but I never imagined it would be this bad. This is worse than anything Maho ever did to me when I was young."

"The enhancement process is always excessively painful at first," the Angel program said. "The patient's brain is adapting to new neural inputs and the use of pain blocking drugs inhibits proper system integration and function. The pain will quickly diminish over the next twenty-four hours."

"Would it help if one or two of us stayed with you?" Blaine said. "Give you someone to talk to, help take your mind off the pain."

"Yes, but just Sahla." Sachi panted as she spoke through the pain. "Just Sahla. And you, My Captain."

***

"How are you feeling, Habiba?" Sahla asked as she entered the Physical Therapy room. "The 'Angel' thing just told me that I am released from care and may leave now." Sachi was sitting at a table in a hospital gown not much different than the type used on Earth during its twentieth century. As a sop to modesty, a pair of loose shorts were included.

"Better now." Sachi had been out of the enhancement surgery for a week now. The red lines that had marked incisions on her arms, legs and even her torso were mostly faded away, leaving vague marks that would be gone within the day. The medical programs had her doing something called 'physical therapy' now. At the moment, she was busy bending a steel bar into a complicated knot. The exercise would test her hardened skin and work to strengthen muscles in her hands and forearms. "The first two days were agony, you remember. Now I'm starting to truly understand what's been done to me. I'm stronger, faster and tougher than ever before. Oh, I can still be killed, cannon shot would do it, but it's a lot harder than before. The 'Angel' program informed me that I've received a standard, covert agent's upgrade package. A Marine's enhancement package would be even more extreme, allowing them to interface directly with their weapons and heavy combat armor. It's a lot more evident that a Marine was enhanced. With me, you can't really tell. You've touched my skin, Sahla. Does it feel any different to you?"

"No, it's just as soft as it always was."

"But now, my skin would easily turn a knife stab or sword blow. Unless the weapon was magical or driven by inhumanly strong muscles. A dragon's claws could still tear me in half."

"Then let us avoid any dragons." Sahla came next to Sachi and carefully took the twisted steel bar out of her hands. "There is another test I wish to conduct." She leaned forward and kissed Sachi. It was a thorough kiss, long and passionate. A tap on the door of the physical therapy room interrupted them before any further 'tests' could be conducted.

***

"Ahem, am I interrupting you two?" Captain Blaine cleared his throat and smiled at the scene. "We need to talk about heading back to the ship. Can you two restrain yourselves long enough to discuss that? I realize it's an imposition, but the Admiral might begin to think we're overdue on this little excursion. Everyone else is in the waiting room. So...?"

"You couldn't just lock the door and wait, could you, William Blaine?" Sahla blushed red but a certain amount of frustration was evident in her voice.

"I could, but wouldn't you prefer one of the rooms we've been using for sleeping areas for anymore, hmm, *strenuous* tests of Sachi's recovery? And, honestly, we need to get back to *Intrepid* as soon as possible."

"You are right, My Captain. We should leave as soon as possible." There was a certain amount of frustration in Sachi's voice as well. She sighed, "Sahla, we are going to have to wait a little longer to indulge ourselves in more...*testing*."

"If not here, then where? On the trail back to town? No comfort or even any privacy there! On the ship? I think there should be even less privacy there! Too many eyes and ears! By the Prophet, it's bad enough when I use the head or try to wash up at least a little bit!" An irritated Sahla nearly snapped. "Where is our next destination, Captain Blaine?"

"Shortest course to Capitol City in Kolbia, six weeks with fair winds, eight or ten with contrary winds or if we get becalmed."

"You will have fair winds, Captain Blaine. I am a Jann of Air. I will see that *Intrepid* has the fairest winds any ship ever had. And when we get to Kolbia, YOU will get us the biggest, most luxurious room in the best inn in the city and it had better have a PRIVATE bathing room. And a proper, Kolbian-made water closet! Nothing less will be acceptable!" Sahla stormed out of the room, then came back in. "And it is early in the day! We will leave immediately! Quan take it!" She slammed the door on the way out of the room as Blaine scrambled to get out of her way.

There were tears in her eyes, I think. I have really stepped in it this time. And I can tell Sachi's furious with me as well. Damn it! I didn't mean for this to happen! I should have just closed the door and walked away. Brilliant move, Blaine!

"That was poorly done, My Captain. You are right, we must hasten, but...I could wish you far away right now." She straightened the steel bar with such force that it snapped in half. "Let me get dressed and then we should leave this place. We can get more than a half day's travel done before it gets too dark to continue. And the Ancestors help anything that gets in our way back to town and the ship."

Apparently, no new creatures had moved into the territories vacated by the creatures they had killed on the way to the PDC, since the rotting corpses of the previous occupants were still there. There were signs some kind of scavenger had been at the bodies, but they were conspicuously absent when the group passed back through the area.

Traquilidamar Sea
KRN *Intrepid* (32)
May 1479, Third Age of Imperial Reckoning

They arrived back in town just after noon on the sixth day since leaving the PDC. They had been gone nearly six weeks. By dusk, *Intrepid* was headed out of the harbor on a perfect seaward wind. Sahla had perched herself on the ship's taffrail and stared intently up at the sails. Blaine could hear her whistling softly, just barely loud enough to be heard. As they moved out into the Traquilidamar Sea, the wind freshened and shifted around to Intrepid's starboard quarter, her best point of sail, driving her on a broad reach. The wind continued to rise, peaking as a near gale, with winds near thirty-three knots. The waves were nearly twenty feet high, white spray blowing from their crests. Intrepid's taffrail log showed a speed of fourteen knots. Blaine walked over to Sahla.

"Is this wind your doing, Sahla?" he quietly asked.

"It is. I judge this wind to be the best for *Intrepid* to make the most speed. I can push it a little harder if that will move the ship faster."

"No, this is nearly perfect, what sailors call a near gale. The increased wave height of a full gale would drive the waves high enough that they would slow the ship a knot or two. The log shows a speed of fourteen knots. The best speed I got out of her during trials was twelve knots. The armor slows her down. Before the refit, with this wind and this sea, I believe she would have reached near to sixteen knots. How long can you keep this up?"

"As long as I am awake, I can control the winds within reason. It would be difficult to push them any harder, but I could do it if absolutely necessary. When I sleep, they will slacken and may veer about. But even then, it would remain a following wind. How long will it take to reach Kolbia, William Blaine?"

"It's late May now, only a few more days to June. Given a following wind and a following sea, sailing close hauled on a broad reach the entire journey, I would calculate we would reach Capitol City the last week of June. Mid-July may be more reasonable. Can you control the winds that way, that long?"

"Unless we encounter a storm, which I judge very possible in the mid-Lanic this time of year, yes, I should be able to do so. My father could control a hurricane, if the Marid, princes of elemental water, did not directly oppose him. I cannot do so; I am not that strong."

"Another question, Sahla. The Imperial fleet is at sea. I doubt even one of their ships-of-the-line can offer a true threat to *Intrepid*. Between our armor, our shell-firing guns and the new rifled guns, well, they'd wind up 'right bastards, sorry and sore,' as

Bosun Beauchamps would say. Could you control the winds well enough to give us the weather gauge and deny it to them?"

"I don't know; it would depend on many things. I shall say 'perhaps' but only that. You need to talk to Silaqui. The last of the poison of cold iron has left her. She has her full powers back at last. She could call down fire and lightning on the enemy, if they're close enough. She might not be able to make *Intrepid* invisible, but I think she could make her a blurry, misty target, hard to see and harder to shoot at."

"She may not be willing to use her magic on an opposing ship; the pirate Je'Libe used her for that purpose for two years. On the other hand, she hates the Empire and may gleefully rain destruction down on them. But I will go talk to her about it. Thank you, Sahla."

"You are welcome, William Blaine. Chalta's Grace go with you." She gave him a winsome smile and went back to softly whistling.

Chapter Twenty

A WEEK OF TRAVEL had them approaching the Gates of the Lanic. The current here was against them and *Intrepid* was only averaging ten or eleven knots, despite all that Sahla could do. And now there was another problem.

"Sail, ho!" came the cry from the crow's nest lookout. "Two sail, dead ahead, due west!"

"That cannot be good. Two Lietelean ships patrolling the Gates? Only two?" Admiral Sartell looked up the mainmast. "Or can we only see two?"

"Admiral Sartell, I'm sending the sailor with the best sight up to look. Sachi, front and center!" Captain Blaine roared out the last bit. She promptly appeared from below decks.

"Yes, sir?" she asked. "You have a task for me?"

"I do, take the number one glass up to the crow's nest and see if you can tell what ships are patrolling in the Lanic Gates. We know there are two of them at least. See if you can determine the types and if there are more than two of them."

"Aye-aye, sir." Sachi dashed off to Bosun Beauchamps' office, grabbed the number one glass and headed up the main mast rat lines. Sahla appeared from below decks and followed her up the mast. Sahla shot herself up the mast, flying right next to the rat lines.

"What are you doing?" she asked when she reached Sachi.

"Headed to the crow's nest to see what my improved vision can see. Come along and I'll have you fly a little higher above the mainmast with this glass and we'll see what we can see." Sachi reached the crow's nest and climbed in over the side of the basket. "Well. Hello, Midshipman Eliss, fancy meeting you here."

"It's good to see you again, Sachi, we missed you. All of us Midshipm..." Evan Eliss stumbled to an awkward halt as Sahla literally flew up over the edge of the basket and landed in it. "How did you do that, Miss...?"

"Calm down, Evan, this is Sahla, a Jann from Darsälaam. And yes, Jann can fly by the strength of their will. I'm charging you to keep her secret to yourself, Evan. Now both of you step back and let me see what I can see. Ah, very good." Minutes passed. She then handed Sahla the glass. "Can you fly up about fifty feet and see if there are any more of them?" Sahla took the glass and flew up, fifty feet about the mainmast.

"Sachi, there are four ships, not just two." Sahla peered through the glass for a few minutes, then flew back to the crow's nest. "The two furthest away only have one mast. The closest two have three masts with four sails on the forward masts. That's all I can see."

"Could you see the hulls of the closest ones? What color were they?"

"The closest ones are painted white, and their flags are black with some red on them. I think they are Imperial flags, like the ones we saw that day near Du Khamps."

"I can see their flags and enough of the hull to have a good idea of what they are. Come, Captain Blaine and the Admiral need to know what we've seen."

Sachi slid down the backstay and Sahla pretended to do the same. Sachi expected that the secret of Sahla's nature as a Jann would be all over the ship by six bells in the afternoon watch. Too many of the crew had seen her fly at one time or another. It shouldn't cause problems, but one never knew. And her beauty was another possible issue, as even a well-drilled and professional crew like *Intrepid's* practically salivated when she walked by. Sachi doubted any sailor on this ship would so much as touch her, but you never knew for sure. Sachi reached the deck and walked over to Blaine and the Admiral.

"There are four of them, not two. They're painted white, so Imperial ships. The two closest are ship-rigged on three masts, frigates, I think. The farthest pair are likely galleys. Sahla got some... extra height, let's say, and saw those two were single masted with a single, square sail. So, galleys."

"I see." Blaine glanced at the Admiral. "Sir, I feel confident that *Intrepid* is the equal of any pair of Imperial frigates, much less a pair of their galleys. My only concern would be getting rammed and boarded by them. There's only eighteen inches of half-inch armor below the waterline and that's only half-inch plate armor. A galley's iron beaked ram would hit below that armor."

"Are you really concerned about that, Captain Blaine?"

"Not really. They'd have to get through at least one, if not two of our broadsides. They'd be wrecks."

"I concur. Do you think they'll attack us?"

"Well, Admiral Sartell, with their entire fleet at sea, it is my belief we're already at war, and that they've attacked Task Force Southron in force and by surprise. I'll not let any Imperial ship within ten miles of *Intrepid* without clearing for action."

"Very well, Captain Blaine, I'll endorse your log on that decision. How are you planning to handle this group?"

"When I can see their hulls from the deck, we'll clear for action and beat to quarters. I'll not fire first, but they won't fire a second time. After that, we'll see what they do. Excuse me, Admiral."

"Carry on, Captain Blaine."

***

"So, you are my friend Sachi's girlfriend?" Toby drew on his cigar and blew out a perfect smoke ring. The ring was instantly snatched away by the wind. "A Bond of True Love, no less, I am told. Good. Very good. She's a lucky girl."

"Thank you...Toby, or should I call you Mr. Wilkerson?"

"No, lass, Toby is fine. Call me Mr. Wilkerson, and I look around for my father." Toby chuckled. "It's funny. Before she left *Intrepid* I would have sworn that she was frustrated in loving Cap'n Blaine. I think she still does. Do you know that?"

"Yes, I know. They both still love each other. They have told each other that."

"Huh, and now you're here. You know Cap'n Blaine is married, right? Well, was married, by now, I guess. His wife filed for divorce just before we raised anchor. Something has changed if they said, 'I love you' to each other." He paused and drew on the cigar. "The Cap'n's wife is, or rather was, well, difficult. She's a social climber of the worst sort, in my opinion. That's based on the way she treated the crew when she came aboard for a fancy dinner during our passage through the Kolbian Straights. Treated everyone except the officers as if we were just drudges, even the bosun. Called him, the bosun, a man with forty years or more at sea, she called him 'boy.' No courtesy at all. Mean spirited woman, I think."

***

"Deck there! The galleys are going upwind under sail and oars. The three masted ships are on direct reciprocal of our course. Range is nigh on four miles." Evan Eliss shouted down through his leather speaking trumpet.

"Well done, Master Eliss. Get back on deck, sharply now!" Admiral Sartell stood next to Blaine, watching Eliss start to climb down the ratlines to the deck. "Admiral, would you please be so kind as to escort Envoy Courtenay below decks. Thank you, sir."

"Of course. Fight your ship, Captain Blaine. If it comes to a boarding action, I will join you on deck."

"I wouldn't dream of denying you the pleasure, sir." Blaine shook hands with Sartell and the Admiral went below.

"Bosun."

"Aye, sir." Beauchamps turned to Blaine.

"I believe I should like to clear for gun action, port and starboard. Sharply now."

Bosun Beauchamps blew three sharp blasts on his whistle and instantly the ship was a kicked-over hive, boiling with activity. Bulkheads were struck down to the orlop deck as were all the furnishings from every cabin. The Marine command element fell in on the quarterdeck, the drummer beating out the call to quarters.

Marines grabbed their muskets and grenades and took their positions on deck. Marine sharpshooters, armed with rifles, took their positions in the fighting tops. Small, one-pound guns were hoisted up to the fighting tops and locked into swiveling mounts and loaded with canister shot. Those guns were short ranged but were only intended to fire down onto an enemy's rigging and top deck.

The main guns, the big Dolmen smoothbores on the gundeck, were prepared for action, loaded with fifty-three-pound explosive shells. These new guns, both the Dolmens and Parkers, had replaced their flint locks with the same 'caplock' ignition system as Willis' revolvers, although their 'percussion' caps were considerably larger and more robust. The Parker rifles were similarly prepared.

"Sir, I beg to report the ship ready for action at General Quarters readiness." First Lieutenant Keith Gustav saluted Captain Blaine.

"Well done, Lieutenant Commander. I told you I'd make you an outstanding officer, ready for his own command." Blaine checked his pocket watch. "The men set a record for clearing for action, twenty-nine minutes. Very well done. Take your position." Blaine went over to the taffrail where Sachi and Sahla stood. "Ladies."

"Captain Blaine, what would you of us?" Sachi asked, "Or of her?" she placed a hand on Sahla's shoulder.

"Sahla, can you whistle up a stronger wind? Those two galleys will be faster than we are in these winds, only moderate breezes. The advantage is to the oared ship under these conditions."

"I will see what I can do, Captain Blaine. I can strengthen this wind, but the air is...heavy here, hemmed in just as the ocean waters are restricted. But I will do what I can. And to do this I must be on deck. And if I remain on deck, Sachi will, as well."

"I expected as much." Blaine turned to Sachi. "Guard her...and yourself well. Against four ships, two of them galleys, this may come down to hand-to-hand fighting."

"Captain Blaine, if I must, I will slaughter any enemy that sets foot on this deck. I will protect my heartmate...and you, William Blaine, with my life. But my intent is that the Imperials do all the dying today."

"I expected no less." Blaine started to turn away.

"William," Sachi spoke just barely loud enough that Blaine heard her. He stopped.

"Yes?"

"I love you." Her voice was low enough that Blaine barely heard her. "Be careful."

"I will." He turned to face her. "And I love you, too."

Traquilidamar Sea
ILN *Malleus Fidelium* (32)
June 1479, Third Age of Imperial Reckoning

Capitan Jean Juste, master and commander of the Imperial Lietelean Navy's thirty-two-gun frigate *Malleus Fidelium*, was rather pleased with himself. His ship had come through a battle with a Kolbian task group of three ships almost completely undamaged. *Hammer of the Faithful*, as the heathen Kolbians would name her, had lost the t'gallant mast and yard when a single hit had exploded against the t'gallant crosstree on the foremast. The topsail yard had fallen as well.

That damage may have saved *Malleus* from being sunk. The Kolbians, one of their big forty-four-gun frigates, a sloop-of-war and one of their infernally weatherly schooners had all been sunk or captured when the Lanic fleet was two days out from the Gates of the Lanic. The frigate had sunk, the sloop and schooner had been captured. Too damaged to be taken as prizes, they had both been burned.

The commander of the Kolbian task group, Captain Logsdon, had been killed in action. His ship, KRN *Renown*, had been dismasted, her hull shattered by the fire of no less than three ships-of-the-line and two of the bigger galleasses. There had been only fifty survivors taken off the sinking wreck.

The Kolbians hadn't gone alone. One ship-of-the-line, ILN *Argent*, was so badly damaged that she was burned. The galleass ILN *Loyal Oath* was heavily damaged as well, but still had her masts and would sail for home with the prisoners aboard. Several galleys had been lost as well. The realization that a Kolbian frigate could stand against a capitol ship was unnerving. Equally unsettling was the truth of the rumor that the Kolbians had devised a way to make their shot explode when it hit a ship.

But the Kolbian flagged frigate they were bearing down on was a single ship and Juste's squadron had more than double her guns...*and* the Kolbian captain did not know the Empire was now at war with Kolbia. Juste's ships would be able to fire first, and the galleys could ram her and send her on the way to the bottom of the sea. Juste would get his own name in the *Journal annuel de la Navio* and be assured of promotion to flag rank.

Traquilidamar Sea
KRN *Intrepid* (32)
June 1479, Third Age of Imperial Reckoning

"They're coming in close, planning to catch us between their two ships. That's when they'll fire. They won't care that we are flying a diplomatic mission flag." The Admiral had come back up on deck. "You think you can do better than Captain Eyles' *Stellar* did against three galleasses?"

"Admiral. Sir. With all due respect and respect for what Captain Eyles did with *Stellar*, these four have only one chance against *Intrepid*, and that's to dismast us. No, they'll want us as a prize, to sail back to Luctini covered in glory." Blaine spat over the rail. "In short, these poor fools are screwed."

"And you have Sachi and Sahla. Not to mention a powerful sorceress who can call down fire and lightning. And a priest who can heal the injured. Not fair at all." The Admiral looked up at the sails. The wind had picked up; it was blowing about twenty-five knots. *Intrepid* had reduced sail to fighting sail, the courses had all been brailed up and reefs taken up in the topsails. Between the reduced sail and Sahla's control of the winds, *Intrepid* was making a decent seven knots.

"I see what these boneheads are trying to do. They're on a direct reciprocal course. They want to catch us between them and give us a broadside that hits both sides of the ship. Now the question is, do I let them, then watch their jaws drop when their shots bounce off the armor plate? Then, give each one of them eight eight-inch shells and four six-inch shells. That'd blow the guts out of them both." Blaine rubbed his hands together in anticipation.

"It comes down to whether or not you trust the armor, doesn't it, William?" The Admiral stood beside Blaine on the quarterdeck. "That's a pair of frigates coming at us. Their frigates are built much lighter than ours are, thinner scantlings and fewer, lighter guns. At least that is what ONI tells us. And I've been a guest on one of their frigates. Only thirty guns and the heaviest guns were eighteen pounders. The spar deck guns were twelve pounders. And, supposedly, that was one of their heavier frigates."

"Any suggestions, Admiral?"

"Fight your ship, Captain Blaine."

"Aye-aye, sir."

***

Sahla leaned against the taffrail, quietly whistling. One of the cased blast rifles was at her feet. Sachi stood close enough that their shoulders touched. Silaqui was bantering with Willis, who had the other cased rifle. Gelman stood just behind the two helmsmen. Aylie was below decks with the Envoy and Lorelei.

"Can you do what Blaine is asking, Sahla?" Sachi asked.

"I can. Whenever he gives me the signal, I can put a strong wind into our sails. A wind that will put our enemies, what did he call it...?"

"'In irons' he called it. The wind shifting enough to blow against their sails, slowing them as it gives *Intrepid* greater speed."

Traquilidamar Sea
ILN *Malleus Fidelium* (32)
June 1479, Third Age of Imperial Reckoning

Capitan Jean Juste grinned as the range closed. He knew the Kolbian wouldn't fire first. The range was down to four hundred yards and all three ships held their course. The range from each of his ships to the Kolbian between them would be close to fifty yards when they passed each other. Slightly on the long-range side for his guns, but close enough to gut the Kolbian. After the two frigates passed by, the galleys *Poing des Fidèles* and *Dragon* would ram and board the crippled ship. Three hundred yards.

I'll have the guns run out when we reach about a hundred yards from her. She's reduced sail to fighting sail, so they are prepared to fight me. But four ships against one? Ships of about the same weight of metal? I can see she has only four guns on the quarterdeck and four in each broadside on the spar deck. I don't know what she has on the gundeck, but it shouldn't matter. No, it won't matter one little bit.

Two hundred yards. *Malleus Fidelium* was making seven knots on the close reach. *Malleus* was slightly faster than *Gladius Dei. Malleus* would be broadside to the Kolbian frigate for less than a minute. Juste would order his guns to fire by division, two spar-deck twelve pounders and two gun-deck eighteens marching down the side of the Kolbian ship. The six spar-deck guns would aim high, trying to dismast the Kolbian. The ten gun-deck guns would aim to blow out her starboard gun deck and prevent any effective return fire. *Gladius Dei* would do the same thing to the port side of the Kolbian.

One hundred yards.

Traquilidamar Sea
KRN *Intrepid* (32)
June 1479, Third Age of Imperial Reckoning

"NOW, Sahla! As much wind as you can!" Blaine yelled. "Up gun ports! Run out the guns! Prepare to fire by division on my command!"

Sahla screamed and the wind doubled in strength, blowing nearly fifty miles an hour, a strong gale wind. *Intrepid* seemed to leap ahead, the taffrail log showing eleven knots in speed, half again the seven knots she had been making. Blaine could hear shouts of consternation from the two ILN frigates, as the wind caught them from nearly dead ahead and put them in irons. Blaine estimated the enemy ships had been making nearly nine knots. Now their sails flapped and luffed in the wind Sahla had created. The wind lasted less than a minute, but that was long enough.

Traquilidamar Sea
ILN *Malleus Fidelium* (32)
June 1479, Third Age of Imperial Reckoning

Juste got up from where he had fallen when the sudden gust of powerful wind shook his ship. *Malleus Fidelium* shuddered as she lost half her speed in nearly an instant. The gust didn't last long, less than a minute, but it changed the dynamics of the three ships. The Kolbian was moving faster now; she was downwind of the gust and leapt ahead. Juste's ship was moving only due to momentum.

Gladius Dei was in trouble, he saw. The powerful wind had snapped her fore topsail mast. It hung from its rigging. She had lost speed and fell off to starboard. The wind ruined his plan of engagement.

"Up ports and run the guns out!" he yelled. "Fire as you bear on my command." In some ways the wind helped *Malleus*, slowing her, and giving her gunners more time to aim the cannons. But, like Juste, the gun crews were scattered and picking themselves up off the deck.

The closing speed of *Malleus* and *Intrepid* was seventeen knots. *Gladius Dei* was trying to get back on course, but the broken fore topsail mast prevented her from keeping up with *Malleus*.

Intrepid and *Malleus* would be broadside to broadside for less than a minute. Less than a minute but long enough to wreak havoc on both ships. *Gladius* was quartering away from the other two ships. She was on a close reach to the wind and was struggling to get back on course to fire on the Kolbian. The bowsprits of *Intrepid* and *Malleus* passed each other and then *Malleus'* first division of guns fired.

Traquilidamar Sea
KRN *Intrepid* (32)
June 1479, Third Age of Imperial Reckoning

Intrepid rang like a bell as the iron shot hit her armor. The *Malleus'* broadside shot hit *Intrepid* with a quarter ton of iron. The gun deck eighteen pounders didn't even put a dent in her armor plate, causing no damage. The spar deck guns did more damage. One shot hit the mainmast fifteen feet above the deck, cutting a perfect half-moon shape out of the white oak that made up the mainmast's lower mast. Another shot wrecked the foremast's fighting top, killing six Marines and four sailors. The last shot that hit anything broke the mainsail yardarm neatly in half. The falling spar killed five sailors serving spar deck gun number two and fouling guns one and three.

"By starboard divisions, fire as you bear!" Blaine shouted. "Give 'em what they deserve!" The first division of eight-inch guns fired as one. Flame and smoke marched down the side of *Intrepid*. The single, unfouled Parker rifle added its bellow to the noise and destruction.

Every shell hit *Malleus'* port side. The Parker rifle's shot punched in the port side and went through the ship, leaving a neat, six-inch hole in each side. Its fuse burned down, and it exploded eighty feet from the ship, doing no damage other than the hole. The quarterdeck carronade's shells added very little to the carnage.

Traquilidamar Sea
ILN *Malleus Fidelium* (32), *Gladius Dei* (28)
June 1479, Third Age of Imperial Reckoning

Eight fifty-three-pound shells blasted deep into her gun deck, then exploded. The spar deck seemed to heave upward. The mainmast leaned drunkenly to starboard. Its rigging snapped and the mast fell halfway over the side, acting as a sea anchor. Moments later the mizzen went, also falling to starboard. The foremast fell forward and entangled the bowsprit and all the jibboom sails.

Malleus was a wreck, her decks shattered, dismasted and her keel broken. The ship's bow and stern bent up into a 'V', as she started to sink. Capitan Jean Juste died on the spar deck, extorting his men to break records reloading the guns. A shell fragment tore him in half. He was not the only fatality. Over ninety percent of the sailors manning the long eighteens on the gun deck were dead, torn to pieces by the explosions. To a man, the rest were badly injured. And worst of all, the shells had started fires. When the fires reached the magazine, *Malleus* would simply explode.

Capitan Carlos de Haes, master and commander of ILN *Gladius Dei* stared in horror at the wreck of *Malleus Fidelium*. His First and Second Lieutenants were on the quarterdeck and were just as horrified and shocked as the Capitan was.

The Kolbians had destroyed her with one broadside. *Gladius* was seventy yards away from *Intrepid*, but he could see the menacing maws of those guns. He turned to the helmsman.

"Hard to port, get the wind on our quarter!" he yelled at the helmsman.

First lieutenant Félix Blanchard was just as shocked at what happened to *Malleus*, but the Capitan trying to avoid action? Was the man that much a coward?

"Mon Capitan! Why do we run from one Kolbian warship? Our orders are to press the action closely."

"That...thing over there destroyed *Malleus Fidelium* with a single broadside! *Malleus* was one of our heavy frigates. What chance would we have? I am the senior officer in this group! I will try to avoid acti..."

***

Intrepid's port side guns thundered. Fire-shot smoke enveloped her port side. It was long range for the Dolmen smooth bores. One Dolman-fired shell hit the forecastle and failed to explode. One punched a neat, eight-inch hole in the mainmast's topsail. Another one moaned like a lost soul as it passed cleanly over the sterncastle. Four were short, plunging into the sea, raising impressive waterspouts. No one saw where the eighth shell went. But not for the Parker rifles. All four of the rifles' fifty-pound shells hit just at the waterline and exploded. The frigate staggered at the explosions.

Gladius Dei's gun deck and spar deck withstood the blasts. She was badly holed at the waterline, but her keel was intact. If the carpenter's mates were quick enough to fother a sail over the hole, it might keep the ship from sinking. Fragments came up through the gundeck and some bigger pieces went through the spar deck's planks, injuring two sailors and ripping open the Capitan's right leg from knee to pelvis, finally lodging in his hip. Blood fountained from the ripped open femoral artery and the Capitan passed out from pain and shock. First lieutenant Félix Blanchard was now in command of *Gladius Dei*.

"Belay that last order, helmsman," Blanchard shouted. "Bring us hard to starboard and lay us alongside that ship. We'll fire one broadside when we reach long pistol shot. Then ram and board her. Once the galleys get here, they'll be able to board her as well. With three crews against one, we'll be able to take her. Sailor! You, yes, you and you, take the Capitan below to the Surgeon." The two sailors took the Capitan below to the Surgeon.

Second Lieutenant Eduardo Rosales stared at Blanchard as if the First Lieutenant had lost his mind.

"Félix, are you insane? That Kolbian throws twice our weight of shot. We'll never survive another broadside."

"If we get close enough, fast enough, those guns won't be able to hit us. We'll be under them. Then we take her by boarding action. It must take some time to reload those monster cannon."

"You are crazy, you know, but you're the Capitan now." Rosales began shouting orders to shake out a reef in the t'gallants on the mainmast and the mizzenmast. "Prepare for boarding action to starboard!"

Blanchard watched the activity on *Intrepid's* spar deck, trying to judge how long it took to reload those big guns.

I hope to hell I know what I'm doing. If they're significantly faster than I think they are, we are all going to die. If I'm right, we'll have a chance. That's a big ship, they probably outnumber us by a fair margin. We need to get a foothold and keep it until the galleys get here.

Traquilidamar Sea
KRN *Intrepid* (32)
June 1479, Third Age of Imperial Reckoning

"They're going to try to get in under the guns and board us. Damn, that's one gutsy captain over there. And those galleys are closing the range quickly. They've hauled down their sails and unstepped their masts. That's a sure sign of a fight to the finish." Blaine took his hat off and ran a hand over his hair before putting it back on. "This could get real hairy, real quick. I give those galleys an hour or maybe less to get here."

"Will the guns be loaded in time?" Sachi was bouncing on the balls of her feet. Silaqui sat on the deck, next to the taffrail in a full lotus, a faint reddish aura around her while she meditated. Sahla leaned against the taffrail, still whistling up the wind.

Sachi stopped and looked at Silaqui, thought a minute and then effortlessly dropped into a full lotus position beside the sorceress. She closed off the outside world, one sense at a time. Finally, she was completely calm, and she visualized the VR world and stepped into it.

"D.A.V.E. where are you?" she sent out the call.

::I am here, Lieutenant Commander Caitlyn Schmitt. You want help with the Lietelean Navy vessels, ninety percent, plus or minus fifteen percent. You are aware that I see everything you see?::

"I know, but is there anything you can do to keep *Intrepid* afloat? And preferably as undamaged as possible."

::There are no weapon system satellites with orbits that can be shifted to allow coverage in the required time limit. In a sense, you are on your own. Do not get killed.::

"Gee thanks. I'll be the one doing the killing. If you please."

::Codicil accepted. I calculate a fifty-eight percent chance of the *Intrepid* successfully dealing with the three Lietelean Navy vessels. Plus or minus thirty-nine percent, multiple variables.::

"You're no help, today. End VR session." She raised her hand and made a pinching motion with the middle finger and thumb.

The VR world whirled away, like angry confetti, kept in their box too long. She reentered the real world, with a deep sigh of contentment. Her friends stood in a semicircle around her, guarding her from any harm.

"Any luck with D.A.V.E. today?" Willis knelt next to her as he asked his question.

"No, he said there were no armed satellites in a correct orbit. So there's nothing he can do to help us out of this mess."

Gelman reached out a hand and helped her up. Sahla threw herself into Sachi's arms nearly weeping from the release of anxiety. Willis was next to join the hug and then everyone was hugging. Everyone except Captain Blaine.

"I know you all were worried about Sachi, but we've got rude company coming," Blaine spoke up as the group parted a little bit, enough to let Sachi breathe anyway.

"They're going to get under the guns and try to board us, aren't they, Captain?" Sachi turned to Blaine after giving Sahla a quick, hard hug.

"They'll close enough that the only thing we can hit will be their masts in a few minutes. And if they're close enough, the exploding shells would damage us as well. They're going to be able to board us, I'm afraid. Fortunately, we have a bigger crew than normal and more Marines too. Thanks to the crew off your sloop and the Embassy Marines. And there's your little group. Can you fight at all, Sahla?"

"I can fight, Captain Blaine." Sahla still wore her Dervish clothing and the CLIBA armor shirt. "My sabers are not just for show." She tapped the blue-hilted sabers sheathed on each hip.

"I kin...damnit...I can fight too," Aylie said. "Captain Blaine. With my knives or with my shotgun here. And as last resort, I can use the blast rifle."

"Those things create an explosion on the target, right?" Blaine asked.

"They do, sir, and they have a very long effective range." Willis held up his cased rifle.

"How long?"

"Over a quarter mile in blast mode." Sachi's eyes glittered as D.A.V.E. gave her the information on the blast rifle. "That mode does the most damage but is relatively short ranged. In beam mode? Well, eventually the atmosphere will degrade the beam. After about four miles it degrades. In the vacuum of space? There, the targeting system is the limiting factor. The beam is theoretically effective out to what D.A.V.E. calls an A.U. or Astronomical Unit. That's the distance between our planet Rybithia and the Sun. Hard to see anything that far away, much less hit it."

"Good Lord!" Blaine exclaimed.

"William," Sachi said, "those ancient humans fought with weapons that could destroy worlds. Their adversary, the Quar'taneeka, they were a species that hated everything that wasn't them. When they found a planet with any life form that might, just maybe, become a threat, well, that planet they destroyed. They didn't destroy Rybithia, but they did do a hideous amount of damage. We've lost so much. The Seekers are like the Quar'taneeka. And they are insane in what they want, the destruction of our world. But now, it's time to fight."

"You're right." Blaine walked forward to the edge of the quarterdeck. "First Lieutenant Gustav, give the order for the guns to go to rapid fire and fire independently!"

"Aye-aye, Captain!" He turned to face forward. "You scruffy lot! You heard the Captain! Rapid fire and fire independently!"

A cheer came from the gun crews. The two port side cannonades fired immediately, one missing short and the other slamming into the base of the jibboom. The explosion severed the base of the jibboom and it fell back against the *Gladius Dei*, held only by its rigging.

Three Dolmen guns fired almost as one, two shells missing long and only putting more holes in the sails. The other shell hit the foremast's fighting top and exploding, sending the men stationed there showering down on the ship in a gory rain. The t'gallant mast was cut in half by the explosion and fell to the starboard side of the frigate.

Gladius Dei's guns fired a ragged broadside, shot bouncing away, turned by *Intrepid's* armor. One twelve-pounder had fired at maximum elevation. The round shot hit the main topsail's yardarm neatly at the crosstrees and shattered the yardarm there. Split in half, the topsail collapsed, the shattered yardarm's pieces falling onto the netting rigged above the spar deck to catch debris. The actual sail fell onto the netting as well but hung over enough to foul the spar deck Parker rifles. The mainmast was damaged there but didn't fall.

The Lietelean frigate kept coming. Her helmsman spun the wheel right and the two ships crashed together. The remaining five gundeck Dolmans fired, smashing eight-inch holes in *Gladius Dei's* side, killing a dozen men on her gundeck. One shell hit an eighteen-pounder gun on the breech and lodged there. Instants later it exploded, blowing the gun, carriage and all, out the starboard side of the ship. The explosion killed another half dozen men and wounded more than twenty Lietelean sailors. The other shells put eight-inch holes in the starboard side of the *Gladius Dei* and exploded a hundred yards away.

With a yell, the Lieteleans hurled ropes with grappling hooks attached and locked the two ships together. A handful of Kolbian Marines met the charging Lieteleans at the rail. They killed a dozen before being swarmed over and went down. Other Kolbians rushed to stem the tide, but the Lieteleans had numbers on their side. They forced their way onto the spar deck. Kolbians met them with belaying pins, ramrods and musket butts.

The battle on the spar deck was slowly being decided for the Lieteleans. Until a black-clad form crashed into their midst. Almost instantly, ten men went down, dead or dying.

Sachi had entered the fray. Three Lieteleans fired pistol shots at her. Fired from less than a foot away, the bullets were all stopped by her CLIBA armor. Her butterfly swords had a mono-molecular edge. They cut through steel just as easily as through flesh. From the quarterdeck, it looked like a tornado of blood was in the Lieteleans' midst.

Blaine killed the man with whom he was engaged and stepped back, mostly to get out of Sachi's way. Behind him he heard *whik-ka-BLAMM, whik-ka-BLAMM* as Willis and Aylie opened fire with the blast rifles. They targeted the closest galley and two hits in the same place were devastating. The galley *Dragon* mounted three very big guns on her short forecastle, the middle one rated as a hundred-pounder and the guns to either side were fifty-pounders. Their ready ammunition, three large casks of gunpowder, was stored in the forecastle.

The resulting explosion blew her bow off. Her sweeps stopped their neatly synchronized rowing as her speed drove *Dragon* bodily under. She sank so fast her only survivors were the officers and men on the poop deck.

Thunder crashed overhead as dark clouds suddenly formed, blocking the sunlight around the ships locked together. Silaqui stood at the starboard corner of the taffrail. She was outlined in a scarlet aura, hands held high above her, her green hair blowing in a wind no one else felt. She screamed in Elvish and ripped her hands down. Dozens of lightning bolts struck the other galley.

Poing des Fidèles, the Fist of the Faithful, was a twenty-gun galley. She exploded when one of those bolts of lightning found the nineteen tons of gunpowder in her main magazine. The explosion tore the ship in half. The sterncastle and the shorter forecastle were blown away from the hull in more or less one piece. That is, until more lightning bolts hit the remnants, killing the few survivors clinging to the wreckage.

"I believe I mentioned that I don't like Lieteleans." She turned and walked onto the quarterdeck, while Aylie and Willis stared at her in shock. She reached out and grabbed Blaine away from the two men with whom he was engaged. They stopped attacking for just a moment, as surprised as Blaine was. That moment was all Silaqui needed. Shoving Blaine behind her so hard he fell and skidded, a dozen bolts of pure magical energy shot from her free hand.

Those bolts unerringly found twelve men and killed them.

She cast another cantrip and lightning jumped from her hand to one Lietelean. He screamed as his skin blackened and his hair burned. Lightning forked out of his body and hit two other Lietelean sailors, with similar results. From those two, lightning forked out again, hitting four more Lieteleans. It forked out one last time and killed eight more sailors.

Her magic broke the back of the Lieteleans. Some turned and jumped back onto their ship, dropping their weapons to run away faster. The rest of them stopped fighting, backing away from their adversaries, before dropping their weapons and falling to their knees, hands in the air.

Sachi stood in the middle of them, her enemies in piles around her, most dead, but there were some wounded. To a man, the wounded ones were missing one or both hands. Silaqui still had the scarlet aura glowing around her. Her hands glowed with power and her hair floated in her aura.

"Move out of the way, Sachi. I'll finish this."

"No, Silaqui, I'll not move. They have surrendered honorably. Let go of your fury and rage for blood. To kill in battle is one thing; to murder in cold blood those who have surrendered is another thing. Do not do this! You remained steadfast after all those years with the pirates and left them to die by hanging, after being convicted by a court. You wanted to torture Je'Libe as badly as I wanted to torture Buckley. I stopped you from blackening your soul then. You stopped me from slaughtering Buckley, so now I will not allow you to tarnish your soul. They may be enemies, but they have done you, yourself, no harm. Leave it be, my dear friend."

Sachi walked toward Silaqui, her hands out. The sorceress took a deep breath. When she let it out, the aura faded away, and she was once more just an Elvish maiden in scarlet. Tears ran down her face and she embraced Sachi.

Chapter Twenty-one

**Mid-Lanic Ocean
KRN *Intrepid* (32)
June 1479, Third Age of Imperial Reckoning**

INTREPID'S LOG REGISTERED SIX knots in a light breeze. She was close hauled and beating to windward. They were two weeks out of the Lanic Gates, and even with Sahla's control over the winds, they had nearly been becalmed more than once. After the battle, it took them most of the next two days to make repairs and bury their dead at sea. The gaping hole at the waterline of *Gladius Dei* had been partly repaired. Between the minimal repairs and several sails fothered over the hole, it was agreed that she should proceed to the nearest port and hope she wouldn't sink on the way there. Only her third and fourth Lieutenants had survived the battle. Blaine had checked their navigation skills and decided they could find their way home by themselves. He hadn't been quite sure what he would do if neither one of them could navigate.

***

It was noon and *Intrepid's* Fourth Lieutenant Ensign Thomas Anderson was instructing the six midshipmen aboard the ship in celestial navigation. Four of the ship's five sextants were in use. The fifth one was Captain Blaine's personal sextant, locked away in his cabin. All in all, a calm, ordinary day. One that was suddenly disrupted by a cry from the crow's nest atop the main mast.

"Sail ho! Many sails in sight! South-southeast!"

"Damn and blast it! Midshipman Wiess! Front and center!" Weiss jumped like he'd been poked with a hot needle, carefully handed the sextant he was using to Ensign Thomas and scurried over to Captain Blaine.

"Midshipman Weiss, sir!" he snapped to attention.

"Go find Sachi, give her my compliments and ask her to report to me on the quarterdeck as soon as possible. She'll probably be in the Officers' Galley with Toby."

"Sir, find Miss Sachi, your compliments and ask her to report to you on the quarterdeck as soon as possible. Aye-aye, sir!" Wiess bolted for the below decks hatch.

***

"You know, Lady Silaqui frightened more than just the Lieteleans with her display of magical power. There's more than a few of our fellow sailors who are scared to death of angering her." Toby was busy cutting fresh bread for sandwiches for the Officer's Wardroom. It was nearly the last of the flour.

"Tell the scared ones that she will harm no one unless harm is threatened to her or her companions. I'm surprised they're not scared of me. I butchered more than a score of the Lieteleans myself." Sachi was pulling the second loaf of bread out of the oven.

"Ah, but you're *our* Sachi. You hold the rating of Able Seaman, given to you by Bosun Beauchamp himself. Sadly, Lady Silaqui was never more than an interesting passenger. A rescued Elf lady was no more than a novelty. A novelty that can summon a storm and shoot lightning from her hand? That's a novelty to inspire fear and terror. Remember, even in the Navy it's a rare sailor that's seen an Elf or magic that's no more than card tricks."

"Miz Sachi!" Midshipman Weiss rushed into the galley, breathing hard. "The Captain's compliments and you're to report to Captain Blaine as soon as possible." It all came out in one rushed breath.

"I see, Johan." She hid a smile at the earnest young man's rapid delivery. "Any idea why?"

"No, Miz Sachi, but the lookout reported many sails in sight."

"Ah, I know what he wants. Do me a favor and go find Sahla and ask her to join me on the quarterdeck. She's most likely taking a nap in her hammock. You know where our hammocks are hung forward, right?"

"Aye, I do." Wiess blushed. Sneaking peeks at the incomparable Sahla was a common pastime for all the young midshipmen "But if she's asleep?"

"Wake her and tell her I need her on the quarterdeck. Get her the number one glass from the Bosun's office. If Captain Blaine wants what I think he wants, we'll need it. Quickly, please." Sachi gave Toby a wave and headed for the quarterdeck.

***

"Able Seaman Sachi reporting as ordered, sir." Sachi gave Blaine a salute with a twinkle in her eyes. A salute which he gravely returned.

"Sachi, you're not just another seaman anymore, you know," he said.

"Perhaps not, Captain, but I choose to be just one more sailor when aboard this ship. It gives me a place every sailor aboard understands. And this ship is like home to me. A comfortable home where I know I'm welcome and wanted."

"Be that as it may, right now this Captain wants you up in the crow's nest. The lookout reports many sails to the south-southeast. Take those superb eyes of yours up there and see what you can see."

"Aye-aye, sir. I took the liberty of sending Midshipman Weiss to wake Sahla and to get the number one glass. Handy, isn't it, having someone who can fly to make observations."

"Yes, it is. But what I'm afraid of is what those sails may represent. Another unforeseen consequence of events you've been tangled up in. The 'line of fire' in the sky, the destruction of

Du Khamps des SouSee. The OADS, what did that mean again, please?"

"Orbital Area Denial System. It launched scores of metal rods that cover a wide area. The 'crowbars,' as they were called, are inert metal rods that move at orbital speeds. Their sheer speed made them deadly. And they seek the biggest target in their area. That attack may have, no, did, wreck most of the Kolbian ships in the area." There was a quiet tension between them but neither of them acknowledged it. Sachi gave Blaine a quick salute and headed up the mainmast to the crow's nest.

***

"Hullo, Miz Sachi." Able Seaman Franklin Kory greeted her as she clambered over the edge of the basket and leaned against the royalmast. The crow's nest lookout basket was constructed sitting just above the mainmast's royal yardarm.

"I guess you're going to insist on calling me 'Miz' aren't you?" Sachi gave the older seaman a dirty look. "Just plain Sachi is fine, that, or Seaman Takahashi. I'm no different from any sailor on this ship."

"But you are different, Miz Sachi, you're an adventurer and a hero. The crewmen that came from your sloop, the one that was burned, they've told us only some of what you've done. The young lady, Miz Aylie, has told us other stories about you."

"I guess it's too late to put a stop to these stories, as they'll have been blown all out of proportion." She sighed. "Now, point out the sails you saw."

He pointed. Sachi stood on the edge of the basket railing and looked to the south-southeast. Adjusting her vision brought the sails closer to her and her face was grim as she made out the Imperial flag flying from a dozen masts. But she couldn't see the hulls. They were still too far away to identify.

"*Habiba*, Captain Blaine told me to come up here and help you. What do you wish for me to do?" Sahla floated up next to the basket. Kory gulped as he realized the beautiful Darsälaamic woman was standing on nothing at all.

"*Koibito*, take the glass, fly up and tell me what you see. I can see many masts and they all fly the flag of the Lietelean Empire. See if you can determine what kinds of ships there are, how many and if they seem to be on a pursuit course?"

"A moment then." Sahla shot up, eighty feet above the very top of the mainmast, three hundred feet above *Intrepid's* spar deck. Raising the glass to her eye, she slowly spun in a complete circle, stopping when she was aligned to the south-southeast. She stayed there for several minutes, then lowered the glass and came back to the crow's nest.

"There are eight ships there. Three of them are very big, with as many as three gundecks. Two others are built like *Intrepid* but smaller, and the last one has three masts and uses oars as well. There are two ships with one mast with a square sail and many oars. They are the closest ones and seem faster than all the other ships. And I would say that they have seen us and are chasing us. Very slowly, but they are coming this way, my *Habiba*."

"Not good news. Let's go talk to the Captain." Sachi leaned out and grabbed the backstay, hoisting herself out of the basket and wrapping both legs around the backstay. She started sliding down the stay, controlling her speed with her hands. The thick rope wasn't rough enough to damage her hands. A normal person doing the same thing would likely want or need gloves. Reaching the deck, Sachi, followed by Sahla, reported their findings to Captain Blaine.

"Sounds like three ships-of-the-line, a pair of their smaller frigates, a big galleass and two traditional galleys. What would you make of their range and speed, Sachi?" Blaine asked.

"A moment." Sachi's eyes glittered with tiny lights. "Twenty-one point nine miles. The big ships-of-the-line are making four point four knots, the frigates are slightly faster than that, five point six knots. Right now, we're faster than their sail-only ships, but the galleass is making six point five knots, and the galleys are coming along at seven point eight knots. If the oared ships can maintain those speeds, they'll catch us some time tomorrow. Assuming no changes in the wind." At that moment, *Intrepid's* sails went completely sack as the wind died away.

"Well, that's not good." Blaine grimaced. "Sahla, can you do anything to keep us moving?"

"I shall try my best, but the air has become very...heavy here." Sahla put her fingers to her lips and blew an ear-piercing whistle. The sails luffed and boomed as they filled with a light breeze. Due to her momentum *Intrepid* was still moving but the log showed her speed had fallen to two knots. "I will keep trying to call up the winds, Captain Blaine, but I think a storm is coming, not today or tomorrow but soon. A big storm."

Blaine checked the barometer attached to the binnacle, then walked over to the lee rail of the quarterdeck, motioning the two girls to follow him. He stood at the bulwark, staring aft, where the pursuers were. He looked up at the sails several times. Obviously, he was considering something. Sachi and Sahla waited patiently for his decision.

"Lieutenant Hanley." He waved at the red-headed lieutenant who had been helping with the navigation lesson. He left the midshipmen and hurried over to Blaine.

"Yes, sir." He saluted.

"Find the bosun and order the topsmen to get the stun'sls on her. Mainmast topsails and t'gallants, the course sails, topsails, and t'gallants on the foremast. Also, get the pumps ready and hoses run up the mainmast. We'll wet down the sails to help them catch the lightest breeze. Ready the longboats to haul out the anchors and their chain, we'll kedge if we have to do so. I would engage a Lietelean ship-of-the-line and figure to beat her, but eight ships is a bit much even for our incomparable *Intrepid*."

"What would you of us, Captain Blaine?" Sahla asked.

"How long can you keep the winds in our favor, Sahla?"

"For as long as I can stay awake. How strong a wind I can call depends on how 'heavy' the air is when I try to summon it. It is the elementals of air that push the wind against the sails, Captain Blaine, not I. The elementals of clear air are very different from the elementals of a strong storm. They are not something I would summon willingly. The Marid of the deep ocean are like as not to try to carry me away, so that they could drain my magic before giving me to the Efreet to utterly destroy me."

"But Sahla, I didn't know, I had no idea what cou..."

"Enough, Captain Blaine, I know you would not put my Heartmate to such risk," Sachi interjected.

"I would never ask such a thing of her. If she told me, as she has, the dangers inherent in such magic. We will seek another way." Blaine reached out and touched Sahla on the shoulder. "You are very precious to someone I love. I will not risk destroying that love bond between the two of you."

"Thank you, William." Sachi's voice was pitched soft enough that only Blaine and Sahla could hear her.

***

For two days the Imperials chased *Intrepid*. The pair of galleys were the fastest Imperial ships. They closed the distance slowly but surely. The winds had been fitful, blowing in one direction and then another. *Intrepid's* advantage was Sahla. The Jann could never get the winds to completely cooperate, but she managed to keep *Intrepid's* speed at a steady average of five knots. The imperial galleys got within long cannon range late in the afternoon on the second day.

***

"The Imperials will be close enough to fire on us in another fifteen minutes, Captain." First Lieutenant Gustav was watching the crew of the closest galley loading their forward three guns, a hundred pounder and two fifty pounders. The glass he was using brought them uncomfortably close. "Those big guns will tear the hell out of us, if they hit us, that is."

"You're correct, Keith. But the question is, can they hit us at two hundred yards?" Blaine was also using a glass. "They won't be firing shells, thank God, but that hundred pounder looks to throw a sixteen-inch ball. I don't want sixteen-inch holes in my ship. Keith, have the chase guns engage the enemy the instant they fire. I'll not fire first on them."

Just as Blaine lowered his glass, the foremost Imperial galley fired its hundred pounder gun, followed an instant later by the two fifty pounder guns. They fired as the galley crested a wave and all three shots moaned like lost souls as they flew past *Intrepid*, missing high and to starboard of the big frigate.

"Well, that answered that question. The gunners may fire at will." Everyone who was standing at the taffrail moved away from the poop deck to give the gun crews plenty of room to service the guns. As soon as everyone was clear, both of the chase guns, long twenty-pounder Parker rifles, bellowed in unison.

***

One shell went high, putting a neat, three-inch hole in the galley's sail. The second shot was better aimed. It smashed through the forward head and exploded just forward of the oar deck. Fragments blasted into the first four rows of galley slaves, pulling on their oars. There were three men to an oar and both the starboard and port foremost oarsmen were killed by the blast wave and by fragments sleeting into their bodies. Fragments injured and maimed oarsmen three rows back and the galley lost way as the delicate synchronicity of her oars was lost. One of the three slave overseers was also killed. The screams of the wounded and dying could be heard very faintly on *Intrepid's* quarterdeck.

The chase guns fired again. Both shells hit the galley this time. One shell hit the port bulwark and exploded there, killing most of the portside fifty pounder's crew. The other shell flew the length of the galley and exploded against the sterncastle's forward bulkhead. Fragments and splinters killed gun crewmen on the aft guns, light eight-pounders mounted on the bulwarks, port and starboard. More fragments blasted through the quarterdeck's decking and killed one of the two helmsmen at the galley's wheel, damaging the wheel itself. The first and third ship's lieutenants were killed, and the captain was seriously wounded with a fragment sticking out of his chest.

Between the loss of coordination in the oar deck and the damage to the wheel, the galley sheared off to starboard, just in time to be rammed behind the forecastle by the following galley. The impact of the ram mounted below the waterline on the second galley tore a gaping, thirty-foot-long hole from just under the forecastle back to the fifth set of oars. Oars snapped like twigs, breaking arms and crushing chests of the helpless slave oarsmen.

The impact sent the masts of both galleys crashing down, the rammed galley's mast going over the port rail, while the ramming galley's mast fell forward, killing and wounding the crews of the guns mounted on both port and starboard bulwarks.

The rammed galley began to list to starboard as tons of seawater poured into her hold. The list trapped the beak ram of the second galley and ripped it off. This caused that galley to begin to flood as water ran into the hold below the waterline. Both galleys lost way as their oars stopped and their masts were down.

***

"Damn good shooting, boys!" First Lieutenant Gustav was ecstatic, cheering the gun crews.

"Belay reloading, boys, those galleys aren't going anywhere but to the bottom of the ocean." Blaine's face was grim; he knew most of the men dying on those two galleys were slaves, chained to a rowing bench. Some of them for the length of their sentence, most of them for the rest of their lives. Lives which had always been nasty, brutal and short. Killing enemies was one thing, but he took no joy in the deaths of men like those helpless men chained to those rowing benches.

"That makes you sad, doesn't it, Captain William Blaine?" Sahla had walked up without a sound, but Blaine was aware of her presence, nevertheless.

"Yes, it does. Galleys are elegant ships with graceful lines. Not that long ago, our navy used galleys not that different from those."

He pointed at the wrecked ships. "Now, our oarsmen were paid enlistees, not slaves or convicts. A man could sign on with the Navy, specify wanting to serve as an oarsman for the first two years of a six-year enlistment and be promoted to Petty Officer Third Class at the end of his first two years. Assuming he had stayed out of trouble during those two years, of course. My steward Toby got his start in the Navy that way."

"Does it trouble you, William Blaine, to kill other men?" she asked.

"Yes, it does. It would be best if humankind could learn to coexist with each other, much less the Elder Races, like Silaqui's people, the elves. Or the dwarves who supposedly live in Montagar. There, the Montagarans are showing the way, that humans can simply get along with the non-humans. Kolbia is trying to show the world that slavery is wrong. And then there are places like the Lietelean Empire. And groups like these insane 'Seekers of the World's Death.' Sachi told me what little she knows of them."

"Why are you in the Navy, William Blaine?"

"I started out as a boy looking for adventure. My great-uncle was a ship captain in the Navy, a very successful one. He bought me a post on his ship as a midshipman, I was, oh, twelve then. Despite how hard it was, I loved the Navy, loved the sea." He paused a moment, looking out to sea. "The storm is coming. Going to be a rough blow, but my *Intrepid* can handle a rough blow, and my girl, here," he rubbed his hand along the bulwark's rail, "she will never let me down."

"The *Intrepid* is a great ship, Captain Blaine. It is an honor to be aboard her."

"It's an honor to have you, Sachi, and the rest of your friends aboard." He pointed to the southwest. "That dark line is the storm coming. The Lieteleans will have a bad way with it. They'll never have a hope in hell of catching us, or of even knowing where we've gone." The sails, which had been nearly slack with the light winds Sahla had whistled up, suddenly snapped and boomed as they filled with the first winds of the oncoming storm. "That's the gust front. A few more hours and we'll be running before the wind with storm sails on the topsails and the t'gallants, and a storm sail on the foremast jib. She'll be lively in a blow like this, but there's a thousand miles of open ocean in front of us. I expect to raise Stark Haven by the second week of July. Excuse me, please, Sahla. I need to get the crew working on getting the storm sails up."

Blaine turned and strode away, calling for his officers. The remaining Lietelean ships were so far behind that only their mast tops showed above the horizon. Sahla looked at the log. It was showing six knots and increasing.

***

She extended her senses out into the storm. She could feel the entities riding the winds. True Jinni rode those winds, Princes of the Air. Jinni who bore a Jann like her no affection at all. She quickly pulled in her senses, striving to make herself as small and unobtrusive as possible. Then she realized at least one of them was aware of her.

The Jinn swept out of the winds, as swift as thought. He stepped onto the deck, assuming the appearance of a giant, blue-skinned human male with black hair and a short black beard. Sahla was vaguely aware of shouts of consternation from the crew of the chase guns and everyone on the quarterdeck, including Blaine and Sachi, rushed toward her.

"I am Hasan al Naseem, a Jinn of the Foremost Rank of the Princes of Air and Wind. Come with me." He flung out an arm and a whirlwind roared around them. Everyone aft of the mizzenmast was knocked flat, everyone except Sachi and Blaine. They both staggered but kept coming. The Jinn gave a roaring laugh and swept Sahla into the sky. A single, one-millimeter flechette shot past Hasan's face, close enough that it shaved hairs off his beard. Sahla could see more of the flechettes being swept away as Hasan intensified the whirlwind around them to the strength of a tornado. Then they were too far away to be threatened by the tiny darts. But she could still hear Sachi screaming with rage and terror.

"LET ME GO!" Sahla struggled to free herself, but the Jinn held her too tightly.

"Not yet, Little One." She heard his voice as the slightest whisper of a breeze and, at the same time, the roar of a hurricane. "The Lords of Air and Wind, the True Jinni of the Noble Courts, will see you before them. And they will judge you there, to determine what your father Ilben alh-Taymyah, a lowly Jinn of the Second Rank of Air and Wind, has created in you."

***

They swept into the eye of the storm and the winds quieted. A score of Jinni waited there, standing or seated on air as they chose. The biggest of them, a giant ten times Sahla's height, stepped forward.

"I am Saahir al Hamed, First Lord of the Courts of Air and Wind. And you are Sahla al Qasim, Flowing Beauty in the tongue of Mortals, a mere Jann. But a 'mere Jann' that troubles the possibility that the World as we know it may be greatly changed or even destroyed. How is it that you are Bound to a lowly mortal, and yet trouble all things that exist beyond the ken of mere mayfly mortals?"

"Speak, child, tell us why you should continue to exist if you threaten our very existence? Threaten the existence of all things imbued with the magic that mortal man understands so poorly, if he understands it at all." Another Jinn spoke, one who wore neither beard nor hair, his blue pate shining in the sunlight.

"Yes, tell us why you should be?" came a chorus of mighty voices.

"Silence!" ordered Saahir, "Give the child at least a bare moment to speak! She is as magical as any of us, a being of lesser Power, but a being of Power nonetheless." The voices subsided. "Now Sahla al Qasim, tell us truthfully, why does the Power of monumental times swirl about you?"

"I will tell you only the truth. If nothing changes, if the holder of my Bond of True Love fails in her Quest, then in forty-seven mortal years, this world will be struck by another world, one launched ten thousand years ago, from the very deepest depths of the Void beyond the Sky. Our world will be shattered into dust, nothing left for either mortal man or immortals of magic. We will all die." Sahla took a deep breath as utter silence descended within the eye of the storm.

"My Bonded does not truly need me to stop this falling destroyer of the world. That, she might be able to do by herself. It is after the destruction of the world killer that we must fear. The power that she will bear is one that has no love for what we are. It has no use for anything but cold logic. There will be no room in the world it will create for a dragon, or a unicorn. Or the Elder Folk, elves and dwarves and other such races. There will be no room for magic. No room for elemental beings such as you, My Lords of Air and Wind. No room for such as me, either. No room for even the power of love."

"And how, Sahla al Qasim, do you figure into this catastrophic time? What is your role in this?" Saahir spoke into the silence Sahla's words had created.

"I figure into this because I love my Bonded with every fiber of my being. It is upon me, and Sachi's other beloved compatriots, it is upon us, to stop this thing, this monster that would remake the world entire. I will be, WE will be the anchor in Sachi's heart, the very embodiment of love that will turn this cataclysm away." Sahla fell silent, looking into the eyes of each of these mighty Jinn, the Lords of Air and Wind. Then she spoke again, so quietly that the Jinni there all leaned forward to hear her. "That is the truth, My Lords. I am a Jann, to the mortals of Darsälaam, my birthplace, an abomination, the doors of Chalta's Paradise closed to me. And I have no place here, in the realms of the immortal Princes of all the Elements. My only place in all the Planes of Existence is at my Belovèd's side. Without me, she will have no care for what the World becomes. That is the Truth, My Lords. I can say naught else in my own defense. You will do as you will, My Lords of Air and Wind." Utter silence fell. Finally, Saahir stepped forward to her side and turned to face the other Jinni.

"The child has spoken well and truly," he spoke into the silence. "I have never before seen a Bond of Mortal to Elemental so powerful, so anchored in a Power greater than any of us. The Power of Love. She will be returned whence she came, with no constraints, no bindings, no let or hold on her Powers. Are there any here who would say me nay?"

There was a faint susurration of sound, but no words were heard.

"Hasan al Naseem, return this Jann to where she must be, swiftly and safely."

"Your will, Great Lord." Hasan stepped forward and offered Sahla his hand. "Come child, let me return you to those who love you." She took his hand, and he drew her through the wall of the storm and into the clear air. There was no storm, only clear skies and strong winds. Far below them, so tiny that she looked like a child's toy ship, was the *Intrepid*, sailing westward with all sails set. Far to the west, only visible due to their height above the earth, the dark line of the storm on the horizon was visible.

"Lord Hasan, how long have I been gone?" her voice shook with fear.

"Not long at all, Child Sahla, eight days by mortal time. Time in the Planes of the Elementals flows differently. Now, let us return you to your Belovèd's side." Hasan held her hand as they arrowed down out of the sky, faster than thunder. "Since I do not want your Belovèd shooting at me again, we will slow and only you will be visible to the mortals when you step onto the deck of the ship. I shall raise a whirlwind to protect me and return to the court of the First Lord."

No one noticed as they came down from the sky, not until Sahla's foot touched the deck. Fourth Lieutenant Anderson had the afternoon watch, and he happened to be checking the ship's taffrail log when Sahla seemingly appeared out of thin air directly beside him. Anderson yelled and jumped sideways a good ten feet in sudden surprise. Anderson's yell drew the attention of everyone on deck.

***

Admiral Sartell and Envoy Courtenay were discussing the effects of the loss of Sahla on Sachi's quest with Blaine and Sachi, when they heard Anderson's yell through the cabin's open skylight. Sachi sprinted out the cabin door with Blaine hard on her heels.

"Oh, thank the Ancestors!" Sachi enveloped Sahla in a crushing, rib-bruising embrace. Sahla hugged back just as hard. "I thought I'd lost you forever! What happened to you?"

"I was taken by a true Jinn, a Lord of Air and Wind, taken into the eye of the storm." She stopped talking and kissed Sachi passionately. Admiral Sartell openly smiled, as did Envoy Courtenay. There was a smile on Blaine's face, an odd one, a mix of both sadness and joy. When the pair came up for air, Sahla continued with her tale. "I was brought before the court of the High Lord of Air and Wind…"

Three hours later, Sahla's tale had been told and retold, discussed and debated. They had moved to the stern great cabin, formerly Blaine's cabin, now the Admiral's, at the beginning of Sahla's story. The cabin was crowded with the Admiral and Envoy Courtenay. Captain Blaine and Dr. Hoff were there, as were the other four members of Sachi's group.

"Well, we've beaten this dead horse into a pulp," Sartell said. "I don't think there's anything else to be learned from Sahla's kidnapping. Anything to add, William?"

"No sir, other than to comment that the winds have been superb. We're sailing on a close reach, *Intrepid's* best point of sail and averaging nearly twelve knots. That's the best she averaged during her trials after the refit. Sahla's control over the winds is amazing."

"Captain Blaine, I have done nothing to control the winds. No, this is the favor of the Jinni Lords of the Air and Wind. They knew I spoke no falsehood before them."

"Well, if we can keep their favor all the way home, we'll reach Stark Haven Bay in about three weeks. Then a day's sail to Capitol

City. I'll be on the quarterdeck if anyone needs me. Admiral Sartell, Envoy Courtenay, the rest of you, would you be willing to join me on the quarterdeck?" Blaine picked up his hat and left the cabin.

Silaqui smiled at Sachi and Sahla, nodded her head, then collected Aylie and Willis with a glance and headed out the door behind Blaine. Aylie grabbed Gelman by the sleeve and hauled him out the door.

Sartell had a slightly confused look on his face. Then Courtenay gave him a look and nodded toward the door to the cabin. Sudden understanding dawned on him.

"Angelina, I'm sure Captain Blaine has important information to discuss with us. Sachi, Sahla, if you have no other duties, we will see you later." He grabbed his hat, held out an arm to Courtenay and they left the cabin. Sachi and Sahla looked at each other and started giggling.

"They mean to give us time alone together, Sahla."

"Yes, they will give us only the scantest bit of courtesy and privacy, as best they can. But even this is not truly private. They mean well, Sachi."

"No, it isn't. And they do mean well. But...there is the Marine sentry at the door, and the skylight is open. I don't want any spectators to our lovemaking. And here we have a bunk which will only fit one and a tight fit at that. And the bulkheads are very thin and carry sound well."

"So, we wait?"

"Yes, we wait. But I will at least taste your lips again." The kiss was the first of many, but nothing advanced beyond a kiss.

Chapter Twenty-two

**Stark Haven Bay
KRN *Intrepid* (32)
July 1479, Third Age of Imperial Reckoning**

Two weeks from Stark Haven Island *Intrepid* had encountered five of the surviving ships of Task Force Southron. The frigate *Repulse* and the sloop-of-war *Resolution*, and three schooners, *Wing*, *Swiftsure*, and *Defense*. *Repulse* and *Resolution* were both heavily damaged, and the three schooners had various levels of damage.

Gelman had gone to *Repulse* to heal as many of the wounded as he could. The priest spent an entire week, going to each ship by boat in turn, healing the wounded on those ships. He also brought back what was known of any other ships of the Task Force.

***

"Three ships-of-the-line lost, at least four frigates, half a dozen sloops, what a disaster!" Admiral Sartell stared at the papers on the desk in Blaine's cabin. Those papers listed all the ships assigned to Task Force Southron. "Five known surviving ships. There were losses to those things that fell out of the sky, they generally seemed to hit the bigger ships over the schooners. Then they were attacked without warning by the Lieteleans' joke of a Lanic fleet. It's easy to win when your opponent is already damaged."

"Diplomatic tensions were already high, but this surprise attack on damaged ships with no warning? The average Kolbian in the street will be enraged. The Tribune and the Proconsul will lose their minds and both the Quorum, and the Council will be out for blood. This will mean war."

"It certainly will." Courtenay was sitting on the couch. She was going through her own set of the papers. "There will be no choice in the matter. Our Navy will sweep them from the sea. There won't be so much as a rowboat flying a Lietelean flag by this time next year."

"That is true, but getting at them on land will be a different matter entirely. Their army is supposed to be the best in the world. And they have a much larger population to draw more troops for replacements or standing up new regiments. If they have both quality and quantity on land, we have a real problem."

There was a knock on the door. The Marine sentry opened it and Captain Blaine walked in. He set his hat down on the sideboard and gave Sartell a salute.

"I'm supposed to salute you, William, not you saluting me first."

"Yes, sir." Blaine poured himself a shot of brandy, looked around the room and quickly swallowed it. "We'll reach Capitol City tomorrow, coming in to dock by noon, I estimate."

"Well, that's good news," Courtenay said, "There's been little enough of it lately."

"And there's another issue to discuss. The three of us are the only ones who know of Sachi's quest and her complete explanation of what will happen if she fails in that. I would suggest that we either keep it solely to ourselves, or inform only the Tribune about this? My choice would be to keep it amongst the three of us. What do you two think?"

"I think the news of the possibility of the coming end of the world would cause a nationwide panic, assuming anyone believed us, that is." Courtenay held out a snifter to Blaine and he poured brandy into it, offered the bottle to Sartell, who waved it off, and poured himself another shot.

"I agree, Angelina." Sartell set down the paper in his hand and leaned back in the chair. "We need to offer Sachi and her friends all the support we can. And that will be difficult in a nation preparing for war. Any suggestions, William?"

"Yes, I do have one. There are ancient ruins on one of the islands in the Kolbian Straights. There are sea stories of fabulous treasure there but anyone who went ashore there either found nothing or was never seen again. Get them a civilian schooner with a Navy crew and take them there and see if they can find what they're looking for."

"That's an excellent idea, William." Sartell leaned forward and rested his arms on the desktop. "And I think that if both Angelina and I speak to Admiral McGowan, we can bring him around to see things our way. And I'll check with Sachi and see what she says about bringing him into the secrecy needed to explain the whys and wherefores of needing to keep this under the table. Any idea where we might find Sachi?"

"I know exactly where she is." Blaine smiled. "She's up on the foremast's fighting top with Sahla. They have as much scant privacy there as anywhere on the ship."

***

Sachi sat with her back against the foremast facing forward, her long legs stretched out in front of her. Sahla sat in her lap, twisted around so they were face to face. The remnants of lunch were on the aft side of the mast and a pair of gulls were scrabbling over the scant bits left over.

"This is nice. Being up here. Away from everyone, where I can kiss you as much as I want to and there's no one staring at us."

"They stare because of your beauty, my love." Sachi leaned forward for another kiss. A long moment later, she leaned back against the mast. "Blaine owes us a very nice, luxurious room—"

"With a luxurious, private bathing room—"

"Yes, of course, you silly, it'll hav—"

"And silk sheets, those 'ten-year' sheets you called them, from Han."

"You may be asking more than poor William can give, my love. Ten-year silks are very rare, but we can look for them, perhaps, tomorrow. In Capitol City, perhaps, tomorrow... I love you, my Sahla."

"Yes, perhaps tomorrow. And I love you, my Sachi."

**END
BOOK THREE**

Author Notes

Sachi meets Sahla, the young woman who will become the center of her life, on a bloody beach. The story follows Sachi's quest to save the world as she first resists and then accepts the magical Bond with Sahla.

Sahla is my own creation whereas the other main characters were inspired by one or another of the old Saturday Night Gang.

This is the third book in what I expect to be a five book series. **To Find a True Course** is planned to be released in June 2025, just before Liberty Con 2025. Book Four is expected to be released in late December 2025 or early January 2026. Book Four is not quite halfway complete and should go to Chromosphere Press in late July 2025. Book Five is very tentatively scheduled for June 2026, again before LibertyCon.

Lots of folks have helped me along the way. LOTS. More than I can mention here. **To Find a True Course** wouldn't exist without that help. Character ideas, beta reading, editing, whew, it's a list.

First and foremost is my publisher and editor, Stephanie Osborn. She is the first to give me a chance. Without her knowledge and expertise, I'd still be vainly floundering around, wondering what to do next. Stephanie is just awesome, both as editor and publisher. She kept me on track and on target. She's the best and I'm lucky to be able to call her a great friend as well.

Lt. Col (USA, ret,) Jon Holland handed me advice and guidance on all things military, especially on Eighteenth Century artillery. He kept me from making some real boo-boos.

Fellow author Lydia Sherrer has been a cheerleader in my corner for years now.

The Saturday Night Gang: Troy Logsdon, my 'brother from another mother'; Louis Nicoulin III, Tom Herp, and Kristy Kannapel. These folks gave me inspiration for major characters.

Last and most important is my lovely wife of 31 years, Kae Thompson. She helped me create Sachi from whole cloth and provided the love and support needed to finish this novel.

About the Author

Reared on a West Texas ranch, A.G. Thompson is a veteran of the US Air Force, having served during the Cold War and earned the rank of Staff Sergeant. He earned Bachelor of Arts degrees in both English Literature and History from the University of Louisville.

He has been a competition shooter for around a decade, is an avid reader (as most authors are), and is extremely knowledgeable in military history, especially as regards World War II.

He is retired from a 29-year career at UPS, a devoted cat-person with a pair of large four foots in his household and has been married for the last 31 years to his wonderful wife, Kae Thompson.